SHE WAS SHERIFF

SHE WAS SHERIFF

MELODY GROVES

FIVE STAR

A part of Gale, Cengage Learning

GALE
CENGAGE Learning·

Farmington Hills, Mich • San Francisco • New York • Waterville, Maine
Meriden, Conn • Mason, Ohio • Chicago

GALE
CENGAGE Learning®

LIBRARY OF CONGRESS CATALOGING-IN-PUBLICATION DATA

Names: Groves, Melody, 1952– author.
Title: She was sheriff / Melody Groves.
Description: First Edition. | Waterville, Maine : Five Star, a part of Cengage Learning, 2016.
Identifiers: LCCN 2016003808 (print) | LCCN 2016009177 (ebook) | ISBN 9781432831998 (hardback) | ISBN 1432831992 (hardcover) | ISBN 9781432831967 (ebook) | ISBN 1432831968 (ebook)
Subjects: | BISAC: FICTION / Historical. | FICTION / Action & Adventure. | GSAFD: Western stories. | Adventure fiction.
Classification: LCC PS3607.R6783 S54 2016 (print) | LCC PS3607.R6783 (ebook) | DDC 813/.6—dc23
LC record available at http://lccn.loc.gov/2016003808

First Edition. First Printing: July 2016
Find us on Facebook– https://www.facebook.com/FiveStarCengage
Visit our website– http://www.gale.cengage.com/fivestar/
Contact Five Star™ Publishing at FiveStar@cengage.com

Printed in the United States of America
1 2 3 4 5 6 7 20 19 18 17 16

To Erin and Haley
for being the inspiring women they are

ACKNOWLEDGEMENTS

Thanks to:
Judy Avila, Phil Jackson and Bart Cleveland

Hazel Rumney:
The Word Smyth Who Stands under the Chestnut Tree,
Pen in Hand

Extra Special Thanks to:
Myke Groves

PROLOGUE:
CRIME DOESN'T PAY?

Boom! Sparkling lights filled the night air. Another Roman candle shot a red trail of fire high overhead. A little girl, perched on her pa's shoulders, squealed with delight. *Oooh*s and *aaah*s raced through the crowd as each exploding firework obliterated the stars.

James Mooney elbowed his way past a bulky man standing in the middle of the boardwalk. Too crowded to make his way easily, he squeezed sideways through the crush—men, women, children—gathered to gawk at the display. Huge throngs were fine with him. More people with their eyes on the sky meant fewer people watching the bank. Exactly the way he'd planned.

Another *boom* and he jumped. A curse, which he thought was under his breath, turned a couple of heads. Damn. He'd have to keep it to himself if this plan was going to succeed. By now, his accomplices should be in place. One at the side of the bank, the other in the near alley with their horses. A quick getaway in the fireworks distraction was key to their success.

And the Chinese community handily provided the cover Mooney needed for his plan to succeed. He considered it queer, the Chinamen celebrating the New Year so late, as much as a month after the real one. Still, taking advantage of their ignorant miscalculations worked in his favor.

Pulling on the cigarito clutched between his teeth, Mooney blew out smoke and glanced into the sky. The fireworks began. He'd have plenty of time to blow the safe, skedaddle out of town with his gang and split the loot in the safety of their hideout. Sacramento would be a little poorer come morning, the price it would pay for letting those foreigners celebrate like this.

Kerosene streetlights, normally lit by now, hung lifeless on the poles. Mooney smiled. The street was dark and nobody was watching. He eased down the boardwalk past the First Sacramento Bank. His heart raced knowing he'd be inside within a minute and richer within two.

Mooney whistled one sharp note. Skulking in the alley's darkness, Amos "Wink" Smith stepped out. Mooney pointed to the pry bar in Wink's hand. Wink edged to the side door, waited for the covering blast of a firework. Two powerful strikes and the door splintered. Wood flew into the bank. Both men hunkered down, Colts drawn, waiting. Would some curious soul come and check out the noise? Mooney knew he'd shoot them if they did.

But nobody came.

After waiting half a minute, they rushed inside, closing the door, now hanging at odd angles. The glow from the bonfires, gas lanterns and fireworks provided enough light to make out the clerk's wooden desk against the wall. They skirted that, then both peered through the windows. Everyone outside seemed fully intent on watching the sky light up.

So far, this bank job was as easy as licking butter off a knife. As expected. Mooney elbowed Wink and nodded toward the back room. The safe room. Both crouched until they reached the tempered iron Diebold safe, standing against the wall.

Mooney ran his hand down the front of the safe. Beautiful. A newer model. But not so new he couldn't break into it. He holstered his Colt, then extracted a poke of gunpowder from his vest.

After holstering his gun, Wink wedged the point of the iron pry bar between the safe's door and frame. He pulled. Then pulled harder, until he'd widened the crack. Mooney poured the gunpowder in and waited.

Flash! Boom! Red and gold splattered the sky. A quick mental count of ticks between "flash" and "boom" and he was ready. There would be another any time now. He waited and counted.

Three. Two. Mooney pulled his cigar to a cherry red and held it to the fuse.

It sparked.

Both men ducked behind a desk and covered their ears. Had he estimated the size of the charge correctly? Too little and it wouldn't even dent the iron. Too much and they'd be blown to bits.

Boom! Mooney glanced at the safe. The door stood wide open, hanging lopsided on one hinge. He coughed in the smoke and then laughed, slapping Wink on the shoulder. His timing was better. Last job he hadn't been so lucky and bystanders had questioned the second explosion. Fortunately, no one had come to check before the gang had scooped up the bank's holdings and were long gone. With great satisfaction, he'd read about it later, in the newspaper.

Mooney yanked the canvas bag from his vest, stuffing bills and certificates into it. He ignored the coins. Too heavy and not worth the effort. Wink, not burdened with this conviction, snatched up coins into a smaller bag. Satisfied with his efforts, Mooney smiled. This had worked better than expected. What holiday was next? Not until the Fourth of July. He'd have to come up with other plans until then.

Bolting for the door, he grunted to Wink, "Doyle's got the horses half a block over." They stepped into the night. "Ride out one at a time."

Wink growled. "I ain't stupid. You already said. Take it slow out of town."

"No need for anybody to get suspicious." Mooney held up

the canvas bag.

"You go first." Wink pushed stringy hair out of his eyes. A greasy hat, pulled low, failed to keep most of the black mop away from his face.

Mooney moved into darkness. "Meet y'all at the cabin." He switched the cigar to the left side of his mouth and chuckled over it.

"And they say crime don't pay."

CHAPTER ONE:
WHO, ME?

"Sorry, Miss Overstreet. Ain't any mail for you today." Wally Cline, hotel clerk of little Dry Creek, California, shrugged, giving me a half-smile. His black hair, tucked behind his ears, curled like worms down to his shoulders. But his eyes were kind. Little crinkles jutted out from the corners.

"When's the next stage coming?" I tapped on the counter. "Wasn't he supposed to be by this morning?" Patience had never been one of my virtues. Besides, I hadn't heard from Eli for ages and surely, by now, he'd located a real postal office, unlike this one, to send me a letter. In it would be his plans for our future and the date he'd come back for me. We'd marry in the church and then be off to start our new lives, together.

Frustrating. That man was purely frustrating.

How long was I expected to wait? It had already been, what . . . two years since he'd ridden away? A couple of letters and lots of tears later, here I was, still waiting. I looked up from my daydream playing on the counter. Mr. Cline eyeballed me.

"Did you hear me?"

Apparently not. I tossed him a smile.

He sighed a bit too loud and a little too long. Guess patience wasn't one of his virtues, either. "As you well know, that rascal Jack McCormick drops off mail from Dutch Flats pretty much whenever he remembers to bring it by. That is, when he's sober enough. Been a couple weeks now, come thinking on it."

Two weeks! Plenty of time for Eli's letter to reach me. It was more'n likely sitting there in Dutch Flats, waiting to be delivered. Or maybe not. I took a breath and tilted up my chin. Fine. Elijah J. Goodman was a rapscallion of the worst kind, stealing my heart like a common thief. On the other hand, he could read and cipher, was handsome, gentle and a really good kisser. Heat crept to my cheeks with the recalling.

"Soon's a letter comes for you, I'll get a kid to bring it over, directly."

Mr. Cline's words spun hope into my chest. I thanked him and stepped out of the hotel and into a bright, northern California afternoon. A lone horse and rider plodded down Main Street. Henry "Pokey" Johnson tipped his hat and continued east. He was headed toward the livery stable, I assumed. Where else would he be going? People around here didn't head anywhere, very often.

My skirt rustled in the spring breeze, bringing a strange combination of warm and cool to my face. It was as if ol' Ma Nature couldn't decide whether to retain winter or bring on summer. Exactly like Eli. Noncommittal.

Rooted to the boardwalk, I stood alone, wrestling with whether to go back home and start supper for Pa and me, or wander around town in search of something important to do. Important? I'd settle for *anything*—interesting, different or challenging. How much longer could I dust, polish, cook, wash and sew for Pa? Here I was looking at thirty behind me, no longer a young woman, pathetically waiting for a man who'd more than likely forgotten me.

Bathed in self-pity, I aimed jealousy at the crows flying overhead. They were going somewhere. Doing something. I sank lower into my mood.

"Howdy, Maud!"

The voice turned me around. Sarah Beth Simpson produced a wide smile.

"Thought it was you." She cradled her newest born, bouncing him gently. Two youngsters hid behind her skirt, tugging and pulling. "How've you been?"

As much as I wanted to share my gloom, doom and boredom with her . . . I lied. "Terrific! Can't complain." I beamed. One look at the baby and my heart melted. I wanted one. Down to the core of my being, I wanted one. And I wanted a husband along with it.

"Maud, I'd like to stop and visit with you, but Ginny's teacher wants to have a meeting during afternoon recess, and little Leroy here's got the sniffles and Jeremiah, well, he's a handful, getting into all sorts of mischief." Sarah took a quick breath. "Thank the Lord the baby's no trouble. Sleeps the night, too. But now, Tom, he's busier than ever at the sawmill. Hardly ever see him."

I took stock of her three children and seriously doubted that last statement. Obviously, she saw him enough. Without that saw mill, there'd be ten kids.

Before I could respond, she continued. "I'm sure it's none of my business, but what brings you downtown?"

"Checking the mail." I thumbed over my shoulder, then gazed into the blue afternoon. "Such a pretty day thought I'd get out into it a bit." Done with the inquisition, I cocked my head. "Gotta get home. Good seeing you."

Sarah flashed a quick smile. "Me, too." She scurried off down the street, her children clinging to her skirts like baby chicks.

If I had been one to grumble as I walked, I would have muttered clear to the coast and back. Thoughts muddled through my bowed head as I marched up the boardwalk. While Sarah was a friend, our lives were too different and I resented her too much to be close. Maybe some day—

"Miss Overstreet?"

I slid to a halt at the man barreling toward me. Now there

were two of us on the boardwalk. Dry Creek's version of congestion.

Harvey Weinberg, mercantile owner and one of three town council members, tipped his hat. I nodded in return. "Mr. Weinberg. Good afternoon." Speaking to three different people in one day! I needed to get out more often.

As I'd been taught, I figured he'd pause, stand to one side as I passed, then continue on his way . . . to somewhere, to something important, I was sure. Well, I had something to go do, too. I needed to start supper. Pa, the town's bank president, liked to eat precisely at six, and I still needed to bake that pie. However, supper was yet a few hours away.

With surprising familiarity, Mr. Weinberg, much taller than me and a nose pointed like a hawk's beak, waited at arm's length. A grin raised his mustache. "Got a minute, Miss Overstreet?"

Of course I did. "Just one," I said. Or two. Or sixty. I had hours. Days. Years. But I couldn't figure out why he wanted to talk. Any time we had spoken, I had to listen carefully. He tended to throw bits of Yiddish into the conversation.

"Excellent." He waved a hand toward the mayor's office across the street. "Would you mind accompanying me to Mayor Critoli's? We've got a . . . *matter* . . . to discuss with you."

"With me?" Why would those two want to talk to me? "Is this about my pa? And the bank?" I ran down a mental litany of reasons they'd want me, as we crossed the dirt street. Nothing sprung to mind.

He chuckled. Something I'd never heard him do before. "No, *balabusta*. This is about you."

Mystified at what he'd called me, I stepped through the door he held open and into Mayor Seth Critoli's office. He was seated behind his desk, while in front sat two men I recognized. Both town councilmen. Ian MacKinney, a red-haired Scotsman so short he looked like he'd been sawed off at the pockets, and Slim Higginbotham, not so slim. The three men's faces turned to me.

Fit and trim and looking all "mayor-y", Mayor Critoli stood before the other two struggled to their feet. Higginbotham, owner of two saloons, held a chair for me and they waited to sit until I was arranged on my seat. I spread my skirt so it wasn't wrapped around my legs, so as not to trip me when I stood. I sat up straight.

Awkward silence. Clearing throats. Growling stomach. I hoped it wasn't mine.

"Miss Overstreet," the mayor said. "I'm sure you're wondering why we asked you here."

My eyebrows arched and I forced a thin smile, but words refused to form.

His gaze trailed over the three town leaders and at last landed on me. From me, he looked at his desk, out the window, back to me. The men squirmed.

I couldn't stand it. "Is there a problem? Am I in trouble?"

That broke the ice. Four men guffawed, shaking heads and squirming again.

Councilman Higginbotham thumbed his mustache and spoke. "Well, Miss Overstreet, as you know, Sheriff Larimore's . . . gone fishing."

"An' he ain't a-comin' back." MacKinney shrugged. "Which leaves our fair town a wee bit shorthanded, when it comes to enforcin' the law."

Still confused, I tried to make sense of the conversation. "But he's been gone almost three weeks. We've been fine."

" 'Tis the truth, you're statin'," MacKinney said. "But 'tis the future what's concernin' us."

"What Ian's trying to say, Miss Overstreet . . ." the mayor said. "We've done a lot of serious thinking about the future of

Dry Creek, and in what direction this town should head. We want to be as ace-high as Sacramento. As progressive as San Francisco. As . . . well, you get the picture."

I didn't.

Harvey Weinberg, who'd been silent, spoke up. "What we're beatin' around the bush is . . . well, we'd like *you* to be sheriff. Take Ol' Larimore's place."

"It'd only be 'til election time, this July." Higginbotham leaned forward. "Think about it. You'd get paid. Have your own office."

"And a badge," said the mayor.

"Right. A badge. An' ye would still have opportunity to take care of your pa's house." MacKinney patted his stomach.

Badge? Pay? Office? They were speaking some manner of English, I was fairly sure, but the words made no sense. I looked from face to face. Serious enough until I broke out laughing. "I get it," I snorted. "This is a joke. Funny." The smile stretched my cheeks. "Had me going there for a minute."

I knew the mayor. He and I had gone on a picnic once where I had discovered he had a mischievous sense of humor. This had to have been his idea. Seth and his friends got me good.

I stood, folding my skirt at my ankles, straightening my hat. The men jumped to their feet, but there were no smiles under the mustaches. Concern was more like it.

"Miss Overstreet," said Harvey Weinberg. "You misunderstand. We're serious. We'd like you to fill in as sheriff . . . until mid-summer."

Mayor Seth eased from behind his desk, moved within inches of me and came close to whispering. "Seriously, Maud. We thought hard about who could fill this position and we chose you."

"Besides," Slim Higginbotham said, "you're about the only adult around here who ain't married, or holdin' down a job."

18

He shifted his weight. "And it ain't like you're busy all the time. You got nothing important to do."

Nothing to do? The resentment of the offense caught in my throat . . . until I realized he was right. On one hand, I had no experience with being a law man. Woman. I didn't own a gun, had never even held one. On the other, becoming sheriff would get me out of the house and give me something to do. Maybe even something *important*.

Mayor Critoli interrupted the maelstrom in my mind. "You're also level-headed and have schooling. Necessary requirements for the job."

Level-headed? Me? They had the wrong person. "But," I said, "in case you haven't noticed, I'm a woman." I sat again and rearranged my skirt. "Doesn't that mean something?"

The four of them mumbled, retaking their seats. "We did, er, notice and did take that into consideration." Weinberg shrugged. "Still, we feel you're the best man for . . . woman . . . person for the job."

Still not really comprehending, I asked, "But nothing ever happens around here. Sure, the Henderson boys stole a couple of pies off Mrs. Gallaway's windowsill, I hear the fellows at the saloons get rowdy at times, but they don't shoot each other. And . . ." Then it dawned on me. "I've never shot a gun."

The men muttered to themselves and then at each other, exchanging glances. Then the mayor produced a half shrug. "Tell you the truth, I can't remember the last time Larimore used a gun, much less shot anybody." He nodded at the other men. "I don't see that as a problem, her not being able to shoot. Do you?"

Heads wagged and more mumbling.

"So, it's settled, Miss Overstreet." The mayor stuck out a hand to shake mine. "We have a deal?"

"No," I said, surprising myself. "It's clear you don't need me."

"Oh, but we do," MacKinney and Higginbotham said in unison.

"Not enough excitement 'round here." Weinberg straightened his brocade vest. "We're thinking that appointin' you sheriff might shake things up a bit." He looked at the mayor, who raised an eyebrow. "It'd surely bring people into town. No other female sheriffs within . . . well, I don't think there is another one."

"And," the mayor added, "the folks who come in gotta eat, stable their horses at the livery, buy supplies and maybe a drink."

"You would be good for business," Higginbotham said. "Dry Creek needs you."

I sat stunned. Good for business? Me? I'd have to run this past Pa, who'd surely say no. He liked things the way they were. As long as he had an orderly house, clean clothes and food on his table, he didn't seem to much care if I was happy. But he was my pa and I, an obedient daughter.

"I don't think so." I choked down concern. I'd never held a job before. Would I even know what to do? "Did you ask Pokey Johnson? He's had schooling and knows how to shoot." I looked from man to man.

The four men squirmed and then leaned back. When it was obvious no one else was going to break the silence, MacKinney spoke. "We know that, Miss Overstreet, and we did consider him. Fact is, that young man's been spending a wee bit too much time sleepin' off his nights in jail. It wouldn't look good for the city council to appoint a fellow like him sheriff."

I understood, I guess.

"You think some more. But, we'd like your decision soon." Mayor Seth Critoli stood and held out a hand. "A day without a sheriff is a day without . . . well, the law. Sure would like to pin that badge on your chest." His face sparked red. "I mean . . ."

Despite my annoyance, I grinned. He was so cute, flustered, sputtering and stammering. I let him dangle for a while. Standing, I took his outstretched hand.

These men had been in the sun too long. Serious or not, I would not be sheriff. I walked toward the door and then turned back halfway. Each man froze, I supposed hoping for me to announce that I'd be happy to oblige. I didn't.

"Gentlemen," I said. "Thank you for the offer, but I won't be your sheriff. I wouldn't know how to do the job. And I doubt that anything you can say or do will change my mind." I reset my hat, which I felt sliding to one side, gathered my skirt, tossed a tight "Good day, now" over my shoulder and marched out of the door.

I got my mutter going as I stormed down the street toward home. How dare they imply I was their last choice? That I had nothing important to do in my life. Who did they think they were talking to? Good for business? *Me?* A circus attraction?

I stomped into Pa's house and slammed the imported glass door.

CHAPTER TWO:
THERE'S NEW LAW IN TOWN

"I . . . Maud Overstreet . . . do solemnly swear . . . to uphold all the laws of Dry Creek, in the great state of California." My left hand trembled as it rested on our family Bible. I raised my right hand shoulder high and repeated after the judge. By now my knees threatened to send me to the floor, but I locked them tight and they held my weight. I considered, for the millionth time, why the town council had chosen me to be Dry Creek's new sheriff. Maybe Old Sheriff Larimore would come back, a string of fish on his shoulder and put that badge back on his own chest. Maybe not.

The three members of the council, along with the mayor, agreed I would do a righteous job. They'd yammered at me for close to a month wearing me down. In addition to being schooled, level-headed and, most importantly, unmarried, they claimed another attribute I possessed: I was strong-willed. All traits they were looking for.

Pa said I was prettier'n Old Larimore. "It doesn't mean you should wear a badge and swagger around this one-horse town like a man. Besides," he'd sniffed, "there isn't any real crime in this part of northern California. No need for a full-time sheriff. One of the town council would be a better choice."

But I'd quit listening to Pa a couple weeks ago. What did he know, anyway? He certainly paid me no never mind. And, by gum, it was time for me to get out of the house and accomplish something on my own. Something . . . important. Maybe make a difference. Okay then, I would become the first woman sheriff of Dry Creek. Probably of anywhere. And it would take more than Pa's patrician disapproval for me to reconsider.

Muffled chortles and snickers rolled out from the crowd gathered in the courtroom. Two days before, the weather had turned exceptionally warm for this time of year. Packed with people, the room, built to hold twenty, possibly thirty, men, now lacked oxygen. Must be forty, maybe fifty, townsfolk inhaling and exhaling, like fish on a stream bank. I struggled to breathe. The men standing in the back shouldered each other and mumbled. The three rows of pews sagged under all the weight.

I glanced over at Pa in the front row, a place reserved for important people—the bank president being one of them. The other part of the front was taken up with the three men who'd convinced me to take this job, "Big" Ian MacKinney, part owner of Dry Creek Mercantile—Harvey Weinberg being the other part—and Slim Higginbotham. Slim towered over most men, but his ample waistline was what most people saw coming first.

Pa's head slowly wagged back and forth, his lowered gaze sweeping the floor sure as my broom sweeps our front porch. Must be trying to figure out where he'd gone wrong.

The Honorable Circuit Judge Andrew Richfield mumbled something. I leaned closer and frowned. Was I supposed to mumble, too? When I didn't say anything, he let out an exasperated sigh and repeated the garble louder. "As set forth in the Code of Conduct in this town of Dry Creek, California, on this fourteenth day of May, eighteen hundred and seventy-two."

His eyes shifted to someone over my shoulder, someone who was more than likely more interesting than me, as I repeated it. He allowed his eyes to rest on mine. "So help me God."

"So help me God. I do."

"Not 'I *do*'," Judge Richfield snapped. "You ain't gettin' married, Maud. Say I *will*."

Sniggers from the assembly. My cheeks warmed. "Sorry. I will."

From somewhere behind me in the crowded courtroom, a voice called out. "Don't worry your pretty little head none, sheriff. We'll all help you catch them pie-stealin' boys."

Chuckles rolled across the room.

"That's right," another chimed in. "Soon's we catch 'em desperados, and soon's we eat them pies, we'll bring 'em right along for you to string up."

The courtroom exploded with a good heehaw. Men held their sides and elbowed each other. The women hid smiles behind fans or gloved hands. Were they laughing at me? No, of course not. Why would they? The idea of stringing up boys for pie stealing was silly. I smiled, too, sure the cackling was exclamations of joy and relief that finally a new sheriff had been confirmed. Dry Creek had been, according to my quick ciphering, sheriff-less for over two months.

Butterflies stomped a square dance in my stomach as I shook hands with Judge Richfield, the three town council members and, lastly, my pa, who gave me a pat on the shoulder. We didn't hug like a normal father-daughter. We rarely even shook hands, but with today being a special day, I guess he felt obligated to show some . . . affection.

Mayor Seth Critoli elbowed his way through the crowd. Above his head he held a metal star with five rounded points. "Here, Maud. We forgot somethin'."

It was rather comical watching him figure out exactly where to pin that sheriff's badge. Even though he had taken me to an occasional church social, our relationship had never gone beyond a quick goodnight kiss. I didn't like him well enough to let him touch me in places reserved for my real beau, Elijah J. Goodman. Regardless, it was because of Eli's absence, wherever he was, that I took this job. Being sheriff of Dry Creek would give me something to do while waiting for his return. Something *important.*

After a couple of cursory yet futile attempts to pin the star on my blouse, Seth grabbed my hand and unceremoniously slapped the tin badge into my palm. "Here. You best do it." He stood back, all toothy smiles. Curved lips slid up both sides of his mustache. With his smooth cheeks, he resembled one of those cherubs. Seth wasn't a bad sort of man. Still, he wasn't all that saintly, either.

Like I'd just won a trophy, I studied that tin star. A tinge of rust threatened a tip, but otherwise, it was in fine shape. Then a closer look—Sheriff of Dry Creek County! Wait one cotton-pickin' minute. I was supposed to be sheriff of the town, not the whole county. No siree, I wouldn't be hornswaggled like that. I searched for Seth, finding him heading outside.

"Mr. Mayor," I hollered over heads. "A word." I waited for him to spin around and take a step toward me.

I held the badge up. "It says right here, county. C-o-u-n-t-y. Not town. *County.* You left out that little bit—"

"Ah, Maud," Seth held my hand with the badge in it. "It doesn't make a difference. Only one town in Dry Creek County and that makes us the county seat. Town. County." He shrugged. "Same thing."

All the wind blown out of my indignant sails, I held my head up. "I knew that. Just testing you." Was that the best I had? Oh boy, this would be a long three months 'til election time.

His explanation made sense. I pinned the badge on the left side of my blouse, polished it a bit, threw my shoulders back and planted a smile on my face. Soon I would have to change that smile to the stern, concerned look I knew the citizenry expected. But right now, I was happy. My cheeks ached, unaccustomed as they were to this sort of prolonged activity.

But it was Pa I was most bothered with. He shook hands and accepted more pats on the back than I did. One would think *he* had just become the first female sheriff of Dry Creek. Right then I resolved to show him I could be a good lawman . . . law woman. That I would make a difference and uphold what I'd taken a vow to do.

When I realized most of the gathering had migrated to the boardwalk to stand around and gossip, I sauntered outside, also. If I was to protect and serve, well, I needed to be where the townsfolk were. All three hundred and eighty-one of them.

Sarah Beth Simpson sashayed up to me with the newest resident swaddled in her arms. Her two-year-old gripped her skirt from behind and peered up at me with big, brown eyes.

"I'm guessing congratulations are in order, Maud. I never thought you'd actually go through with it. I mean . . . you being a woman . . ." She shot me a quick frown. "Guess you'd already thought about that, though."

She pulled down the wrap around the baby so that I could get a better look at his angelic face. The familiar ache again tugged at my heart. I still wanted one. When breathtakingly handsome Eli had come along, I was convinced a ring and children were right around the corner. I'd even practiced writing my new name—Mrs. Elijah J. Goodman. Curlicues looked good on the *J*s. Life couldn't have promised any better. That is, until he followed his own dream and the road out of town . . . without me.

I wrenched my thoughts back to the here and now, stumbling over my words. "He's adorable, Sarah. You both look great." My jealous side was about to rear its ugly head. If I didn't leave, I'd most likely burst into tears. Not the way to show off my new law woman potential.

Sarah cuddled the baby. "He's such a good boy. And so advanced for his age, too. Why yesterday—"

"Excuse me," I spotted Pa talking to a farmer he knew. "Need to talk to Pa. It'll only take a minute."

Running a gauntlet of well-wishers, I shook hands and endured endless back pats while making my way toward Pa, now standing in the middle of the street.

"Miss Maud!" Doc Monroe's youngest boy ran toward me, waving a piece of paper and hollering like he'd found gold. "Miss Maud, wait up!"

I stood, waiting for him to catch his breath. He wagged the paper up to my face. "Here. This's for you. Mr. Maguire said it's real important."

Rune Maguire was the town's telegraph operator and if he said something was important, more than likely it was. Not an idle word escaped the man's lips. He didn't rattle easily and I'd never known him to start gossip or rumors.

I read the telegram. *Urgent. James Mooney Gang seen riding toward Dutch Flats and Dry Creek.* Signed, *U.S. Marshal, Sacramento, California.*

It didn't mean much to me, so I read it a second time. I realized the youngster still stood in front of me, I guessed waiting for a penny tip. I shook my head, patting my pocketless skirt. "Sorry. Don't have a cent on me."

He kicked at the dirt, turned on his heels and marched off, grumbling under his breath. I caught the words *skinflint* and *no good,* but I turned my attention back to the note. *Marshal in Sacramento!* And who was this James Mooney? Must be outlaws. And headed this way . . . Uh-oh. Before I had time to process the implications, a cowpoke came roaring up the street.

"Fight! Fight! Up yonder at the Tin Pan." His arms flailed like a wild herd of cattle was about to stampede down Main Street. "Get the sheriff!"

I looked around for someone to take charge and all eyes turned to me. What exactly did they expect me to do? Though I was tall for a woman, a thumb over five foot eight and plenty strong from working around Pa's house, chopping wood and tending the garden, I sure was no match for those bull-strong men who got liquored up and beat on each other.

And I didn't have a gun. Or know how to use one.

Mayor Seth slapped me on the back and pushed harder than I thought he should. "First order of business, Sheriff. Go break up that fight." He pointed toward the Tin Pan Saloon, one of five in town and, from what I'd heard, the rowdiest of the bunch.

He leaned in close. So close that I choked on the Bay Rum cologne he'd bathed in. It announced his arrival half a block away. "Arrest those miscreants."

"Arrest?" I didn't even know where the cell keys were. Right then, it dawned on me I was woefully unprepared for this job. When the brawl was stopped, I'd have to spend some time in the office finding my way around. There was probably some paperwork or something for arresting people.

"Sheriff? They're gonna kill each other!" The young cowboy danced on one foot then the other, pointing and spitting his words. "Come quick!"

I hiked up my blue, calico skirt and trotted up the street, citizens on both sides cheering. Their support and good wishes made my heart thunder and my feet take flight. I was the newly appointed sheriff of this town and, by golly, nobody was going to ruin my first day.

Chapter Three:
A New Day

Though I was in my mid-thirties, I had never stepped foot inside such an establishment. Rarely had I even walked by, preferring to pass on the opposite side of the street, as proper ladies do. However, today was a new day.

From outside, the Tin Pan looked like all the other saloons. A hastily-built false front fashioned from roughly-hewn lumber, it was painted in whitewash with orange and black letters proclaiming the name. I wondered if Councilman Higginbotham chose the name himself when he built it. Smoke roiled out the door along with the stench of alcohol combined with tobacco. My nose twitched involuntarily. A sneeze was in there somewhere.

On tiptoes in front of the batwing doors—the only thing separating breathable outside air from questionable inside air—I peered across the room. Kerosene lanterns and the scant natural light from frosted window glass kept the room dim. Smoke fog made it difficult to see who was in the room, but, with my eyes narrowed, I distinguished male from female. At last I discerned individual men.

Sawdust covered the floor. The bar, running parallel to the longest wall, sported rags hanging from underneath, spittoons at men's feet. Five or six cowboys leaned against the bar while whooping and hollering. The bartender scooped bottles and glasses from the mirrored tower of glassware behind the bar, shoving them under the front counter.

I straightened my shoulders, held my breath, and pushed the batwing doors open, holding them wide as I stepped into Lucifer's Workshop. The stench of used tobacco and warm beer combined with kicked-up sawdust attacked my nose. I sneezed and coughed at the same time. Sure enough, two men, bruised and winded, took turns swinging at each other. Other men lazed against the bar, drinks in hand, shouting out bets as to the victor, while others stood on the other side egging on the contenders.

"Two dollars says you can take 'im, Frank!" A ranch hand I recognized from the Lazy Cross Bar held up a couple of silver coins overhead between his index finger and thumb.

A cowboy across the room yelled, "Two? I'll bet *three* Willie there clobbers old Frank!"

"I'll take that bet," the Lazy Cross Bar hand hollered back.

"Nobody's winning anything, fellas." Surprised that I sounded so sheriff-like, I moved in closer to the bartender. I thought his name was Sam, but I wasn't sure. I used it anyway. "Sam," I said. "What's going on here?"

His eyes grew wide and I thought he would choke. He coughed and pointed at the men. "Old Frank and Willie come in here to blow off steam. Got a little out of hand. Thank goodness you're here, Sheriff."

A couple more teeth-rattling whacks got my full attention.

Sam slid a bottle of amber liquid under the bar. "Better break it up quick before anybody else joins in."

"How?"

His eyebrows shot toward the ceiling. "Like Larimore used to." Sam pointed to the brawlers. "Go tell 'em."

By now, everyone in the place cheered, jeered or chanted encouragement to their chosen fighter. I couldn't hear my own thoughts, much less whatever else Sam had to say. I moved in a bit closer and held up my hand. "Hold on, men. No need to fight."

Nobody stopped. Nobody took notice of me.

I stomped on the floor. "Stop it!" The sawdust puffed around my foot and absorbed the definitive effect I had hoped for.

Frustrated and now a bit angry, I stepped within arm's reach and managed to grab Frank's vest as he reeled past me. "Right now!"

Wobbling in place, his glassy gaze traveled up and down my body. "Darlin'," he muttered, a grin stretching up one side of his face.

"I'm the sheriff," I corrected.

" 'Scuze me, *Sheriff* Darlin'."

The bar crowd roared. Willie swung at Frank, who stepped sideways and plowed into me. I sailed back, bouncing into a table, which scooted toward the bar. Slipping on the sawdust, I crashed to the floor and came to rest against a spittoon. Most of its targeted contents were splattered around its rim.

All right. I was sheriff and they were going to do as I said, or they'd both go to jail. I struggled to my feet, pushing my way over to Sam. "You got a gun?"

"You gonna shoot 'em?" His eyes widened.

" 'Course not," I said. "Need something to get their attention."

Sam hauled out a clean bar rag. "This. Get in close, and wave it like you're calling a truce." He flashed me a knowing wink. "That's what Ol' Larimore used to do. Works every time. Guaranteed."

This method seemed a bit tame and inefficient to me, but what did I know about barroom brawls? And if Larimore did it, I would, too. I held up the white rag and waved it. "Stop it! This minute!" I waded in as close as I could without being on the end of a fist. The rag fluttered. "See this? You're supposed to stop." I stomped my foot again for emphasis.

Willie glanced my way, but before I could say anything else, he danced Frank backwards and up against the cherry-wood bar. I waggled the rag harder. "Stop it!"

Frank pushed off from the bar, bent over and grabbed Willie around the knees. And in a move I'd never seen before, lifted Willie and heaved him up and over the bar and into the mirror.

Crash!

I realized why the bartender earlier had been sequestering his glassware. Sam slammed the bar rag onto the counter and glared. "That's it! Fun's over!" He looked down behind the bar at where I supposed Willie lay, as I couldn't see him. Sam snarled, "Get up!"

I don't know what surprised me more—Frank's strength or the fact all the men froze. You could've heard a mouse sneak across the floor, it was so quiet.

It took a bit for me to come to my senses. By then, Sam and Willie stood behind the bar, Sam's face a black thundercloud and Willie's one of delight.

Frank wiped a trickle of blood from his lips and stretched across the bar offering Willie his hand. "That was some right fine flying you did."

Willie picked a glass shard from his hair and offered it to me. "Souvenir of your first bar fight." He swung his gaze around the room. "Courtesy of the boys."

Sam shoved Willie from behind the bar. "You worthless, no-good sodbusters," Sam said to the two men. "Get this place cleaned up. You promised 'no breakage.' Who's payin' for it?"

General mumbling and grumbling ensued, but, to my surprise, the men righted the tables and used their boots to push broken glass under sawdust piles. Jokes flew over the mild curses. Remembering I had a job to do, I edged up to Frank and Willie.

"I should arrest you both," I said to Willie.

He cocked his head at me. "Yeah? What for?"

While I wasn't exactly sure of the correct wording, something else I'd have to look up, I knew the general gist. "Disturbing the peace and quiet of this town, that's what for."

"Peace?" Frank raised an eyebrow at Willie and smiles spread on both faces.

"You want peace, Frank?" Willie elbowed him. "Yeah, me, too."

Willie stepped nose to nose with me. The liquor on his breath took mine, a small gag catching in my lungs. He scanned me head to toe. "A little piece of you'd be fine with me."

Understanding what he meant and not willing to go down that line of reasoning, I stepped back and ran into Frank. By now, everyone in the bar had gathered around, hoisting their glasses to me.

"Here's to you, Sheriff Darlin'."

"Hey, Sam. Why don't you hire her for upstairs? She's mighty pretty."

"Hell, boys, she already got a job."

"She needs one she's good at. You know . . . what comes natural."

The thunderous roar pounded my ears and threatened to bring tears to my eyes. I wanted to cry, but I didn't. I wouldn't let them see me upset. What I wanted to do was to turn and run, but I didn't do that either. I slid sideways from between Willie and Frank, and inched back toward the safety of the batwing doors, threatening the men with arrest if they didn't behave.

I glanced over at Sam behind the bar. He held up a half-empty glass of beer high toward me. "Here's to you, Sheriff."

An ear-shattering cheer erupted. Smiles and pats on backs were offered to Frank and Willie. The two men hitched up their britches, plopped their hats back on their heads and walked over to me. Frank stuck out a hand. "You done good, Sheriff Darlin'."

"Overstreet," I said. "Sheriff Overstreet."

Chapter Four:
Being Level-Headed

Plucking the pinfeathers from a just-boiled hen, I mulled over the real reason why the town council had selected me as sheriff. Nothing I hadn't already thought about came to mind. Still, I was glad they had, as I'd secretly wanted to be in charge of something other than Pa's house. And I wasn't in charge even of that. I fixed supper his way, cleaned house the way he wanted it, even planted a garden and flowers the way he approved.

I floured legs, breasts, wings and thighs, dropping each into the grease that rumbled hot at the intrusion. I stood at the stove, fork in hand, watching the chicken turn a deep brown. No matter which way I turned the pieces, I still couldn't figure out why they'd chosen me. Unless . . . nah, it wouldn't be to play a joke on *me*. Had to be a better reason.

I scraped supper out of the pan and onto Pa's plate, adding a big helping of mashed potatoes. The giblet gravy was full of chicken liver and gizzard pieces, the way he liked it. I'd never cared for it fixed like that. Pa waited at the table, napkin already under his chin. A quick nod of approval, as I set the plate in front of him. I took my chair, he said grace. I shook out and placed my napkin on my lap, then asked what'd been on my mind all day. "You suppose they hired me because of what Seth told me?"

"Which is?"

"That I'm 'levelheaded.' " The chicken had no taste. I could've been eating my shoes and not tell the difference.

Pa ate in silence. Maybe he was thinking over his answer or maybe he was thinking about how good his chicken supper was. Or some problem at the bank. Either way, his not giving me an answer or any conversation made me cranky. I didn't like being ignored.

I pressed on. "Don't know what being 'levelheaded' would have to do with sheriff-ing. I mean, you don't have to think deep to read all the papers the county sends or even to arrest somebody. I'd think all you'd need to know is how to shoot a gun or fight." I rested my fork against the rim of my plate. "And I sure don't know either of those things."

Pa waited to answer until he'd finished sopping up all his gravy with the biscuits I made every day. He patted his mouth and mustache with the red and white checkered napkin. "Can't speak for the town council, Maud. But, I wish you'd said no." He placed the napkin next to his plate. "Don't need to be doin' a man's job."

"I haven't done anything yet." I wadded up my own napkin and tossed it at the table. "I've spent two days sweeping out the jail cell and the office, sorting through Larimore's old wanted posters and putting up with a parade of people stopping at the door to gawk."

"Curious is all." Pa picked his teeth, a habit I hated. "Your sweeping and sorting's cheating the town out of its money. Seems to me you oughta be earning your pay."

I considered his criticism. I was doing my job, and earning pay was the least of my worries. Pa provided well enough, being president of the only bank within twenty miles. We never went without food, clothing or shelter. Even when we'd moved here to northern California fifteen years ago, right on the heels of the gold strike, we'd had a fancy wagon and good horses. Ma, God rest her soul, had said over and over again she'd married a fine man.

I stood, gathering dishes. "I don't cotton to cheating. You know that, Pa. I'll work for my wages."

Pa scooted back from the table, the chair legs screeching across the wooden floor.

"Wouldn't expect anything less." He disappeared into the parlor, tossing the final word over his shoulder. "Chicken's a bit dry. Grease was too hot."

If I could get the dishes washed and dried within the next half hour, I'd still have time to weed part of the garden before the sun went down. There was always something to do. Don't know why I thought I could be sheriff and run the house at the same time. There weren't enough hours in a day or enough hands on my body to do all the things necessary.

The sun rested on the western horizon as I pulled today's new sprouts of dandelions out of their hiding places. It seemed like every time I turned around, another weed found a spot to grow—always where it wasn't welcomed. Late spring brought warm weather and rain. It was close to harvest time for my early crops. I'd have lettuce, radishes and green onions pretty soon.

Down on my hands and knees, I muttered to the invaders as we did our tug o' war.

"Sheriff Maud?"

I about jumped out of my shoes. Raring back on my knees, I frowned up at Pokey Johnson. His thin mustache did not hide his twenty-five years. He chuckled.

"Guess you thought your plants there was talkin' back to you." He tipped his hat. "Sorry to startle you, Sheriff."

I liked Pokey. There didn't appear to be a mean bone in all of his body, which wasn't quite as tall as me. While he was not skinny, his roundedness showed he hadn't missed many, if any, meals and he enjoyed a good belch now and then. That didn't endear him to me much, but he had other, better qualities.

Besides being too young, he wasn't my type. Meaning, I suppose, he also wasn't Elijah J. Goodman.

The way my skirt bunched under my knees made standing awkward. Pokey gripped my arm, lifting me up. I swiped at what I was sure was dirt on my cheek. "What can I do for you?"

"Well, ma'am . . . sheriff. Sheriff ma'am." Pokey stammered his way through several variations of the title before moving on. "Down at the Empire Saloon. Well, there's a fella there I know is cheatin' at cards. He's been playin' poker since before noon, and he's already made a pile of cash."

"How do you know he's cheating?" I asked, wondering how long it would take me to learn poker. Another thing I figured a sheriff should know how to do.

"Oh, he's cheatin' all right. Nobody can make that kind of money without cheatin'." Pokey looked left and right, like somebody was watching and listening in on our conversation. "Plus, he beat ol' Charlie. And nobody beats Charlie."

"Charlie?"

Pokey let out an exasperated sigh like I'd asked him to recite his ABCs. His ample eyebrows shot up. "Charlie O'Tennessee. You know. *Charlie.*"

"Right." But I didn't know. However, I wanted not to look dumber than I already was. I wiped my hands with my apron. "So you want me to go down to the Empire and arrest some fella for winning at poker?"

"When you put it that way, Maud, it don't sound like much." Pokey sighed again. "But he's cheatin'. We all know he is. We want you to catch him doin' it and arrest him." He shrugged. "That's all."

"Well," I said. Maybe this was another game to watch me make a fool of myself. "Guess I better make my way down there. Let me put on a clean bonnet."

I froze. Bonnet. Sheriff. Arrest. Poker. Those words didn't

mesh together. One had to go. I glanced at the sun and it was going down fast. I wouldn't need a bonnet, although I had to have a hat. No one went out without a hat.

A few blinks unfroze me. Pokey still stood, his hat in his hand, an expectant look on his face. I smiled. "Be there soon's I can."

Pokey plopped his hat back on his head, and whisked off as silently as he'd come.

CHAPTER FIVE:
CHEATER, CHEATER

We lived a short three blocks from Main Street, so I didn't have to bother hitching up the buggy. I dashed inside the house to tell Pa I had to go out. Snores emanated from his favorite chair in the parlor. Instead of waking him, I left a note. With my new shiny badge pinned on my blouse and my Sunday church hat pinned firmly on my head, I pulled the door closed and stepped into a warm, northern California evening.

Poker, poker, poker. Could it be that complicated? Look who played it. Still, I should know the details. Tomorrow I'd have to get Pa or Pokey to teach me. But, tonight, I had to figure out if this new-to-town fella was cheating. Or, if they were pulling my leg again. How I was going to do that, I hadn't a clue. But Seth said I was levelheaded. Maybe this was one of those times he was talking about. A test, so to speak.

Given that I'd been in the Tin Pan, another immoral devil's outpost, two days before, I'd made it a point to scout out the other "viper pits" in town. While I hadn't stepped inside, I did know their locations. The Empire sat in the middle of town.

Standing again outside the batwing doors, I gazed into the gloom. It looked a lot like the Tin Pan, only darker and smokier. The stench of stale beer, kerosene, tobacco and something I declined to identify rolled over the doors and hit me in the face. My eyes watered. The view, cloudy as it was, revealed four or five tables, men seated around each. I located Pokey at a table near the back. Men lazed at the bar while a couple of the bar maids flounced around, laughing and sidling up to the customers. One woman pounded at an upright piano, such as it was. I thought I recognized *Camp Town Races*. It was so out of tune, it could've been *Sweet Genevieve*.

Holding my breath, I stepped in and made my way over to the bartender. I didn't want to single out Pokey, asking him to point out the culprit. No need putting my informant at risk. Maybe the bartender could tell me.

I leaned across the bar. "Who's the fella been playing cards, winning all day?"

The bartender stepped back, gave me a long up and down inspection, and frowned. "We don't allow ladies in here." His frown turned smirky, one eyebrow arched. " 'Less you're lookin' for a job."

"Already have one," I said. That in itself was an odd feeling. I'd never had a real job before. "Need to know about that fella is all."

He snorted. "And who exactly wants to know?"

I pointed to my new badge. "*I* do." Little butterflies fluttered in my stomach. That was kind of fun.

He squinted closer through the smoke. "Oh, it's you, Maud. I know your pa. Sorry, didn't recognize you."

"I'm Sheriff Overstreet." I liked the way saying "sheriff" made my name sound. Almost as official as "Mrs. Elijah J. Goodman." I refocused my attention.

The bartender bristled a bit at my correcting him, but he pointed toward a table in the corner, back by the steps, which led to the second floor. Enthusiastic sounds of "negotiable affection" fluttered down the stairway. I chose to concentrate on the shuffling of cards and the tinny piano.

Four men slumped at the table, three looking miserable—drunk, but miserable—and the fourth was downright jovial as he scraped a pile of money toward his other sizeable pile. He

41

looked up at me, a tree limb–sized cigar clamped in his mouth. He spoke around it.

"Sit down there, Missy. You look like a woman who knows her way around a card table."

Any semblance of bravado I'd faked escaped through my toes. Something about him scared the living beejeezus out of me. Could it be his dark eyes running across my face? Or his long fingers playing with the cash as he stacked it? Maybe it was that smarmy leer peeking out from under a curling mustache resembling two seahorses kissing. The image of a man who hated to lose.

My mouth turned into the Mojave Desert. I tried to speak, but the only sound which came out was a stammer and stutter. Before I could try something else, Pokey Johnson appeared at my shoulder and pressed a mug full of beer into my hand.

"Here, Sheriff. This'll wet your whistle."

Like a five-gallon water bucket, it hit me. This was another prank the town boys figured to pull on me. Another initiation. Not one to shirk my duties and to appear the mountain canary—those donkeys used up in the hills—in front of this card sharp, if indeed that's what he was, I needed to drink. I looked at Pokey and sipped. More like sour milk.

I coughed . . . and sipped again. Second time was not as bad. Two more sips and I handed the glass back to Pokey. Pushing down beer remnants clinging to my throat, I warbled to the stranger who continued to smirk at me.

"You new in town?" What a dumb thing to ask. Of course he was new in town. I knew pretty much everybody and he was new.

Cutting narrowed eyes up at me, he plucked the cigar from his lips. "You asking me out on a date, Sheriff?"

The barroom exploded. Even the piano stopped playing long enough for my face to heat up. I gulped the rest of the swill

Pokey handed back to me.

"Simply asking where you're from, sir."

The room warmed.

That oily fella patted the table where an empty chair waited.

"Sit yourself down right here, Missy, and I'll tell you my story." He paused for effect. "I'll even buy you a drink."

More snickers and laughter rolled across the room.

I glanced at Pokey, who shrugged. All right, I'd play along with this little game. Guess I'd have to trust Pokey not to let me down, even though, more than likely, he was in on the joke.

"All right, sir. I'll sit with you, but I don't usually drink when I'm on duty." I sauntered toward the empty chair, my bravado in place.

The man held up two fingers and hollered at Sam. "Two whiskeys. One for me and one for the lady who don't drink."

I sat up straight. "I'm not a lady, I'm the sheriff."

Snickers waved across the room as everyone watched.

When the shot glasses arrived, the man held one up. "Here's to you, Sheriff Missy." He tossed it back like water. All eyes stared at me until I knew I had to reciprocate. I brought the glass up to my nose and my eyes watered. I sipped.

Fire.

It slid down my throat like a singed cat, claws out. I choked and sucked in air while everyone whooped and hollered.

It took three deep breaths and Pokey pounding my back before I could see again. I couldn't understand what was so intriguing about whiskey. People drink this stuff on purpose?

One of the saloon girls slid a cup of coffee under my nose. "Here, honey. This'll help." While it was hot, it didn't burn like that whiskey. I produced a weak smile of appreciation to the woman. I recognized her from church.

"Now, I'm assuming this's a social visit, Sheriff Missy." The gambler tossed a coin at the bartender, who'd delivered two more shots. He threw back the brimstone, knuckled the center of his curled mustache and looked at me. His dark eyes danced. "What can I do for you?"

"You seem to be winning a lot. I think it's time to give it a rest. Maybe move on to another town?" I wasn't sure he needed to leave, but I wanted to make it clear that he'd taken enough money. At least for today. And I was tired of this fun-poking at me.

He leaned back, sighed and flipped open his jacket to reveal a pocket pistol lashed against his chest. The single-shot gun would kill at close range. Even I knew that.

"Well, Sheriff, there's no law saying I can't sit here and win at cards. Any fellas who ran to you crying are bad poker players. That's all. They're not *winners* . . . they're *whiners.*" He picked up a deck of cards and shuffled them, staring at me instead of them. "Can't stand whiners."

Was that what they really were? I'd have to talk to Pa.

"You play cards, Missy?" He squared the deck and tapped the top. "Cut 'em."

I looked up and around. The ten or so men and women who'd gathered around leaned in closer, as if watching a rooster fight. I wouldn't be surprised if they'd laid bets on who was going to win: the fella who had scooped up his money and pocketed most of his winnings, or me—the new lady sheriff.

Before I touched a card, my eyes trailed up to his derby pushed back on his forehead, down to the man's silk brocade vest, and finally rested on long, slender fingers. They were dainty, in fact, too much so for a man. But what I truly took note of was the cuffs of his white shirt. Now most men I knew used leather cuffs over their shirtsleeves, supposed to keep them from fraying, but this fella's leather cuffs were black and thicker than I'd seen. I leaned closer and squinted. Something white stuck out under his left cuff. Looked like the corner of a card. I lowered my voice, figuring he'd put it there on purpose.

"Looks to me like a card got stuck to your sleeve, sir."

"What?" He followed my gaze.

I pointed. "You've got a card stuck under your cuff." His black eyes flew to mine. I grinned, expecting a roar from the crowd with wide smiles all around. A few thumps on the back from people admitting their joke. I win this time. But, instead, the crowd gasped and scrambled back. Guns flew out of holsters. The metal on metal grating of hammers cocking brought me to my feet. The fella jumped up, jerked out his pocket pistol and stuck it to my head.

He hollered. "You shoot me, I shoot her."

I couldn't breathe. If this was a joke on me, it was a good one. Sure felt real.

"Put your guns down," he waved his weapon toward the back of the room. "Everybody. Move back there. Try anything funny, she dies." Everyone did as instructed.

Pokey's eyes grew wide and the beer in his hand sloshed. This was no joke. Now, I wished it was.

Satisfied he had a clear path to the door, he clutched my arm. Together, we backed across the room, navigating vacant tables and chairs.

Our shoes scuffling through sawdust, my heart thudding and the fella's hot breath on my neck were the only things making sense. We backed through the doors and out onto the boardwalk.

"No need for anybody getting hurt, sir." I tried reasoning with him. Since I was supposed to be "levelheaded," I offered a solution. "How about returning their money and you riding out? No pursuit." I hoped he'd take the deal. "Or . . . you can give me the money and I'll return it."

"Like hell!" He removed his pistol from my head and shoved it into my side. He grabbed my wrist. Hard. I flinched. His words hissed in my face. "You'll come with me 'til I know we ain't followed. If you play nice, Sheriff Honey, I'll let you go. Maybe."

I didn't like the "maybe" part, but what choice did I have? None, really. I didn't like being a hostage and made a mental note to get myself a gun first thing in the morning. I chanced a quick glance behind me as we marched up the street toward the livery stable. A few of the patrons followed, but most stayed behind in the saloon.

Maybe I could trip and fall and roll out of his clutches. Maybe a horse would kick him.

Maybe I could scream and help would come running. No, wait—I *am* the help.

I didn't know my legs would carry me so far and so fast but, within a couple of minutes, we reached the stable at the south end of town. A golden glow from the kerosene lanterns lit the inside, giving it a warm and cozy feel, while the smell of fresh hay made me sneeze.

I let out a good one. Another on the way tickled my nose.

As I bent over for a second sneeze, the stable owner, the only Negro in town, Swede Swensen, moseyed out from a stall. He hung a kerosene lantern on a peg head high. "Howdy."

The scalawag spun around at the man's baritone voice and released my arm. Since I was bent over anyway, I hit the ground and rolled, careening right into his legs, toppling him and his fancy boots. When he thudded, little puffs of dirt and hay blew up around him and his gun skidded into a stall. I scrambled for the weapon the same time as the card sharp did.

We were a tangle of legs, arms and skirt, rolling in the dirt. He wasn't giving up and I wasn't giving in. Over my grunting and sneezing, I heard shouts and men's voices. I was going to get that gun, take the cheater to jail . . . do my duty.

We rolled back and forth, my strength surprising me. Guess you can hang on when you have to. Tumbling around wasn't getting me anywhere, I struggled to my feet. The fella had the same idea and pushed me hard against the wood stall. My arms flew up, one hitting the lantern and next thing I knew, it flew off the peg. Glass shattered. The hay burst into flames. Shouts erupted.

"Fire! Fire!"

Orange flares danced at my feet. Flames engulfed the stall. I grabbed the fella's flimsy vest. He wasn't using a fire as an excuse to get away. My grip remained like iron.

"Maud!" Mr. Swensen hollered. "Your skirt!"

The bottom of my brown skirt sizzled in flames. I danced backwards until Mr. Swensen shoved me to the ground, beating out the flames with a horse blanket. Dust and hay flew into my face. I sneezed. And rolled. And sneezed.

Pokey rushed in and tossed a bucket of water near me. Within seconds, other men with buckets tossed while others led wide-eyed horses outside.

A moment later I was out, but it took another minute or two to extinguish the rest of the fire. Men spread and stomped the hay, checking for errant embers.

Mr. Swensen, muscled ebony arms, shirtsleeves pushed up to the elbows, pulled me to my feet. "Thanks," I said. "That was close."

He wagged his head, mumbling, and walked away, the smoldering horse blanket in his enormous hands.

By the time I could gather my "levelheaded" wits, the gambler had vanished. Escaping into smokey chaos. I looked everywhere for him—in each stall, up in the hayloft, even outside. But he was gone.

All I could do was stand there as the men walked away, grumbling and mumbling. Only Pokey waited at my side.

"You done good, Sheriff Maud."

"Thanks." But I knew I hadn't.

Tomorrow, I'd learn to play poker.

Chapter Six:
Deserving Dignity

All right. A gun pointed at my head and then being caught on fire caused more than a sleepless night. I'd tossed and turned until daylight crept into my room. I fought the need to toss back the bedcovers and wake up to a new day. I would have given almost anything to hide under the covers.

Despite misgivings, I threw off the sheet and let my feet hit the floor. I'd face the day and my new job with the dignity it deserved. And the dignity *I* deserved.

I sipped a final cup of coffee and scanned the littered breakfast table. Pa had lit out earlier, citing important banking business, which left me, as usual, to tidy up. As I waited for a pan of water to heat on the stove, I pumped water into the sink. I thought about last night and how things could have been different. With no good answers at hand and the water hot, I immersed the dishes and utensils into sudsy, warm water. Just doing dishes this morning, my hands, deep in familiar territory, was oddly soothing. As I scrubbed, I considered. If I'd had a gun and used it, maybe I could've defended myself.

Which brought me to a life-altering conclusion—I'd have to buy a gun.

And learn how to use it.

Pa, I knew, wasn't willing to teach me the finer points of shooting. He maintained no woman needed a gun, and it was "downright embarrassin' to see a woman doin' what a man had a God-given right to do." His masculine pride wouldn't let me into his world, so I had to seek my education elsewhere. Curiously, Pa was more than grumpy lately. Close to hostile. But worrying about Pa's feelings wasn't at the top of my "to do" list.

First off, I'd have to visit Dry Creek Mercantile, where I knew Harvey Weinberg sold guns. Then, I'd need somebody to teach me how to operate it. Parts of me tingled with anticipation alternating with worry that I'd shoot myself or somebody else, accidentally. I suppose secretly I'd always wanted to shoot a gun, but, until now, I'd had no need to even hold one.

Today was a new day.

Once dishes were dried and the remainder of the kitchen cleaned, the ironing finished and two rugs hung out to air in the day's delicious warmth, I made sure I was dirt-free myself and walked toward Main Street, hoping to locate a teacher. Pokey had offered to help me with the fine art of shooting, so I went in search of him. Since he worked part-time at the mercantile, he would be the one to fix me up with an appropriate gun.

I checked the mercantile, the office, even church. No Pokey. About to give up and go home, I found him bellied up to the bar at the Tin Pan, leaning against it, beer glass in one hand, flinging the other arm around, explaining something vitally instructive to the bartender.

The accomplishment of walking across those sawdust-strewn floorboards pulled my shoulders back. Women didn't come in here unless they worked here. I wasn't a woman. I was the sheriff.

All heads turned as I sidestepped a glob of something black and coated in sawdust. Smells of beer, whiskey, cigars and kerosene mingled, making it impossible to figure out what the black goo was. I didn't really want to know and I was careful my skirt didn't drag in it.

By the time I made my way to the bar and stood next to

Pokey, a couple of men gathered their courage to make snide comments.

"Look what the cat done drug in, Clyde." The words were slurred but I understood.

"Why, looks like she's been out runnin' with the dregs of the she-herd."

"Guess the only way she could throw a loop to catch herself a man is to be one."

The entire saloon roared. My cheeks burned. Humiliation came with the badge, I figured, but I hadn't prepared myself for it today. I focused on Pokey, who seemed oblivious to the barbs.

The taunts continued.

"Bet she'd make damn fine blanket company." With that, two groups at the tables lifted their glasses, saluting me and offering to show me how it's done. I reached Pokey and turned my back to the room.

"Howdy, Sheriff Maud, ma'am." Pokey's beer-soaked words dribbled down his chin.

One eye twitched while it tried to focus on me. "What cha doin' here?"

With as soft a voice as I thought he could hear, I explained. "Last night . . . got me to thinking. I need a gun. Learn to shoot."

A smile blossomed under his mustache and both eyes twinkled. He slapped me on the back, sending me against the bar. "That's a swell idea, Maud. I mean Sheriff, ma'am. Maud, ma'am." He held up his beer glass, his voice rising above the saloon's din. "Here's to you."

Most of the room cheered and saluted with raised glasses, not that they needed much encouragement. Pokey ordered another glass, while I declined his offer to buy me one. He sampled the new brew, wiped the foam off his mustache and turned one bleary eye on me, the other not bothering to follow.

"Wait a minute. You got me a'wonderin'. Now, if I'm teachin' ya to shoot, where's your gun at?"

I realized this was not the day for Pokey to teach me . . . anything.

CHAPTER SEVEN:
IT'S A DATE

While Pokey slept off his beer-laden morning, I had to figure out who else could teach me. Somebody I trusted. I strolled the boardwalk, mumbling a howdy to the fine citizens I passed. The answer struck me.

Mayor Seth Critoli.

I backtracked up Main Street to his office and found him leaned forward in his chair, hunched over his desk like a question mark, poring over some sort of document. It looked official and important, but *my* business was official and important, as well. I knocked on the partially opened door and waltzed in as he looked up and smiled.

I explained my predicament and he raised both eyebrows.

"You're staying in the job?" he said. "I figured after last night, you'd be ready to quit."

"I don't scare easily." My shoulders straightened. Fact was, I did scare, but I would never admit it. "I took an oath that I'd be sheriff till at least summer and that's what you'll get."

"Knew I could count on you." Seth stood and pointed to an empty chair. "But a gun at your head could make you question your occupation."

"Know what I think?" I fisted my hands on my hips and remained standing. "I think you and the town council didn't know what you got yourselves into when you appointed me."

Part of a smile dimpled his right cheek. "Aren't you finding it hard to keep house and sheriff, too?"

"You got somebody to replace me?" I eased for the door. "All I came over here for was a simple favor and didn't expect, or need, an attitude. If you and that town council of yours want this badge, you'll have to run me out. I'm here to stay."

Seth held up a hand.

"Besides," I said, not done yet. "I came to ask if you'd help me buy a gun and teach me how to shoot. If you don't think—"

"Didn't say that, Maud." Seth touched my hand. "I'm pleased you're taking an interest in your position."

"What does that—?"

"It means," Seth said, "that I understand you've had no reason to learn—before now."

My temper simmered. Maybe he'd teach me. "I'm staying sheriff. You and everybody else in this town better get used to the idea."

"What about James Mooney? Aren't you afraid—"

"He doesn't scare me. I've pondered on him and, well . . ." I hunched one shoulder hoping to give a "don't care" attitude, but mostly I spoke through fake disdain because after looking through the wanted posters, Mooney *did* scare me. "Being as I'm so 'levelheaded,' I'll think of something, if the time comes." I emphasized "if."

Seth recoiled, slightly, stifling a grin.

One hand on hip, I pointed the other over my shoulder. "You gonna help me learn to shoot or not?"

Seth held up a hand. "Be glad to, *Sheriff.* And I know what I'm doing 'cause I've been handling weapons since I buttoned up my first britches. Guns and me are natural together."

Inside the Dry Creek Mercantile, Harvey Weinberg stood behind the counter, arms folded over his ample stomach, while Seth examined a gun in his hand. He turned it over and over, caressing it with the gentlest of touches.

"A thirty-six Navy revolver's the workhorse of weapons," he said. "Shoot, it'll knock down about anything you hit." Seth turned a wickedly seductive grin on me. "This'll be perfect."

I eased it out of his grip, butt first. Heavier than I'd imagined, it fit my hand like someone had built it with me in mind.

At first, I was afraid to touch it, certain the thing would go off. Then, upon holding it and figuring out which end to point, instantly, I was in love. My gun! My own weapon!

Pa would have to understand.

Etchings depicting a scuffle between the Mexican and Texas navies encircled the cylinder, giving the gun its name. I liked the balance and its weight, a bit under three pounds. Seth called it a "single action", which meant it could be fired only as fast as I could cock the hammer and pull the trigger. The ammunition was black powder, poured into paper cartridges, and a lead ball seated atop the chamber. I'd have to learn how to tamp the powder into the cartridges. Make my own bullets.

"Most important, Maud," Seth said, "is keepin' this baby clean. When you fire it too many times, there's a buildup of lead and grime and it fouls the action."

I looked at him. Was he speaking English?

"What he means," Mr. Weinberg said, pointing to the gun, "is that fouling can slow or even stop your gun from shooting. Might get you shot while you're fumblin' around."

I nodded like I understood what he was saying. "I'll take it," I said to Mr. Weinberg. "You got ammunition?"

"*Ech.* Of course I do. What kind of store do you think this is?" Mr. Weinberg could be testy at times, and this was one of them. He eyed Seth. "Maybe we should find somebody else."

"She's doing fine, Harvey." Seth tossed me a wink.

Mr. Weinberg turned his back on Seth and me, searched through a few racks and drawers and brought out black powder, cartridges, balls and caps.

A short lesson from Mr. Weinberg and Seth on tamping powder into the cartridge and fitting the ball, cap and nipples in place, and I was ready to become the next shooting legend. I paid for everything with the last of my saved money. Seth and I thanked Mr. Weinberg and stepped outside.

"Wanna do it right now?" Seth asked.

"Absolutely."

Seth pulled his watch from his vest pocket, inspected it, snapped it shut and replaced it. "Got one errand to run, but I'll meet you in your office, directly. All right?"

"Fine. I'll be ready." He leaned close and kissed me. Right on the cheek. Confused, I alternated between being ecstatic to wanting to smack him in the face. How dare he presume?

I fumed and flustered my way back to the office. As I examined my gun, I thought about the possible meanings of that little cheek peck. Was it a "we're merely friends"? Was it something he did with all the women? Was it going to lead to . . . other things?

One thing I knew for certain—I enjoyed it. Thoughts of Eli crowded in, and being I was a one-man woman, dismissed Seth's kiss as a friendly "good-bye."

Seth Critoli stepped into my office ten minutes later. He greeted me as if nothing had happened. I'd play along and pretend nothing of mention had happened, as well. Maybe nothing *had* happened. I'd heard he was dating Miss Pearl McIntyre, the school marm, and I wouldn't impose myself on Seth. *It wasn't the proper thing to do*, I heard Ma's heaven-sent voice say. I hated when she intruded.

Seth peeled off his jacket, hung it on the hook by the door, and flashed that politician's grin he was so practiced at. "That loaded?" He gestured to my gun as he strolled over.

"No." I swung it in his direction and he leaped to one side, grabbing the gun as he moved. "Don't ever point it at somebody."

"But there're no bullets in it."

"Still. Not a good idea." He rolled the cylinder checking each empty chamber, then, satisfied, handed it butt-first to me. "Even if you know for sure, don't point that thing, unless you mean to fire it."

First lesson learned. I found the box of combustible paper cartridges and held them out. Seth leaned in close. So close, his bay rum aftershave made me wrinkle my nose.

He inspected the cartridges. "Yep. They'll do nicely."

"Great," I said. "What're we going to shoot?"

Seth pursed his lips, making his mustache stick out over his top lip. "Don't want to scare anybody in town and sure don't want to stampede the horses." Seth pointed behind us. "We could put up some targets over in that little box canyon. It's far enough we shouldn't bother anybody."

"I'll dig around for some cans." This adventure was getting better. I'd heard the *plinking* before, and now it would be my gun making that noise.

"And I'll check with the Tin Pan for bottles," Seth said. "Meet you there in half an hour?"

"It's a date," I said. We both stopped for a split second, looked at each other. He grinned. I frowned. What was I thinking?

Chapter Eight:
Becoming Proficient

Seth was already there by the time I showed up. He'd lugged a gunnysack full of cans, along with a couple of cracked whiskey bottles. I'd found four tins at my house, then went door to door, until I had enough for one lesson. I counted my bullets. One bullet per can. Should be enough.

He removed the cylinder and started with the basics, using his *I-have-to-use-simple-words-for-this-moron* voice I'd heard him use with slow-witted council members. "Now this is a thirty-six, which means the caliber, the measurement, of the inside of the barrel is thirty-six millimeters." Seth peered inside the barrel like it held a picture. "Pretty standard for today. That size'll do enough damage to stop a horse, or a man."

I looked in. Too narrow to see much, but with the cylinder gone, I spotted a pinpoint of daylight coming through the other end.

He clicked the cylinder back in and handed the empty gun to me. "Now point it like you were gonna shoot it." I aimed at the row of cans we'd set up. "Both hands," he said.

I fumbled a bit, trying to figure out two. Slick as mud in the spring, Seth moved behind and put his arms around me.

"Like this," he said. He cupped his hands over mine and suddenly, we had four hands holding one gun. His warm breath in my ear did nothing for my concentration, but I needed to know what to do. I wished he hadn't been so close. He was a distraction.

Seth and his dimples stood back approving. "Look like a professional, Maud. Yes, you do."

We spent the remainder of the day *plinking* toward the cans and bottles. By late afternoon, all but two of the cans sat unscathed and both bottles remained intact. But I'd had fun. Now I knew how to put the cartridges in and how to remove the spent ones. Come to find out, there was a spring rod that ejected the empty cartridge. He spent some time showing me how to load the cartridges—again.

"Once the powder's poured in and a ball seated atop the chamber," Seth said, "the rammer then pivots on the bolt connecting it to the barrel, and as the lever swings down, it forces the bullet into the chamber."

I sort of followed his instructions.

"Now, when a percussion cap's placed on the nipple at the rear of the cylinder, like this," he demonstrated, "the chamber's loaded."

Firing the gun was fun, but I was tired by the end of the day. Who knew target practicing was so hard? It took all my concentration plus some I dredged up from my toes. Before we parted, Seth grunted his satisfaction.

"Did good today, Maud."

"Thanks." Would I admit it was harder than it looked? No. He probably had already figured it out. "Let's leave the cans and bottles here. I'll come back tomorrow morning to pick 'em up."

Seth finished arranging his bullets in a canvas pouch. He cut brown eyes sideways at me. "Wanna try a shotgun?"

"Who wouldn't?" The grin took over my entire face.

CHAPTER NINE:
READIN', WRITIN', 'N 'RITHMATIC

The major item on my mind was learning how to shoot my gun. I'd spent most of the morning cleaning and oiling it and replacing the parts. This I did at the office. I hadn't told Pa about my gun, waiting for the right moment. At least half an hour sailed by while I tried to get the cylinder back in place. Harder than Seth and Mr. Weinberg made it look yesterday. Besides learning to shoot, another part of being sheriff came to call late that afternoon.

School marm and Seth's "friend" Pearl McIntyre stopped by the office on her way home. Merely seeing her made me envious. I'd always wanted to teach school, but Pa said only women who either couldn't get a man or who were too homely to find a husband were teachers. He talked me out of applying when the position came vacant some years ago. He told me school marms would remain old spinsters and, if I ever wanted a man, I should learn how to run a house, not teach children to read.

Fat lot of good that piece of advice had done me. I didn't know whether to be angry at Pa or myself.

But Miss McIntyre was a gentle soul, bringing with her a breath of fresh air when she stepped into the office. And there was not a shred of "homely" about her. A broom straw under my height, she was close to skinny, her reddish-blond hair always tastefully held in a bun at the nape of her neck. I'd seen her wearing glasses, but not today. Today, her blue eyes shone, despite the dust storm swirling around outside. Somehow she left all the dirt at the door. Her smile was contagious and I found myself enjoying our visit, despite not knowing her much at first.

By and by, she got around as to why she'd come. She glanced out the window. "My students bring up your name often. Can't get over the fact that we have a woman sheriff."

I felt my eyebrows knit while I cocked my head. "What's wrong with that?"

"Oh, nothing. I think it's a noble thing to do."

Noble? I'd never put such a moniker on my job.

"The reason I came . . . would you mind spending a few minutes out of your busy day to explain to them what a sheriff does? And they'd like to know how you got to be sheriff."

Of course I'd like to come. I explained to Miss McIntyre, "The town council asked me to be sheriff and I said yes." Pretty simple, I thought. What I left out, but would include during my big reveal, were the persuasive visits of the town council.

"I'm sure there's more to the story than that, Sheriff." Pearl McIntyre sashayed for the door. "Friday morning all right?"

She left and I got to thinking, with summer coming on and school about to be out in a couple of weeks, I should get to know some of the youngsters. I knew a few of the older boys liked to steal pies and tip over a privy or two, so, for everyone's sake, I'd go meet what I might have to deal with.

In the summer, most children would be busy working on the farm, helping out where needed. But with sun-drenched, warmer weather, there didn't seem to be enough work to fill up their long days. Getting into a bit of mischievous fun was part of their youthful enthusiastic duty. Keeping a lid on it was mine.

The big day couldn't come soon enough. I got stomach flutters like I did all those years ago, waiting for school to start in the fall. I loved playing with my friends, learning letters and numbers, thinking new thoughts. When I felt the days turn a bit crisp, I knew school's starting would be right around the corner.

Friday came. As soon as I opened the schoolhouse door, all heads turned. Part of me wanted to back up and run, the other half couldn't wait to get to the front of the room and begin talking. I'd spent hours figuring out how to introduce myself—I'd ask them to call me "sheriff" and I'd tell them they could ask any sort of questions they'd want. I needed to come across as a friendly, yet strict, law officer. So, for once, I was prepared.

On my freshly pressed blouse I had pinned my sheriff's badge, its star shining like the ones at night. I'd left my new gun back at the office—school wasn't a place for weapons. I had an example to set, although I knew about half those fresh-faced children could shoot a whole lot better than me.

Miss McIntyre said nice things as she introduced me to the class, many youngsters I recognized from seeing around town. I started off with what I'd memorized. "Thank you for having me here this morning. I'm sure you're wondering what a sheriff does all day."

A hand shot up. I pointed at him.

"Even though you're a girl, can you arrest outlaws?"

"Yes, I can. But I haven't had to arrest any, so far."

Another hand reached skyward, this time wiggling.

"You gots a gun?" The little girl took a breath. "My ma says no self-respectin' woman would be seen dead with a gun and my pa—"

"Laurie Dyer," Miss McIntyre said. "Let the sheriff finish her presentation."

I smiled and went on. "With our small-sized town, we don't have anybody that steps outside the law very often. And when we do, a good talking to by the sheriff usually sets them straight." I looked the little girl in the eyes and bent down closer to her level. "Precisely like your pa talks to you when you're misbehavin'."

"I'm never mishavin'," she said. "Besides, I got two brothers and three sisters and *they're* always in trouble. But not me. I'm never—"

"Thank you, Laurie," Miss McIntyre said.

A young man who looked to be at least thirteen raised his hand inch by inch. I called on him, when it got above his head.

"Sheriff Overkill?"

"Overstreet."

"Sheriff Overstreet, ma'am?" His eyes flitted back and forth like he was watching a fly buzz around his head. "Well, my pa says the only reason you got to be sheriff was 'cause nobody else would take it." He sat a bit straighter. "That true?"

Before I could figure out how to answer, because I'd asked the council and nobody had told me, another hand shot up, and he didn't wait for me to call on him.

"My pa says hiring you was a joke on the town and on you. And once you get done with playin' at it, the town's gonna get a *real* sheriff." The youngster looked from face to face, as if seeking confirmation.

"How much they pay you?" A little boy leaned forward.

"A dollar, I heard," another boy said.

"She don't even have a gun," a third boy said as he eyed me.

"I *do* have a gun," I said. "A Navy Colt. And I know how to use it." Why was I defending myself against a ten-year-old?

"But you don't gots a horse."

"What kind of sheriff don't got a horse?"

This was going to be a long morning.

CHAPTER TEN:
GOTTA GET A GIDDY UP

Enough was enough. I'd endured as much humiliation as humanly possible. Tired of ridicule and sideways glances, I turned my thoughts to what I needed to know to become a "real" sheriff. I now knew how to shoot, but who knew I'd need a horse? As I explained to Seth, I'd always ridden in buggies, stages, even taken a train once, never needing to sit a horse. Although I had been on one when I was six. Guess that didn't count.

Seth's mustached mouth melted into a frown when I told him I didn't know how to ride. Despite what I was sure numbered a thousand misgivings, and no need to tell the council members, he agreed to teach me.

We stood in front of Swensen's Livery Stable, smells of warm horses and hay wafting out. I stifled a sneeze threatening to form.

Seth looked down at my calico skirt. "That's gotta come off."

"Excuse me?"

"I mean . . . that didn't come out right." Even in the cloudy sunlight I could see Seth's cheeks catch fire. "I mean, you need to be wearing trousers, or you'll have to ride side saddle."

"Women don't wear trousers, and *I* don't wear trousers." Shock and outrage mingled in my head. Worse than being sheriff, wearing trousers would bring gossip and scandal to not only Pa and me, but to the entire town.

"You'll have to find a side saddle." Seth shrugged. "Don't

think there's one in town."

I'd never seen one around either, which meant I'd either have to borrow Pa's trousers or figure out how to straddle a horse while wearing a skirt. Neither prospect appealed to me, but I had a job to do. Nobody ever said being sheriff would be easy. Then again, yes, they had. In fact, it had been Mayor Seth Critoli, standing at my right shoulder, who'd said being sheriff was like eating cake—nothing to it but sweetness. And I'd believed him. Now, I knew better.

"Can we use one of these horses, right here?" I pointed to the wagon hitch, waiting on the street. They weren't saddled, but they did have bridles on.

"Nope. There're horses trained to wagons, some trained to the plow. Others are trained to ride with a saddle. You can't mix 'em." Seth wagged his head like I should've been born knowing that.

I shrugged. "Guess I never gave it much thought." That went for a lot of things, apparently.

"Tell you what." Seth jerked his thumb over his shoulder. "Let's go inside, find Mr. Swensen."

"You think he'd have a horse I could ride?"

Seth gave me a long look. I wasn't sure what to make of it, but I felt confident with him around. I would learn how to ride and life would be good. I'd be a real sheriff.

"Mr. Swensen rents horses, Maud. That's a good chunk of his business. We gotta find a horse doesn't mind having a skirt all over it." Seth nudged me inside.

Mr. Swensen produced a thoughtful mutter and pursed lips as he looked me up and down. I'm not sure what he was measuring, but he was the expert. "Got de nag you need." He aimed a gnarled finger toward the stalls. "Dis way."

Seth and I followed him through the stable, smelling of old manure and fresh hay, to the far end. My nose twitched. The stable owner stopped and regarded the horse.

"Dis here's May Belle," he said. A dappled gray rump stood in the stall. "She'll do ya fine." Swensen's eyes cut to mine. "She's a mite slow, but she's good natured and reins soft. Don't never recall her buckin', neither."

Bucking? I hadn't given that little gem a twinkle of thought. I needed more information than simply the fact nobody had seen her do it. "You think she might? Why do they buck?"

Both Swensen and Seth chuckled, like they were in the all-knowing man's club and I was an outsider.

"Horses are afraid of only two things," Mr. Swensen held up his thick index finger. "Dose dat move." He held up a second finger. "And dose dat don't."

"Anything'll scare 'em." Seth's words were clear. "A snake. Gunfire."

Swensen pointed his stubbled chin toward me. "Your skirt. Dat's why May Belle's good for you." A low rumble that could've been thunder or a chuckle rattled in his chest. "She's a mare, like you."

I chose to ignore the comment. "She doesn't wear a skirt, though, Mr. Swensen," I said. "Can we introduce her to one? Or at least let me sit on top of her?"

"Reckon so." He backed May Belle out of her stall. Her shoulders were a bit higher than mine. She seemed the perfect size. "Any time you're 'round a horse dat don't know you, you gotta let 'em smell you. Rub 'er neck and nose, scratch 'er back, talk to 'er. Comfort 'er you're not gonna hurt 'er."

"I'd never hurt her."

"But she don' know dat."

Though I didn't know how to ride a horse, I'd been around them enough. I had an idea.

"Mr. Swensen? Can't we get May Belle used to a skirt by hanging one on her?"

Mr. Swensen pondered for a moment. "Great idea. My woman's got a extra skirt hanging up in de bedroom. I'll run home ta get it." He started off, tossing a quick directive over his shoulder. "You and May Belle get 'quainted whilst I'm gone. Won't be long."

Seth and I talked sweet nothings to the horse. She blinked back at me with her big, black eyes, as I stroked her long neck, appreciating the bluish-gray hair with black speckles. What they called Grulla, Seth said. There *was* something about her that was special. But would she buck me off? I pushed that image away. I didn't need any more doubts squeezing into my brain, right now. No, I needed only positive, good thoughts.

"Miss Overstreet."

The voice in my ear startled me so badly I jumped. There stood Harvey Weinberg, town councilman. "Understand you're learning to ride." An Ashkenazi Jew, he followed the tradition of wearing bobbing curls on either side of his face, with a flat round hat perched atop dark hair speckled with gray. A long, black coat fulfilled the requirements of his trousseau.

Recovering, I said, "Thought I should." I wondered how he'd discovered that I didn't know how to ride.

"Got hit op di naronim!" Harvey said.

Seth and I exchanged puzzled glances.

"God watches over fools," Harvey said.

I clenched my teeth, not willing to let this man's comments get under my skin. So, I didn't know everything they did. Not yet. But I would.

I wagged my head and went back to stroking May Belle. The men grunted and huffed at each other in their special kind of man-speak. Mr. Weinberg stepped away and stopped, turned to me.

He pointed to May Belle. "Learn to ride and you may keep your badge past mid-summer elections."

Great. I waved good-bye over my shoulder. May Belle was all I needed. Her and a lot of luck.

Mr. Swensen returned with a faded calico skirt, which looked like it'd seen better days, at least five years ago. But it would work. May Belle stood in her stall and accepted the skirt like it was one of her own. Her eyes grew a bit wider when Mr. Swensen flicked the material, but she didn't shy or rear back.

"What about a saddle?" I glanced around the darkened stable and spotted one perched on a rail, not far from the horse. "What about that one?"

"Should fit you fine." Swede Swensen pursed his lips. "One dollar a day for horse and saddle. Won't find no better deal, anywhere."

"A dollar?" Seth moved in closer. "That's a lot of money."

"You can parcel it out, Mayor," Mr. Swensen said, his ebony hands extended palms out. "Fifty cents a day for de horse, fifty cents a day for de saddle. You can pick one or both. Up ta you."

A dollar a day was a bit much, especially being as I didn't know how long I'd be gone. And I didn't think the town would pick up the bill. "You think maybe Pa's horse would carry me all right?"

Both men shook their heads, at once.

"His horse is used to pulling a buggy," Seth said. "You need a horse that's saddle broke."

Mr. Swensen pulled the skirt off May Belle. "The mayor's right. Dis's de mount you need. She'll treat ya good, if you treat 'er good."

By now, I was in love. May Belle and I had equinely connected, and I vowed to treat her like I would a real person. "You'll get your dollar a day, Mr. Swensen. Now, show me how to saddle her."

CHAPTER ELEVEN:
ME AND MAY BELLE

It took a few more minutes of walking and stroking, but I was confident May Belle and I would get along fine. The skirt would be another issue, but I'd have to figure out the easiest way to mount the horse without getting tangled up in my own clothes. Now, I saw a reason to wear trousers. But still, I wouldn't entertain the notion.

Seth patted May Belle's gray neck and looked at me. "Best if you rode her a bit right now. Get used to her before you *have* to ride."

I'd had the same notion, but exactly how did I get into the saddle? The stirrup hit just below my waist. No way could I get my foot up so high, swing my other leg over and put my rear in the saddle. Not and retain a shred of dignity.

Apparently, he saw my dilemma. "Once you're in the saddle, we'll adjust the stirrups. They go up and down, you know."

"I know." Truthfully, I'd suspected, but hadn't given the subject much thought.

Seth locked his hands together and bent over next to my knee. A dainty woman I was not, and it showed. I grabbed hold of the saddle horn with one hand, using the other to pull up my skirt enough to clear the top of my high-top, button-up shoe. Would Seth contain his composure at the sight of my ankle, or would such a lurid sight distract him from our purpose? What choice did I have? I put my left foot in Seth's hand-sling, and, with his lift, hoisted my way into the saddle. Grunting from both of us helped.

Yep, nothing dainty or graceful about me.

Ever the gentleman, averting his eyes, Seth lowered the stirrups a few notches, while I tugged and pulled at my skirt. He stood back, his gaze roving over May Belle and me. It felt good and I gave him a nod, setting my heels to May Belle's sides. "Giddy up!" I said and we lurched forward, the horse walking, me gripping the saddle horn and reins. It *was* glorious.

We walked around the stable and out into the yard, Seth quick-stepping by my side.

"Sit low in the saddle, Maud. Like you're part of the horse." He straightened his shoulders. "But sit up tall."

I tried to picture my rear melting into May Belle's back yet trying to sit up straight. Three turns around the yard, I knew I could ride. Maybe not well, but I could more than likely stay on.

"Good job." Seth shot me a hundred-dollar grin. "But it's late. Gotta get back to work."

I agreed and urged May Belle back into the stable. I managed to slide off the horse and stay upright, despite my legs trembling. I pulled off the saddle, which seemed to weigh almost as much as me, then the blanket and led her back to her stall. Looking into her eyes, I stroked the blaze on her muzzle.

"We're gonna get along fine, May Belle," I said. "Yep, real fine."

Chapter Twelve:
Putting Dry Creek on the Map

Despite having success learning to ride, the school children's comments plagued my thoughts. Why me? As I marched down Main Street toward the mayor's office looking for a definitive answer, I thought about these past few days. I liked being sheriff—I was capable—and I'd be darned if I'd let anybody run me out of my badge.

It was hard work balancing care of Pa, the garden and the town and, except for being a hostage, I found meaning in my job. More meaning than I'd ever expected in a job or in my life. So far, though, I hadn't really been put to the test. I mean, no James Mooney gang had robbed the town, no drunken drovers had come riding in a whoopin' and a hollerin' 'cause they'd just got paid. No, it had been peaceful.

"Maud? Sheriff Overstreet?"

I slid to a stop at the voice. My hand shaded my eyes from the bright afternoon sun. A silhouette rushed toward me.

"Maud. Glad you're in town."

As the figure neared within a few yards, I recognized Elizabeth Gallaway, a woman older than me, but not by much. I'd known Beth for fifteen years, when I'd first moved to town, and counted her as a friend.

Touches of gray in her black hair jutted around her ears. With her hair pulled back in a bun and her green eyes shining, she reminded me of a cat ready to pounce on a mouse.

"I was hoping to run into you," Beth said. "I've been so busy

71

cooking, cleaning, mending and now the garden's coming in, well . . ."

She was never one for getting right to the point, so I helped her along. "What can I do for you? I've got a meeting . . ."

"Of course you do." Beth smoothed her green gingham skirt and pulled at her sleeves.

She was a lot of woman to cover and I fleetingly wondered how much fabric it had taken to make that dress.

Beth glanced over her shoulder, turned back to me and lowered her voice. "I have an idea for Dry Creek." She paused. "We need us our own postal service."

"A post office?" I'd never given any thought to it, always figuring our telegraph office was sufficient. And what little mail we did get, Dutch Flats sent it over and left it at the hotel, a central point where men and women alike could enter.

"And, well, after thinking on it, I'd like to be in charge," Beth said.

"You?" I knew it came out like I thought she was the last person on earth to manage a position of responsibility, and I sure didn't mean it that way. But she was a woman. I reconsidered. If I could be sheriff, she could be a postmaster. Or was it postmistress?

"Like I said, I've given it a lot of thought, Maud. A lot," Beth said. "Dry Creek's growing. Why, you remember last week that new family from Oregon moved in, and they've got five young 'uns, and another on the way, and—"

"I'll go pay them a visit, next day or two."

"Good idea." Beth pointed back over her shoulder. "It's because of new families like theirs we need to get our own letters, packages, newspapers. Postal mail that's addressed to us, not to Dutch Flats and hauled over here, whenever Jack McCormick sobers up enough to come this way. You know sometimes he simply throws the mail at the hotel doors. Doesn't even bother to take it in."

"But, the hotel—"

"Also thought about that. Talked to Mr. Goldstein at the hotel and he's thinking a postal office might be a good idea. Fact is, he's been complaining to me that people are always coming in, demanding their mail, which he doesn't have, it's always so late. They get 'testy' he said. He hopes we *do* build a postal office and he said he'd be the first to help build one."

"Tell you what," I said. "I'm heading over to the mayor's office right now. You want me to suggest it?" Now, I wasn't sure Seth would decide having a post office was a good idea, but the least I could do was ask.

"Would you?" Her tone implied she'd never thought about it before, but I knew better. I played along.

" 'Course. It's a post office, not like a fight's gonna break out or get robbed or anything."

I believed those words, too. How many post offices had brawls? None, that I knew. This was a safe bet and it would put Dry Creek on the map.

What could go wrong?

CHAPTER THIRTEEN:
GOING POSTAL

"I already told you, Maud. You got selected by the town council 'cause you were most qualified for the position." Mayor Seth Critoli threw up his hands as he paced the length of his office. Fortunately, that involved only a few steps. Nobody's business was important enough to take up much space. Even my office was small.

He turned to me. "How many times do I gotta tell you?" One hand rubbed his eyes.

"I think this is the first," I said. "And I don't know why I'm more qualified than anybody else."

"Anybody else? You graduated school. Tenth grade, didn't you?" Seth frowned at me.

"And finished a correspondence course in bookkeeping."

"Right." His Italian heritage glowed with each overly zealous gesture. "And you're strong. I mean, look at all the gardening you do and work around the house."

There were plenty of men stronger than me, who weren't chosen. So far, I hadn't needed to be muscle strong, and I still wasn't sure how it was a qualification for a sheriff, but I let him go on.

"And, most importantly," he said, "you ain't married. Not tied down with a husband or children."

"Just how many men did you ask before me?"

Seth mumbled into his chest.

"How many?" My voice rose higher than I'd wanted.

Clearing his throat, he blinked. "Most of the men around here are married, as you well know. Their wives said no."

So that was it. I qualified because I hadn't landed a husband yet. Maybe I was more "man" than the male population of Dry Creek. I didn't know whether to be pleased or insulted. I suspected it should be a bit of both. I let him stew for a beat.

"But, just so's we're clear," I said. "I'm not giving up my badge. Not for nobody. It's just that . . ."

Seth's gaze wandered around the room before settling on my face. One end of his mouth drew up under his trimmed mustache, and I remembered how he kissed. Kind of sideways. In all fairness, that had been the only kiss between us, and a year or so back. I'd been sitting next to him, not in front. And I hadn't planned to return the kiss, especially since he wasn't Eli.

"Maud. You know I like you and think highly of you." Seth moved in close—so close I knew he'd had one of his ma's famous pastrami sandwiches, with mustard, for dinner. He lowered his voice. "I'm glad you like being sheriff. I knew you were the right man for the job."

"But I'm not—"

"I *know* you're not a man." His eyes roamed down my chest, but knowing he was caught, sprung back to my face. "Believe me."

He was charming despite his practiced politician's way of speaking. Smooth and sincere-sounding. I believed him.

Seth glanced at his watch, shoved it back into his vest pocket and turned another disarming smile on me. "So glad you stopped by." His grip on my upper arm nudged me toward the door. "We'll have to chat again."

I stopped at the closed door and faced him. I wasn't done nor ready to go. "I have another matter to discuss."

His eyebrows narrowed, putting a cute dimple between them. For an instant, Seth was the handsomest man I'd ever seen. Images of Eli crowded in. However, Seth Critoli was right in front of me and Elijah J. Goodman was . . . well, I didn't rightly know where he was. I focused on my mission.

"You know that Dry Creek's growing," I said.

"Uh huh." Seth inched toward the door.

"Every day new families are moving in."

"Uh . . ." He grabbed the handle.

"We need us an official post office. One where we can receive and send real mail. One where we don't have to rely on Dutch Flats to send Jack McCormick over with our packages and letters. One—"

"Great idea, Maud." Seth turned the door handle and pulled. "Let's talk about it—"

The door swung open. "Oh!" Pearl McIntyre's eyes grew wide as she grabbed for the receding door handle. "I didn't realize you—"

"Miss McIntyre?" I must have blinked thirty times before getting my eyelashes under control.

Seth stepped back, opening the door farther. "Miss McIntyre. What a surprise."

The school marm flashed him a dazzling smile, turning a polite one on me. "How nice to see you again, Sheriff. Funny meeting you again, so soon."

"Funny's a word," I said. Seth's face turned whiter than usual as his eyes flitted from woman to woman. I liked him well enough to help him along. "I need to see to Pa's supper. But, Mayor, we need to talk about our own postal office." I stepped onto the boardwalk.

"Post office?" Miss McIntyre bunched her perfect eyebrows at me. "Post office," she said as if trying on those words for the first time. "I think that's a grand idea. We've needed one for quite some time." She turned her sparkling blue eyes on Seth.

"We should do it."

"We?" my brain echoed as I brushed past. "*We?*"

CHAPTER FOURTEEN: THE PROPOSITION

It wasn't long before Seth, Pearl, Beth and myself sat down to hammer out postal office details. We agreed that Beth would be well suited as postmistress, although Seth questioned her ability by citing the fact she was female and married. The three of us set him straight and he quickly acquiesced, without further argument.

Once our plan was in place, we presented it to the three town councilors. Within half an hour, they agreed, citing the lack of consistency on the part of Jack McCormick and thus causing the need for our own postal service. They went as far as hinting that some of the mail may have been opened before reaching our hotel. No telling what, if anything, went missing.

They did, however, approve only if it didn't cost the town money. Otherwise the deal was off. We assured them the postal office could sustain itself.

So, with the council's blessing, Beth, Pearl and I spent Saturday marching around town, peering into one building after another, searching for a place for our new postal office. The mercantile didn't have enough room for the packages and letters and newspapers we were sure would be arriving. We ignored the saloons as women would not consider entering them. Even the livery stable, a logical choice with a stagecoach or wagon bringing the mail, didn't have enough room.

We marched back and forth, up and down Main Street, until I knew I'd worn holes in my shoes. We took lemonade at the

Shoo Fly Restaurant and spent the next hour discussing our options. It wasn't until we stood on the porch, out of the sun, tasting the remainder of the third glass, that I spotted our solution.

The telegraph station.

What had we been thinking? It was perfect. Near the end of town, the wagon had room to stop in front and the driver could pick up any telegrams that'd come in or needed to go out. It was already a central spot of communication.

"The telegraph office," I said. "That's it. All we gotta do is tell old man Maguire he's got company."

"Not going to be easy," Pearl said. She pursed her lips, picking off a piece of lemon pulp stuck there. "He's mighty possessive."

Beth cocked her head. "He's been a widow for some time now, hasn't he?"

Time sure passes quickly, I realized. "At least eight years, if I remember right."

A gleam took over Beth's eyes and lit up her face. "Follow me."

Off we went, the three of us. On a mission. By now, I was determined to use that space, but a bit nervous about how we were going to do it. I let Beth lead. She seemed to have a plan.

We marched across the street and down the length of the town before stopping in front of the telegraph office. A mischievous gleam caught in Beth's eyes. "Let's do it."

I didn't know exactly what we were going to do, but I was all in favor. I hadn't had this much excitement since being held at gunpoint and this didn't feel nearly as dangerous. What was the worst that could happen? He could say no.

I stepped in right behind Beth and Pearl followed me. She shut the door as Rune Maguire peered up from his desk. The man looked to be at least a hundred and ten, but he wasn't much older than me. "A hard life in Ireland," it was said. I figured he looked old because he was so ornery.

"Yeah?" Maguire tilted his head to one side, but he didn't bother to stand or walk over to the counter, which was about four feet away.

"Mr. Maguire?" Beth's voice took on an official, yet sweet, tone. "We got a proposition for you."

He shot up out of his chair and bolted toward us. I backed up a step.

"I tain't tha' kind o' man," Maguire said, his Irish brogue still thick, despite the years he'd spent in this country. "And up 'til now, I didn't think you were tha' kind o' womens."

The three of us, I'm sure, pulled in all the air in the room, shaking our heads as fast as we could. Beth came to her senses first.

"You're right about that, sir," she said. "What I meant is we're looking to do some business with you."

"Beth, that didn't sound right, either." Pearl turned her blue eyes on Maguire, who seemed now to be using the counter as a shield. "What she means is we're looking to set up a postal office for Dry Creek." She looked around, then back to Maguire. "We're hoping to use this building."

Maguire stared at his feet, at the ceiling, scratched his head and then his beard as if thoughts would jump out and form words. A bit more staring and scratching, he looked first at Beth and then me.

"You all off yer nut? T'will bring nothin' but trouble. As it is, we got enough with this telegraph station." He huffed into his beard, hitched up his britches and aimed his indignation at his chair, as if he'd dismissed us.

"But Dry Creek's growing and *needs* a postal service," Pearl said. "This location would be ideal."

Maguire spun around and glared. "This location is mine. I bought this buildin'. I own it. Tis *mine.*" His brown eyes narrowed. "G'day now."

Beth wasn't one to take "no" so quickly and, as of yet, I hadn't seen her plan in motion. She straightened her shoulders and sidled up to the counter. "Mr. Maguire? When's the last time you had a woman-cooked roast beef supper? I mean with all the trimmings? Gravy, mashed potatoes, fresh green beans—"

"Right out of the garden," I said. I'd figured out where she was going with this, and I realized she was close to genius.

"Wha' kinda gravy?" Maguire said.

"Brown," Beth said. "Fresh blueberry pie?"

Rune Maguire ran his tongue over his bottom lip, following it with his hand. "Canna say exactly, last time I et like tha'."

"Mr. Maguire," Beth said. "I'd be delighted if you would come to my house for supper tonight. With only me and my husband left at home—and Jacob Junior off in the gold fields—well . . . When I make a roast I prefer serving it to more than just two." She turned to Pearl and me. "Sheriff, would you and Miss McIntyre like to come as well?"

Of course I would, but I remembered Pa. He hated to eat alone and would starve unless I sat at the table with him. "But I'd bet Miss Pearl here would enjoy someone else's homemade cooking."

Pearl smiled.

"Then it's set," Beth said. "I'll see you both at six."

Chapter Fifteen:
A Job for Pokey

Two roast beef dinners, a full blueberry pie, an apple pie with crumbles on top, one pork rib supper complete with ham beans, my famous three-meat stew, fried chicken and a buttermilk pie later, Rune Maguire reluctantly agreed to let us set up a postal office in his building—for a price, of course.

He rolled out a phrase in his native Gaelic, but none of us understood until he switched to English. "A chicken egg for a goose egg."

So, in addition to fifteen dollars a month rent, he asked for a homemade supper every couple weeks or so. I threw in a pie every other Wednesday, to seal the deal. *"Is maith an t-anlann an t-ocras,"* he'd relinquished, the final resistance drained. "Hunger's the best sauce," he interpreted.

The first thing we did was devise a schedule—mail would come in on Monday, Wednesday and Friday. We set a price. A dollar an ounce was fair, considering the Pony Express had charged five dollars for half that. Of course the Pony Express was out of business, thanks to the telegraph, but a dollar still seemed reasonable.

Would we accept payroll? As long as the company sending it paid us, we'd take coin and cash, bank notes, too, sort of making us an express company. But mostly we expected to be hauling newspapers and letters. How big of a wagon would we need? The trip from Dutch Flats to Dry Creek was more than twenty miles, but there were only a couple of steep hills to navigate, so we figured a four-hitch team and a good sturdy wagon should do fine.

Mr. Swensen at the livery stable agreed to rent us his big box wagon and four matched horses for what Pa said was a good price. Now all we needed was a driver. I didn't know anything about driving a team. And, being sheriff, I needed to stick around town, in case . . . In case of what, I wasn't exactly sure, but still, I couldn't be the driver.

Pearl couldn't drive, as she was teaching school, and Beth's job was to be in town to receive the mail. Which left Pokey. All right, so he drank a bit. Couldn't be as much as Jack McCormick over at Dutch Flats. And I'd keep an eye on Pokey, I told the others. While he didn't do a lot of deep thinking and had unusual ideas, I felt he'd make a good driver.

After some discussion, they agreed.

On Tuesday I searched all over town checking out his usual hangouts, the Tin Pan Saloon, the Shoo Fly Restaurant and his own room in the back of Dry Creek Mercantile. The last place I would have suspected, I found him in my office, sitting at my desk—asleep.

I left the door open so he wouldn't startle and jump up at the bang. Surprised he didn't come awake at the squeak, I eased across the room and tapped his foot, planted on my desk.

"Pokey?"

He jumped like he'd been prodded with one of those sharp sticks I'd seen the cattle ranchers use. His feet lifted up and he leaned back, his arms flailing like he was trying to fly. I grabbed an arm before he went over backwards and landed on his head. That righted him and I waited for both feet to hit the creaky floorboards. Watching him laying out straight, boots waggling and his body trying to stay in the chair, I laughed.

He didn't find it so funny. In fact, he glared at me.

"What'd you want to go and scare me like that, Maud?"

Pokey stood, dusted himself off, rubbed sleep from his eyes and ran a trembling hand through his tousled hair. Locating his hat on the floor, he dusted it off as well and fit it to his head.

Stifling a chuckle, I offered what I hoped was a concerned furrowing of eyebrows. "You all right?" I could tell he was—only his pride was ruffled—but I struggled not to laugh. "Need to talk to you about something important." I pointed to an empty chair in front of my desk and I took the one Pokey had warmed up.

"Before you do, I been thinkin'," Pokey said as he poured two cups of coffee, added sugar to one and handed it to me, probably as a goodwill gesture, and eased down to the chair.

His brown eyes trailed over my face and one side of his mouth curved up. Like that, he was almost nice looking.

I couldn't imagine what Pokey had been thinking all on his own. He'd always been an odd sort of duck out here in the wilderness of northern California, and he constantly surprised me. "What's on your mind?" I hoped it was quick because I was purely excited about our new postal office.

A sip and a long stare into his cup, he raised his eyes to meet mine. "Sheriff, you need yourself some help. A deputy."

"A what?"

"That's right," he said. "Deputy. And I want to be that deputy." Pokey rushed his words so I couldn't get any of my own in. "I'd be a good one, too. I'd keep this office clean and I'll teach you how to shoot like I said I would. And—"

"But there's not enough for you to do. I, myself, don't have enough as it is. And I already know how to shoot." And ride, I thought. "I doubt the town council's willing to hire a deputy." I shook my head and I'm sure produced a frown, feeling my face contort and my eyebrows pull together. "And we haven't had gunplay, robberies or even . . ." I dropped my voice because I knew this would sound silly. ". . . pies stolen off Mrs. Gallaway's windowsill. There's nothing going on."

Pokey snorted and lowered his eyes. I tried to ignore his little-boy stance. "I don't think—"

"With all I done for you, you're not even gonna ask?" Pokey stood so quickly I flinched.

He plopped his coffee cup on my desk, its dark liquid spilling onto the ever-present pile of not-so-important papers. Before he marched all the way across the room toward the door, I found my senses.

"Wait. Won't do any harm asking," I said. "You'd make a fine deputy and I'd like to have you by my side." At this point, I discovered myself standing. What was I thinking? I needed a deputy like women need a mustache. But my words were out and I sure couldn't take them back. .

Pokey's smile lit up the entire room. The bear hug took my breath.

Chapter Sixteen:
I See by Your Outfit

True to my word, I went to Mayor Seth and to the town council. As I suspected, they declined the enticing opportunity to employ Pokey Johnson. A couple of weak reasons were he wasn't very well educated and, as mentioned before, tended to drink a bit. I hadn't had to lock him up yet, I explained. But they agreed, still, he was an odd duck and not one the town would approve of, even as deputy.

I countered with the facts he could shoot and knew how to play poker. And, at his age, mid-twenties, he could stay awake all night. However, those valuable justifications didn't sway their opinion. The crowning blow came when they pointed out there wasn't enough money in the town's coffers to pay him a salary. I figured he'd work for free, but I saw clearly, if he was going to lay his life on the line, literally, there should be some sort of compensation.

I conceded, reluctantly, and said I would give him the bad news. I didn't want it coming from anybody but me.

Pokey had waited in my office while I visited with the town officials. As I walked back, I thought about how I would tell him. By now, his heart was set on being deputy and I hated to be the one to break it. But the council had made their decision despite the outstanding qualifications I'd cited.

I guess my poker face was not in place because, the moment I stepped into my office, Pokey sighed loud and long.

"Ain't fair, Sheriff Maud. It ain't fair." Pokey threw a

telegram he'd been holding. It sailed to my desk. "How come you get to be sheriff and I can't even be a deputy? Huh? Why you and not me?"

I didn't have an answer I was willing to discuss with him, so I chose to simply relay the main reason presented by the town council. I eased down behind my desk and realized the chair was warm. I guess Pokey had been trying it out for size. Well, he wasn't getting my badge any time soon. But I did feel sort of sorry for him.

"They said there wasn't enough crime and misdeeds going on to warrant the expense of a deputy," I said.

"Expense?" Pokey fisted one hand. "What's so expensive about a deputy?"

"Also," I said, ignoring that question for the moment, "they explained having a sheriff *and* deputy would be overkill. Nothing ever happens, and the good people of Dry Creek might get to thinking hiring a deputy was one lawman too many, and they wouldn't pay for two walking around."

"That's crazy," Pokey said. "I could be a deputy on Friday and Saturday nights. That wouldn't be too expensive. Would it?" He yanked off his hat and pounded it against his thigh. Dust flew. "Plus, you've seen the Tin Pan when the cowboys come in."

Actually, I hadn't, but I'd heard about the one time a rancher had hired extra hands and when they got paid, they let off a little too much steam. A couple had been thrown in jail and the rest slept it off behind the saloon. Other than a few horses spooked and three new bullet holes added to the saloon's ceiling, nothing too bad had happened. I could handle it alone, if and when men pulled out their guns and got lively again.

"Pokey, I'm sorry," I said. "I agree with you, but the Council's made up their minds."

"What'd you tell them?" Pokey paced to the door.

"What you and I talked about. But they wouldn't budge."

"Sure could've used that pay," he said. "Damn them anyway."

I ignored his bad language. "Tell you what." I leaned forward and put my elbows on the desk. I pointed my chin toward the telegraph/post office. "You know, we got us a postal service about to be started, don't you?"

He shrugged a yes.

Knowing I was in charge of scraping his feelings together, I continued. "But there's one problem."

"You don't got no driver for that big ol' wagon gonna be hauling the postal mail." He stared out the window. "So?"

"How about *you* be the driver? Dry Creek's first postal carrier."

Thought furrowed his forehead. "No. Thanks anyway. I just wanna be deputy."

I'd tired of his whining. Life didn't always treat everyone right, but we were offering him a job—a pretty good one at that.

He paced back and forth a couple times, mumbling. His boots thumped on the wooden floorboards, which squeaked in rhythm to his footfalls. He was like a one-man band. I watched until the telegram he'd tossed on the desk caught my attention. It had to be new; I didn't recall reading anything like this before going to the council's office.

While Pokey stewed, I read. It was from a marshal's office in San Francisco. The James Mooney Gang had robbed a train near there and their trail was leading up toward our neck of the woods. We needed to be on the lookout for this notorious group of thugs.

"When'd we get this?" I held the paper out for Pokey, who stopped pacing long enough to glance at it.

"Few minutes ago. While you were over at . . ." He cocked his head toward the mayor's office. "You know."

I pursed my lips, which was an odd thing for me to do. It was out of character, but, again, I hadn't been sheriff very long and I was beginning to do many things out of character.

"You see anybody you don't know around here?" Pokey had grown up in Dry Creek and knew everybody. This second James Mooney warning was setting my nerves tight. Maybe there was something to this.

Pokey let out a long sigh and played with his shirt buttons. "Nah. Nobody that's stayed more'n a few minutes. Mostly, they pass on through."

"What about gold? Any talk in the saloons about finding gold?"

A smile stretched his cheeks. "Ah, Maud. You'd be one of the first to know if they'd found anything. Hell—" His cheeks fired red and he ducked his head. "I apologize for the language. I get carried away some times."

"No harm done. I've heard it before." He had turned into an eight-year-old in front of me. Those downcast eyes, looking everywhere but at me. I realized we got along as well as two pups in a basket.

He swallowed so hard his Adam's apple bobbed up and down. He continued. "Anyway, those fellas would be all whoopin' and hollerin' so loud the whole town would know. Finding gold ain't something you can hide."

He made sense. For once in his life, he made sense. I changed the subject.

"Dry Creek still needs somebody to drive our postal wagon." I smiled at Pokey hoping my sincerest raised eyebrows would convince him. "Sooner we get somebody on the seat, the sooner we can start getting mail."

Pokey's eyes narrowed. "If I drive, can I still be deputy later on?"

"Don't see why not," I said.

"All right," he said. "If I can't be deputy now, then guess I'm your man." Hooking his thumbs in his suspenders, he announced to the room, "I'm gonna be Dry Creek's first postal carrier."

I thought for sure his vest buttons were gonna pop with all the strain they had holding the fabric together.

"Thank you, but there's one other little problem," I said and his face clouded. "Although the United States government's supposed to be in charge of this adventure—paying salaries and all—there's no way they'll be coming all the way out here to run our little office."

He sat and leaned forward. "What you're beatin' around the bush tryin' to say is I ain't gonna get paid for drivin', neither?"

"No. What I'm saying is you're not gonna get paid very *much* to drive," I said. "Beth and Pearl and I think twelve dollars a month—to start—is all we can afford. But, in a few months, if we're making money, we can give you a raise."

That hangdog expression of his—those brown eyes drooping, the lips melting, the big sighs got to me.

"Tell you what," I said, thinking about our agreement with Maguire. "How about I throw in a home-cooked supper once a month and a pie whenever I can?"

That got his attention. He rubbed his stomach. "I like to eat." He stuck out a hand. "You got yourself a driver. I'll tell Mr. Weinberg I can only work every other day."

We set the next day as official mail-coach inspection day.

CHAPTER SEVENTEEN:
TO HAVE AND TO HOLD

Getting married was something I'd thought about the moment I realized there were girls and there were boys in this world. I must've been six. Before then, they were simply the kids I played with. Some of us liked catching frogs and some liked playing with dolls. But one day, out of the blue, there I was making a mud pie in my front yard and, all of a sudden, *wham!* Thaddeus Jefferson Williams became a boy. Right in front of my face. He looked at me with big blue eyes, mud smeared on his nose and mouth, probably from sampling my pie before it was "cooked," and smiled. One of his teeth had come out, but despite his snaggle-toothed grin, he was appealing right then.

Of course, I didn't know what to do with those feelings or with Thad. He and I followed each other around for months, me making pies—him chasing me with lizards—until the fateful day when a big wagon pulled up in front of his house. I watched his ma and pa bring out furniture and cases and boxes and pile it all in the wagon. My heart shredded at the thought of his moving, and I tried to keep the tears back. I didn't do a very good job hiding my feelings.

I waved good-bye to Thad, dragging myself home. I never knew a body could cry so hard or so long. Ma slid her arm around my shoulder, and told me it wasn't the end of the world. I would find another boy to like.

I didn't believe her, but within a few weeks school started back up, and I discovered there were other boys. Lots of them.

They didn't know I was a girl, but I tried my best to look pretty. For Sunday school and with Ma's help, I'd curl my hair using little strips of rags. To get gussied up, I'd wear my best church dress, the one with little pink rosebuds that ran up and down the skirt, and I'd shine my shoes until they gleamed.

But it wasn't until I was thirteen that a boy looked at me again the way Thad had done. It had taken seven years to become a girl. That year, both Juan Ramirez and Peter O'Shea had tried to sit next to me for Easter service, but Ma took one side and Pa the other. Squeezed in the parental middle, all I could do was sneak smiles at those boys and wish it was one of them next to me.

"Maud?" Pa's voice made me jump. "You daydreaming again?"

The iron in my hand had gone cold and my blouse under the metal now sported a V-shaped burn mark on the shoulder. Shoved back into the present, I jerked up the iron. The kitchen, big enough to hold me, the ironing board and Pa, shrunk. The smell of singed clothes brought me full around. Pa cocked his head.

"You been awful quiet lately. Somethin' on your mind, gal?"

No more than usual, I shrugged. "Just thinking. Pretty excited about the new postal office. Today, Pokey and I're going over to Swensen's to look at his wagons." I set the iron on the stove and held up my ruined blouse. It had been one of my favorites, but now it would have to make a good dust cloth.

Dusting. Another chore I'd neglected.

Pa raised both eyebrows. "Best be thinking someplace else, or you'll likely burn down the whole house." With those words, he wagged his head and disappeared. The front door opened and closed before I selected another blouse to ruin.

I'd been sheriff a couple of weeks and had spent a good deal of time looking at and cleaning my gun and learning to ride.

That was the pleasant side. The other side involved a man pointing a gun at my head and then fire enveloping my skirt. Nothing else bad had happened, though. Pokey Johnson spent his off hours trying to teach me the finer points of poker. I'd asked Pa last night, but he said, "No proper woman should be seen with a deck of cards in her hands. Or alcohol." When I reminded him I was a sheriff now, he simply raised one thin eyebrow, huffed and returned to his newspaper.

Today was Tuesday, ironing day. Pa liked his clothes done exactly so. Maybe later this afternoon, when dinner was cleaned up and supper planned, I'd get down to the office. I'd find Pokey and we'd inspect our mail wagon.

I continued ironing until only one of Pa's shirts lay in the basket. A glance through the window at the lack of shadows told me it was almost noon. Pa would be wanting his dinner within minutes.

I smoothed his shirt on the ironing board and gripped the iron hot off the stove. The front door opened, the high-pitched squeaking hinges announcing a visitor better than any bell in a store.

"Dinner'll be ready in a few minutes," I hollered.

"Maud? Sheriff Maud?"

The feminine voice jerked my head up, almost losing my grip on the iron. Instead of Pa standing in the doorway, there stood Annie Perkins and Thomas Clarkston, blinking at me.

Not understanding why these two people were in my kitchen, I took a step back.

Mr. Clarkston clutched his hat. "Sorry for the intrusion, Sheriff." He used it to point over his shoulder. "But Mr. Overstreet . . . your pa . . . said to come on in."

I knew who my pa was. Oliver Lamar Overstreet, president of the Sacramento Security and Trust Bank. Sent by the Sacramento bank's owner to open a branch in Dry Creek.

That had been fifteen years ago and Pa seemed to revel in being president.

Recovering, I set the iron on the stove. "That's fine. Welcome." I pointed to the parlor. Whatever it was they wanted, I couldn't conduct business in the kitchen.

They settled on the settee and I perched on the edge of Pa's chair. "What can I do for you?"

The two of them made me smile. Younger than me by several years, Annie had her share of boys follow her around, but I knew she'd been courted by Mr. Clarkston for a few weeks. In a small town, everybody knows everybody's business. She worked in the bank as one of Pa's tellers, but I wasn't sure how Mr. Clarkston made his living, since he was new.

Annie blushed while Mr. Clarkston hemmed and hawed. I let them find the words. "Well, ma'am," he said at last. "Annie and me want to get married."

A smile pushed my cheeks up toward my ears. A wedding would be fun.

"Congratulations, you two." Was I being invited?

More fidgeting from both; furtive glances exchanged. My smile melted. "When's this big occasion?"

Annie straightened her skirt. "Whenever it's convenient for you, Sheriff."

"The sooner the better," Mr. Clarkston said.

I thought for a bit, finally able to offer a possibility. "Church's probably available next Saturday. That soon enough?"

Annie frowned. "We were hoping for this afternoon."

Now that was a surprise. How could they get the preacher, a ring, the crowd of well-wishers and the buggy all ready in a few hours?

"Today?" I blinked faster than usual.

Mr. Clarkston slid an arm around Annie's shoulders. The ends of his mouth curved up, like pictures I'd seen of elves. "If not today, how about first thing tomorrow? We're kind of in a hurry."

"I see," I said, but I didn't really. What was the hurry? What difference would a day or two make? I ran down a mental calendar and found my afternoon open. I guess learning to shoot could wait until their wedding was over.

"This afternoon is fine," I said. "What time?"

Giggles and cuddling erupted on my settee. Mr. Clarkston stood, hat clutched in his hand.

"Four o'clock. Does that work for you, Sheriff?"

"Fine. I'll be there." I gave Annie a quick hug and shook Mr. Clarkston's hand.

I walked them to the door. "I'll see you at four at the church. Bye now."

Annie and Mr. Clarkston froze, then, like they were melting, turned back. "Church?"

"Isn't that where you're gonna have it?" I couldn't imagine anywhere else.

"You use the church?" Annie's eyes widened.

I shrugged. "Doesn't everybody?"

Annie and Mr. Clarkston looked at each other, then back at me. His shoulders drooped. "We figured to do it there in your office. But if you do it at the church, then we'll be there."

It hit me like ice water on a hot day. "You want *me* to marry you? I'm supposed to officiate?"

Two heads bobbed.

"Can I do that?" Why was I asking them? I'd never once given it a thought I could perform weddings. If this was true, it would be a side of sheriffing I'd enjoy. It sure beat breaking up bar fights or policing card cheats.

I had to be honest with the blushing couple. "Tell you what. I'll find out if I can marry you two and, if I can, I'll see you down at the office at four. If I can't, I'll see if I can get the preacher." It was the least I could do.

Annie hugged me again and Mr. Clarkston shook my hand. "Thanks again, sir . . . ma'am."

As I closed the door, that's when something inside me rose up . . . and hurt. Envy? Doubt? I pushed it down. My turn would come some day. I had to believe.

CHAPTER EIGHTEEN:
LET NO ONE ASUNDER

Annie wore the prettiest white dress I'd ever seen. Lace covered the bodice and ran down both sleeves, cascading from her shoulders to her wrists. The full skirt rustled as she walked and more lace at the hem swept the ground. Mr. Clarkston, dressed in his Sunday go-to-meeting finest, had bathed since I'd last seen him, along with a shave and his newly-cut hair slicked down with sweet-smelling pomade. A hint of Bay Rum and cloves circled him.

It would be my pleasure uniting such a good-looking couple. I finished the ironing and the noon meal in record time. On my way to the office, I asked Pokey Johnson and he agreed to be a witness, as had mayor Seth Critoli, who'd confirmed that one of the duties of a sheriff was, indeed, marrying people. I rummaged around in the desk for a marriage manual. Finding none, I hustled to a couple of married ladies I knew to get the right words. I jotted them down, adding my own where holes seemed to be. This would be an event worth remembering.

Do I wear my new gun and holster to this wedding? And, if I wore it, exactly where? Should I tuck it under my skirt waistband and let the walnut handle stick out, or wear my creaky leather holster over my Sunday skirt? I tried both ways. A wedding was no place for a gun, even if I was sheriff. So, sure the Colt had at least one cartridge in the chamber, I laid it gently in the top drawer of my desk.

At four o'clock, Annie, escorted by her pa and teary-eyed

ma, stepped into my freshly-swept office. Mr. Clarkston had already arrived a couple minutes earlier. Pokey, hair slicked down and shirt and trousers brushed, looked almost presentable, though his wide eyes and open mouth made him look more nervous than Mr. Clarkston. The two men stood side by side, facing me, while I motioned for Annie to come stand beside her soon-to-be husband.

Sniffles from Annie's ma flooded the room. Mayor Seth pushed open the door and tiptoed in, followed by about half the town. People pushed and shoved, elbowing their way into my office until the blushing couple and I were jammed up against the desk. I would get this over and done quickly, so I could breathe again. It was hot.

"Dearly Beloved," I started. The crowd continued jostling. I repeated myself shouting, and the crowd at long last stopped fidgeting. I lowered my voice and deepened the timbre into a soothing tone. "We are gathered here today to join this man and this woman in the bonds of holy matrimony." So far, so good. Nobody had shot at me or tried to take me hostage at gunpoint. This was fun.

I regarded my notes and continued. "Marriage is a union of two people who share goals and love." I went on about how love makes the impossible possible and how it makes us whole.

Annie grew redder by the second and Mr. Clarkston cleared his throat and fidgeted. I was losing my audience, so I skipped down to the important part.

"Do you, Annie Perkins, take Thomas Clarkston for your lawfully wedded husband?"

"I do." The vow was so low I had to lean forward and we were less than a foot away. Annie's ma sniffled louder.

I continued, but something welled up behind my eyes and pushed. "And do you, Thomas Clarkston, take Annie Perkins for your lawfully wedded wife, to have and to hold so long as you both shall live?"

"I do."

Feeling my heart would burst with overwhelming good wishes, I hurried. "Give her the ring."

He slipped the gold band on her finger as tears streamed down her cheeks. I straightened up and touched them each on their shoulders. "I now pronounce you husband and—"

"Thomas Clarkston? You in there?" A screechy female voice hollered from outside. A fist pounded on the window. "Tom, you no good, cheatin' . . ."

I looked up and realized there was no way anyone else could squeeze in. We were at capacity. But that didn't stop the woman from pushing her way into the crowd. She elbowed and shoved to the front, sputtering threats and curses.

"Thomas Clarkston!" the woman's voice sailed over the mob. They stared at her as though she'd dropped down from the moon.

Mr. Clarkston's face drained of all color. He stepped sideways, holding Annie in front of him. He mumbled, "Virginia?"

She bulled her way up to Mr. Clarkston and stood within inches, Annie sandwiched in between. "So this is where you run off to?" Virginia narrowed her eyes and shook her finger at Clarkston. "Couldn't do any better than this hick town? This one-horse, dried-up poor excuse for an outhouse?" She aimed her glare at me. "What're you looking at?"

Murmurs and whispers grew louder. This was not what I had envisioned as the finale to my first wedding. But I had to take charge. "Ma'am, you need to calm down."

"Calm down? Calm down?" Virginia exploded. "I haven't even started yet!" She took a deep breath, turned and scrutinized Annie head to foot. "Let me guess. You're supposed to marry him."

Annie's blue eyes grew wider, if that was possible.

Virginia turned back to Mr. Clarkston. "Think you can simply take off?" She speared a pointed finger at his face. "Think you could run and I wouldn't find you?"

Mr. Clarkston's head wagged back and forth.

Virginia pointed at Annie. "Run off with this . . . this *trollop?*"

"Trollop?" Annie moved in closer, which I didn't think was possible. She held her left hand under Virginia's nose and pointed to the ring. "I'm his wife!"

"Wife?" Virginia's eyes went wide.

"Ma'am?" I said, my voice louder now. "I need you to calm down."

She turned on me. "Mind your own business. This's 'tween me and my husband."

Well, I hadn't seen that one coming. I probably blinked faster than Mr. Clarkston. Virginia pushed Annie aside and got right up into his face.

"You got another thing coming, Mister. I know you. You can't hide from me." She held out a hand, palm up and shook it. "I want my money and I want it now! All of it! You . . . you two-timing loser!"

Thomas Clarkston turned his pitiful brown eyes on me. "Sheriff. This woman's been following me everywhere I go, demanding money. She's crazy. Arrest her." He backed away as far as he could, but people pushed forward, craning necks to catch a better glimpse of the fracas.

"Ma'am," I said, holding up one hand at the crowd and the other on her shoulder. "You've interrupted a wedding. Wait 'til it's over. We can talk later."

"You don't get it," Virginia screeched. "Tom's *already* married." She turned her pointed finger on herself. "To *me!*"

Annie hollered. "Ain't either. He's married to *me.*"

If Mr. Clarkston could have melted into the floor, he would

have. I've seen dead people with more color. He stuttered and stammered, turning pleading eyes on me. "That's not true. She thinks we're married. We're not. She's crazy, plumb loco!"

The crowd clucked and chattered until I couldn't hear myself think. I looked at Mayor Seth, who shrugged, his eyes dancing. Pokey Johnson, still standing next to Mr. Clarkston, swung his head from side to side as if trying to clear the voices rattling around in there.

Annie again pointed to the ring. "This says we're lawfully married and that's good enough for me. And who do you think you are? You . . . you hussy! Leave my man alone!"

"Hussy?" Virginia's shoulder bumped Annie. "Harlot!"

Annie shoved Virginia hard enough that both women twisted forward. "Doxy!" Annie growled.

I grabbed sleeves. "All right, ladies. Pull in your horns."

Paying no attention to me, Virginia fisted her hand and hauled off with a roundhouse at Annie. Fortunately, with so many people in the room, the strike missed and Annie didn't go to the floor. Instead, she recoiled back, bounced off Mr. Clarkston's chest, ricocheting into Virginia.

Both women clutched each other's hair and sunk to the floor, rolling up against legs, which tried to step over them or get out of the way. Annie's ma cried louder, her pa grabbed at his daughter, Mr. Clarkston shouted at both women, Pokey offered suggestions and Mayor Seth laughed.

I grabbed wedding dress, hats and hair, arms and legs—anything within reach. The women crashed into anyone who wasn't quick enough to move. Annie's dress bunched up around her waist, showing off her new bloomers. Virginia's blue skirt lay in shreds as the women shrieked and tumbled.

Seth was now doubled over, holding his stomach, and Pokey had managed to shrink back into the crowd. Which left me to restore order and dignity to the solemn occasion.

101

"Stop it!" I couldn't even hear myself over the din. I clutched Virginia's blouse as she rolled by. "Stop it, I said!" The material ripped, but I didn't let go. Instead, I grabbed her arm and tugged. It was like separating two hungry bears fighting over the same carcass. Neither was willing to let go.

Drastic times call for drastic measures. I shoved my way around the desk, grabbed my brand new gun, pointed it toward the ceiling, squeezed the trigger and *bang!* Bits of plastered ceiling rained down on my head.

The crowd froze. I glared at Virginia and Annie.

Annie lay like a statue that had fallen over, and Virginia, her scratched face turning red, stared up at me, her mouth open. I lowered the gun and waved my empty hand at the two women.

"I'm arresting both of you." Surprised at my words, nevertheless, that's the way I felt. Both needed cooling-off time. I pointed first at Virginia, then thumbed behind me toward the cells. "You, first."

We threaded our way through the gasping throng and into the back area of the office, Pokey handing me the keys hanging on the peg behind my desk. I opened the iron door, squeaking as it swung. Virginia griped and complained the entire time, telling me—loudly—she was indeed Mr. Clarkston's lawful wife and he'd taken all of her money and skipped town.

"I can explain, Sheriff." Mr. Clarkston's voice sailing over the crowd's noise caused Virginia to shriek louder.

I clicked the door locked and stood back to take a good look at my very first prisoner.

Brown hair hung down over her right cheek, the other starting to bleed. Her green eyes flashed anger, frustration and a smattering of disappointment. She marched from end to end of her iron-barred cell, muttering words I couldn't understand.

I returned to the crowd for Annie. She was now sobbing into Mr. Clarkston's chest while he patted her, telling her it would be all right, that it was all a misunderstanding. Hating to do this, but knowing it was right, I took Annie's arm and tugged her out of his embrace and into a wedding night never to be forgotten.

"You can cool off back here, Annie."

"Let me explain." Mr. Clarkston threaded his way behind us. His arms flapped like he was trying to fly. "I can explain."

I ignored him. Annie didn't put up any resistance, but her ma wailed so loudly I turned around and pointed at the door.

Without a word, Annie's pa slid his arm around his wife's shoulders and the two disappeared outside. The rest of the crowd wasn't about to go anywhere. They shoved and elbowed their way behind my desk and into the hallway where the holding cells were.

I locked the second cell with Annie inside and turned to find myself face to face with half the town.

"Go on home now. There's nothing more to see." I waved my hands and stepped forward. The crowd backed up, much to my amazement. Another step forward, they backed again. Three more steps and by now men and women were filling my office, not the hallway.

As the crowd turned to go, screeches grew behind me.

"Harlot!"

"Cow!"

"Doxy!"

"Bandy-legged biddy!"

"Biddy?"

"Trollop!"

"Jezebel!"

I shut the door.

Chapter Nineteen:
Nothing but the Truth

Pokey Johnson leaned back in his chair and sipped the coffee I'd made earlier that morning. Boiled here in the office, it tasted better— stronger, bolder. The coffee I made for Pa was good, but this was better. I knew. I'd had four cups long before dawn.

Even though I'd tried to stay awake all night, sure that one of those women would try to escape, or, even better, somebody would try to break them out, long after midnight, I gave up and rechecked the locked door. I put my head in my arms at my desk and closed my eyes. Definitely not the most comfortable sleeping arrangement, but through my semi-dozing I listened to the night sounds of crickets and coyotes.

After an hour or two, maybe more, I stretched and yawned, then stood, peering out the window as false dawn turned the dark world grayish purple orange, like it couldn't decide which color to be. Surprisingly, faster than I realized, the sun peeked its head over the horizon and the world burst into flames of gold and pink. There was a whole new day ahead, waiting for me.

However, keeping my eyes open had proved to be a struggle, and, even now, on the heels of a sturdy breakfast and more coffee, the weight of a fitful night slumped my shoulders. I held my empty cup toward Pokey. "Any more in that pot?"

He eyed me the way Pa did when I'd asked for a second helping of mashed potatoes. The look made me squirm. Wait a minute. It was my coffee, my office and, more so, I was tired.

Pokey reached over and used a mitten to pick up the hot pot.

"You're liable to be awake for days." He poured the warm liquid and handed me the cup.

A hesitant sip. The coffee helped. I had prisoners, females, and there was no way I could've gone home and slept in my own bed knowing that Annie and Virginia were here, unguarded. Pokey had offered to stay the night, but it wouldn't have been proper.

With no bed in my office and no cot I could locate, I'd spent most of the night drinking coffee and going through paperwork. Mounds of paperwork. I found wanted posters, some five and six years old. I looked at each face wondering if I'd seen it before. None looked familiar. And it seemed that U.S. marshals loved to send reports back and forth. All of those were jammed into the back of a bottom drawer. I even found some fishing lures—one with a dried up old worm.

It appeared former Sheriff Larimore hid all the papers and brought them out only when the town council or other important people came to call, probably thinking it would make him look busy. Otherwise, nothing got thrown away or acted upon.

As I sat at the desk, I thought about one bit of information I came across, which was interesting. It seemed, according to a report from down around Sacramento, the James Mooney Gang, the ruthless gang of cutthroat outlaws I'd already been warned about, were terrorizing small towns. Prime targets were the local banks, with the citizens paying the hefty price. James Mooney was described as around six foot, mid-to late thirties, close-set brown eyes and shoulder-length brown hair.

My shoulders slumped as I let out a sigh. That description fit about half the men of Dry Creek. The report said the gang, more bold and brazen by the day, was getting handsomely rich off of other people's money by targeting towns which had struck gold.

That left out Dry Creek. Nobody panned for gold here. We couldn't find gold if all the women took off their wedding bands and put them in the middle of the street. Our creek hadn't run in at least fifteen years, the old timers said, and even in those days it was a trickle. So we were safe from the infamous James Mooney gang, I hoped. But still, his name sent shivers up and down my spine.

Turning my thoughts to something more pleasant, like Eli, I compared him to this Mooney character. Eli was about the same height, only a couple inches taller, and his hair was a light, sandy brown—the kind of brown you see on the bark of new saplings. And his eyes. Eli's weren't narrow brown. They were green-brown wide, and sparkled when he laughed. My favorite parts of his face, in addition to his lips, were the little crinkles racing away from those eyes when he smiled at me.

A familiar hollow ache filled my chest again. I pushed it down and turned better thoughts to my job. I stifled a yawn and glanced at Pokey, busy reading one of those new Beadle & Adams dime novels. I hadn't realized, until then, he could read. Guess I wasn't too good at knowing people. I'd have to work on that.

Last night, my two prisoners had called each other every name I'd ever heard and then some—I think they made up most of them because Annie was too much of a lady to repeat those words even if she had heard them, which is doubtful. Who uses that kind of language with a respectable lady? They stewed for a good long while, finally quieting down. I checked on them every couple of hours throughout the night, giving each a blanket and pillow Pa had reluctantly brought from home. They slept peaceful enough, each on a lumpy cotton-stuffed mattress. I hoped ticks and other tiny vermin had taken the night off.

What I couldn't figure out was Mr. Clarkston. He'd peeked in the windows a time or two in the evening and once again this morning, but he hadn't come in. When Pokey had gone to fetch the prisoners' breakfast, he spotted Mr. Clarkston at the Shoo Fly Restaurant. But the new husband, if that's what he was, refused to recognize Pokey and shoveled in his eggs and biscuits. That was close to an hour ago and we still hadn't seen him.

Pokey drained his cup, plopped it on my desk and groaned up to his feet. While he wasn't very tall, an inch or so under me, Pokey's too-short, blue vest hitting well above his waist made him look even shorter. His dark-brown hair, hiding under a narrow-brimmed black hat, stuck out like a scared mop. But his unfettered enthusiasm for life made up for his lack of stature.

He stretched, bringing both arms above his head and twisting his torso at the same time. "What're you gonna do with your catch back there?" Pokey rocked his head side to side, I guess hoping for either his neck to pop or for his head to come loose. "I mean, they're not really criminals, are they?"

I'd already thought about this and was way ahead of him. " 'Course they're not criminals. Haven't done anything much wrong, except maybe wrestling around in good clothes." I poured myself another cup of brew and stared out the window. "I gave little Bobby McCormick a penny to tell the Perkinses to come fetch their daughter." I turned to Pokey, who stood with a soft look on his face, like he approved of what I was doing.

"And, once they take Annie, you'll release Virginia?" He shook his head. "She's a scrapper, ain't she?"

That wasn't the word I would've used to describe Virginia Bouvier, of the San Francisco Bouviers. No, I'd describe her . . . well, I hadn't decided how I felt about her. She'd opened up last night and told about meeting Mr. Clarkston, how he said he'd come from a wealthy family and swept her off her feet by proposing marriage. Her family, which happened to be well-to-do, agreed to the union. A quiet marriage in a church in Clearwater and a sizeable wedding gift later, Clarkston promised he'd invest the good sum of money, and he'd be right back.

Six months and, until last night, Virginia Bouvier Clarkston hadn't seen her new husband in all that time. Annie had listened and sobbed through parts, mumbled about losing her family's money, too, tugged off her new gold band and threw it across the jail cell. I picked it up, holding it for a moment like it was mine. That's when I noticed a V-shaped chip in it, probably from hitting the wall. Closer inspection showed it was a cheap ring, the gold tarnished and parts turning green. But it was Annie's and I'd keep it for her until she wanted it. I nestled it in my top drawer, right next to my treasured gun.

Maybe it was a good thing Thomas Clarkston hadn't been brave enough to come in last night. If I had known the true story then, I would've locked up all three in one cell and . . . well, it would've been interesting.

Even if Pokey had known the full story this morning when he spotted the miscreant, I couldn't charge Mr. Clarkston with anything. Breaking ladies' hearts was not a jailable offense.

I sure would like to hang him, though.

CHAPTER TWENTY:
MAUD, THE MAGNIFICENT

Pokey and I had delayed our mail coach inspection a day. Now with the jail empty, we could concentrate on something more fun. For late May, it was chilly the next morning when Pokey and I met at Swensen's Livery Stable and inspected the team.

"I can handle a four-hitch wagon like Pa taught me when I was knee high to a stump," Pokey claimed, his gaze cascading over the horses' backs.

The horses were big. In fact, they intimidated me. As for driving a wagon, I was no help, being raised by a bank president and a socially prominent ma. Pokey was on his own. But he would do fine.

Inside the barn, Mr. Swede Swensen, originally from Pennsylvania and a born-free Negro, shook hands with Pokey. The three of us circled Dillon, a big roan gelding, standing at least sixteen hands. One of his legs sported a white sock, making him look lopsided.

"Fine shoulders here, Maud. Look at these muscles." Pokey slid his hand across the short dark hair mixed in with white and down the blazed leg. "He's a fine animal. Fine."

"Dese two smaller ones over here . . ." Mr. Swensen led me over to the end of the stable and pointed at the rears of two brown horses standing in side-by-side stalls. "Dese two, Abner and Bob, dey're right for your leads, being as dey don't have ta be as big and strong as your wheelers, like Dillon and Jasper."

He pointed at two horses, their rumps looking wide and muscled.

I chuckled. "Who comes up with those names? I mean, *Abner* . . . *Jasper*?"

Mr. Swensen's calloused hand scrubbed his grayed stubble. "Sometimes my grandchildren name 'em, but mostly dey jest come dat way." He tossed me a sly grin. "Bad luck to change horses' names."

While mulling over that tidbit, I turned my thinking around. Now was the time to ask what I'd wondered for years. "Mr. Swensen," I hesitated, not sure whether he'd answer or not. "No disrespect intended, sir, but seeing as you're well . . . Negro . . . and Swensen isn't a Negro name, how'd you come by it?"

A long gaze traveled across my face; he leaned in closer to me. He lowered his voice. "Long story."

A turn and he stepped into a nearby stall. Apparently that was all I was going to get.

Pokey led Dillon and then Jasper outside and tied them to a hitching rail. He and I inspected every inch of the beautiful animals. I guessed they had to be well over a thousand pounds each. They would be wheel horses, meaning that they would be hitched closest to the wagon. They would do most of the pulling. The other horses would be in charge of guiding, leading the parade, so to speak.

I couldn't wait to see them harnessed and ready to go. Mr. Swensen brought out the other horses for Pokey and me to inspect and to do a fair amount of patting. All in thrifty condition, as my pa would say.

Tearing ourselves away from appreciating fine horseflesh, we wanted a look at the mail coach in a barn the next block over and the opposite end from our postal office.

Mr. Swensen walked in front of us. "Watch out for dem . . ." The livery owner stumbled over a couple of words as he pointed to steaming piles of fresh "used up hay," as Pokey called them. I'm sure he called them other things, like my pa did, but I let him be a gentleman. Now, I knew that Mr. Swensen owned the barn behind the stable, but until right that minute, I'd never had any cause to go inside. With only a couple of small windows and one wide door, it was dark and a bit unnerving. In front of me, I could barely make out a bigger-than-buffalo-sized object. I squinted and peered hard.

"I'll be gettin' a lantern lit, so's we can see where we're goin'," Mr. Swensen said. He turned to me, cocking one eyebrow up and the other down. "Dat is, if'n you can stay upright. No more rollin' around in de dirt."

I blew a thunderous sigh as I rolled my eyes heavenward, but resisted the bait. I flashed a thin, forced smile.

Within moments, golden light pooled on the ground and spread up the wooden barn sides. The cavern warmed. Now that I could see better, I recognized our mail coach, which could also handle passengers. A tingle raced up my spine. This was real. We were actually going to do this.

I'd seen our stagecoach before, but only in passing. I'd relied on Pa and his eye for things like this. So, it was with great interest I inspected our mail wagon. Of course, we weren't buying it, same as the horses. We couldn't afford much. But with Mr. Swensen's generous rental fee, it felt like it belonged to us.

"This here's a Celerity. Some call dem mud wagons. Finest made. Clear over in New York." Mr. Swensen opened and closed the coach's door. "It's lighter in weight dan dose passenger coaches, de Concords, and dat make it better to run along de road. Horses like it better, too."

The wheels looked mighty narrow, and for the first time I noticed the front ones were smaller than the back.

"For running over rocks and dirt like we've got, dose narrower wheels work best. An' the front," Mr. Swensen said, "well, it's lower in front but you'd never know it when you sit. It's to help balance the coach." He opened a door. "Here, step inside and you'll see what I mean."

I hadn't been in a stagecoach for many years. Immediately, I remembered the excitement of the ride and the thrill of the ground rushing past me. I found myself smiling as I snuggled down on the dusty seat. Maybe I could go with Pokey on his first run. Now, *that* would be fun.

Pokey and Mr. Swensen sat opposite me, facing the front of the coach. On the outside, it looked similar to a stagecoach, but inside, it didn't have the jump seat in the middle, where extra people could sit. It did have an extra large boot in the back, where packages would be placed. I'd been told sitting under the driver's seat, facing the back, was the best place to be, except for the driver, who had the best seat—as long as the weather held. As the coach moved, the throat-strangling dust streaming in through the windows tended to attack the people facing forward, leaving the seats facing backward not quite as dirty.

The coach rocked while Mr. Swensen and Pokey climbed out, chatting about leather straps and weight distribution and facts and figures, which bored me. The door slammed shut and left me all alone, inside. I relaxed back, took a deep breath and closed my eyes. My imagination took charge.

Four sets of reins intertwine in my fingers. Horses' hooves pound while I sit high on the drivers' bench, tasting sweet mountain air. Commanding a hitch of four horses is a tough job, I know, but I won't let the company down. My hat snugged down tight keeps the wind from tangling my hair, and my long sleeves keep the sun from frying my skin. The sun's warmth burns my cheeks but, as the horses run, the exhilaration of being in control of the stage and the team leaves me bursting with pride.

In front lay a narrow mountain trail. I sit up straighter, knowing it is a test mastered many times, but still and always a challenge. I check the horses. Abner and Bob pull like champions and the wheel horses follow them well. Jasper and Dillon gallop like kings of the road.

"*Whoop, whoop. Eyyee!*" To my right, I spot five or six Indians, bows and rifles held high. They gallop down from a low hill, all the time hollering. An arrow whizzes past my head. I duck, slapping the reins hard over the team's back. The Indians' painted faces sneer menacingly at me, as they ride closer.

I yell at the horses, "Giddy up!" The reins snap, but it isn't enough. The Indians are gaining on us. I lean forward, connecting with my four horses. We become one powerful machine—me and them.

"When you plannin' on needin' dis?" A voice shot in through the window.

I jumped. My heart pounded so hard I couldn't breathe. Fighting to make sense of where I was, I swallowed and blinked at Mr. Swensen and then Pokey, who held the door open. When the current world came back into focus, I took a deep breath.

"What?"

"Must've dozed off dere, Sheriff." Mr. Swensen's eyes twinkled in the golden light. "I asked when you'd be wantin' dis rig."

Pokey chuckled at me. "Must've been a good dream." He pointed. "Both your hands're all fisted up."

Sheepish is the word I'd use. As much as I wanted to deny it, my mind had been elsewhere. A couple fresh breaths and I was again in the barn, sitting in a parked and dark stagecoach, talking to Pokey and Mr. Swensen. I turned full attention on the mail coach owner.

"How about next Monday?"

Chapter Twenty-One: Pull the Front Trigger

I couldn't get the rush I'd imagined, that stomach-clenching excitement of driving the stage, out of my mind. Here it'd been a full day and still the image seized my soul. Of course, I was concerned about the attacking Indians part, but nowadays, with them settling more or less peaceably on reservations, such a scenario didn't happen often. Driving the stage was safe. As I pushed around more wanted posters, I made up my mind. I would ride shotgun on the inaugural run. Again, I feel the wind whipping my hair and the sun warming my cheeks. In two days I'd get to ride on top of the stagecoach.

Being sheriff did have advantages.

It rained. And rained. And then it rained some more. What the old-timers called a *frog-strangler*. The deluge settled in over our little town, and no amount of mild oaths changed the sky's mind. High time I learned to use a shotgun, especially since I would ride guard with Pokey.

Seth and I met in the livery stable. Deciding we'd have to shoot indoors and some place with plenty of room and no horses, we moved down to Mr. Swensen's coach house a few blocks over, where we figured we couldn't do much damage. All he kept in there was our mail wagon and a buggy.

Seth set up several levels of hay bales, and I balanced the cans that I'd recovered this morning, placing them like a pyramid. He'd borrowed a shotgun from a friend of his and bought some shells. He handed them all to me.

Heavier than I'd expected, the double barreled Belgian must've weighed well over five pounds. It was heavier than my revolver, which in its own right weighed more than it looked.

Seth stuck with explanations that even a cowboy could understand. "See these two holes in the end of the barrel?"

Before I looked down the end of a shotgun, I knew enough now to see if the thing was loaded. Seth cracked it open between the wooden stock and barrel, and pointed to the empty holes where cartridges usually went. I peered into the black abyss and spotted pinpricks of daylight at the other end. Satisfied, I nodded and he flashed me another heart-stopping smile.

"I'm proud of you," he said. "You looked first." He patted my back.

He showed me how to insert the two paper cartridges, much bigger than my .36 ones. He snapped the shotgun together and handed it to me.

"All right," he said. "Put that baby up against your shoulder, tuck the stock against your cheek, sight down the barrel, and pull the front trigger." He breathed in my ear. "The front trigger connects to the shell in the right side."

I fumbled around like a ham-fisted little girl, until he once more put his arms around me.

"Like this," he breezed.

Concentrate, Maud. Concentrate. I sucked in air. My finger closed around the front trigger, exactly like he'd instructed. Pulling both at once would result in a double discharge, probably a waste of ammunition. No problem; I wasn't coordinated enough to shoot two at once. Both of our fingers, however, rested on the triggers.

I spotted the cans on the hay bales ten yards away, aimed the shotgun in their general direction and sighted down the barrel.

"Gentle now, Maud." Seth's candy-sweet words, his strong arms around me, tingled my body. His essence enveloped me like a warm milk bath. As he stepped back, one hand slid up my extended arm.

Boom!

I jerked backwards like invisible hands had shoved me. Losing my balance, I knocked Seth back and down and splatted on top of him, shotgun hitting the dirt. With the wind knocked out of me, his body under mine, I struggled to figure out where I was. I shook my head.

My world swam like trout fighting upstream.

"Yah awwlll rrrttt?" From the barn door, Mr. Swensen hollered something I didn't understand. He bolted toward me.

More voices from behind him. Silhouettes bobbed through the smoke, their voices rising. Were they speaking English?

A cacophony of sound encircled me, while I lay on Seth.

Before I could make much sense of anything, Mr. Swensen offered a hand and pulled me to my feet. I turned and looked down at Seth, lying still, eyes closed.

A couple men knelt beside him, checking to see if he was dead, I guessed.

"Somebody get the doc."

"Where's some water?"

Muffled voices echoed from far away. I strained to make out what they said. Bells rang and it wasn't even Sunday. A high-pitched whine replaced the babble. I leaned close to Mr. Swensen. "What'd you say?"

"I said he's out cold, Sheriff."

"What?" I heard what he'd said, I couldn't believe it. I knelt beside Seth, held his hand and rubbed. No response. "Seth?" I looked up at Mr. Swensen and a couple of men peering over his shoulder. They shrugged.

An eternity passed. Seth pulled in air, wiggled his legs and fluttered his eyes. He rolled to one side as Doc Monroe rushed in.

"What happened?" Doc helped Seth sit up and turned his dark-blue eyes on me.

Words refused to form. My head tilted one way, my hand pointed the other and my eyes had their own game plan. I grunted sounds, until I forced them to make a word.

"Shotgun."

A collective *ooohhh* erupted from the crowd, which now included several women and two children.

"You shot de mayor?" Mr. Swensen frowned at me, down at Seth, back at me.

Another *aaahhh* raced around the group.

I shook my head until the last of the rattles and whines vanished. "I knocked him down."

Oooohhhh.

"The shotgun. Kicked my shoulder and I—"

"I'm fine, Doc. Help me up." Seth offered both arms. Doc tugged and I pushed until the honorable mayor of Dry Creek stood upright.

Doc Monroe inspected the back of Seth's head. A lump the size of a medium horse dropping made Seth's hair stick out. Doc poked at the bump while Seth grimaced and cut his eyes at me.

"I'm sorry," I said. "Guess I pulled both . . ."

My gaze caught someone standing over to one side, arms crossed. Pearl McIntyre.

CHAPTER TWENTY-TWO:
WESTWARD 'HO

I figured, with a few more lessons, I would be proficient at using such a weapon. And the purple knot in my shoulder was turning to a dinner plate–size green and blue bruise. Now it throbbed only when I touched it or moved my right arm. Complaining got me no sympathy. Besides, Seth was worse off.

And Pearl McIntyre wasn't yet speaking to me.

Days earlier, back at the "event" in the coach barn, when bells had quit ringing in Seth's head, he'd wobbled over to her, where she'd lectured him, loud enough for me to hear, about shooting in enclosed buildings and some other drivel. She fawned and fussed over Seth. His big eyes turned downward, and he whimpered enough she promised to take him home to take care of the "nasty bump" on his head. They walked out of the livery stable with him on her arm. I'd staggered out alone with the shotgun, one arm hanging limp and numb.

But right now, some of the vinegar in my veins turned to molasses, as I thought about tomorrow's adventure with Pokey. Was he the right man for the job? Was he reliable enough to get the mail through three times a week? Was there anyone better than him for the job? That made me stop to reconsider.

Hadn't the town council said that about me? Not that I was good, but there wasn't anybody else?

Now *that* was a depressing thought.

★ ★ ★ ★ ★

Rain had at long last quit sometime during the night. Between the chill, the overcast skies and the mud, my outlook on this new venture was rocky. I hadn't slept well, if at all, and this morning I rushed to get Pa's breakfast and make a sandwich for his noon meal. If things went according to schedule, I'd be home in time to fix him supper. That was the plan.

So many doubts rattled through my head I barely heard Pa wish me good luck. There was probably an added comment or two, but I'd already closed the door and had focused on the day ahead.

True to his word, Pokey was at the new postal office by the time the sun peeked over the hill. There sat the mail coach, hitched to the four horses we'd rented. The start of our ground-breaking adventure. The ensemble reminded me of a giant sailing ship, ready to navigate around the world. And I would be at the helm. Almost.

Pokey seemed a little twitchy. He spit and circled the half-full sacks of mail and the coach like a dog circles a rug before lying down. Swede Swensen, Rune Maguire, Beth Gallaway, Pearl McIntyre, Mayor Seth and I kept pace. There couldn't have been a dust speck we didn't know about.

"This postal office, great idea, Maud," Seth said. "I mean, Sheriff Maud. I'll be waiting for you, when you get back this evening."

Wanting to take credit, but knowing it was truly Beth Gallaway's idea, I said, "Don't thank me," raised eyebrows at her and nodded. "It *is* a great idea, Beth. Thanks for thinking of it."

Beth's smile lit up Dry Creek. "I can't wait."

Pearl glanced at me sideways, looking less enthusiastic.

I knew if we didn't get going, I'd plumb burst. As it was, I had to visit the privy out behind the postal office before climbing up on the wagon.

Mr. Swensen held my elbow and pushed until I found my balance and footing on the coach. I'd been on one before as a youngster, but today I discovered scrambling up on top was a lot harder than fitting me and my skirt inside. Now, sitting on the left side of the mail coach, up on the wooden bench, my shoulders straightened and chest tightened. Exactly like I imagined a captain would feel taking his ship out on its maiden voyage. And, from up here, I could see for miles.

Maybe not miles, but at least half a mile. I spotted the Clarkes' fence running along their house bordering on the creek. Not something I saw normally from the ground. Behind me, the town lay spread out. Muddy Main Street didn't look so long any more. And more and more people stepped out of stores and alleyways to watch the launching. A regular party.

Seth stepped up to my side of the coach. "Forget something?"

I took quick inventory. "Don't think so."

He held up the shotgun.

My face burned. I was such an idiot. How could I forget my shotgun, when I'm the *shotgun guard*? "That'll come in handy." I reached down for it. "Thanks. And . . . sorry about your head."

He dug in his pocket and came up with two shells. "It's not loaded. You might need these." His eyebrows narrowed again and one dimple appeared. If I could've leaned down without falling off, I would've planted a big kiss on his lips. Instead, I plucked the ammunition out of his slim hand.

As sheepish as I felt, I gave an official sheriff-like bob and deepened my voice. "Thanks again." Then I remembered. In my jacket pocket was my .36 Navy revolver. I pulled it out, held it up at the assembled crowd, like I'd known it was there all along. "We're gonna be fine."

Why didn't I feel fine? Throwing up was an option, but I was determined it wouldn't happen and embarrass myself further in front of the town.

Pokey clambered on board and took the four reins in hand. He looked like he knew what he was doing, and I sat up straight, as though I did, too.

"Let's go," I said.

Pokey released the brake with his foot, flicked the reins over the team, and hollered, "Step up now." We lurched forward, the team looking for synchronization. I turned around and waved.

Holy smokes! Here I was sheriff of a whole town and riding shotgun on top of a stagecoach! The early morning sun on my back warmed me.

Seth trotted next to the slow-moving coach and shouted up to me. "Watch out for robbers and outlaws. That Mooney gang's around these parts, you know."

Great. Just when I'd managed to push that rascal to the back of my mind.

Chapter Twenty-Three: Mr. Friendly

Despite my worries about James Mooney and his band of cut-throats, the rest of the first mile was joy. From up on the bench, the wind ruffled my hair and an occasional ray of sun beamed down. Heaven, I knew, had to be a lot like this.

The second mile was a little less heavenly and a lot more bumpy. By now we were well out of town, with no houses or ranches or farms within sight. I missed the children running alongside whooping with excitement. Not even a dog nipped at the horses' heels. A time or two we hit chuckholes so hard that, in coming down, I had to grab Pokey's arm to keep from bouncing off the seat and sailing overboard.

"Should we stop for a couple minutes?" I bounced and lurched. "I could use a get-down." However pleased I was with my new terminology, I wasn't about to admit my rear end was sore and my legs cramping.

"Gotta keep on schedule, but we can probably stop in a bit." Pokey glanced at me, then returned his steady gaze to the road.

We jounced along, me trying to stay in my seat, Pokey whistling.

Now, with five miles behind us, and fifteen to go, Pokey pulled back on the reins, letting the horses walk instead of gallop. "We'll get over that big hill, then we'll let the hitch rest a mite."

Sounded reasonable to me. By now, my rear had bounced against that wooden bench till it ached like I'd been swatted by the meanest teacher in the world. Not that I had ever been swatted, but I could sure use a stretch. I glanced at Pokey, adjusting the reins intertwined among his fingers. He was driving like a professional.

He cut his eyes sideways. "Up ahead, half mile or so. We could stop for five minutes. There's a wide spot off to the right. Luke's Pond's just on the other side. You remember it?"

I most certainly did. Tingling butterflies landed on my chest, tickling my memories. Eli and I had fished there a time or two spending more time lying in the grass watching the clouds than actually trying to pull supper out of the water.

"Maud?" Pokey shoulder bumped me. "That all right? Five minutes. Got a schedule to keep, you know."

"Fine." I could hike off the road and make sure "our" pond hadn't changed. Besides, five minutes downtime wouldn't make much of a difference. What would make the difference, however, was this muddy road. We about got stuck a time or two, but our strong horses pulled us out. If it got worse, though, no telling how long it'd take to unstick us. I'd have to push, probably. And my skirt would present some difficulty.

At long last, I spotted the wide place in the road and Pokey pulled on the reins. "Slow now. Slow." Easing to a stop, Pokey stepped hard on the wooden brake, wrapped the reins around the end of it and jumped down. With the shotgun in one hand, I gathered my skirt with the other and waited for Pokey to help me down. His strong hands around my waist kept me upright.

We twisted our bodies, rubbed our lower backs and walked a bit, shaking out complaining leg muscles. Pokey headed off to find a large bush that needed watering; I ambled toward the pond, knowing he would eventually find me there.

I'd walked halfway when my nose pulled in smoke. Not a lot, just enough to tickle. Stopping, I sniffed. Campfire, most likely. Somebody else wanted fish for supper. A couple of steps farther, the smoke stronger now. A distinctive click, metal scraping against metal, echoed through the trees.

I froze. Immediately, my throat closed and went dry. I swung my head side to side looking, hoping it was my partner. Instead, a man stood there, a gun the size of Mount Shasta pointed at my chest.

"Name?" A thick accent I didn't recognize flowed from under his black mustache.

I blinked.

"I asked your name."

"Maud . . ." I said, swallowed again and started over. "Sheriff Overstreet from Dry Creek. We're starting a mail run over to Dutch Flats. Simply stopping for a breath."

"You the driver?" The man edged to where I could see him clearer—brown eyes, grizzled face, leather skin. Homemade clothes, which had seen many better days, hung on his rail-thin frame. He might've been about my age. Maybe not.

I clutched my own shotgun by the barrel, forgetting it was loaded, and that I knew how to use it. I shook my head. "The guard. My driver's over . . ." Well, I wasn't sure where my driver was. I hoped he wasn't lost. Or dead.

"Here, Sheriff Maud." Pokey stepped from around a pine. He walked up to me until we stood shoulder to shoulder.

The man eyed me. "If you're really the sheriff, show me your badge."

Had I even worn it? I looked down at my chest expecting to find nothing but buttons. Opening my jacket, I was pleased to discover the badge. I guessed by now it had become second nature to pin it there every morning. I pointed at it. "It says 'Sheriff.' "

"Hmm." He breathed so deeply I figured he'd float away, being so full of air. But he stayed grounded. He turned his pistol, which could've been a Smith and Wesson, on Pokey. "She lyin'?"

"No, sir. She's really the sheriff."

The man grinned. "Woman, huh?" He pointed to my shotgun. "Get any squirrels with that thing?"

I glanced at the forgotten weapon gripped in my hand and held it up, not really intending to shoot, but knew I could if need be. Tired of his questions and not wanting to play his game, I tried on my best menacing stare. "Now, look. We both have guns. How about you put yours down and we'll call it even?"

As if he didn't hear me, the man turned to Pokey. "You the deputy? Got at least a man for that?"

Pokey shuffled his feet before answering. "I'm the driver for Dry Creek's first postal office, but soon enough I'll be deputy."

The man waggled his gun at my badge. "You haulin' just mail in that buggy?" His elbow pointed toward our coach.

Hadn't I just explained? Maybe not. "Letters. We'll offload these at Dutch Flats, pick up mail for Dry Creek." Why was I tolerating this fool? The gun in his hand was why.

"You aimin' on comin' back this way?"

Of course we'd have to come back this way. I didn't want to argue the finer points of travel with this fella and we didn't have the time. Instead, I said, "Best way to fetch the mail, I figure." The shotgun heated in my grip and I wanted to raise it up to my shoulder, but figured he might shoot if I did.

From somewhere deep in my stomach, I pulled up courage. I nodded at his gun. "Put that thing down, Mister. Otherwise, you'll be heading off to jail. Or shot."

He didn't move.

"You can have breakfast in jail or at your camp," I said. "Your choice." I had no idea what I'd do if he chose to be arrested. And I'd sure hate to shoot him. "Now, like I said, lower your weapon."

"All right, Sheriff Lady." Like a snow pack melting in early spring, he eased back the hammer, and his arm inched downward. "Didn't mean you no harm. You comin' back through *today?*"

"Maybe."

Pokey cocked his head toward the team. "We gotta go. We're apt to be late as it is."

For once Pokey's head was on tighter than mine.

"Stop by here on your way back, an' maybe there'll be some fish to fry." The man's eyes narrowed.

I threw sarcasm over my shoulder as I turned to go. "Thank you for your kind invitation, but most likely not."

Pokey and I about ran to the mail coach. Laying the shotgun on the seat, I scrambled up without much help and was glad when he flicked the reins over the team's back. With a jerk, we trotted down the road.

Several long looks behind us revealed no one riding up hard. The skinny man wasn't following. My insides flip-flopped. Now besides James Mooney and his miscreants, I sensed I should add this new fella to my worry list. Why didn't I get his name? Hours of checking old wanted posters was definitely in my future. What would I find?

Chapter Twenty-Four:
Dutch Flats

Farms any gardener would envy dotted the hills for miles lead-ing into Dutch Flats. Entering the town, we passed at least two restaurants, one dining salon tucked between two mercantiles, more saloons than I could count, a church complete with a sky-sweeping steeple, a dressmaker, a blacksmith's, two livery stables and, finally, the postal station. The town, more than twice the size of Dry Creek, was the biggest congregation of humanity I'd seen since leaving Sacramento, some fifteen years before. Now I was extra-glad I had come along.

Butterflies fluttered in my throat. I hadn't felt this much excitement, except maybe when the fella's gun was to my head. My cheeks burned from the grin stretching them.

Pokey reined up in front of the postal station situated near the far end of town. Two women on the boardwalk stopped to stare. Several people stepped out of the various businesses to gawk. Even children froze. I guessed they'd not seen a mail coach this fine up close.

I scrambled down from the bench seat, not quite as grace-fully as I'd have liked, and spotted an official-looking man ambling out of the station.

"Howdy there." A thin hand stretched out of a well-starched shirt sleeve. "Been 'specting you."

Pokey joined me by the side of the coach. He shook with the man after I did.

"Name's Napoleon Bonaparte Dean," the postmaster said, a

127

twinkle creasing the sides of his blue eyes. "But most people 'round these parts call me Bert. Reckon you can, too."

"Pleased to meet you, Bert." I introduced Pokey and myself, as I took in the extra long main street of Dutch Flats.

"Napoleon Bonaparte?" Pokey frowned. "Heard o' you, but don't know from where."

Bert's face blossomed, years melting off what had to be at least sixty. "Original one was a great French leader, he was. My pap wanted a general in the family, figured the only way to get one was to name me that." He chuckled, letting loose a belly laugh.

With a windmilled arm toward the post office, coupled with his lanky frame and awkward gait, Bert reminded me of puppet marionettes I played with as a child in Sacramento. "Come on in," he said. "Make yourselves t'home."

We stepped inside, where mounds of envelopes ran from the floor to the top of Bert's desk, their magnitude almost as high as the Sierra Nevadas. Packages sat in front of his desk.

"These ours?" I pointed to a sizeable stack labeled "Dry Creek." More than I'd expected, but I figured there might be enough room in the coach.

"Yep," Bert said, thumbing at another sack and a pile of newspapers. "These . . . and these, too." He chuckled. "Ol' Jack ain't too good at gettin' every little stack, especially when I ain't around to check on him."

Pokey's frown mirrored what I felt, but I knew if we were going to be the postal service, we'd have mail. Up until now, I hadn't realized how much. Dutch Flats's deliveryman, Jack McCormick, hadn't been too reliable, and no telling how much he hadn't bothered to bring.

Or what got "misplaced" along the way.

"Oh. And back there's a package for you. Came in yesterday." Bert lowered his voice and leaned in close. "Addressed to Sheriff

Larimore, though."

He plopped an inch-thick brown paper package into my hands. A quick glance at Pokey before I studied the return address. *USM, Sacramento, California.* I tore it open.

Wanted posters. Looked to be at least twenty of them. A scribbled note on top was from the U.S. Marshall. *Thought you'd want these.*

The top one caught my eye and took my breath. James Mooney. The drawing of him, wide mustache and menacing eyes, his name emblazoned across the top, made my hands shake. I couldn't let Pokey or this Napoleon Dean fella see my reaction. It wasn't sheriff-like.

I cocked my head toward the towers of awaiting mail and packages. "What d'you think, Pokey? Think it'll all fit?"

Pokey's eyebrows narrowed and he gave everything a good sweep. Seemed like mountains were left over from what McCormick hadn't delivered. "Yep. Got us a big coach. We could purt'n near fit in—"

"Newspapers can ride in the boot," I said. "Everything else we'll tuck in here and there."

Right then, a small noise from my stomach reminded me breakfast had been a long time back. No doubt Pokey was starving, too. He was always hungry.

I turned to Bert with one more question. "I see you've got at least two restaurants. Any recommendations?"

"Ready for some grub, are ya?" Bert rubbed a skeletal hand over his mouth, a thin mustache doing a poor job covering his upper lip. "Good one's right down the street, 'bout half a block." His voice lowered, turning serious. "Word of advice. Watch out for Jack McCormick."

"Any particular reason?" Pokey asked, his attention now full on Bert.

"He's been drinkin' and complainin'."

"Complaining?" I asked.

" 'Bout you," Bert said. "You took his job . . . one of 'em anyways. With you drivin' to Dry Creek now, that leaves him only a couple other short runs. Went berserk when I told him. Claimed, and rightly so I reckon, that you're stealin' money from him."

"Never thought much about his losing his job," I said.

"Didn't lose all of it. Like I said, still got a couple other runs, but that was a goodly chunk of it." Bert wagged his head. "He ain't none too happy with y'all. I'd stay outta his sights, if I were you."

"He dangerous?" My sheriff badge warmed.

"Drunk, mostly. But . . ." Bert's eyebrows reached for his receding hairline. "I hear tell he had something to do with helpin' Juarez run the French outta Mexico few years back. He knows which end of a gun shoots. And . . ." He lowered his voice. "Don't take much to set him off."

Pokey's summer tan turned a lighter shade.

Bert snapped gnarled fingers. "Near plumb forgot." He glanced right, left and lowered his voice. "Local bank here's got a small sack of notes and bills for ya. Regular shipment. Need to get to your bank . . . today. They're expecting it."

I was uncomfortable knowing we had United States of America currency with us. "Anybody else know we've got this?"

Bert shrugged. "Doubt it. Keep things like this quiet. Only ones who know are the bank and Jack."

"Terrific," I said. I'd stick it under the driver's seat.

"Be sure it gets through," Bert said. "Had a couple complaints your Dry Creek bank didn't get the right amount. Or none at all."

Pokey gave Bert a hard look. "You think maybe Jack McCormick took it?"

Bert shrugged. "All I know is, *I* didn't take it." He dismissed us. "Enjoy your dinner."

Tucking the wanted posters under the driver's seat, I gripped the shotgun, thanked Bert, asked him to get a boy to water our horses and told him we'd return directly. We went in search of the restaurant. I knew I was in a big town when I had to choose which place to eat. We selected the recommended one, *Angel's Eatery,* which sported lace curtains on the windows, a novelty by any Dry Creek standards.

As Pokey opened the door and I stepped inside, everyone froze, eyes riveted on us. Forks and conversations stopped midair, while Pokey and I took our seats. It wasn't the scrutiny I minded so much, but I wasn't sure my table manners would be up to snuff.

From our corner table, my chair faced into the room. I leaned the shotgun against the corner, hoping a weapon of such a size wouldn't be so conspicuous there. I smiled at each person. Pokey studied his fork until a waitress took pity and rescued us with paper menus.

Back home, there was no choice as to the fare. No need for a menu. They served the same thing to everybody. But in this town, it looked like there was more choice. I scanned the listing and surveyed the other diners' plates. Most contained remnants of fried chicken and mashed potatoes and a couple sported trout with a helping of carrots. I knew immediately I'd like to try somebody else's fried chicken, tired as I was of my own cooking. This was going to be a first-class treat.

Pokey ordered sliced ham with turnip greens.

While we waited, I glanced to the patrons who continued to stare. Conversations were hushed or nonexistent. I fidgeted. The wanted posters were no distraction. Maybe if I kept James Mooney's surly mug face down, he'd stay away from my thoughts so I could enjoy my dinner.

Each squeak of the door's opening made me jump. Was it

Jack McCormick coming in to kill me? Then again, I didn't know exactly what he looked like. I'd never been around when he deposited mail at the hotel. A quick check with Pokey. He didn't know either. Now we were really in trouble.

One couple stood to leave, but stopped at our table on their way out. The man addressed Pokey. "Excuse me, sir. Are you by chance the new driver for the Dry Creek mail?"

Pokey's chest strained buttons. He sat tall and answered with a refined air. "Yes, sir, I am. Started our first run today."

The woman smiled at me. "How nice your husband let you tag along. I'm sure you're glad to get out of the sun."

I opened my jacket and flashed my badge. "Ma'am," I said, "I'm not 'tagging along.' I'm the sheriff of Dry Creek."

The man shrunk back like I had the pox, his eyes traveling up and down my body. He glanced at his wife. "Who ever heard of a woman sheriff?"

She lowered her voice to a venomous whisper. "Simply not done. Not by *proper* ladies."

I wanted to explain things, but she turned before I knew where to start. The man huffed and followed his wife, words trailing behind him. "A woman sheriff? Next thing you know, they'll be wanting to vote. I tell you, Clara, this world's going to hell. Pardon my language." The door banged shut behind him.

I bolted halfway out of my seat, ready to "explain things," but realized it wouldn't make any difference. Men would have to get used to the idea women could do about anything.

Our meal came and I chose to focus on my fried chicken dinner instead of a narrow-minded man with backwoods ideas.

CHAPTER TWENTY-FIVE:
HOLED UP

The noon meal filling my stomach, hoping no one was looking, I undid the top button of my skirt. Whew! That chicken was delicious. I made a mental note to try frying my chicken the same way. The lingering taste of spices tantalized my brain. Was that perhaps ginger? Too expensive for me, so maybe I'd try more pepper.

With Bert's help, Pokey and I loaded the mail, all the while keeping an eye out for Jack McCormick. He had reason to be sore. I'd be, if somebody took my employment. Yeah, he did indeed have a right to be angry, but not a right to hurt anybody.

Toting and arranging took longer than we'd figured, but within an hour we waved good-bye to Bert Dean and trotted away, safe from the likes of Jack McCormick—at least for the moment.

Clouds played peek-a-boo with the sun. The hills, covered with yellow and purple flowers, sprung to attention as we loped past. With the sun's warmth on my back, a full stomach and the horses' steady pace, my eyelids grew heavy and threatened to close.

My head dropped, my shoulders slumped, but the chuckhole we hit jarred me upright. I glared at Pokey. "My backbone's about up around my ears. Can't you at least miss one of 'em?"

He chuckled. "Nope. Got 'em all so far."

"So far."

I recognized the hill coming into view. Luke's Pond and the

crazy man stood on the other side. On one hand, I knew we were about five miles from Dry Creek and, judging by the sun's slant, we were making good time, despite the mud. What if the man was waiting to hold us up?

"Are we stopping?" I said. "The horses probably need a breather, but I'd rather not do it there."

"Agreed." Pokey tightened his grip on the reins and narrowed his eyes toward the hill, coming into sight.

Trees, hills, the pond off to the left and a chipmunk skipping across the road ahead of our team—not team, *hitch*, Pokey had instructed me. Clouds darkened another part of the world, so the blazing sunlight now caused me to squint despite my hat's wide brim. But the warmth felt good. In fact, *I* felt good. Maybe I could go again some other time.

"Hold it! Right there!"

The cold words sent chills over every part of my body. Off to our right, up ahead, stood a man, rifle cradled against his shoulder and aimed our way. To our left, another man, pistol pointing at us, moved in closer.

Pokey gripped the reins and pulled. His boot on the wooden brake jammed it against the wheel as we skidded to a stop. Bandanas covering their faces did little to disguise the skinny one who had confronted us on our way to Dutch Flats. The same shabby clothes, a threadbare yellow plaid shirt, laced in front with rawhide, hung on his skeleton frame. His pants sagged, held up by a string around his waist, giving the impression he was wearing his pa's hand-me-downs.

"Down!" the man growled. His pistol waved at me and Pokey. "Sheriff Lady, I said 'down'!"

Before my shoes touched ground, he rushed toward me, grabbed my shotgun, tossing it into the dirt behind him, and hefted the Colt out of my skirt's waistband. He wedged the revolver into his own gunbelt. I was really glad I'd put only one bullet in it, figuring if he was a poor shot, chances were good he'd miss me. There would be no second chance.

"*¡Arribas sus manos!*" The other man, fatter than the first and taller, shook his rifle at me. While I didn't understand a lot of Spanish, most of it I'd learned on the playground, I knew what he wanted. My hands needed to be reaching skyward.

Should I tell him I was the law? What kind of difference would that make? The skinny fella already had called me "sheriff."

Pokey's voice sailed over from the other side of the coach. "That lady over there's a sheriff. Of Dry Creek. You got no right to hold us up. She's gonna arrest you, then hang you."

Great. Like they needed reminding.

Feet scuffling, a *whump*. Moans. Chuckling from the other side of the coach. Pokey?

Before I could call out, the Spanish-speaking bandit sidled up close. He'd had a considerable amount of whiskey, recently. Not only was it on his breath, despite the greasy bandana over his mouth, but his clothes reeked, too. A bath in it was a strong possibility.

"Sheriff, *¿verdad?*" He reached for my jacket, I guessed hoping to find my tin badge. As he moved in close, I grabbed the rifle barrel gripped in his hand. Using it for leverage, I spun it upside down and smacked the man in the face. The wooden stock slammed into his jaw. Teeth clacked as he reeled backward.

I scrambled for his weapon, which he released with a groan. Grabbing it, I jammed the rifle close against my sore shoulder, and aimed at the fallen bandit.

"Don't move," I said.

"Drop it!" Pistol in hand, the yellow-shirt attacker rushed around the horses, slid to a stop by his partner and cocked the pointed weapon. At me. The man on the ground holding his cheek moaned louder this time and pushed up on one elbow.

I eased back a few paces and aimed the rifle toward his chest.

"*You* drop it. I'm arresting you both." Was Pokey all right? And was my voice as high as I thought? I hadn't heard a gunshot, but moans I figured were his sounded serious. No telling what had happened when I was busy clobbering this fella.

"You . . . *mujere* . . . *niña.*" The man wobbled up to his feet, the red mark on his face glowing against his tanned skin. The tattered scarf hung loose like a worn baby's bib.

I gripped the rifle harder, while my legs—all on their own—took a wider stance.

Both men stood side by side. "T'aint but one of 'er," the scrawny bandit said. He lifted a shoulder toward the coach and raised a crooked sneer to his partner. "You done took care of t'other."

Like lions hunting their prey, they edged toward me.

"Stay right there," I said. My finger touched the cold trigger. *Bang!*

I lurched backward, bouncing off the mail coach. Anger strengthening my "girl" muscles, I kept my feet. Smoke lazed in the air, as if cloaking them. But I could still make out one man's skinny frame, his fingers clutching a blood-soaked shoulder, the useless gun hand empty.

"You shot me!" he hollered, jerking my Colt from his gunbelt. He aimed at my head. "Gonna give ya what's comin' ta ya."

Bang! A bullet whizzed past my ear. Bits of wagon wood exploded.

"*Gringo!*" the Mexican yelled. "You almost shoot me, too." He fired.

I ducked. Two bullets were two too many. Refusing to go down without a good fight, I cocked the rifle, hoping it was still loaded, and brought it up to my shoulder. Before I could pull the trigger, a hatless and bleeding Pokey materialized behind them and bear-hugged the skinny one, knocking the revolver into the dirt.

"Gotcha!" Pokey held up the pistol like a trophy. "He won't be needin' this anytime soon."

The other outlaw glanced toward his partner. That split second of inattention was all I needed to get the drop on him. I rushed forward and jammed the rifle in his stomach. *"Manos arriba,"* I said. Surprisingly, he raised his hands.

The outlaw in Pokey's grip wriggled like the proverbial fish on a hook, but to no avail.

Had I brought handcuffs? No, didn't have any, but we could use the saddle strings on their saddles to tie hands. Keeping an eyeball on the fella at the end of my rifle, and with my heart in my throat, I plucked my gun out of the dirt.

It was indeed a glorious day—I'd saved the mail, saved the bank's money and shot well, but not killed anybody. All level-headed actions. Now . . . if I could breathe and keep my heart from exploding from my chest.

CHAPTER TWENTY-SIX:
ALIAS SMITH AND DOYLE

With the two desperados secured behind thick iron bars, I hunkered down at my desk looking for any wanted posters on them. After threats of death and various torture techniques, none of which we'd actually use, Pokey, Seth and I managed to wheedle out the true identities of these desperados. Amos "Wink" Smith and "Slap" Jack McCormick. Odd that he spoke Spanish and yet used the Irish name McCormick.

Thumbing through the stack I'd brought from Dutch Flats, as well as those left behind by my predecessor, I considered the few photographed faces. Those glared at the camera, looking as if they modeled for *Outlaw Gazette*. The rest of the posters had either bad pencil drawings or vague descriptions. From what I read, they were scoundrels of the lowest kind, and, surprisingly, many were younger than me. Must be the outlaw way of life took years off these men, and many didn't live long enough to get old.

One grabbed my attention as I read the description.

Wanted: Amos "Wink" Smith. Five foot ten, skinny, black hair. Last seen in Texas. Cattle rustling, robbery, murder.

Could that be the fella I had locked up? I shivered, wondering how strong the iron was on those cell bars. How about the lock? A glance at the keys hanging on the wall made me feel a mite better. The murderer hadn't tried to escape. But would he? Moreover, he and McCormick had only been in jail less than an hour. Locking them up, I'd told them both the circuit judge would be coming in about three weeks, and I'd insisted they "rest up" in my jail, until then. Three weeks was more than enough time to plan and execute . . . more shivers at that word . . . an escape. I'd have to be on guard all the time. Maybe I really did need a deputy.

A glance at the Regulator on the wall revealed I'd need to wander over to the Tin Pan in about twenty minutes to check on Pokey. He'd insisted a stiff one would get the dust out of his craw and twenty minutes gave me plenty of time to continue my outlaw-poster searching.

I studied each poster for one on McCormick, but nothing came to light, except one. Was this who I thought it was?

Wanted: Juan Doyle. Alias Pancho Romero. Half-breed, light skinned. Five foot eleven, dark eyes, black hair, speaks Spanish. Cattle rustling, bank robbery, double murder, escape from jail. Ties to James Mooney Gang. Reward $500. Dead or alive.

I reread the first line. Juan Doyle? The rest fit. Maybe. Possibly. Had to be.

And a reward? Pokey earned it and I, being a lawperson, was ineligible for the reward. I looked forward to bearing the happy news to him. I would do so this evening.

Doyle was obviously one bad hombre, somebody I was extra glad to have behind bars. And, to think, Pokey and I had captured him.

Now coming on toward suppertime and, despite my urge to let them go hungry, I knew I couldn't. They'd been quiet enough up 'til now, but cat calls and whistles, muffled by the closed inner door, interrupted my concentration. I sat up straighter, pulled the revolver out of the desk drawer, checked on the single bullet still in the cylinder and, gun in hand, marched back toward the holding cells. I guess they'd heard me coming. The floorboards squeaked under every step.

As I twisted the inner doorknob, both spoke louder so I could hear them.

"You afraid of *la mujere* out front, Wink?"

"The one that got us locked up? Thinks she's a law dog?" A snort. "I'm shakin' in my boots."

"*Yo Tambien.* I bet she's real fearsome at the cook stove."

I opened the door and stepped into the hallway. Each outlaw received my best glare. "You got something to say?"

Wink leaned back on his bunk and propped one foot on the cot. "Not me, Sheriff." He rubbed his bandaged upper arm. "This here bullet wound's painin' me somethin' fierce. Need the doc again. Whiskey'd be even better."

The smirk on his face and gleam in his eyes betrayed his complaint.

I shook my head. "Doc's already said it was a graze. You'll live."

Juan Doyle or Jack McCormick, whatever moniker he went by right then, eased off his bunk and slunk toward me. As much as I wanted to back away, I stood my ground. They weren't going to see me afraid.

"I gots a question, *bruja.*"

As close as I was to him, it was easy to spot his rotted teeth, gray with a few black ones. His breath stunk like rotten tomatoes and onions. I turned my head hoping to avoid gagging. "You Jack McCormick? From Dutch Flats?"

"*Si.* You . . . you stole my job."

"And you stole from the post office and the bank. Over several years. You're looking at federal offenses. Jail time," I said. "Maybe hanging."

"You got nothing on me. I never stole nothing." He cut his eyes to Wink. ". . . except, maybe some girl's heart." McCormick turned his gaze on me. "Your *papa* know you're out? He know you're playin' grown-up? He's probably worried about you, *tambien* . . . it's gonna get dark soon. You best run on home."

"Hell, Doyle," Wink pointed his scraggly chin toward my Colt. "Looks like this Law Dog gots a gun. Just 'cause she was lucky with that rifle, bet she don't know how to use that two-dollar pistol, there." He eased to his feet like a snake slithering off a rock, and glided to the iron bars, all the while making a hissing chuckle.

"Probably never even shot it." Doyle looked at his partner. "Suppose she's got bullets?"

"Nah," Wink said. "Probably scared she'll shoot herself."

The two outlaws leaned within arm's reach, iron bars the only thing separating us.

"Shoot herself?" Doyle said. "*Mierda*, Wink, I been thinkin'. You know any other girl sheriffs?"

Wink scratched his head. "Can't rightly say I do."

"Know what I think? I think she can't get herself an *hombre*, so she's gotta get one at gunpoint."

Wink held up one hand, the other arm in a sling, his false baritone voice irritating. "Don't shoot me again, Sheriff. I'll marry you."

Both men rolled with laughter. Doyle's breath about took mine away.

Doyle choked down chuckles. "No. She shot the old sheriff and took his job." His dark eyes slid down to my chest and stayed there. "Only way a homely *vaca* such as herself can get a man's job."

"You're right there. For a half-breed Mex, you think good." Wink licked his chapped lips and lowered his voice. "Either shot him or bedded him. Either way, poor fella lost out."

I had to take control, right now.

"You done?"

"Ay, no, we ain't," Doyle said.

I wouldn't let them see me rattled. "Huh. Looks like your

grub's gonna be two more hours."

I turned and marched through the door, slamming it behind, cutting off their protests.

I'd make sure their food was cold by the time they got it.

CHAPTER TWENTY-SEVEN:
. . . TO POKEY!

Outside the Tin Pan Saloon, I stood on tiptoes peering over the top of the batwing doors. Pokey leaned against the bar, beer mug in one hand, a woman in the other. Happiness exuded from him. I didn't know anybody could smile so wide or so long.

"Here's to Pokey Johnson." Mayor Seth's raised glass sloshed as he saluted my almost-deputy. "The man who saved not only the mail, but Sheriff Maud's life."

"Hear, hear." Congratulations sailed around the room followed by loud gulpings and *aahhh*s by the crowd, and a couple of slaps on Pokey's back, propelling him to the middle of the room. If I didn't know him better, I'd say he'd taken wings and flown to the moon. If his buttons strained any more, he'd be shooting them clear across the room.

"Speech! Speech!" One man started the chant. More well-wishers joined in.

The batwing doors squeaked open, swinging wide as I pushed. I stepped in with all the bravado I could muster, hearing Pa's words in my head, *"Ladies don't drink or ever consider going into those dens of desire."*

Up until a couple weeks ago, I had no idea what a *den of desire* was, but I'd figured it out pretty quick. I'd come into one . . . again.

Pokey derailed Pa's admonitions by pulling my attention to himself. He held up his glass. "Come join us, Sheriff Maud. I'll buy you a beer." His smile danced in his eyes. "You earned it."

I certainly hadn't liked the only beer I'd ever had. Memory of its bitter, sour-milk taste made me wince. But if a man could do it, I could. "All right," I said as I elbowed my way in next to him. "I'll drink one with you."

I gripped the glass someone'd brought over. Cool, but not warm, the way I'd heard beer used to be before they figured out how to store ice all year round.

We clinked glasses, I closed my eyes, held my breath . . . and chugged. It all went down in one long gulp.

"Hooray!" The crowd exploded as I raised the glass above my head.

Pushing down the foul liquid, I found my breath and voice. I patted Pokey's arm. "You were about to give a speech." I glanced around the room at the crowd of well-wishers. Most I recognized, a couple I didn't. "Let's hear it."

Pokey ducked his head, his bruised left cheek turning red, and shot me a sideways glance.

I nodded encouragement, although curious as to what he was about to say.

I was happy for him, but I had also helped subdue those bandits. If it hadn't been for me shooting the skinny robber, well, Dry Creek would be without its mail and the bit of currency we'd carried. While it was Pokey's day, his time to shine, it was also mine. I was the one who shot the outlaw and put an end to the robbery. I deserved at least some of the credit.

I waited to see what Pokey had to say.

He put down his beer, his gaze taking its time traveling from face to face. The crowd of at least twenty-five people, mostly men, grew silent.

He drew in a deep breath, let it out, then rested his eyes on me. A crooked smile and he began. "I didn't do anything other than what any man would do. What any of you all would've done. Once Maud . . . Sheriff Overstreet . . . got their attention, heck, it was easy for me to capture both of them outlaws."

Capture? Him? Wasn't I the one who faced down Smith? Wasn't I the one about to shoot Doyle? Saving Pokey's hide?

I interrupted Pokey's speech. "*We* got the drop on those men, Pokey. You *and* me."

"Ah, let Pokey tell the story, Maud," someone shouted from the edge of the crowd.

"Yeah. 'Sides, you're a girl," another man added. The crowd snickered, their heads bobbing. A couple of glasses clinked in a toast.

Anger warmed my cheeks. Why wasn't Pokey defending my honor?

A woman dressed in an above-the ankle, light-blue skirt and low-cut blouse, a couple feathers sticking out of her brown hair, pushed her way through the crowd and sidled up to Pokey.

"You're awful brave. Did you get hurt?"

His cheeks, which had started returning to normal color, pinked up. He frowned and shook his head. "Naw." Apparently changing his mind, Pokey rubbed his shoulder a bit, rotating his arm, and turned his frown into a hang-dog expression. His eyes drooped. "But I did get kinda banged up fightin' those bandits." He rubbed his right arm.

"You poor thing," she said. "Here, let me take care of you."

"Thank you, darlin'," Pokey said, then as if being hit by the good manners wand, raised an empty glass to his friends. "Just wanted to say I appreciate your kindness . . . and beer."

The crowd roared, wishing him more success and alcohol. The floozie pulled him toward a far table.

Chapter Twenty-Eight: A Reason for Celebrating

I tugged on Pokey's arm, pulling him toward me, out of her grasp. "Hate to spoil a good time," I said, pushing down tingles of outrage. I dropped my voice. "Need to tell you something."

"Tell me somethin'?" Pokey's voice rose above the din. "What kinda somethin'?"

"Not here." I eyed the lady planted against Pokey's side. "Back at the office." I leaned around behind Pokey and spoke to the woman. "I'll return him later. Town matters need looking to right now."

Pokey was drunk enough he didn't need much coaxing to go anywhere. He wasn't stumbling, rather sort of gliding as we walked across the barroom.

"See ya later, Pokey," one man said.

"Good job, Pokey," said another.

"Congratulations, again!"

I gripped his arm as he swayed. We pushed shoulder to shoulder through the batwing doors into the cool early evening air—air clean and pure, not filled with cigar and kerosene smoke.

We made our way down Main Street and across it, stopping in front of the office. I wanted to be sure the information about the reward money stayed outside—I didn't want Smith and Doyle to know who earned it.

"You remember those fellas we arrested this afternoon?" I felt the need to remind Pokey of the reason for celebrating.

" 'Course I do, Sheriff," Pokey said. "Can't never forget

146

somethin' like that." His words slurred, but they sounded soft, like a kitten purring.

"I've got some good news." I glanced side to side. We were alone, no one within shouting distance. By now most people were home either fixing or eating supper. A thought about fixing Pa's supper pranced across my mind, but I pushed it aside. "I came across wanted posters on our men in there."

"So they're really bad men? I thought maybe they were gonna hold us up seein' as we'd come through earlier." Pokey sounded more sober.

"Both are wanted for murder, so be careful." I drew in a deep breath and let it out an inch at a time. "Turns out, that fella McCormick?"

Pokey bobbed his head. "Slapjack?"

"I think his name is Doyle. Got a price on his head, too." I let it sink in. "You've got a reward coming."

"I do?"

I patted his arm. "Congratulations."

Pokey's eyes blinked as he frowned. Words started and stopped. He blinked some more and cocked his head. "Reward?" He spoke as if trying on the word for the first time.

"Yep. Five hundred dollars." I liked sharing this kind of news, and hoped I'd get to do it again. "I'll send a telegram to Sacramento and as soon as they authorize payment, you'll get it."

Pokey held both my shoulders and looked into my eyes, his own blinking independently. For a second there, I thought he was going to kiss me. But instead, he smiled. "You know what this means?"

I mirrored his smile but shook my head.

"Means I can be deputy now." Pokey's cheeks stretched. He stared over my shoulder as if already counting his money. "I'll be damned! *Deputy Johnson.*" Without another word, he wrapped me in strong arms. We whirled and sashayed down the boardwalk, his feet and mine tangling like a drunken octopus.

Stopping to catch his breath, Pokey released me. Confused as to how he figured the windfall made him a deputy, I asked.

Serious now, Pokey again gazed into my eyes and explained, as if I were seven years old. "Town council said they couldn't afford my wages, right? Right. Well, now they don't have to pay me. Hell, Maud, five hundred dollars's like a year's pay, right? Right."

I followed his reasoning but wasn't sure of the ciphering. "I guess."

"So, since they don't gotta pay me, I can be deputy." Pokey picked me up and whirled me around again. "I can even buy my own badge. This is the best damn day of my whole damn life!" He stopped and lowered his voice. "I apologize for the language. But I'm about as happy as a flea in a doghouse. Why, I ain't never—"

"Congratulations, Pokey," I said. "But if I were you, I wouldn't go around telling everybody—yet."

"You wouldn't?"

"Nope. I'd wait until Slapjack . . . Doyle and Smith go to trial and get carted off down to prison. No telling what they'd do if they found out it was you who got the reward money."

Pokey's Adam's apple bobbed up and down. He bear-hugged me, again. With a long, deep, self-satisfied sigh, Pokey slowly slid down my chest, past my badge, bumping his chin on my gunbelt on the way down, and melted into a limp puddle, right there on the boardwalk.

Like the Cheshire Cat, only his grin remained.

CHAPTER TWENTY-NINE:
THESE BOOTS ARE MADE FOR WALKIN'

One problem I hadn't given much thought to was who'd stay at night guarding the prisoners. Pokey volunteered for a night or two and borrowed a cot from his part-time boss, Harvey Weinberg, owner of the mercantile store and also one-third of the town council. The other nights, it would be me. Sleeping probably wouldn't happen, since I was determined not to have a jailbreak. No, I'd spend my nights at the desk, fully awake, writing up reports to send to Sacramento. I'd have to stock up on coffee. Strong coffee.

That whole next week, the lawbreakers perched in their cells and called out disparaging remarks every time I brought them their grub. If I wasn't a nice person, I'd've spit in their oatmeal.

Seeing as they were busy doing a great deal of nothing, I'd wheedle some information. Kind of get to know them, informally. I wanted to know who, exactly, I had locked up. The posters didn't say much. But what I needed to know, most of all, was about this James Mooney criminal and his gang. I figured if they would let me in on some of Mooney's secrets, maybe I'd discover if he was planning to ride into town, shoot up the place and spring them out of jail. I also knew if I plain asked outright, they'd lie.

So, one day, while they were pushing supper, their "four o'clock" meal, into their faces, I stood nearby, leaning against the wall. Doyle glanced up. *"¿Qué quieres?"*

I didn't respond.

"He asked if you want something, Missy." Stew dribbled out of Smith's mouth as he talked.

With my heart in my throat, I tried to sound casual. I'd practiced on the way over, that morning. I was ready. "Grub all right?" My voice was strong, not shaking like I felt inside.

A shrug. "Good enough."

"They have this kinda stew where you're from?" I glanced over at Doyle, who shoved bread into his face. Carrot bits covered with gravy clung to his beard. "What's your favorite kind of food?" I asked.

Now that was a stupid question, one I hadn't rehearsed. But it popped out like a naughty child slipping out of bed.

Both men stopped and peered up at me.

One side of Wink Smith's mouth curved into a grin. "You askin' us out on a date, Missy?"

No need to get rattled, I told myself. This is simply conversation. I shook my head and forced a breath. "Nope. Wondering where you grew up. Curious. You know . . . for conversation." Did that sound casual enough? I hoped so.

"Ain't never had a sheriff ask personal questions before." Smith spoke over his last bite of bread. "All right, Miss Nosey. I grew up all over the place. Pa moved us from camp to camp, always lookin' for that damned gold." He slurped his coffee. "Died tryin'."

I turned my attention on Juan Doyle. "Is that when you joined the James Mooney gang?"

"¿Mande?" Doyle about choked and Smith chuckled out loud.

Doyle swallowed and shook his head. "James Mooney? No. I was six when *Papa* died." He shot a knowing look at Smith. "Mooney don't let six-year-olds ride with him."

"Kinda particular that way," Smith said.

A beat and I asked, "You ride with Mooney a long time?"

"Long enough," Doyle said.

"How about you, Mr. Smith?"

He laid his bowl aside and eased to his feet, kind of like a cat ready to pounce on an unsuspecting mouse. His dark eyes locked onto my face, while he oozed up to the bars. "How come you're so all-fired interested in our lives? 'Specially about Jim. Why don't you come right out and ask what you're beatin' around?"

Fair enough. But I'd have to ask it just right. I chose a soft approach. "Well, being in law enforcement, I see Mr. Mooney's name come over my desk. And you're the first men I know who've actually ridden with him. I'm curious is all, especially being he's famous."

Doyle joined our intimacy and leaned against the cell bars. He and Smith stood less than two feet apart. Four dark eyes stared through me until my entire insides turned squirmy.

"Famous? Jim Mooney?" Smith let out a long, sour breath and pressed up against the iron bars. "Honey, who you gotta be scared about ain't Jim Mooney."

"*Sí,*" Doyle growled. "*Mujer,* you best be scared about *us.*"

I was, but I'd be darned to let them see it. "Is Mr. Mooney planning to attack Dry Creek?" Dark eyes stared at me, almost boring a hole clean through my own. Wink Smith cocked his head.

Silence hung like a thick blanket. Enjoying the tension, Smith spoke in measured words. "Mooney molests folks only where and when they ain't lookin'."

Right then I knew I had to do more target practicing.

CHAPTER THIRTY:
POKER FACE

Besides rattling me, the only other thing my two "guests" did was play poker. Pokey sat in a time or two, staying outside of the bars, while Smith and Doyle scooted close to each other in their individual cells.

This afternoon Pokey shuffled, his soft fingers fluttering the cards like he knew what he was doing. An unlit cigar stuck out the side of his mouth. The only time I'd ever seen him with a cigar was when he had cards in front of him. He gummed it thoughtfully. Doyle cut the cards, wooden matchsticks were tossed onto a stool near Pokey, and it began. The mumbling, the eyes sliding sideways from man to man, the grunting. From what I'd observed, it was all posturing. I listened in and watched, when I could.

With the inner door open, it was easy to eavesdrop. From my chair in the office I heard Pokey's voice, louder than usual.

"Two pairs, gentlemen. Read 'em and weep."

"*¿Cómo?* Third time today?" Doyle's scratchy, Spanish-laced, deep voice made me sit forward. He was sounding more agitated than usual.

"Can't help it if I'm lucky." Pokey's chair squeaked, a sign he was leaning back. "Fact is, tomorrow's gonna be even luckier."

"Yeah? How's that?" Smith's voice echoed slimy as ever. He sounded like a singer who'd reached too high and strained his vocal cords, then drowned the pain with cod liver oil and kerosene.

"I'm gettin' rich."

I bolted out of my chair hoping, praying I could get to Pokey before he spilled the beans. He sat, leaning back in his chair, munching on a big cigar, his eyes shining. He cocked his head toward me.

"Yep. Gettin' rich thanks to Sheriff Overstreet here." Pokey smiled around his cigar.

Smith slapped down the deck of cards. "You mean she's payin' you to babysit us? To take our matchsticks?"

"Pretendin' you don't know how to play?" Doyle eased to his feet as if going for his gun. The one I had locked in my desk. Maybe he'd forgotten it wasn't strapped to his hip.

Easing to his feet also, Smith backed away from Pokey. "You cheatin' or a poker clergy?" He turned to Doyle. "Either way, we've been had."

I held up a hand, trying to save Pokey's reputation and wanting to have a word with him in private. "Nobody's a cheater or a ringer. You've both had a bad turn of cards." I glared at both men. "Besides, it's just matches." With a clenched jaw, I turned to my sidekick. "Need to see you in the office . . . *now!*"

I sat at my desk, Pokey taking a chair across from me.

"Maud, I wasn't gonna tell 'em about . . ." Pokey lowered his voice to a whisper, ". . . you know. I was thinkin' about the pie and meatloaf you always cook for me, when I get back from a run. Tastes like my ma's when she was alive. And anyhow, home cookin's almost better 'n money."

For the first time in the last hour, I relaxed. How could I be angry at such a gentle soul? I cringed at the thought of Pokey handling all that money by himself. Then again, if the only people who knew were Pokey and me, maybe he'd make it all the way back to town in one piece. Plus, I figured, I had the two big-time outlaws in my jail. They wouldn't be out robbing mail coaches.

No, Pokey was safe. Probably.

Chapter Thirty-One:
A Visit from the Magi

Standing on the boardwalk in front of my office, I waved good-bye to my almost-deputy as he drove off. His flick of the reins and command, "Step up now, fellas," sailed over his shoulder as the hitch pulled together. They left no cloud of dust this morning. Run number six, and I felt confident he would have no trouble. Still, something caught my breath as the coach trotted away. Maybe it was the warm June morning heating up the hitch's fresh pile of droppings. Maybe it was last night's supper. Maybe . . . it was simply too perfect.

Pa's breakfast was going to be later than usual. But I had to see Pokey off. For some reason, recently, Pa seemed to be more understanding than usual when his meal was late, an occurrence happening more and more often. I'd rush in from doing sheriffing business to fix dinner or supper only to find Pa already seated at the table, newspaper in hand. A time or two, he'd even set out the napkins and forks.

Knowing the inner door was as secure as it could be, my prisoners sleeping and the cell key in my pocket, I gave the office a final survey. All tidy—the way I liked it. I turned to leave, but the moment I pulled open the outer door, in tumbled the three town council members. Big Ian MacKinney, Slim Higginbotham and Harvey Weinberg.

"Got a minute, Maud?" Slim's stomach ballooned over his waistband, straining his suspenders until I feared they'd break.

I pointed over their shoulders and out the door. "Need to get home to fix breakfast, but I've got a couple." Their faces were drawn and immediately I feared the worst. Was somebody dead? I eyed each man. "What's wrong?"

Hemming and hawing, the men shuffled their feet and looked everywhere but at me. I couldn't stand the suspense. "Something happen to Pa? Or Pokey?"

All three shook their heads, but it was Harvey, his long hooked nose dwarfing his dark, pinched eyes, who stepped closer to me. "We've been talking and . . ." He paused until the other two shot him urging looks. "Well, we think now with you having *real* prisoners locked up . . . it's time for a man to step in as sheriff."

Slim Higginbotham stuck out his sizeable chest. "And I've agreed to fill the job, until election time."

"So, if ye'll jest turn over yer badge," Ian MacKinney said, red hair sticking out from under his modern bowler, "ye can rest easy in yer own hoos, tonight. No more havin' ta walk the streets, when it's dark oot."

"Your papa will be happy to have you back, I'm sure," Harvey said.

"Badge." MacKinney looked at me and stuck out his hand, palm up. He wiggled his stubby fat fingers like crazed grubs. "Dinna worry yerself. We'll take over, noo."

I realized my mouth had flopped open only when I had to close it. I took a deep breath and swallowed. "What?" They'd never once insinuated I wasn't doing a good job. In fact, this was the first time they'd even been into my office. "Did my pa put you up to this?"

Harvey cocked his head toward the closed inner door. "Those are coldblooded miscreants you've got locked up. No telling what they'll do."

Slim waddled in closer. "It's a man's job."

I took a longer, deeper breath and stared down each man.

"No." I refused to hold the office only when it was convenient for *them.*

"No?" All three frowned.

"I said 'no.' " And meant it. Nobody was taking my job and badge away. Not now. And especially not the town council, with or without Pa's encouragement. Not when I had to prove to the town I was a capable, levelheaded, worthy sheriff. Being a woman shouldn't matter. I'd been duly sworn in and I'd see this thing through until election.

Right there cemented my idea to seek re-election. I was sheriff and I'd *stay* sheriff. "Gentlemen." I pointed toward the inner door. "You're going to have to do better than a couple worthless troublemakers to scare me off. I can handle them."

Harvey frowned. "Now see here, Maud. We only appointed you—"

"Enough's enough, Maud." Ian MacKinney's thick accent boomed across the room as he stormed closer to me. "We gave it oot an' we'll be havin' it back!"

"You said until election time." I'd also had enough. "Besides, you've all established and agreed there *isn't* anybody more qualified. I'm doing a good job. Haven't had anything I couldn't handle."

Slim Higginbotham lowered his eyes and voice. "We'd feel real bad if you got hurt, is all." He shrugged to the other men. "The town's had its fun."

"Goody for the town." I crossed my arms. "Nobody's getting my badge."

Ian and Harvey turned to each other. "Got an election comin' up ourselves, next year," Ian said.

"And if we fire a popular sheriff, *ech,* we might not get re-elected." Harvey wiped a hint of perspiration trickling from under the curls.

"Nae, canna risk that," MacKinney contemplated. "The dog

is mair important than the collar."

"Howsomever," Slim said, "she *does* give everyone something to talk about. A distraction, as it were." He turned his shining eyes on me. "In a good way, you understand."

I didn't really, but I knew I'd kept my badge. At least for now. Pulling my horns in a bit, I said, "I can handle this job. You trusted me before . . . trust me *now*." I led the threesome to the door. "Thank you for stopping by. Good day, now." There was no way I could stifle a smile as I closed the door on those three blowhards.

Undecided whether to be mad they thought I couldn't do the job, or glad they were concerned about my well-being, I could only shake my head. My shoulders did straighten a bit knowing I'd stood my ground and won.

I double- then triple-checked that the cell door was locked and then the outside door. With Pokey on his mail run, I had no one to stay at the jail. I would've asked one of those windbag councilmen, but they'd made me mad. It would be a cold day in hell before I'd ask one of them to take over my duties, even for an hour. Caught between sheriff duty and daughter duty, I'd rush home, do what needed to be done and rush back to work.

I scurried home, fixed eggs, fried ham and baked biscuits. Pa fed at last, I washed up the dishes, straightened the parlor and took a moment to tuck some loose strands of hair back up into the twisted braid pinned to the top of my head. I looked into the mirror as I tucked. My light brown hair set off my green/blue eyes. Was I really homely like Doyle said? And why did I let such a cruel remark get to me?

So, I wasn't twenty anymore, but the small crease fanning out from my left eye certainly didn't make me an old hag. That mark more than likely came from all the sunny days I'd spent squinting into the yard working in my garden. Or reading the

Good Book in poor light. Or waving good-bye to Eli . . . and now Pokey.

I couldn't talk to Pa about this. He'd agree with the town council and would only continue to nag me to quit until I gave in. No, I'd give him no ammunition to bolster a new attack.

Still on edge and grumbling over the three wise guys' visitation, I hung up my apron, smoothed my calico dress and said good-bye to Pa, relaxing in his favorite chair in the parlor, newspaper in hand. I wanted to slam the beveled-glass door but, instead, merely closed it *firmly* behind me.

As I marched down the street, office in sight, I knew, just *knew,* they'd escaped. Somebody had broken them out and right now they were robbing the bank. I *knew* it. However, when I opened that inner door, a big sigh and smile escaped when I spotted their two surly faces glaring at me.

I untied my bonnet, poured a cup of coffee, then eased down to my chair. Papers on the desk beckoned, but I chose to ignore them. A few minutes of quiet wouldn't hurt anyone.

Within moments, the door opened and in stepped Mayor Seth Critoli. His smile stretched his smooth cheeks, sending his mustache almost up to his ears. Was that my heart pounding a bit harder? Why was he all of a sudden good-looking? Why hadn't I noticed before? It felt as if the more I worked with him, the more desirable he became. And why hadn't I realized that when he first came courting?

And where did Eli figure in with my newfound feelings for Seth?

It didn't matter now, anyway. Seth was seeing Miss Pearl McIntyre, the school marm. Pa was none too happy about it, figuring Seth and I should be an item and a mayor would be a good catch. I figured we'd be hearing wedding bells in the not too distant future—but they weren't going to be mine.

That thought didn't exactly lift my spirits. However, it

159

dawned on me Pearl had left town to visit her sister in Sacramento, now that school was out. She'd be gone at least a month. While I wasn't one to elbow my way into a budding romance, now I did have the opportunity to talk privately to Seth without worrying about Pearl popping in. But this was town business. Official. No guilt here.

I waved my coffee cup toward an empty chair. "Coffee's still hot. Help yourself."

"Good to see you, Maud." The smile relaxed as he sat. "Haven't seen you for a few days."

"Been keeping a close eye on those prisoners," I said. "With Pokey away so much, there's nobody else to guard the jail."

His lips pursed and he shot a glance my way. "Nothing wrong with hanging up your badge, Maud. You've served well, and now—"

"You knew about that?" I jerked forward in my chair. "Their little visit this morning? How come you didn't come by, too? Afraid I'd throw you out, as well?" My frustrations surfaced and most of me didn't want to control them.

"You threw them out?" Seth chuckled, then thought better of it. He smoothed his mustache as if wiping away his lack of respect.

"Yes, I did. And you well know it. They scampered right over to your office and the four of you sat around figuring out another way to take my badge." I rose menacingly from the chair. "The badge you gave me." My fuse was lit and I wagged my finger in the direction of the mayor's nose. "Let me tell you one thing, Mister. I'm doing the job as well as anyone who wears trousers. It'll take more than you and your . . . your *posse* to make me quit."

"I—"

"How'd *you* like it, Mister Mayor? Huh?" I jerked my finger toward the door. "How'd you like it if the town council came for your gavel, asking you to resign? How'd you feel about it?"

He rose from his chair. "I—"

"That's right. You wouldn't like it, one bit. And I don't, either." I turned, stomped the few feet to the door. Grabbing the handle, I faced him. "Don't come gunning for me again, unless you want a real fight on your hands!"

"Wait, Maud." He grabbed for my arm. "Sorry," Seth said. "Didn't give it much thought."

"Thought? *Thought?*" I was spurting now. "Men! You don't ever *do* much thinking!"

"Appears so." Seth glanced out the open door. He sighed. "I wanna show you something."

He must've been truly sorry, judging by his downcast eyes. It took some of the wind out of my sails. "All right. What?"

"I got to thinking, and I feel bad that Pokey's gonna use his own money to be deputy." His face lit up as he fished in his vest pocket. "I had Swede Swensen make this for him. That blacksmith can do anything."

He held up a tin five-pointed star, which looked, not surprisingly, like mine, and handed it to me. Imprinted in small letters was *Deputy, Dry Creek.*

"He's gonna love this," I said, softening. For the first time that day, I smiled. "Does he know you've got this?"

"Nope. Gonna be a surprise. Thought I'd come over to your office this evening when he gets back and pin it on him, like I did for you."

"He'd like that." I returned the badge. "Nice of you to do this."

Seth nodded toward the street. "Want to go get some lemonade?"

"I do, but somebody's gotta stay here and guard the prisoners."

Seth's shoulder's sagged. "They were all right alone earlier this morning when you fixed your Pa's breakfast."

I nodded, knowing I really should stay. Then, I remembered the framed daguerreotype of Pearl McIntyre on Seth's desk. Our eyes met.

"Sure," I said. "Just for a couple of minutes."

CHAPTER THIRTY-TWO:
ABRACADABRA

We sipped our cool beverages in the Shoo Fly Restaurant, Dry Creek's one and only culinary palace, such as it was, and spewed out a greeting to folks stopping to chat with the mayor and sheriff. I chuckled, thinking *two important people.* Uh huh. Real important. Out on a date. I had to keep reminding myself this was an informal business meeting, not shenanigans behind the backs of Eli and the school marm.

Why did I insist on feeling guilty? Pushing negative thoughts aside, I endeavored to relax and enjoy the moment. This didn't happen very often and might never again.

We spent the better part of an hour pulling on our lemonades and swapping stories, some true and some not so much. Losing track of the time, we laughed and enjoyed ourselves. I told him about the latest dime novel I was reading, how the sheriff seemed to walk on water and the outlaws were more dastardly than humanly possible. He waxed about the differences between the serialized stories of magazine articles and the questionable plots of novels.

It was over too soon. Seth dug into his vest pocket, pulled out a pocket watch and frowned.

"Gotta go. Got a meeting with a new lawyer passing through. Mr. Fenniman," Seth said. "You met him?"

"Fenniman." I shook my head. "Can't say as I have. Is he opening an office in town?"

"Don't think so." Seth pushed back his chair. "Think he's a

traveling lawyer. Kinda like a traveling judge."

That made sense. Curiosity piqued, I was dying to know Seth's business. I beat around the topic. "Hope you're not in trouble."

"Nah. Nothing like that." Seth guided me outside and we paused on the boardwalk. He pointed down the street. "See you soon."

"Thank you again for the lemonade and most enlightening conversation."

"My pleasure." Seth touched the rim of his narrow-brimmed hat and was gone. No sideways kiss, no peck on the cheek, no whispered words of a promised clandestine meeting. Not even a handshake. Nothing. I settled for a wave of his hand and a view of his back disappearing into the small crowd.

As I ambled up the boardwalk, I considered my life, thus far. Was this where I wanted to be? Maybe. It felt good being in charge of something important. I knew down the line, in a few months, I'd be up for re-election. Right now I was filling out Larimore's term, and with him being an elected official, that meant I would have to be elected, too, eventually.

Again, I realized I *wanted* to be sheriff. Which meant I needed to start campaigning. I'd have to learn how to drink, and more than likely learn how to play poker. I drew the line at smoking cigars. But I was already good at shaking hands and kissing babies. And . . . now I knew how to shoot. Next time I saw Seth, I'd have to ask him about running a campaign.

Before I knew it, I found myself at the office. When I stepped in, it felt different. I don't know what it was, but something was . . . different. With the office so small, it didn't take long to survey the room. Potbelly stove in one corner, the coffee pot on top. My desk in the opposite corner, wanted posters tacked to the board near the door. Perhaps the feeling was due solely to my newly-found confidence.

The inner door to the cells was still closed. Nothing missing.

My legs mired in quicksand, I made my way across the office to the inner door. I did a lightning-quick mental rundown. I patted my skirt. Keys jingled in my pocket. I stood and stared at the closed door. What would I find on the other side? Hope against hope, two disgruntled bulls would be sitting there, cursing me as usual for keeping them penned up like cattle with no decent fodder.

I drew in and let out a deep breath, turned the doorknob. It swung open. That's when I spotted the pry mark on the jamb just above the lock. I peered into the darkened area.

Two cells. Both empty. The doors stood open, black smudges around each keyhole. A matchstick on the floor.

Icy cold shivers raced up my spine and imploded in my brain. "No!" I said out loud.

"Damn and double damn." Cursing was a sin, but at that moment I didn't care. It was times like this cursing was meant for.

"What the hell?" Had I said that out loud? I knew they didn't have gunpowder and matches when I left, so they must have had an accomplice. That was the only explanation.

Could it have been James Mooney himself? More cold shivers walked down my spine. Was he watching right now? Would he stroll into the office and shoot me, right where I stood?

My gun. My first ever, honest-to-goodness gun. I'd left it in the top drawer, along with Annie Perkins's almost-wedding ring. I jerked open the desk drawer. Both gone. Her beautiful chipped gold band. How could I tell her—assuming she'd ever come back asking for it? But, more importantly, my gun! My expensive, first weapon! How could I be sheriff without a gun? I cursed Smith and Doyle.

I forced myself to turn my attention to the gun rack, where I kept the shotgun. Next to it was the peg where I'd hung Smith and Doyle's gunbelts. Empty. Sheriff's guns and bandits' guns—gone.

I plopped down in a chair and stared through the big window facing the street. People walked past as if they had no cares. Of course they had none, because all the cares were in *here,* with me.

Beyond feeling sorry for myself, I had no idea what to do next. I'd have to wait until Pokey came back. Maybe tomorrow we'd go on the hunt. Or maybe I should go right now. I'd have to tell Pa and he'd be furious his girl had to chase escaped criminals. And he'd want to have a meal before I left.

A couple of minutes reflecting on what to do and I figured it out. Talk to Seth. It was still an hour or more before Pokey was due in, and I'd spend part of the time at the post office, waiting. The other part I could spend talking to Seth. Or buying a new revolver. And shotgun.

I stepped outside, shut the door and turned at Mr. Swensen's voice.

"Maud, wait up." He bounded across the street, navigating around a buggy heading into town.

This wasn't the time to discuss riding or the city paying for the use of the horses. That process took weeks. Before I could say anything, he jumped in.

"Two of my horses're gone. Stolen."

"Stolen?" This was not boding well.

He nodded. "Went off ta dinner; when I come back, two of 'em 're gone."

"They didn't wander off?" I hoped he'd agree, but the anger on his face said otherwise. He didn't bother to answer.

"I'll look into it, Mr. Swensen." I spotted Seth marching toward me as the livery man huffed, fisted his meaty hands a time or two, did an about-face and roared off.

"Just coming to see you," I said, not wanting to spend more

166

time worrying about the horses. I knew who had them.

"Got a problem," we said in unison. I knew mine was much more important, but I let him go first.

"That lawyer I told you about? Argus Fenniman?" Seth pointed up the street. "He's missing."

"Missing?" I said. "You mean like dead missing or not-at-his-desk missing?"

"I hope he's not dead. I waited and waited, but he never showed." His eyes grew wider. "Then I stopped by the hotel." Seth shrugged. "He checked out. No forwarding address."

"There's an epidemic of that around here today." I thumbed over my shoulder. "My prisoners 'checked out,' too. And two of Mr. Swensen's horses."

"What?" Seth about shouted. "They escaped?"

"Keep your voice down; don't need everybody knowing." I glanced left to right, but nobody was within range. "Yeah, while we were out . . . lemonading, the prisoners somehow broke out."

Tears pushed against my eyes. I sniffed and turned away. Did this mean Pokey didn't get his reward money? Didn't get to be deputy? Would I lose my job, after all? Go back to being the homely old-maid daughter, not a levelheaded sheriff?

Resolve swept over me. I was sheriff, doggone it. *Nobody* was going to break out of my jail and take my job away from me. If it killed me, I'd hunt down those escapees, haul them back into town, and see the judge and jury convict them. I'd sit in front of their cells for days, if I had to.

Seth's arm slid around my shoulders and he pulled me tight. Aromas of his mother's famous Gremolata lamb dish swirled around my memory, but, right now, his nearness only served to remind me I was a woman. I didn't want to be a woman. I wanted to be a sheriff.

I pulled out of his embrace and noted the surprised eyes taking me in. In any other moment, I would have been incredibly forward and kissed him, but right now I had bad guys to catch. Romance would have to wait.

"Tell me about this Fenniman," I said. "Think there's a connection?"

"Maybe," Seth said. "Probably . . . probably not." He frowned and stepped back. "I mean this fella's a lawyer."

"You know that for a fact?" In my mind, it all made sense. I saw the immediate connection. "Did you see a license? Or official papers?"

It was Seth's turn to cogitate. His mental math wheels turned slowly. "Sure did. At least they looked official."

"Uh huh." I knew I was on to something. Would it get me elected? "So, he appears shortly after Doyle and Smith get locked up. Odd coincidence, wouldn't you say?"

Seth ran his hand across his face, glanced up and down Main. "You calculate he waited until your office was empty, then swooped in, opened up the door and the three of them waltzed out?" His eyebrows arched. "That what you think?"

It was. And more. It's what I *knew.* Call it women's intuition, or flat paying attention, but I knew. What I didn't know was where they'd gone. Then it hit me. Pokey. More ice water up my spine.

"Darn!" I said, not excusing my language. "Pokey."

"My God. You think they're gonna rob the mail coach? *Again?* Did Pokey tell 'em about his reward?"

Averting my eyes, I shrugged and hoped for the best. "If nothing else," I said, "for revenge."

CHAPTER THIRTY-THREE:
GET THE TAR AND FEATHERS!

Pokey was due in any minute and Fenniman's gang had had several hours' lead time. There was no way we could get to Pokey before they did. No way. Unless we guessed wrong, which I doubted.

Seth and I had discussed rounding up a posse, but getting more than two men together for anything other than a beer had proved difficult for Larimore. Probably same would apply to me, probably harder. So we waited. And hoped.

Stepping into the street in front of my office, I peered up toward the post office. No coach waiting to offload mail and packages. It was still early yet. But not by much.

We marched to the post office, Seth by my side. We made a good team, I realized. He'd backed my every play, even from the moment he tried to pin the badge on me. When this was all over, I'd have to find an appropriate way to thank him. His ma, being full-fledged Italian, fixed mouth-watering veal, ravioli and somehow turned ordinary vegetables into a heavenly meal. My mouth watered thinking on it. Guess I'd have to offer an apple pandowdy. I hoped she'd not mastered that, yet.

Beth Gallaway and Rune Maguire's laughter poured out of the building before I opened the door. They'd become good friends in the month or so we'd been in business together, and told great stories. I enjoyed listening in when we sorted mail. But not this evening.

Beth stepped in from the back room when I opened the door.

169

"Oh, it's you, Maud. Thought you were Pokey."

Seth came in right behind me and closed the door. Neither of us spoke, both looked around like we half-expected Pokey Johnson to jump out from behind a box and yell "Boo!"

"What's wrong, Maud?" Beth said. "You're looking kinda funny."

Seth explained before my brain could form words. "We think Pokey's been held up."

"Aye?" Rune Maguire moved in next to Beth. "How's that bein' possible?" His Irish brogue turned thick.

I took in a deep breath. "Smith and Doyle escaped, this afternoon, and we believe they're after Pokey's reward."

"We hope we're wrong," Seth said.

"I hope ya are, too." Maguire shot a concerned look at Beth.

Half an hour passed. No Pokey. What I wanted was to go looking, but with the waning daylight, there was no way I could follow tracks. Fact was, all hoof prints looked the same to me and there were hundreds in the street. Last night's misty rain didn't make differentiating the tracks any easier.

We'd have to wait until morning to search for Pokey and the escapees. Stepping out of the postal office to check on Pokey's arrival for the umpteenth time, I reined in Ben Dooley, one of the town's overly active boys, who thundered by. I elevated his deportment further with the tidy fortune of two pennies for his sending word up to Pa supper would be late tonight and so would I. No explanation as to why, simply . . . late. He'd have to rummage around in the cupboard or he could go hungry. I was in no mood or position to rush home and fix a meal.

The best use of my waiting time could be spent over at the mercantile purchasing a new gun. I hated the idea of not having my trusty Navy on my hip, so I had to have another. I reached the store shortly before Harvey Weinberg closed.

I looked around the premises. One other customer stood at the counter, a sack of flour under one arm. He tipped his hat to me and left with a second glance over his shoulder. I shut the door behind him.

"Need another gun, Mr. Weinberg." How exactly I would pay for it was anybody's guess. But I needed it *now*.

He turned the *Open* sign around to read *Closed*, then cocked his head at me. "Something wrong with that Colt Navy you bought?"

I shrugged. "Stolen."

"St—?"

"Don't tell anyone, but the mail coach bandits?" I lowered my voice.

Harvey rolled his eyes. I took that as an agreement.

"Broke out. Took my gun."

"Got in Himmel!"

Before he could start an in-depth interrogation, I hurried to the glass counter where he displayed a wide variety of weapons. Several looked like mine, but I wasn't sure.

"That's a helluva thing, Maud," Harvey said. "Excuse my language." He wiped a bead of sweat lining his forehead. "*Oi*, we were afraid something like this would happen."

An icy tingle crawled up my spine. If I told him the escape wasn't my fault, I'd only be making excuses. If I admitted to dereliction of duty, he'd have my badge, for sure. I took the middle ground, and waffled. "What're you getting at, Mr. Weinberg?"

Harvey moved behind the counter, slid a revolver from the case but, before handing it to me, issued a big, long sigh. Too big. Too long. "Think it's time to take your badge. Those mensches MacKinney and Higginbotham will concur, I'm sure."

"Well, I don't!" I wanted to yell at and curse him, but I restrained myself. "Look, we've been over this. I'm doing the job, and doing it well. Those two could've broken out of anybody's jail. Even with a *man* guarding them."

"A man—"

"*I* will get them back, Mr. Weinberg." I pointed to the gun. "Now, *please,* let me see this one. I don't have much time."

He scrubbed at the sweat, eyed me and then the gun. *"Oy, vey,"* he sighed. Another long pause. "This 'ns like yours. Colt Navy. Came in yesterday. Bought it off a fella—"

"It works?" I asked. Right now I didn't need the pedigree. Maybe some other time.

"Sure does," he said and extracted it from the display. "Same price as the last one." He turned questioning eyes on me. "At least ya still got ammunition?"

New *loaded* gun tucked into my waistband, I trotted back over to the postal office, where I was determined to get Seth and the two of us start searching for Pokey. Darkness be damned. Was cursing part of the job, too?

"Give it a couple more minutes," Seth said. "He'll be here soon, I'm sure."

"Besides, it's dark," Beth said.

"Pokey be our friend, too," Rune said. "But no need to be ridin' out after them tories this time o' night, Maud. Don't make us a'frettin' about you, too." Rune Maguire handed me a stack of mail. "Sort this. Time . . . passes better when busy."

Their arguments didn't convince me but, truthfully, I hesitated to start out in the dark, alone. Plus, I hadn't ranged this gun yet and wasn't sure of its accuracy. I let them talk me into staying a while longer. Our pathetic attempts at keeping our minds off the problem failed. Every horse that passed, every odd sound brought us to the door. No Pokey.

"I can't stand this anymore," I said. "It's been almost an hour. I'm gonna go look for Pokey. It's—"

I was going to say . . . *all my fault* . . . but the clatter of many hooves stopped me.

Could it be? I was first out the door, followed on my heels by the others. Sure enough. Our mail coach slid to a stop in front of the building.

Up on the seat, reins in one hand, sat Pokey—slumped over, gripping his side. He wobbled like a child's wooden toy, while tying the leather reins around the brake. Seth sprang up to the seat.

"Pokey, you're hurt." Seth gripped Pokey's arm. Rune scrambled up from the other side.

"I'm all right," Pokey said.

But he didn't look all right. Yellow light from the kerosene lantern I held danced on Pokey's bruised, bloodied face. Seth and Rune eased Pokey down to the ground where his whole body shook.

"Let's get you inside." Elizabeth held the door wide. "I'll send someone to fetch Doc Monroe."

Pokey's hesitant steps, his pinched face, his labored breathing knotted my stomach. We set him on Rune's chair and gathered around. A quick look at his face—red and purple knots on his cheeks, a split lip, a cut above his right eye—made me angry. How could anybody do this?

Pokey gripped his right shoulder. "I been shot." He turned his sad eyes on me. "And they took my reward money. Smith and Doyle took it. Now I can't be a deputy."

I figured he'd cry if it had been only us. But more townsfolk who'd come for their mail were waiting for Pokey, and had elbowed their way in and crowded around. I stood and turned to them.

"Pokey's going to be fine." I hoped my lack of confidence wasn't obvious. "He got held up, but we'll be on their trail at first light."

173

A man in back spoke over the murmurs. "Smith and Doyle? Ain't they locked up, Maud?"

Murmurs erupted into full-blown questions. I had to be honest with the good citizens. I held up a hand. "They . . . were. Busted out late this afternoon." An eruption of concern ensued.

"How could you let that happen?"

"Told you she weren't no good as sheriff!"

"Hide the women and children!"

More questions and accusations flew around my ears. I figured panic was right around the corner. "Obviously, they've high-tailed it out of here," I said. "Don't worry."

Seth held up a hand. "You're all safe. Please go on home."

People mumbled and even threatened first, to take my badge for allowing dangerous men to escape, and, second, mayhem to whomever did this to Pokey. They trailed outside, leaving the five of us alone.

I vowed to find that elusive posse and leave at first light.

One problem. Where to find one?

CHAPTER THIRTY-FOUR:
A POSSE . . . THE MAKING OF

A posse. How exactly was I supposed to get one? That was the big question. Too bad there was no "sheriffing book" with a chapter on posse roundups. I puzzled. Let's see . . . I'd need at least ten men, maybe more. I glanced up and down the darkened street, deserted this time of night. Could I go door to door, knocking to see if the man of the house would join me? Noble knights for a noble quest? More than likely, well-intentioned men, thinking I'd come to rob them in the dark, would shoot me.

So, where did men hang out en masse, in the middle of the night? Seth stood at my side, scratching his chin, gazing up the street toward the Tin Pan Saloon. Ah! The mother lode. No doubt a ready group, eager to chase the bad guys. And how could they refuse their civic duty?

"I'm going to the saloon," I said to Seth. "Wanna come?"

He slapped me on the back. "Always knew you were my kinda woman!"

"To get up a posse." I tossed him an over-the-shoulder frown, as I took off down the boardwalk.

The ubiquitous smoke, laughter and wince-inducing piano music wafted into the street, the various noises and odors forming their own nebulous cloud. Without much thought and no hesitation, I threw open the batwing doors and strode in. A few heads turned, but nobody challenged my right to enter. Fine with me. I was in no mood for a fight. I needed a posse.

At the bar, Seth ordered two beers. I assumed one was for me, although I wouldn't have been surprised if he drank them both. The Tin Pan was full, but not crowded. A few of the men slurred their hooting and hollering, making them well past posse material. I recognized town councilor Slim Higginbotham at one table, cards in his hands, and a man who worked with Pa in the bank. Two or three others from church. The rest were faces.

Now was my opportunity to speak. How to get their attention? I certainly wasn't going to wave a little white bar rag. No, I pushed that embarrassing memory to one side, choosing instead to stand on my tiptoes and holler.

"Men! Men? I need your attention!"

Nobody acknowledged my presence. Seth sipped.

Frustrated, I pulled out my gun. Seth stood upright. "You gonna shoot 'em?"

Banging it against the wooden bar at least sounded like a judge's gavel. Conversations ebbed, then sputtered into silence.

"Thank you," I said. "I need a few good men—"

"Hell, Maud, we're *all* good men!"

Catcalls and whistles split the silence. Thunderous laughter swirled over rude suggestions.

"I'm man enough for ya!"

Holding up my hand signaling for quiet, I was grateful it shielded my face, undoubtedly blossoming into a lovely shade of crimson. "For a posse. Those two hooligans escaped—"

"Escape with me, darlin'," one man offered, his bowler canted sideways. He held up a hand and staggered upright.

"I saw her first!" Another man jumped to his feet, his hands fisted like a besotted prizefighter.

Seth stepped up next to me. "Listen to what the lady has to say, would ya?" To my surprise, both drunks sat immediately, like children who'd been scolded.

"We've gotta ride at first light. Prisoners escaped! From your town! Ride with me and get 'em back!" I hoped my enthusiasm for this quest showed. "I may be your sheriff, but you're the citizens. Together, we can bring these men to justice."

Heads turned, swiveled, the inebriated mob eyed one another.

"Not riding with no female sheriff," someone hollered. "No telling where we'll likely end up."

"Hell . . . all she'll do is talk! Yak, yak, yak!"

"No wonder them ol' boys escaped. She probably near melted their ears right off!"

"Women shouldn't be doin' men's work." That voice came out of the corner.

"Yeah. Why don't you go bake a pie?" Cheers went up.

A frowning Seth gave the entire room his famous "hairy eyeball" glare. Long and probing. Pretty much everyone ignored him, the voices remaining boisterous, coins continuing to clink.

Seth whipped around to me. "Gimme your gun."

"What?"

"Your gun." He held out his hand, expecting me to hand it to him.

Which I did. "Don't really shoot 'em."

He aimed at the floor.

Bang! Sawdust flew up, scattering woodchips like plucked chicken feathers.

The piano melody slowed, card hands folded, beer mugs clanked to the tables. Low curses and mutterings echoed off the walls. All eyes turned to Seth and me.

Now I had their attention. "We need about ten of you to ride with us," I said. "How many of you can bring your own horse?"

Silence.

"How many can provide your own gun?"

Blank stares.

A couple of heads pivoted, looking around the room, but that was the only movement.

"How about if the town loans you a horse?" I was desperate now. Sure didn't want to track those men alone. "And a gun."

Seth leaned in close. "Maybe offer to pay them."

Before I could consider such a ridiculous idea, Slim Higginbotham scooted his chair back enough so the legs screeched across the wooden floor, pushing sawdust into tiny mounds. "They dangerous, Maud?"

"Yes, I do believe they are."

" 'Specially if you're a sack of cash," another man said.

Chuckles and guffaws again raced through the crowd. As much as I wanted to smile, too, it wasn't my job to laugh at a time like this. If I was going to be a leader, then they'd need to see I was serious.

"Some of you saw what they did to Pokey, today," I said. "And last week, the first time they held up the mail coach, they made it clear they weren't afraid of me."

"Hell, Maud, none of us are." A fella I knew from church hoisted a glass.

More chuckles and guffaws.

I couldn't decide if that was a good thing or not, but I sure knew it was true. At least none of them had threatened to take away my badge—again—yet.

Slim grunted to his feet. "Pokey's a friend of mine. Not only that, but as a duly-elected and sworn-in official of this town," his gaze trailed over his fellow bar patrons, "*I'll* step up to be in your posse."

Was that a sigh of relief welling up from my chest or the sound of my eyes rolling skyward? Politicians. I fought for composure. What I wanted was to grab each man at the lapels and shake him until he agreed to join up. What I managed, however, was a raised eyebrow at Slim.

"Thank you, Councilor," I said. "Anyone else?"

The silence was not inspiring.

At least I'd have company.

Sunrise next morning at the office, I was surprised to see ten less-than-enthusiastic individuals, a bit hung-over, standing out front, outfitted horses tied to the hitching rails. Mayor Seth Critoli waited at the door, chatting with councilman Higginbotham, both with coffee mugs in hand.

As I stepped up onto the boardwalk, I caught Slim's eye. He gave me a knowing tight grin as he hooked a thumb into his suspenders and puffed out his draft-horse chest, if that was possible. I guessed he'd "furthered the discussion" in the bar last night, after I'd left. I realized owning a saloon had its advantages—a good way to raise a posse. Promise free drinks afterwards or threaten to withhold drinks. Either way worked.

And . . . May Belle was already saddled and waiting for me. I turned to the men in the street. Faces I recognized. Most I knew their names. Men who had something at stake or something to prove. I took a deep breath, squared my shoulders and produced what I hoped was a smile.

"Thank you for being willing to serve on a posse. We're looking for two, three men. Wink Smith, Juan Doyle and possibly Argus Fenniman—if that's even his real name. Couldn't find any wanted posters on him, so I'm not sure. But he's the fella who came bounding into town saying he was a lawyer, and hasn't been seen since about the time Smith and Doyle escaped."

Murmurs of agreement.

"Let's mount up, head west toward Dutch Flats. I know a cabin on the way, where they might be holed up." I gave another long look at the assembly. Good, honorable men, who perhaps thought today would be a lark. Maybe they viewed it as a good excuse to get out of work or, at the very least, away from their wives.

Seth touched my arm. "Be careful. We both know these are really dangerous men you're chasing. Don't do something to get yourself hurt."

"You're not coming?"

He shook his head. "Somebody's gotta watch the store, while you're gone. With Pokey laid up and you chasing fugitives, no telling what sort of riffraff's liable to wander into town." Seth slapped me on the back like he would an old fishing buddy. "I'll keep Dry Creek dry 'til you get back."

Caught by surprise and not particularly pleased with Seth's announcement, I faked a nonchalant shrug. What could I do? "Fair enough."

With Seth's boost, I mounted May Belle without much skittering. She still wasn't thrilled having my skirt drape over her, but she seemed to remember when she and I first met, and calmed in a moment or two.

Seth stood by my side, squinting into the rising sun. "I borrowed a shotgun for you. It's tucked into your bedroll, behind your saddle here. Sorry it's not the quality of the Belgian they took." He pointed behind me to the bundle of wool, which very well might be my bed for the next few days. Protruding was a weathered stock, split and held together with several wraps of rawhide string. "There's beans, biscuits and bacon in your saddle bags, and I filled your canteen." It hung in front of my right knee.

I leaned over and touched him lightly on the shoulder. "You've thought of everything." Truth was, I hadn't given much thought to provisions or bedrolls. But I did have my newest Colt Navy tucked in my skirt waistband. My gun on my person at all times was a lesson learned.

The hard way.

I hadn't really slept last night, but my thoughts hadn't been on food. They'd been on Pokey and his assailants and not having a posse and what to do about Pa and . . .

I sat up straight, pulled Pa's hat I'd borrowed as low as I could and thanked Seth for taking care of me. "Be back soon's we can." I tapped May Belle with my boot heels.

As she sprinted from the nudge, I pulled on the reins until she clip-clopped at a reasonable speed through town. A fast walk was fine with me. I turned and waved at Seth, who waved back. Still turned, my eyes trailed over my posse, now following me. Which meant . . . I was the leader! I suppressed a smile.

I faced forward and set my sights on the task at hand. As we reached the edge of town, I spotted Pa standing in front of the postal office.

Pulling up, I braced myself for a lecture. Most times, he'd given me the silent treatment. But being the dutiful daughter I was, I'd left enough fixings for meals for a few days. He wouldn't starve.

He walked up and patted my skirt-covered leg. "Take care now, Maud." Pa's eyes misted. "Come back in one piece."

As much as I wanted to lean over and hug him right then, I couldn't bend down that far without falling off the horse. I would *never* live that down, so we settled for an awkward sort of handshake. Was he starting to understand me?

"I'll be back before your supper gets cold," I said. Pa stood back and I put my heels to May Belle. We trotted off, the posse still dutifully behind, me bouncing hard and gripping the saddle horn to stay aboard.

This would be a long day.

Chapter Thirty-Five:
The Chase

Tracks in the dusty road allowed us to gallop along like we really knew where we were going. Though a few extra-hard bounces took my breath, I felt so official I wanted to sing. Probably not a suitable sheriff-like thing to do, so, I stayed quiet. This was serious business and I was leading ten men who might end up being shot or killed. The thought sobered me.

There was little talk among the company as we rode. Perhaps they also realized this was no lark. Intent on our targets, we rode heads straight ahead, glancing left and right only on occasion, sitting up straight in the saddle.

The first five miles sailed by. For most of those miles, I'd watched May Belle's ears, like Swede Swensen and Seth had told me. Positioning of the horse's ears meant certain feelings— the horse was bored, scared, excited, attentive. Mostly, her ears perked forward like she was listening for the jingle of a distant feedbag. Only once did they flap sideways as a bird skittered from a bush and took flight. Satisfied there was no threat, her ears returned forward.

I was thinking we'd missed the cabin when the first high hill came into view. It sat on the other side. I held up my hand and everyone stopped behind me.

"Up a ways," I pointed due west, "is the cabin I told you about. There's a good chance it's their hideout. We don't want to ride in and give them a turkey shoot."

Mumbles of consensus rumbled through the group.

"So I'm gonna take a look-see. If they're in there, I'll come back and we can strategize." That sounded official to me and I hoped they would agree. How could I be a leader, if no one followed? Head nods assured me they were happy to stay put and in the saddle.

With a fist knotted in my stomach, I gigged May Belle off of the road and tied her close to a hundred yards back in the trees and scrub, well out of sight of both cabin and posse.

Dismounting after a long ride proved much harder than I'd anticipated. While it wasn't so much the getting off my horse that was hard, it was the standing on non-moving ground, which proved next to impossible. How could my legs shake so hard? I gripped the saddle horn, hoping, praying my knees would keep me upright. My ribs were tender but I didn't need them so much as I needed my legs right now.

I stretched and did a couple of quick knee bends, while holding onto the bottom of the saddle, ironically called the "skirt," according to Seth. I could walk . . . sort of. I wobbled over to a tree, affording a good view of the front door. With my newly-purchased gunbelt cinched around my waist, revolver loaded, I clutched my rusty shotgun. I was ready. At least, I tried to convince myself so.

Using bushes, scrub and a few saplings as cover, I zigzagged my way to the front of the house. A deep breath, I pressed my ear against the wall. Silence from inside.

I hollered. "You in there! In the cabin!"

No response.

I hollered again. "Sheriff! Come out with your hands up!"

Still nothing.

"Maud?" Slim hollered from behind the cabin.

I jumped, fumbling my gun. Why hadn't he stayed back there? Before I could answer, he edged around the corner of the cabin and stopped at my shoulder. "You're supposed to stay with the group," I whispered, loudly.

"Sorry." He lowered his voice to the same volume as mine. "No horses around. Looks empty."

He was probably right. I shoved the door hard and it flew open. No shouting from inside, no scrambling of boots, no nothing. A quick survey and, indeed, the cabin stood quite empty.

Slim and I shuffled back to the posse. "Not here."

A groan of general dissatisfaction rumbled through the fellas. I knew it'd been too easy. We'd have to go on. A good look at the sky revealed clear blue in the still-early morning. "The tracks appear to be holding up, especially if it doesn't rain."

One of the men studied the road. "Looks like they're still heading west." He sat up and straightened his shoulders. "They oughta be gettin' tired about now. For sure their mounts are."

"We'll catch 'em, soon enough," Slim grunted as he climbed up into his saddle.

"Guaranteed," I said, struggling. My shaky legs threatened to rebel, but I refused to give them the chance. I had escaped prisoners and holdup men to catch.

We rode hard all morning. Several miles from the cabin we came to a fork in the road. The hoof prints we'd been following, some obviously from maybe six or seven horses, continued on toward Dutch Flats. But two sets took a narrowing path. Had to be our fugitives. We turned north and stayed on it through trees and around hills. We rode nose to tail. The tracks, now fading into hard-packed dirt, wound down into a small meadow. A stream meandered through it, tall grass and wildflowers flanking both sides, spreading to the base of pine trees. The tableau demanded a picnic.

Something told me to stop. Riding into a clearing, no matter how idyllic, ringed with bushy trees, didn't seem a good idea.

"Wait here, fellas," I said, holding up one hand. "Anybody see prints?" All I saw was drying mud.

Shrugs and mumbles.

"I'll ride on and see if I can spot anything. Stay here and keep quiet." I looked at Slim. He looked sternly at the men. I gathered as much bravado as possible and gently tapped May Belle's sides.

Hugging the tree line, I picked my way through the pines, one eye on the stream, the other for anything that moved.

And then I spotted it. Movement. By the stream. I squinted. One saddled horse. One? Probably a stolen one. Its body slumped and head hung like it was either sleeping or standing up dead. A tail brushed at flies. It held up its right foreleg. White patches on its rump confused me. Hair?

Slim trotted up behind me and whispered. "Been rode hard. Salt from the sweat's dried on his back." He wagged his head. "Looks like he's 'bout run to death." He cocked his head toward the animal. "And he's come up lame."

It was then I noticed the reins dragging in the dirt. Not even tree tied. This poor animal wasn't going anywhere and Doyle and Smith knew it.

But where exactly were Smith and Doyle? And the money? As much as I wanted to capture my fugitives, I wanted Pokey's money more. I dismounted and squatted near a tree, using low branches as much for stability as for cover.

"Got more tracks over here, Sheriff." One of the posse men pointed toward the flats. "Just one horse."

Slim rode close to me. "Means they're riding double." He glanced skyward. "They've been riding, what, twenty hours now? Lame horse. Good horse is exhausted. Really slowed them down."

Good news for us. I had it figured out. "They're slow or maybe, by now, on foot." My shoulders naturally pulled themselves back. "We'll catch 'em soon." I groaned into my saddle and then gigged May Belle. "Let's go."

And just like that, we were on their trail again. One of the men, who said he knew how to follow tracks, took the lead. They were pretty easy to spot, but I didn't mind having somebody else out front for a change.

We rode following those hoof prints until my stomach grumbled, my back ached and my legs numbed. Soon, we'd have to fill our bellies and let the horses rest. A get down sounded like a terrific idea. I opened my mouth to order a rest, when the fellow in the lead held up a hand, pulling his horse to a stop.

He turned in his saddle. "There's a horse up ahead. Been rode to death."

All kinds of bad words entered my head, but fortunately I was lady enough not to say them out loud. So that meant Smith and Doyle were on foot. More good news for us. Bad for the horse.

I climbed out of my saddle and studied that poor creature sprawled on the ground. White lather covered its side, and its gray-black tongue lolled out of its mouth. Eyes stared wide and innocent. When I got my hands on those two men, I'd like to run them to death. See how they liked it.

Slim touched my shoulder. "Boot prints go off this way." He pointed southwest.

Before I could remount, which I wasn't looking forward to, another posse member rode back to me. "They're down by that creek, yonder," he whispered. "I don't think they seen us."

"What are they doing? Sleeping?" I hoped they were.

He shook his head. "Taking a drink."

Good enough. I turned to everyone. "What's say we round up these miscreants and head on home?"

I quickly calculated I'd have to get on the horse, off and then back on, and it was easier to tie my horse here and walk down to the creek. I wrapped the reins around a nearby tree branch and headed off.

With my gun in hand, and knowing ten men were behind me, I crept through the bushes as quietly as humanly possible. Apparently, I'd had a good idea to leave my horse behind because everyone else did, too. I spotted the two escapees, kneeling by the creek, slurping away. Any second now they'd get up and start off again, so we'd have to grab them now.

I nodded to Slim next to me. Breath sucked in, I hollered with the biggest sheriffing voice I could muster. "Hold it right there. You're surrounded!" Maybe not surrounded, exactly, but close to it. As if on cue, the rest of my posse stepped into sight, guns drawn. Smith spun around, his gun out of its holster so fast I swear it grew in his hand. Doyle turned, growling something in Spanish.

"Hands in the air!" Hopefully, I sounded as confident as I felt. "Slim, take their guns!" It was fun ordering around a town councilman. I took careful steps toward the escaped prisoners. If they ran, I wasn't sure I could actually shoot them. Surprisingly, they both held their arms over their heads.

Wishing I had the real handcuffs I'd forgotten instead of the rawhide strings on my saddle, I'd make do with what I had. As if reading my thoughts, one of the posse produced two strands of latigo and stepped behind Smith.

Maybe I moved in too closely, maybe Smith stepped toward me. Whichever the case, Smith brought his hands down, like he was willing to have them tied behind him. Instead of complying, he grabbed my gun and spun me around. I gripped his hand, kicking his shin.

"Gimme my gun!" I shouted at Smith's red face. I called upon every muscle available to retrieve my weapon. Like two off-kilter ballerinas, we danced toward that stream.

Using maneuvers I'd never seen before, he threw his arms around me, spinning me around, pointing my own gun to my head.

"Stop or she dies!" Smith hollered.

Not again. No way would I be taken hostage, *again*. Like a horse, I kicked back, this time connecting with his kneecap. Smith loosened his grip and I spun in his embrace. Both of us now teetering on one foot then the other, we pirouetted past the exhausted men. Then, like a constricting snake, my skirt wrapped itself around my ankles and encompassed his legs. Tangled beyond hope, we twisted into the stream.

No way to brace the fall, I plunged face first into the water, little rocks and a small boulder scraping my chin and cheekbone. The water—like ice. Tumbling over and over, dashing arms and body against rocks, I gulped a mouthful of cold. Twice. I sputtered, gasping for air.

Hands grabbed at me. Hands grabbed at Smith. Words flew around my head. Words I didn't comprehend. I had to get my gun, get my prisoner and keep my life. I fought the hands like a crazy woman until Slim's voice battered through.

"We got 'im, Maud, we got 'im! Just calm down!"

I calmed. Lying in the stream, I focused on Slim and his outstretched hand. He nodded. "Got 'em. Both of 'em."

Sitting up, water washed over my lap. Smith lay prone on the bank, two men pushing down his shoulders, another with his knees in Smith's back and a gun to his head. Farther behind them stood Doyle, that smarmy smirk erased from his face, men gripping his arms.

I took Slim's hand and staggered to my feet. Water dripped into my eyes while I slicked back my hair. The weight of my waterlogged skirt yanked at the waistband and I was sure it would slip off any moment. I wrung it out, revealing an unavoidable amount of ankle, and stepped onto the bank, alternating a glare at Smith and a smile for my posse.

While I shook from cold, fear and a let down of muscles, my men tied Smith's hands behind him. A cup of hot coffee would help about now. Since there was none, I chose to get on with the task at hand: get myself and the rest back to town by dark.

Using a small towel someone had pulled out of a saddlebag, I patted my scraped cheek. I blinked into reality and moved in closer to my prisoners.

"The money you took." I held out a skinned but dry hand. "Hand it over."

"Ain't talkin' to no damn *she*-riff," Smith said. He spat at my feet.

Slim, pushing a gun into Smith's ribs, leaned in close. "You show proper respect when you're talking to a lady and the law." He cocked the revolver. "Understand?"

"Let's try it again," I said. "Where's the money?"

"What money?"

Slim raised his heavy Navy Colt above Smith's head. "I swear I'll beat you 'til you don't recognize your own boots."

Smith shot a look at Doyle. "He took it."

I turned my attention to Doyle. "Where?"

Two men held up saddlebags. "Gotta be in here, Sheriff."

Despite Doyle's protest, they searched the saddlebags. Nothing but an old pair of socks, a can of potted meat and a skinning knife. I was tired of their subterfuge. My legs were shaking and I was cold. Honestly, all of me was shaking. My temper turned short. "I'm gonna shoot you myself, Doyle. Where's the money?"

Doyle let out a long breath, a mumbled curse spitting his words at me. "How *stupid* you gotta be to be sheriff? *¡Basta!* We already tol' you. *He took it.*"

That was it. I moved within inches of Doyle, but experienced

189

a whiff of his putrid breath and thought better of it. Edging over to Smith, I brought my gun up chest high. Patience gone, I tried loud and succinct. "I swear I'm gonna use this. Who is *he*?"

Slim stood at my shoulder. He looked nervous, as though I might actually shoot this man.

Wink Smith spoke through gritted teeth. "Our pard."

"Partner?"

Smith and Doyle shrugged.

Of course, a third man was involved. Had to be the one who broke them out. As it was, we'd seen only two sets of tracks. I frowned. "So where's this supposed partner?"

"Ain't here," Smith said, his nose tilting skyward.

Doyle let out a long hissing cackle. "Idiots! You're all blind, as well as stupid. By now, he's got it tucked outta sight and he's high-tailin' it."

I was tired. And hungry. And fed up with these games. With Smith's hands trussed, I moved closer, desperate not to breathe in. "Who's your partner and where is he?"

Silence.

Undoubtedly feeling like he still had the upper hand, Smith chuckled. "Thought he'd pull one over on you. Had a grand plan, he did. Ride into Dry Creek, give the place a once-over, then figure out how to bust us out of your piss-poor excuse for a jailhouse."

I frowned at Slim. A sinking knot in my stomach alerted me. Now I knew who "he" was.

Wink Smith wagged his head. "Sprung us out when you was off cuddlin' with the mayor."

Slim blinked at me, opened his mouth, but apparently thought better of requesting details. I chose to ignore the "cuddling" comment while my cheeks warmed. Now that the posse had heard it, I knew they would spread enough gossip to fill the entire county. But I let it simmer, for now.

Doyle's upper lip raised his thin moustache into his turned-up nose. "And takin' money from your driver was easier'n takin' candy from a *niño.*"

The pieces fit together, but I wanted to make sure. "You mean to tell me the lawyer, Argus Fenniman, is your partner?" I eased back and also eased down the gun's hammer.

"Argus Fenniman?" Smith and Doyle let out discordant cackles. "That's what he called hisself?" Smith shoulder bumped Doyle. "Good one, no?"

Doyle glanced at Smith. "Last time, he was Dunsford . . . Benjamin Dunsford."

"Argus," Smith said like he was trying on the name himself.

Doyle shook his head. "*¡Magnifico!* But no, not his real *nombre.*"

I figured on thumbing through wanted posters for days before finding the right one.

"What is it then?"

Smith chuckled. "Jimmy Mooney."

Chapter Thirty-Six:
There's Gold in Them Thar Hills

James Mooney had Pokey's money. And I had to chase him.

The whole trip back, I fretted. Would James Mooney try to waylay us before we made it back to town? Or break these yahoos out later on, once they were again behind bars? Was he watching us right now? How could I have let him wander around town for a day or two? Why hadn't I figured out who he was? Would I have recognized him from the wanted poster? I tried to recall. There was only a poor drawing on his poster.

And where had he gone?

I would have liked to meet this so-called counselor, as I like to know who comes and goes in Dry Creek. But in learning how to shoot, how to arrest people and feeding Pa, I hadn't gotten around to it.

And now, I'd have to pay for my slip-up. It wouldn't be pretty. Especially when the town heard about my supposed "cuddling" with the mayor. Pa would be hurt, Seth would be none too happy and, for sure, Miss Pearl McIntyre would be livid. She rode out of town to visit her kin the day following my not-entirely-successful shotgun lesson with Seth. There was no way to squelch such rumors and I knew the more I protested, the more I'd sound like I was denying it. It was best to keep quiet, but, as soon as I could, I'd let Seth know who had said what.

"He's coming for us, *bruja*. Witch." Juan Doyle's voice broke my thoughts as I rode.

I regarded this man, riding double in back of one of the posse.

Doyle's gut-wrenching breath coupled with a stomach-turning arrogance. "What makes you think so?"

"We're *familia,* Jimmy and me." Doyle's shoulders jiggled as he chuckled. "An' Smith might as well be family, we all been together so long."

A glance at Wink Smith, who spat, then turned a smirk on me. "It'll be right soon, too. He don't like his kin locked up. No, siree." He peered around Slim toward Doyle. "Do he, Juan? 'Member last time?"

"Remember? That ol' sheriff ate lead, did he not? In cold blood. Not a pretty sight, neither. *Sangre . . . muchas* blood. Blood splattered all across that law dog's office." Doyle's bushy eyebrows dipped. "Smelt something awful, too, when the office burnt . . . and him in it!"

I felt the blood drain from my face.

Smith chimed in. "Sure did—"

"That's enough chatter," Slim said. From then on, it was quiet.

It was getting on toward full dark when we rode into Dry Creek. Shadows spread their fingers into every crevice and alley. Small fires set up and down the street lit it up, making the town appear smaller than it was. Most of the houses sat lined in rows behind the main street, and by now supper was on the table. Soon, candles and kerosene lights would be extinguished as the households retired to bed.

But not me. I had bandits to jail and that all-consuming paperwork to finish. I also wanted to check on Pokey, make sure he was mending.

I said thanks and good-bye to the posse, shaking each man's hand. They in turn busied themselves with congratulations for a job well done, with most heading for the Tin Pan. Slim promised them a free round as soon as he returned Mr. Swensen's horses.

It had been done well. Nobody'd gotten hurt and only a few shots fired. A good thing. But, I admitted, it was not what I'd expected. I thought there'd be at least a brief chase, either on foot or horseback, highlighted by a rough-'n-tumble capture. I figured I'd collect at least one banner bruise in the melee I was sure would ensue. But I had nothing but sore muscles to show for my day.

But I did have the two fugitives. And, even better . . . those windbag councilors would have to admit I was a good choice, after all.

We tied off the horses in front of my office and Slim slid Juan Doyle, alias "Slap" Jack McCormick, from the saddle. In case old Juan would kick out and try to escape, one of the other men held a gun on him. I stood by Wink Smith, hand on my gun, waiting until Doyle was inside and locked up before getting Smith out of the saddle. With hands tied behind him, Smith didn't try to break away. Both men seemed to take their recapture in stride.

I locked the two outlaws in the same cells as before, pulled on the iron doors, ensured they were secure, held up the keys, jangling them at the morose prisoners, and closed the inner door behind me. Slim extended his hand.

"Good job, Sheriff." He cleared his throat and looked away. "Guess I was wrong about you."

"Oh?" I hoped I knew where he was going, but let him choose his words in time.

"You were brave. It's rather, uh, unsettling to ride in on outlaws." He brought his eyes down to meet mine. "You're good to ride with."

A compliment. All on their own, my shoulders straightened. "Thank you, Slim. But I was only doing my sheriffin' job," I said, trying to kill a smile of pride. Maybe I'd keep my badge.

The outside door opened and I spun around, my hand flying

for the Colt in my gunbelt. With those two desperados locked up again, not more than fifteen feet away, guess I was a mite nervous. Who knew when James Mooney would show up.

In stepped Mayor Seth Critoli, lines rippling across his forehead. "Heard you were back. So soon?"

Like a front-row schoolboy, Slim jumped in.

"Sheriff Maud herself tracked down those desperados. 'Cause of her, we swooped down on 'em and arrested their sorry behinds." Slim looked at me. "Excuse my language, ma'am."

"That's all right," I said. "Heard it before."

Seth pulled up a chair near my desk, plopped down in it and leaned forward. "I want to hear all about it. Spare me no details."

"I gotta get home to the missus. Might be holdin' supper," Slim said. "Sheriff'll fill you in." He touched the brim of his hat and was gone.

Before relating the day's events, I wrapped a blanket around my shoulders, the warmth settling my nerves. I then told Seth about the "cuddling" comment. He laughed . . . I didn't.

"Aw, Maud," he said. "Gives 'em something to talk about. They'll forget all about it in a day or two."

I wasn't so sure.

Seth settled back in his chair. "Now, serialize me the adventures of Sheriff Maud Overstreet of Dry Creek, California."

CHAPTER THIRTY-SEVEN:
RUMORS

A day or two later, it seemed the only topic of conversation in the entire town was Seth's and my supposed illicit love affair. According to rumors, we'd run off and got hitched. Pearl had left town with a broken heart. But, my favorite: Seth and I had children together, hidden away in a northern California orphanage. Apparently, we were scoundrels. Pa had remained silent, only shooting me questioning glares now and then. Seth laughed it off, but I still wasn't so sure.

And, during those first two days, thanks to having been on my horse for so long, I could barely walk. Or breathe without my ribs complaining. I entertained the notion of not wearing a corset, but then I may as well have worn trousers. Little shallow breaths were all I could manage and my usual stroll down the town's boardwalk turned into an endurance marathon. My legs still quavered and ached in places I didn't know I had.

In the meantime, I'd wired the Sacramento office—again— we had Smith and Doyle—again. They'd wired back they'd let the judge know—again— the outlaws were waiting for a trial. Two more weeks.

Two long, creeping weeks with me jumping at every shadow, waiting on dastardly Mooney to spring his boys. I kicked myself more than once for having not gone over to meet our newest lawyer. Another lesson learned. *Greet each new person arriving in town.*

I also figured Mooney had scoped out the various enterprises, while in town, learning how the town operated. Which meant the bank, the general store and our postal office weren't safe, now. I'd have to keep an extra alert eye on those three sites.

With Pokey hurt, I managed to find a couple volunteers, former posse members, to stay in the office, while I was patrolling. They agreed to stay overnight a time or two. I listed that in the "win" category of my life.

While Pokey's body healed, his feelings did not. Every day, I made it a point to visit him in his room behind Dry Creek Mercantile.

A soft knock on his door, a mumbled response, and I let myself in. Pokey sat in a chair, his back to the window, which looked into the alley. Each day more color appeared on his cheeks, but his mouth stayed turned down. His healing shoulder slumped.

"Never gonna be deputy. Not never." Something caught in his voice. His words turned soft.

"No such thing as never." We'd already had this conversation . . . three times. Word for word. "Once the judge comes and those men are convicted, I'm sure they'll send replacement reward money."

Pokey wagged his head. "Here I was supposed to be like a deputy, and they took it from me." He mumbled, but the words were clear. "How can people trust me, when I can't do something as simple as not get held up?"

That was a good question, and not one I could readily answer. As much as I wanted to cheer him up by telling him Seth had a badge waiting, I held my tongue. It wouldn't do any good showing him something he couldn't have. Maybe the town council and I could raise the money.

Or James Mooney could give it back.

Or maybe I could rope the moon.

Chapter Thirty-Eight:
Never Kiss and Tell

The days flew by, visiting Pokey, chatting with Seth—on official business, of course—and rejoining abuse from Smith and Doyle.

I consulted Seth and other town officials and realized tracking James Mooney would be close to impossible. Neither Smith nor Doyle would tell us where he went, and no one in Dry Creek was much good at following two-week-old hoof prints.

But I knew . . . *knew* . . . Mooney would be back. And soon.

So it was, this sunny June morning, with Mooney in mind and Pa fed, I'd do a bit of spring house cleaning. Things were quiet in town and, although Pokey was still on the mend, he now could at least guard the prisoners for a bit, allowing me the opportunity to tend my neglected house. My postal office partners found someone else, one of the big strapping, teenaged boys, out of school for the summer, to drive the mail coach until Pokey regained his strength. Maybe as soon as next week—about the time the trial would start.

So far this morning, I'd beaten two rugs, hung Pa's long underwear to air out and washed the kitchen curtains, now on the line, drying. Time to weed the meager garden. Meager because I hadn't time to do real planting. Come harvest this fall, I'd have to can everything I had, and buy fresh vegetables from other farmers. I couldn't get to all of my duties— domestic or otherwise.

My favorite sunbonnet tied under my chin and my yard-work skirt on, I set to pulling out dandelions and chickweed from between the corn and squash plants. I'd be needing to harvest the onions and garlic soon, but that chore would have to wait. Weeds begged to be yanked. I obliged, thankful for both the distraction and a recent rain's softening of the soil.

I set to work on my knees, pulling and tugging, lost in the rhythm of the earth, when an ear-splitting *yaw hoo* came barreling up from Main Street. More *yee haws* followed, along with several gun blasts. Not from shotguns—I knew that sound—but from a revolver.

James Mooney? Had to be.

Every nerve in my body prickled. How would I deal with him? I'd planned to make a plan, but hadn't yet. My lack of foresight now was coming back in a hand of spades.

A flurry of blinks, my muscles thawed and I stood. I had a job to do.

Neither taking the time nor having the wherewithal to change clothes, I hollered at Pa I was heading into town and took off. I sprinted the long three blocks in record time.

At the end of the street, in front of the Tin Pan, a fella sat his horse, spinning it in circles.

By all accounts and descriptions I'd read and heard, he was not James Mooney. I let out a long breath.

The man raised his revolver skyward and fired off a couple of rounds.

Bang!

"Gold! I found gold!"

Bang!

Up and down the street, horses shied, tugging at their tethered reins.

"Where?" People shouted. Throngs of men and women rushed him.

"You sure?" More hollered.

"Sure, I'm sure," the man yelled back. "I know what gold

looks like and I found it!" He held his leather poke high overhead. "Whoo hoo!"

Bang!

"Holy Hoppin' Hannah!" A man I recognized from church waved his hat and trotted toward the gold-toting stranger. "Gold you say? Where'd you find it at?" He stood by the horse's side, gazing up at the man, whose wide-brimmed hat sat back on his head, kind of like a halo.

"Think I've gone plumb loco?" The stranger swung a leg over his saddle. "I ain't tellin' nary a soul where I got this."

*Ooohhh*s and *aaahhh*s raced around the gathered crowd.

Both feet on the ground, the stranger tucked his poke under his shirt. He turned his beaming face on the crowd. "But what I *will* tell ya, is . . ."

People wiggled in close.

The stranger pointed to the saloon. "First round's on me. I'm buyin'."

A whoop exploded and men slapped each other on the back, elbowing their way through the batwing doors. Of course, I followed, though the rest of the ladies remained discreetly in the street, clucking among themselves. Not willing to be left out, I wanted to see what it felt like to be in the middle of such a commotion. This was exciting, and I couldn't help but smile at the fella and his enormous good luck. Secretly, I hoped that he'd tell me where he got it, seeing as I was sheriff. I figured if he told anybody, it should be me.

Easily six men deep at the bar, I chose not to push my way to the front. I'd wait my turn. At least nobody was giving me a second look. I think by now they sort of expected me to walk into the bar, have a drink and maybe even play poker. I hadn't mastered cards yet, but with Pokey and Seth's tutorage, my game was improving.

With the out-of-tune piano bawling noise, the working girls' shrieks of laughter, the kerosene and cigar smoke, the men cussing and spitting and spilling beer on the floor, as well as on each other and me, I couldn't make heads or tails of what was going on. Determined to talk to the stranger and retreat as soon as I could, I squeezed between men, one by one, until my stomach hit the bar. At last, I stood where I had aimed for.

"What'll it be?" Sam reached for a beer mug.

The stranger followed Sam's gaze to me. Sun-crinkled eyes danced. He downed his beer in one long gulp, at the same time staring at me over the frothy rim.

"Howdy, honey." He slammed the empty mug onto the bar top and swiped away his sudsy mustache. He started a fresh brew, then held up the mug. "Here's to findin' El Dorado."

*Whoo hoo*s and *yee haw*s sailed around the room. Pushing and shoving toward the bar, the crowd was oblivious they were squeezing me to death. I pushed for room, but gained none.

"Wait. Wait." The stranger held up a refilled mug. "Give the lady some room."

"She ain't no lady," someone yelled.

"Yeah, she's the sheriff."

The stranger smiled ear to ear, revealing his lack of front teeth. "Then here's to you, Lady Sheriff."

Now I had no choice but to share a beer with this fella. And half the town. The first couple of rounds went fast, but when the stranger quit shelling out gold dust and the men had to start buying their own, most professed they had work to get to, wives to see or some other form of pressing business to attend to.

I stayed put, at his elbow, shooing off a succession of saloon gals whose job was to get men to buy drinks and gamble. The fallen angels selling "negotiable affections" were upstairs.

I introduced myself and he tipped his hat. "Name's Grant."

"Pleased to meet you." I knew my manners. "Tell me, if you

don't mind. Where about here did you find this gold?"

Grant lowered his head and glanced around the room. He crooked his finger at me, until my ear was inches from his mouth. "Like what my mama always told me. Never kiss and tell."

He stifled a burp.

I liked this man. Judging by his rough, calloused hands and dirty, broken fingernails, he'd done his share of hardscrabble work. He deserved to keep the location to himself. I was more concerned for his welfare and for the town's. Now that there was gold discovered somewhere around here, outlaws and riffraff would flood into Dry Creek, shooting and hollering, tearing up the peace and quiet.

And that was simply for starters. I knew Dry Creek would never be the same.

"You planning to put that bonanza in the bank, Mr. Grant?" I pointed toward the small leather poke tucked in his waistband. "We don't have an assay office around here."

"Kiss and tell," he said. "Kiss and tell." Grant slid an arm around one of the painted ladies, flashed me another toothless grin, turned and ushered his new distraction to an isolated table in the corner.

Evidently dismissed, I navigated around the celebrants and pushed outside in search of daylight and fresher air.

Chapter Thirty-Nine: The Letter

"There's a fella in town, Pokey. Says he found gold." We stood on the boardwalk in front of the office. "I'm worried."

"It's good for business." Pokey's bruises had turned a sickly green and the purple faded into gray. His arm rested in a sling Doc's assistant had fashioned for him. He was on the mend. "It's about time we get new people in here."

"I'm afraid it's gonna bring the wrong kind."

Pokey produced a smile, one I hadn't seen him use since before the holdup. "You worry too much, Sheriff." He thumped my arm and limped off toward the saloon, where I considered he'd been spending too much time. But, to his credit, he'd always been sober when it was his turn to guard the prisoners.

The jail birds. According to the last telegraph, I'd have to babysit those fellas another four days until Circuit Judge Andrew Richfield rode into Dry Creek, set up court, found Doyle and Smith guilty, then rode out with them. Half a day, I figured. A full day, tops.

I stood on the boardwalk enjoying the warm sun and the slight breeze, which kept most of the flies from landing on me. I thrilled in the feeling I was doing a job. Something that not only earned me pay, but made me feel worthwhile. Like my life meant something.

My philosophical meanderings probably would have continued for some time, except for Clara Emerson's boy, Clyde, hollering at me from the center of the street.

"Sheriff Maud! Sheriff Maud!" He waved a piece of paper. "Got something for you!"

At fourteen years old, Clyde stood taller than me and I was tall compared to other women. As skinny as he was, I hoped some day meat and muscle would attach themselves to his body. And when they did, he'd be one big man. But today, he was still a walking flagpole.

"Sheriff, this here letter come for you. Mr. Maguire over to the postal office asked me to run it over to you, personal." Clyde shuffled his feet. "Even give me a whole nickel just for walkin' it up the street."

I took the proffered envelope, fished into my skirt pocket for change and handed him another nickel, a generous tip by anyone's standards. "Tell Mr. Maguire thanks for this. And thank you, Clyde."

A grin and Clyde spun around, leapfrogged over a barrel, sailed over a mud puddle and sashayed his way down the street. I looked at the return address.

Elijah J. Goodman
General Delivery
Sacramento

Eli? I'd almost forgotten about him. Well, maybe not forgotten, but he'd certainly been shoved to the back of my mind, recently. It all came flooding forward. Elijah. Eli. The man I loved more than anything.

Right when I had pushed him into a dark corner. Right when days had gone by without his image interfering, he stampedes back into my heart. I reread the envelope, quivering.

Read it here or take it back to the office? That was easy. I didn't want anyone to see me break down, if the news was bad. I could cry unseen in the office.

I tore open the envelope as I walked, absently acknowledging people passing me on the street. My heart thudded in my chest and, by the time I opened the office door, it throbbed in my throat. I swallowed hard, hoping to push it back down to its accustomed neighborhood and to clear the cobwebs from my head that had veiled Eli's memory.

At my desk, I sat gripping the letter. It was the first tangible piece of evidence I'd had he still existed. The first in over a year. Trembling fingers pulled the slip of paper from its container. I recognized his scrawled handwriting.

Dearest Maud,

Meet me Thursday, June 6, at our special place. Noon. Can't wait to see you again.

Yours tenderly, Eli

Thursday? That was . . . tomorrow. Uncertainties paraded through my head. Why didn't he come into town? Where had he been? Should I take Pokey? Seth? Pa? And what did he mean by "tenderly"? Where was our special place? That cottonwood down by the river? No, I remembered. The clearing near old Smith's farm.

But, the most important question . . . what would I wear?

CHAPTER FORTY:
ELI'S COMIN'

There was no way I could sleep. More and more "what ifs" marched through my head. And when my head was full, they paraded around the bedroom, until I couldn't hear myself try to sleep. I tossed and turned, getting more and more tangled in my sheets and nightgown.

It didn't take much thought not to tell Pa Eli was near. Last time my beau had come courting, Pa made it clear he didn't approve. Pa's words to him were something like: "No man's good enough for my daughter. And you ain't even a man." Of course, I'd been in tears when Eli told me he would seek his fortune elsewhere. What kind of man would up and leave his woman?

But Eli did leave and I'd received a mere handful of letters from him. He'd been all over California, up and down the coast, through the mountain ranges—the San Gabriels in the south, the Sierra Madres in the east, and even navigated the big city of San Francisco. He'd been to Sutter's Mill, where the first California gold strike was claimed. Half of me envied him traveling so much, but the other half was happy to have a home and the same pillow under my head every night. In my heart, I preferred staying put.

My brain struggled to provide images of Elijah. Dusty blond hair swept his collar. I remembered a little curl at the end of his locks. He hated it, but I'd enjoyed teasing him. At close to six feet tall, he was above average height to most men. And he carried no extra weight, only muscles. I loved running my hands down his arms, tracing those muscle bumps. He would beam that half smile I knew was saved specially for me. His lips, which always curved up a bit on the ends, remained dry and chapped, because he was outside so much. But his face was smooth, except for a thin mustache, his skin soft with a light tan. I thought it sort of glowed. His eyes, brown with green flecks that sparkled, seemed to dance whenever I gazed into them.

A sigh brought me out of my reverie. I peeked out the bedroom window. The sun had barely cleared the eastern horizon. It would still be a full six hours until our clandestine meeting. Those unanswerable questions invaded my head again. Why so secret?

Maybe he wanted to be alone with me. Maybe he had something to discuss that needed privacy. Maybe . . . he was ready to pop . . . "the question."

But was I ready? If he asked me to elope, would I? A lot had changed since he'd left. I was now sheriff and had responsibility . . . a job. And did I want to trade in my badge for a husband? But, first, I should find out what he wanted. I'd have to make a decision—but not right now.

I spent an hour choosing the right outfit—skirt or dress? Dress. The blue calico one with little flowers on a soft blue background. The neckline was modest, not too high so as to choke me, but certainly not too low exposing anything. The waist nipped in. I could move and breathe, but it set off my figure, especially with the corset snugged up a notch.

My hair was another issue. Up or down? Standing in front of the hall mirror, I pinned my brown tresses up in a braided twist. No, too old and sheriff-like. I took it down and waggled my head. Hair bounced in all directions. No, too floozy-like.

I settled on pulling the top part back and clipping it. The rest would hang well below my shoulders. I smiled. This style fit an unmarried woman my age.

I rushed through my household chores, then charged down to the office, where I relieved Pokey.

"You look terrific, Maud." Pokey circled around me like he was inspecting a horse. I swear he sniffed at me.

"What's the occasion? It's not your birthday."

There was no way I'd tell him what was going on in my life. I went on the offensive. "Can't a girl get dressed up, once in awhile?"

He shrugged.

"I felt like it, is all." I cocked my head toward the inner door and the cells. "Thanks for your help last night. Those fellas stay quiet?"

"Sure did. Threatened them with no supper."

I sat at my desk and picked up a stack of mail. "Good idea." Accepting the cup of coffee he poured me, I held it up and saluted him. "Thanks. Go ask Mr. Harsburg to come by before noon, would you? I need somebody to babysit those prisoners while I'm out."

Pokey's eyebrows hit his hairline, while he nodded. "Where you going?"

"Just an appointment to keep." I played coy. "You know, a woman thing." I knew that would keep any more questions at bay.

"He's over at the stable, helping Mr. Swenson. I'll fetch him." Pokey thumbed over his shoulder.

"Thanks," I said. "Then go get some sleep. I know you're feeling all right, but you still need rest."

"That's what the ladies at the Tin Pan say." Pokey grinned, opening the outside door. "See you later, Sheriff Clotheshorse."

He closed the door before the pencil I threw hit it. No matter how hard I concentrated on the mail, my head was filled with Eli. I swept the office, checked on the prisoners, cleaned my gun—again. The hands of the Regulator, tick-tocking on the wall, refused to move.

Seth Critoli opened the door and stuck his head inside. "Got a minute?"

I did. In fact I had exactly sixty of them before I needed to leave to meet Eli. I waved him in. Seth took the seat in front of my desk. His gaze traveled across my face, over my paper-littered desk, down to his hands. He swallowed hard, his Adam's apple bobbing like a hungry chicken pecking at flies.

I couldn't stand the suspense. "What's wrong?" As much as I welcomed a distraction, I didn't want him to take up too much of my time. On second thought, I was glad he was here. In the past two months, he'd become a friend. I wavered on wanting more, but right now Eli had popped back into the picture. I was still a one-man woman. Eli's woman.

". . . not sure if that's what I should do," Seth said.

What had he said? I chided myself for not listening. Oh boy, this would be tough to recoup without asking. I chose a middle-of-the road response. "What're your options?"

"Do nothing. Keep going like we are." Seth twisted his fingers, while staring at his lap.

"We?" He had my full attention, now.

He took his time answering. Without looking at me, he mumbled, "I really like her." He raised his eyes to me. "And I think she likes me, too." Seth turned and stared out the window.

"It's just that . . . she's gone and I miss her. Should I go after her or wait?"

Ah. The "we" was Seth and Miss Pearl McIntyre. I let out a silent sigh, tinged with a shred of jealousy. I liked Seth, too. Why wasn't he mooning over me and not Pearl? I deliberated. I was going to rendezvous with my mysterious boyfriend in less than an hour. Why was I upset Seth liked Pearl? A while back, he'd made it clear they were a couple.

Abruptly, I had no idea what to do. My head and heart galloped in opposite directions. My heart wanted both Eli *and* Seth. But my head told me to be reasonable, to wait. Right then, I didn't want to wait or be reasonable. I wanted—

"Maud?" Seth leaned across the desk and took my hand. "You all right?"

Snapped back to reality, I gave a perfunctory nod.

He released my hand and stood. "I shouldn't have come to you with this. I mean . . . after all . . . we . . . um . . ."

I stood, suddenly feeling sympathy for him. It was awkward. "I'm glad you did. I think you should wait until she comes back from visiting her family before you make any firm plans."

With that darned dazzling smile, Seth wrapped me in a bear hug. "I knew you'd have the answer. Thanks for being so . . . levelheaded." He squeezed, let go and traipsed out the door, all his cares lifted.

Levelheaded, my . . . I bit my lower lip.

I checked the Regulator. Time for Billy Harsberg to show up. Billy was strong, came from a good family and seemed to know right from wrong. He'd watched the jail a time or two before and I trusted him. I wished he'd show up.

Finally, at last, he pushed in, his wide chest straining the shirt buttons.

"Thanks for coming on short notice," I said. "Shouldn't be but an hour or two." I handed him the cells' keys and nodded at the gun he wore. He'd make sure nothing happened.

"Take your time, Sheriff. The boys and me'll be just fine." His baritone words relaxed me.

I closed the door, turning my thoughts from what was behind me to what lay ahead.

No matter the time now, I'd head on down to Eli's and my secret place, the clearing near a towering tree, where we had shared our feelings. Butterflies invaded my belly, as I walked past the outskirts of town, east down a long hill and over a couple of pastures to a forest of Ponderosa pines. An ax-felled clearing made several years ago created a hideaway. By the time I found our place, I knew it was close to noon, judging by the lack of shadows.

I didn't wait long. I'd barely had time to examine our initials Eli had carved on a tree, when I heard a familiar voice.

"Howdy, Maud."

I jumped, spun around and almost plowed into Elijah J. Goodman. A ghost from my past. A darn fine looking ghost, too. His hair, now darker and longer than I'd remembered, still curled in those soft waves. A full beard covered his handsome cheeks and chin. If I didn't know this was Eli, I wouldn't have recognized him. Although an extra crinkle or two had taken up residence near his shining eyes, he was still a fine specimen of man.

As much as I wanted to throw my arms around him and squeeze, a voice in my head urged caution. Furthermore, it had been a while since I'd heard from him. Five years since actually laying eyes on him.

Eli opened his arms. A smile radiated over his entire face.

All my reservations dissolved.

I moved closer and leaned my head against his chest, my arms encircling his narrow waist. He pulled me against his warmth, until I snuggled up into our familiar embrace. Our hearts beat together—again.

After what felt like two seconds, but in reality was probably closer to a minute, Eli held me out at arms' length. His beautiful brown-green eyes scanned me from top to bottom. "You're looking great, Maud." Eli's mouth curved up. "New dress?"

Four years ago it was, but instead of explaining, I sighed a soft yes.

He pulled me back against his warm body and spoke over my

head. "I'd forgotten how beautiful you are. I've missed you."

"I've missed you, too." I craved particulars, but simply basking in the moment was enough.

We found *our* old spot under the tree and sat. He held my hand with that gentle touch I'd become so accustomed to, and forgotten I needed. He hadn't changed.

Eli looked across the meadow toward town. "What's this crazy talk I hear about you being sheriff? How'd that happen?"

"How'd you know?" I'd wanted to tell him the exciting news myself.

"Word like that travels far and wide." Eli squeezed my hand. "So, how'd it happen?"

"They asked me and I said yes."

"But, you're . . . a woman."

"Thanks for noticing."

"I mean . . ." Eli stammered, "arresting people and breaking up fights and maybe even shooting somebody." His eyes locked on mine. "You can't do that."

"Already did."

"You learned to shoot?"

My head bobbed, a poor attempt at trying to keep from grinning too broadly.

"You ever arrest anybody?"

A shrug. I'd skip my first arrest. Crying, spurned women, who assumed they were married, didn't count. "Got two desperados behind bars as we speak." Could I share all of the news with Eli? I plowed ahead. "They escaped once, but my posse and I recaptured them. They're sitting in jail right now, waiting for the circuit judge."

Eli blew a quiet whisper while his sensuous eyebrows pointed down. "You at least got a couple deputies? You know . . . to help out?" His body close to mine exuded concern. "Don't want you hurt in any way."

"Don't need any help." I chose not to tell him about Pokey being an almost-deputy. "I can handle things around here."

"Even when there's a shooting or a fight?" Eli lowered his voice. "You go in a saloon?"

I raised both eyebrows. Like Pa, he'd flat have to understand. "Bank robberies?"

"Nothing I can't handle," I said, patting Eli's hand. His obvious concern for my safety made my insides mushy.

Eli sat quietly for longer than I liked. What was he thinking? Used to be I could tell, but not now. So we sat, enjoying the company. Finally, he squirmed.

"Can't stay long, Maud," he said. "Just passing through."

"Through?" I'd hoped for longer than an hour with him.

"Yeah." Eli's gaze strayed to the distant hills, finally returning to me. "This cattle outfit I work for. We're driving them a few miles outside of town."

"Cattle?" There hadn't been any errant cowboys coming in off the drive, shooting up the town. Besides, Seth hadn't mentioned anything about seeing drovers around town, nothing about a big cattle drive. He always had before. "Where're you bedding them down?"

Eli cocked his head to his right. "Over yonder. A ways away."

That wasn't much of an answer, but one I'd accept. "Why didn't you come on into town? Visit my office? I want to show you the postal office we opened." I felt like a little girl wanting to show off her latest needlework. I was proud of what we'd done the last few months.

Eli hesitated and cleared his throat.

"You remember how your Pa and me . . . the last time we . . . well, I didn't want to get into it again, with him." Eli hugged me. "Didn't want to put you through that one more time."

I had to agree with him there. It had been an ugly scene, one I'd worked hard to bury.

His straightened shoulders told me he was about to leave. The strange thing was, as much as I'd yearned for this day, to be with him, I didn't feel the connection we'd had before. If we could spend more time together, maybe it would return.

Easing up to his feet, he helped me up and took me in his arms again. "I'll be back, Maud. I promise it won't be so long. Promise." A long, deep kiss, and a whispered, "I *will* be back."

But I wasn't so sure.

Chapter Forty-One:
Rain, Rain, Go Away

Lately, it seemed *rain* was all the sky knew how to do. Clouds, wind, rain. One day resembled another. Sunshine grew into a sad memory—like Eli. I still didn't know what to do about him, if anything. We had left it at a "see you later" and, knowing him, I half-expected never to see him again. I was conflicted. Part of me felt like it had died. But another part felt rejuvenated— reborn.

I wandered up Main Street, toward an unusually boisterous crowd of men. Pokey had been right. The gold strike was good for business. Dry Creek was certainly jumping, growing like a watermelon patch during a rainy summer. We'd had to make some changes. We added two more weekly mail runs to Dutch Flats, which gave Pokey added wages. Two new general stores opened and an assay office set up in a canvas tent. In fact, Pa had to work longer hours at the bank, there were so many transactions.

Almost overnight, three more saloons popped up. Two of them brought tents large enough to hold a couple of barrels with a plank across it, and enough room for twenty men to belly up to imbibe. More men and more saloons meant more whiskey. It continued to flow like water. Like the rain.

The distillers took up residence a couple blocks over from Main Street, assembling their contraptions in apple and peach orchards near town. Each orchard owner I visited said they'd allowed the whiskey makers onto their property—for a cut and free samples, of course.

They even made apple whiskey. On occasion, one of the stills would blow up, but within hours two more were up and running. In order to make the liquor more palatable, I was told, the moonshine manufacturers added hot sauce brought up from Mexico, tobacco juice and other unappealing, disgusting ingredients. Even gunpowder. But the gold-seekers didn't seem to mind the bitter taste.

The patrons used colorful names, when referencing their drink of choice: Tarantula Juice, Tonsil Varnish, Sheepdip, Taos Lightning, Gut Warmer, White Mule, Corpse Reviver, Tangleleg and others I couldn't bring myself to repeat. My favorite, though, was Jig Juice. As far as I knew, it hadn't killed anybody. At ten cents a shot and about twenty shots to a bottle, I figured the liquor dealers were raking in a fortune.

It was my job to be sure everyone stayed relatively safe. A lopsided sign at the top of the canvas tent proclaimed *Thompson's Finest!* Probably rotgut, I figured. But this crowd was loud and sounded like they were about to get unruly. I waded into the middle of the men bellied up to a makeshift bar.

"What's going on here, fellas?" I shouted to be heard over the din. Two men turned to look at me, but most ignored my inquiry. I elbowed my way up to the bar, a whipsawed piece of pine thrown across two barrels.

Before I could gain the bartender's attention, a husky man dressed in a faded plaid shirt and grease-smeared corduroy pants hauled off and planted a roundhouse into another man's weather-beaten face. He spun and crashed into me. Cheers, jeers and *yee haw*s erupted all around, encasing me in a balloon of tauntings. My ears rang as I was rocked back and forth, caught in the flurry of excitement.

"Hold it!" I yelled to nobody in particular. And, of course, exactly nobody paid me any attention. I wasn't about to wave a little white rag, like I'd done before, so I pulled out my gun, aimed straight up and pulled the trigger.

Bang!

Quiet quickly ensued as a piece of canvas flapped. All eyes turned to me.

"I said 'hold it'!" Holstering my weapon, I delivered a frown at the man who'd started the ruckus. "Seems to me you might need some jail time. Cool you off a bit."

"No, ma'am," he sputtered. "Sorry. This fella and me's discussin' things. No need for jail." They both shook their heads fervently.

The punching bag's wide blurry eyes and stringy hair hanging to his shoulders, plus the glowing fist mark on his cheek, almost made me laugh. But I used my "mother" voice. "I'll be back in a few minutes. No more fighting." I pointed my finger in his face. "Hear me?"

Both nodded, the rest *hoo-rah*ed, and the place picked up right where it had left off.

I had to re-elbow my exit.

CHAPTER FORTY-TWO: PRISONER OVERLOAD

Three days before Judge Andrew Richfield was due, I needed more cell space. I had to move Doyle and Smith into the same cell. Not something I looked forward to doing. Doyle, breathing on me, held onto the bars when I ordered him into Smith's cell.

"No, *bruja*. I no go in there. Unless *you* come, *tambien*." Doyle's breath stunk worse than usual. "Me and *mi amigo* could use a bit of blanket company."

"Hell, Doyle," Smith whined, "she's all used up. Why not wait 'til we bust outta this fly-infested rat hole and get us some fresh meat, elsewhere."

I cocked my gun, the feel of it in my hand growing warm. "Get along now, Mr. Doyle. Won't be for long."

"Jest waitin' for James Mooney to come spring us out." Doyle slithered into the next cell. "Or've you forgot about him?"

I hadn't. His name was at the front of my brain all day, every day. But I wouldn't let them see me rattled. "Mooney? You mean that two-bit horse thief? Left you two out in the cold to get caught? Took all the stolen money?" The key in the lock clicked loud. "You mean *that* Mooney?"

While their mouths flapped open and closed, searching for something pithy to say, I walked away. Mentally patting myself on the back, I'd won this sparring session.

So, with all the drunks shooting off their guns in the saloons, I'd hauled a bunch of them into my jail, to sleep off their celebrations. I sure didn't want the undertaker to be the most prosperous citizen in town. As it was, we'd already had two men shot and killed before I could intervene. These were men new to town, so we'd had small, lightly attended funerals for each. The names were either first or last, neither had both. I hated the idea of men buried in Dry Creek and their mamas or wives never knowing what happened. That was a problem I promised myself to work on.

When I had time.

I'd again approached the trinity of the mighty town council and asked for a deputy—full time or otherwise. Even one only on Friday and Saturday nights would be a help. I couldn't believe how pint-sized councilman Ian MacKinney responded.

"Ach, lass, we'll hav' tae cogitate on it. Tis an expensive proposition." MacKinney scratched his red-hued beard. "Le' me explain, so tha e'en ye'll understand."

The hair on the back of my neck prickled. Before I could protest, he continued.

"Ye've been doin' an adequate job, keepin' the peace. And besides, yer prisoners h've nae escaped . . . again."

Slim shrugged. "But, Maud, you've been arresting people left and right."

"They were drunk. Disorderly." I jammed my pointed finger toward the closest saloon. "They were liable to shoot somebody."

"We understand." MacKinney leaned forward, his knobby elbows planted on the desk. "But tha means the town of Dry Creek's got tae feed those men, yer 'guests.' "

Harvey Weinberg played with one end of his mustache. "When you keep 'em overnight, gotta give 'em breakfast, at least. At thirty-five cents a man, times two, *ech*, it adds up."

I hadn't tallied the expenses, but obviously Harvey had. "Jail meals for prisoners," I ticked off on my fingers. "Breakfast is a half loaf of bread, half a pound steak, potato, coffee. Then supper is the other half loaf of bread, half pound mutton stew, beans or stewed fruit, potatoes, tea."

"Twice a day?" MacKinney asked.

"Eight-thirty and four," I said. "But maybe if we charge 'em a dollar . . ."

"And," Harvey said, ignoring me, "the longer they're locked up in your little jail, the less time they have to spend money in town. Think about how much whiskey they're not drinking. That's real money."

Slim leaned forward. "And how many whores —" his eyes widened. "Err . . . flour and sugar and picks and shovels they aren't buying. It all adds up."

MacKinney chimed in, leaning back with both thumbs hooked into his imported leather suspenders. "Aye, 'mony a *mickle* maks a *muckle.*' "

Harvey put it succinctly. "Maud, arresting drunks is bad for business." MacKinney picked up a pen from his desk and pointed it at me. "Tell ye wha'." He glanced at his associates. "Ye can ha' a part-time deputy . . . *or* prisoners." His eyebrows raised, as his eyes met mine. "Canna have both."

"More importantly," Councilman Weinberg said, "you flat don't seem to need a deputy."

Slim Higginbotham shrugged. "I've seen what you can do, Maud. You're more than capable. Maybe we should wait 'til there's a real crisis." He elbowed Weinberg on his left. "If that happens, *we'll* be temporary deputies. Kinda like when I rode in that posse."

Harvey Weinberg spoke over his clenched cigar. "Sure would save the taxpayers some dollars." He extracted the stogy from his mouth and waved it at Slim. "That's a whale of an idea—us bein' deputies. We'll get re-elected for that, *tahkeh*—guaranteed."

"Aye, e'en the Sassenachs would think us bonny!" MacKinney tossed out, more to himself.

My shoulders straightened and I stood tall as I pulled in air, blazing eyes boring holes into each of these three self-important braggarts.

"Next time there's a saloon fight or shooting, I'll be sure to deputize one of you fine gentlemen to intervene. That shouldn't take more'n, what? An hour?" Knowing I'd lost this battle, I started for the door. "Assuming I can even find you."

My right eye twitched. I *knew* I heard chuckling as I slammed the door. I forced my thoughts back to the present and fought down the temptation to call them bad names . . . out loud.

But, right now, I had a trial to prepare for. An honest-to-goodness prosecuting lawyer had come to town and agreed to represent the town of Dry Creek. The court always assigned a lawyer like that. Of course it irked me to no end he'd struck a deal with the council for remuneration. He explained I'd have to testify on behalf of the town, and Pokey would give his side of the story, too. Pokey and I sat down and went over what had happened in the first holdup and subsequent escape, and Pokey's robbery and beating. We took notes to clear up any gray areas.

I heard an additional lawyer, paid by the court, was being brought in from Dutch Flats to represent Smith and Doyle. I hoped he'd get here before things got started.

By the time the sun set the day before Judge Richfield's stagecoach was scheduled to arrive, Pokey and I were ready. I'd even washed and pressed my best skirt and blouse. The stage would arrive at nine in the morning, and I hoped to have the trial underway by ten. Should be over by one, I figured; we'd go home for dinner and Smith and Doyle would be on their way to Sacramento and the prison there.

And, maybe, it'd quit raining.

CHAPTER FORTY-THREE:
DELAYED STAGE

It rained all night. It was still raining at nine the next morning. Pokey and I stood under the porch in front of the Dry Creek Overland Stage office and waited. And waited. A few people scampered by, dodging the relentless precipitation and wind, but most stayed indoors. The main street looked more like a creek than Dry Creek itself did. It was certainly wider . . . and deeper. A couple of men threw rough-hewn boards onto the street so crossing from one side to the other was easier. Otherwise, shoes and boots were sure to be lost, bogged down in the mud that lay under the street/river.

The only part of the day that wasn't miserable was the temperature. What normally bordered on hot, cooled to lukewarm. Not bad for June. Pokey and I made small talk, discussing the newest dime novels we were reading, then . . . nothing. Nothing left to say while we waited.

Long about half past ten, Rune Maguire trotted down the boardwalk, waving a piece of paper.

"Maud," Rune said. "Just got word. Stage's delayed due to this bucketing weather. Won't be in 'til tomorrow."

"What?" If it wasn't one thing, it was ten others. Darn this rain, anyway. "Thanks Mr. Maguire." I let out a long breath, taking most of my energy with it. "Thanks for letting us know. Guess I would've stood here waiting . . . 'til it got dark."

"Tha' ya would've. Been foosterin' till the cows come 'ome."

Maguire thumped me on the arm and marched back up the street.

"Guess I'll go on down to the Tin Pan," Pokey said. "My shoulder," he worked it around and kept his eyes downcast like a pathetic puppy. "Still painin' me some."

Instead of stomping my foot and whining about this rotten turn of events, I patted his good arm and tried to sound sympathetic. "I'll let you know if things change." Another long sigh escaped me. "Enjoy yourself."

CHAPTER FORTY-FOUR:
HOME, SWEET HOME

Instead of trudging back to the office, and with Pokey aiming for the saloon, all I could envision was going home for a couple of hours. With all the law-breakers currently behind bars, I'd had to get volunteers, like Mr. Harsburg, to watch the jail while I was out. I enjoyed the freedom knowing responsible eyes were on Smith and Doyle. For extra measure, I'd handcuffed them to the iron bars.

But, at home, there was always something needed doing. I could finish mending Pa's trousers, iron my shirts or wash up the breakfast dishes.

With our town doubled in size, Pa and the rest of the bank officers kept busy. It seemed that everyone wanted to open an account, get a loan or check to see how secure the vault was. He was so busy, often he ate dinner in town, which freed me up from having to rush home before noon to cook.

As I foot-slogged to the house, the wind enticing my umbrella to free itself and fly away, I looked forward to having some time home alone. Instead of anticipating chores, I envisioned myself with my feet up. Or maybe lying on the couch, like Pa before supper. A short nap called. So, it was a surprise when I heard voices coming from the parlor as I opened the door. One was Pa's, the other I didn't recognize. I knew it was a woman's.

Curious as to whom my Pa had visiting, especially a woman, I took off my hat and rain shawl and hung them on the peg in the entryway, leaned the umbrella to drip in a corner, then slipped into the parlor. Pa sat in his favorite chair and across from him, a woman I'd never seen before. A relative? Someone Pa was sweet on, but had failed to mention to me? A business client?

I extended my hand and produced a sheriff-like, yet warm, smile. "Howdy," I said. "I'm Maud. Daughter."

The woman stood. Easily four inches shorter, she outweighed me by twenty pounds. The coiled brown hair perched on top of her head and her brown eyes sparkled as she gave me a long look. I instantly liked her. She appeared to be somewhat younger than me, maybe by ten years.

Pa stood also. "Maud, this here's Mrs. Stevenson. She's new in town. Came by the bank today, said she was looking for a job."

The woman smiled. I wasn't sure where this was going. The bank had plenty of tellers and other people who ran things. They weren't looking to hire, as far as I knew.

Pa's head cocked toward Mrs. Stevenson. "I've hired her to be our housekeeper." He paused, while one side of his mouth inched upward. It could have been a smile, but I wasn't sure. There was a devil inside him at times, and I wondered if this was one of those.

"Housekeeper?" This was the first I knew of his wanting household help. My initial impulse was to be outraged. Hadn't I done a good job cleaning, cooking, sewing, mending? Running the house? Did I need to be replaced?

My second impulse was one of joy. No longer did I have to do the cleaning, cooking, sewing, mending. I could be full-time sheriff.

"I know you're surprised, Maud." Pa stepped in closer to me and put his hand on my shoulder. "I've thought about it and when she came into the bank, I figured it was time you had some help."

Pleasantly taken aback, I kissed his cheek, then turned to Mrs. Stevenson. "You cook?"

One eyebrow raised as she cocked her head. "My pot roast . . . well, my man says it's the best he's ever tasted. And my peach pie. He says if he don't get a second piece, he'd just as soon die."

I looked at Pa, who looked quite satisfied.

Mrs. Stevenson pointed toward the kitchen. "Now, if you'll show me where you keep the pots and pans and then your iron, I can start right away."

Yep. This was gonna be swell.

CHAPTER FORTY-FIVE:
BAUBLES, BANGLES AND BEADS

The drizzling afternoon slogged by. Me in my office doing sheriffing business, Pa in the bank doing banking business, Mrs. Stevenson in my house doing housekeeping business. Maybe the stars were beginning to align in my favor. That would be a nice change, because it seemed lately they'd all been scattered out in the sky somewhere, blinking, causing nothing but chaos and confusion in my life. I was ready for something to work out.

Now that Eli had walked out of my life—again—it was starting to look like Seth was the fella for me. I'd made all sorts of excuses to see him, asking his advice, and even delivering his mail.

I was pathetic.

Like a love-sick schoolgirl, I'd gone to doodling hearts in the dust on my desk. Once even trying out: *Mrs. Seth Critoli.* Or was that *Mrs. Seth Riccardo Critoli? Mrs. S. R. Critoli?* I liked that one the best.

Pathetic, indeed. Mooning over somebody I couldn't have. I sat up straight at my desk and tried to concentrate on my work. A waste of time. Was being unmarried . . . alone . . . my destiny? Did I choose this life? Maybe that was the whole idea. First it was Eli, a "bad boy." I'd known deep down in my heart he wasn't the marrying type. He and I would never settle down and raise a family. And, now, with Seth . . . couldn't have him, either. He already had a girl, a serious one; he was more or less off limits. While he'd be more likely than Eli to put a gold band on my finger, the chance of that ever happening was exactly . . . zero.

And, the closest I'd come to a gold band had been taken from my desk drawer.

It hit me. I'd chosen men with whom I had no chance of a future. I was safe from a lifetime with either of them. Apparently, I'd outsmarted myself.

I sunk into major despair, while absent-mindedly pushing wanted posters and U.S. Marshall messages around on my desk. Seemed like all of a sudden, nobody wanted me. Not Eli. Too busy herding his stupid cattle. Not Seth. Too busy running Dry Creek and counting the days 'til Miss School Marm returned. And, not even Pa, busy running the bank, with somebody else to cook and clean for him.

I was an outcast. Worthless.

The more I pondered on it, the deeper I enveloped myself with the blue cloud of misery.

Certainly the wind and dark skies didn't help. I needed sunshine. I got rain.

Purposefully, I pulled open the desk drawer and withdrew the latest Beadles and Adam dime novel I had been reading: *Outlaw Trail*. It was something of a page turner, with really, truly awful bad guys running from town to town holding up banks. Sometimes the banker would get killed, other times buffaloed. The sheriff or marshal, always square jawed and incredibly handsome, would take off after the criminals. So far, they hadn't been caught. But I wasn't finished, yet. What did strike me as interesting, however, was this group of outlaws waited until some sort of festivities happened in town—New Year's, Chinese New Year's, Fourth of July—and under cover of darkness and fireworks would blow open the safe, ride out long before the townspeople suspected.

The idea was brilliant. If you were a robber.

As I sat pondering this shiny plot, Mayor Seth Critoli glided into my office. I wasn't ready to have him waltz in, late that afternoon, or for his cat-eating-a-canary smile. I was on the verge of tears and any minute they would fall. A good cry was overdue. But I knew the mayor and the rabble locked up behind me would claim bawling made me incapable of being sheriff.

How many male sheriffs sat at their desks and carried on over love lost?

Using his foot, Seth pushed the door closed and practically danced over to my desk. He was way too happy. Couldn't he see I needed to be left alone?

He pulled a chair up close to my desk, sat and leaned back, his arms spread wide. "Great day, isn't it?"

"It's raining."

"Yep." He glanced outside. "Good for the crops."

"Everything's a soggy, muddy mess. Gonna take weeks to dry up."

"The sun'll come out soon." Seth leaned forward and patted my arm. "We've put more boards across the street. No need for your pretty skirts to get dirty."

I couldn't think of any more doom and gloom. As much as I hated to admit it, Seth and his smile were my needed rays of sunshine. The world looked brighter. Maybe we could have lemonade.

Before I could suggest it, he pulled his pocket watch out of his dark-gray vest and compared its display with the Regulator's. He gazed at the hands as if they were speaking to him. "Almost time." He slid the watch back into its concealment.

"For what?" The stagecoach wasn't due in until tomorrow, and today was not one of our regular mail runs.

"Pearl's coming back. Maybe today, I hope. Maybe tomorrow. Her family rented a coach for her—with a driver. Seems they have money."

Great. Just what I needed. Miss Pearl McIntyre: school teacher, *bonne fille,* nemesis. Now *rich* nemesis.

"I stopped by because I value your opinion." Seth dug into his pocket and extracted a small wooden box, tied with a red ribbon.

It had to be a diamond ring. A big one. With lots of small diamonds surrounding a huge one. Probably expensive.

He tugged at the box's ribbon until it came undone and floated to my desk. "If you think it's too much, tell me. I'll get something else."

Hating the idea of Pearl getting a ring and not me, still I was curious what he'd chosen. Dry Creek had no jewelry stores like I remembered seeing in San Francisco, when I was a child. I assumed he'd ridden over to Sacramento.

He lifted the lid and pulled out a bracelet. Silver, with one little bangle. A silver heart.

Harmless enough.

"These are all the rage with Queen Victoria." Seth held it up to the dim light struggling through the window. "They're called—"

"Charm bracelets," I said. "I know."

He shot me a quizzical frown, both eyebrows lowered like the black clouds outside.

I frowned back. "I *am* a woman." For the first time in an hour, I chuckled. "I know about jewelry and pretty things like this."

His eyebrows returned to their normal perch. A smile pushed his mustache up. "So, what d'you think? Will she like it?"

"She'd be crazy not to." My sense of relief overwhelmed my sense of propriety. "If she doesn't want it, I do."

Seth froze, blinking at me, the charm bracelet dangling in mid-air. His mouth opened and then snapped shut. His eyes darted from the bracelet to me, then back again. His shoulders slumped as he thawed.

"I'm . . . sorry. I forgot . . ."

We focused on the bracelet, avoiding eyes that would force further explanation. Seth put the bauble back into the box and cleared his throat. "You heard from Eli?"

I shook my head, unable to put into words what I really felt. Whatever that was. I only knew if I sat there any longer, I'd cry . . . or scream.

"Wish I'd been around to meet him," Seth said, obviously trying to placate me. "From what you've said, sounds like a nice enough fella."

"He is. Or was." There was no way I could figure out which was which right now. "I think you moved into town a week or two after he left. But Pokey knows him."

Seth's eyes danced. "Then I'll have to talk to him about this famous Eli."

Tired of my breaking heart, I offered an outing. "How about a glass of lemonade? We can talk politics and act official."

"Better yet." Seth retied the red ribbon and returned the box to his pocket. "Let's get one of your volunteers to watch the jail and us have a beer. I'll buy."

What? An invitation into the saloon . . . a man's retreat? So, Seth considers me one of the boys. A pard rather than a paramour. Well, that's certainly disappointing. But my newly acquired taste did make a beer sound better than lemonade. More fortifying. Best of all, I didn't have to rush home to fix supper, and I certainly didn't relish the idea of spending another lonely hour or two drawing in the dust. Dust that I should have dealt with. And Pokey was already at the Tin Pan.

I pushed my chair back. "I'll clean up here, you find Mr. Harsburg."

Seth closed the door before I could stand.

Gunbelt cinched around my waist, loaded gun in the holster, I checked the cells again—Smith and Doyle lay on their cots as if asleep—and double-checked the keys hanging on the hook. Right where they should be . . . and should remain.

Within moments, Seth and Billy Harsburg stepped in. Seth explained, "Billy was just finishing a late dinner. I convinced him to help out."

"Glad to, Sheriff," Harsburg said.

" 'Preciate it." I plopped a hat on my head, closed the inner door and opened the other. Once outside with the office door firmly shut, I lowered my voice near Seth. "I'm buying the second round."

CHAPTER FORTY-SIX:
A NIGHT TO REMEMBER

When Seth and I stepped into the Tin Pan Saloon, a few heads turned, and I thought I heard a few whispered words, but I shrugged them off.

We were on official business.

Kind of. Officially, I needed to remind Pokey that tomorrow was Wednesday and he'd be driving the mail coach run to Dutch Flats, again. Of course, he already knew that, but otherwise I had no good reason to be in the saloon.

Pokey, Seth and I took our beer glasses to a table near the back of the room and sat under a kerosene lantern. From here, we could watch the patrons without interfering with their fun. There was always a certain amount of tension when the law walked in. Kind of like having your teacher at your birthday party.

But, as usual, they didn't pay me much notice. They whooped and hollered at each other, sang along with the piano—*Carry Me Back to Ol' Virginny* repeated endlessly—hoisted glasses and sloshed beer, without concern for spilling on the floor. It was covered in fresh sawdust, anyway, the intent to soak up these spills and from the men spitting on the floor, as the spittoons filled up regularly. I was also told men didn't always make it to the privy out back when the beer overflowed their bladders, so they let loose into the galvanized trough below the front bar.

This little gem of information was more than I wanted to know, but Pokey exulted in telling me—loudly and exuberantly.

233

My cheeks warmed.

My first beer went down with only some effort. Was I beginning to like sour milk?

Tummy now warm and my body relaxed, I ordered another round for the table. Pokey, who'd had a couple ahead of us, drank his with a bit more restraint than Seth and me. I was here to drown my sorrows, or at least to encourage them into a long swim.

Somewhere between the second and third rounds, Seth also bought us whiskey shots. I held up the shot glass of amber and studied it.

Seth leaned close. "Romance the drink." His voice was smooth. "Like this." He sipped and grinned.

I could do that, I figured. I closed my eyes while the nectar slid down my throat easily—the cat, declawed. Two beers and one whiskey now tickling my belly, I realized I should have eaten supper. The room tilted. What was I thinking? I wasn't a drinker, but my pity-pot seemed to have sunk to the bottom of the sea.

Halfway through the second beer and more whiskey shots, nature called. It was my turn to find my way through the saloon and out back. I stood. Or tried to. The table bumped up against my leg and the people tilted to my right. Their images blurred as my stomach turned.

"You all right, Maud?" Seth gripped my arm.

"Uh huh." But my lips—numb. I poked them. Not only my lips but also my cheeks and nose. I poked harder and giggled. "I can't feel my face."

Pokey peered closely. "I can't feel your face, too."

Seth, Pokey and I roared. We poked each other's faces. I was about to wet my bloomers, but, for the life of me, my ankles wouldn't let their legs head for the privy. The more I laughed, the more the urgency.

My feet eventually unglued themselves from the floor, and my knees and I wobbled toward the back door. Fortunately, it wasn't far. Seth walked me through the door and to the privy, holding the umbrella over us both, waiting outside until I was done.

He slid his arm around my shoulder as I stepped into the night air. "You're swell, Maud. Just swell."

Right then, life was perfect. Warm and perfect . . . especially with dry bloomers.

"You're purty swell, too, Seth."

His lips planted themselves on mine, and I think we would've stayed like that, supporting each other, enjoying the kiss, but Pokey pushed past on his own urgent voyage to the privy.

"Gangway!" And, then, over his shoulder, "Wondered why you didn't come back."

Seth and I pushed away from each other and frowned. My stomach roiled, but the rest of me was happy. No, not happy, ecstatic.

I closed my eyes and my world turned, but I knew another beer would make everything perfecter. "Pokey's buying the next round," I said.

Arm in arm, Seth and I traipsed back into the Tin Pan. Pokey soon joined us and we continued our little party, me ignoring most of the stares and comments of the other customers and the saloon's "hostesses." What did they know about being sheriff? All the pressures it entailed? Of my pitifully lonely life? And why should they care?

By our fourth round, Seth, Pokey and I challenged each other to a burping contest. Loudest won and would buy the next beer. Pokey squeaked a small one, while mine turned a couple of heads and brought outrageous laughter. Seth's rivaled mine, but not by much.

Bang!

Gunfire in the street.

Bang!

I looked at Seth as if he knew what was happening. Like it was written on his forehead. I switched a blurry gaze to Pokey, who shrugged.

Realizing it was me who had to see who was disturbing the peace and maybe even shoot someone, I stood, patting the revolver on my hip. My thighs felt as wobbly as my first time on a horse. I eased back down to my chair and grinned.

"Legs are numb." I laughed, accompanied by Seth's and Pokey's giddy chuckles. "I drink I'm stuck."

Even to my inebriated ears, that didn't make sense. I tried it again. "I'm stink. Stunk. Stuck."

Holding our sides, we laughed. Tears blurred my world, bubbled from my eyes and cascaded down my cheeks.

Bang!

Another gunshot gained my attention. I pushed to my feet, while Seth and Pokey did the same. They stood better than I did, which wasn't saying much. Seth swayed. We tossed coins on the table, though we'd already paid for our beer, and wobbled our way out the door and into the cool evening air.

A couple deep breaths helped clear my head. Kerosene lanterns hanging high on poles up and down the street replaced the smaller fires. It was now easier to navigate the boardwalks with overhead lighting. What wasn't any easier to navigate was the mud. The rain had stopped, but things were still sloppy.

Men milled around in front of the other saloons up and down Main Street. Everything blurred, but I could still make out buildings and distinguish people from horses . . . sort of.

From up at the end of the street, a man on a horse shouted, *"WHOOPEE!"*

He shot his gun into the air, reined his horse around and galloped into the night, trailing more whoops and hollers. They faded into the dark.

I shrugged at Pokey and Seth.

"Pro'ly shou' ge' back . . . office." I pointed down the street, then changed direction, when I realized the office was the other way.

"I'll walk you." Seth offered an arm.

"Me, too." Pokey offered another.

We ambled down the boardwalk, three abreast, like old army pals who hadn't seen each other since the war.

"Camptown ladies, sing dis song . . ." I sang. "Doo dah, doo dah."

"Camptown racetrack five miles long . . ." The three of us belted it out at the top of our lungs. "All de doo dah day."

"Gwinna run . . ."

We stood at the board crossover to get to my office. Two wide, but not enough to accommodate three people, especially those who couldn't walk a straight line.

"You go first, 'cause you're like . . . like a girl." Seth released me and waved at the planks.

It was nice to know chivalry hadn't died. I bowed to him and started across, one foot mostly in front of the other.

The first four steps were easy. With my feet staying firmly on the boards and my skirt held high, I would remain unsoiled. Make it across. No problem. I turned to look at my friends.

Forgetting I had my skirt in hand, I raised it high enough to wave.

I showed ankle and leg to both Pokey and Seth, who whooped and whistled, their precise comments lost in my embarrassment. I dropped my hand and skirt, turned my attention to the other side, and took another step . . . right off the board.

Ankle deep in mud, I tried to pull my foot out, but lost my balance and plopped down on the board, now slick as molasses, and slid into the mud. I didn't know whether to laugh or cry, but my floundering only made matters worse. Now all of me was in mud.

Pokey, first on the scene, tugged, laughing, trying to assess if I was hurt. Seth offered a hand and toppled when I pulled. Pokey managed to catch a coattail, as it glided by. All three of us landed in the mud, wallowing like a bunch of four-year-olds.

I'd never been so dirty. Not even when I was in the middle of spring planting. Not even when I'd fixed mud pies for Thaddeus Williams. We sat there, the three of us, laughing until we couldn't breathe.

Some of the alcohol's effects wore off in the mud. I shivered. Despite it being June, the mud was cold. I studied it, considered the nearby tethered horses, and then realized I didn't want to know what else was under me, in addition to wet dirt. Feeling like a pig in its sty, I struggled up to my feet.

A female voice called from the boardwalk, on the far side of the street. "Seth? Is that you?"

Pearl McIntyre.

Immediately, I "level-headed" up and I saw Seth did, too. With great effort, we pulled our bodies out of the muck and slogged to the dry boardwalk. Sure enough, there stood Miss Pearl McIntyre, school marm, fisted hands on hips, glaring at Seth.

"What're you doing? Why didn't you meet me?" She sniffed toward Seth. "Are you drunk?" Pearl's eyes roved up and down Seth, over to Pokey and finally landed on me. "Maud, you're a mess."

I burst out in hysterics, tears again clouding my vision. I hiccupped. Levelheaded be damned, this was the best evening I'd ever had, including nights out with Eli. Pokey and Seth, despite themselves I'm sure, bent over, allowing chortles, cackles and outright guffaws to pierce the night.

Footsteps sounded behind me.

"Sheriff Overstreet?"

I spun around, covering my mouth with a mud-encrusted hand. "Yep."

The man peered at me like I'd turned green, and took a step back. His thick eyebrows shot up. "I'm Judge Andrew Richfield. You were expecting me."

Chapter Forty-Seven:
Court Is Now in Session

A firm hand shook my shoulder. "Maud? Don't you have to go into the office today?"

I mumbled something intelligent. Maybe not.

"Sun's been up a while, now. I hear tell the judge's in town."

That got my attention. I pried one eye open and recognized Pa. A slow survey of my surroundings revealed my bedroom, muddy clothes strewn over the back of a chair and piled on the floor.

A closer inspection revealed the room more nearly resembled a war zone—Gettysburg from what veterans had told me. I certainly felt like a soldier who'd survived a battle. Barely. However, even though my head pounded like hammers on rusty nails into new lumber, and my stomach gurgled like baking soda in water, my soul felt happy. Happiest it had been in months. Maybe even years.

Getting out of bed proved much harder than usual. Pa lingered at the door, a worldly smirk turning into a frown. It paraded across his face.

"Had yourself quite a time last night." Pa folded his arms and leaned against the door jamb. His nose wrinkled. "Down at that . . . saloon." He spat the last word.

With as much courage as my spirit allowed, I unraveled myself from the covers and sat on the edge of the bed. I nodded. I think. Maybe I held my head and let out a long breath of stale beer and whiskey. I figured Pa wasn't happy, his little girl having spent most of the evening drinking at the saloon.

Well, this little girl was an adult *and* sheriff of a bustling little town. It was time she made her own decisions. Not so convincing, when my head throbbed and my mouth tasted like I'd eaten my feather pillow.

Pa shot me "the look," which at any other time would have caused me to apologize. But not right now. He muttered, "Almost nine. Stage's due."

Good grief. Nine?

"Raining?" I squinted against the sunshine pouring through my window, realizing it had been a stupid question.

Pa shook his head, turned and disappeared. The front door squeaked open and closed before I could stand and wave goodbye. At least he was speaking to me. Sort of. Which may or may not be a good thing.

While I was deciding which it was, the chinking of a key unlocking the back door compelled me to stand. Had to be Mrs. Stevenson, ready to start her day cleaning, cooking and washing. I wobbled my way through the kitchen to the door and sure enough, there stood my angel of mercy.

While she removed her bonnet and shawl, her gaze strolled up and down my nightgown, decorated with splotches of mud. One long streak ran near the neck. I chose not to explain.

Instead I pointed to the stove.

"Need coffee," I said. "I'll start some."

Of course, Pa hadn't made any. I assumed he'd buy a cup in town, instead, as I didn't think he knew how to make it. I would've appreciated having a cup ready to pour over my head and another into my mouth, but now I'd have to make it myself and wait.

Mrs. Stevenson pointed to my bedroom. "How about I make the coffee and you go get dressed? I hear there's a trial in town, and I assume you need to be there."

Definitely my angel. I could've kissed her, especially now I could feel my face, and I was pretty sure my lips worked. But, instead, I pointed toward the kitchen.

Trial. Judge. My fuzzy mind peeled back images of Richfield, the judge who'd sworn me in as sheriff, standing there looking down his nose at me. How had he managed to get to town, yesterday? His account played in my head. *This young lady was nice enough to let me ride along with her.* It wasn't bad enough the judge had come early, it was terrible that he'd come with Pearl.

My day had nowhere to go but up.

Mud-free and dressed in my best sheriff outfit, I gulped two cups of perfectly-made coffee. Despite the avalanche headache, I told myself I was all right. I could walk without bumping into furniture, speak without slurring words and maybe even carry on a semi-logical conversation. I practiced on Mrs. Stevenson to be sure.

Downtown beckoned. I had a job to do.

A small crowd of some twenty men and women milled around outside the courthouse.

Several stood in the doorway gawking. I elbowed inside, threading my way up to the front. On one side sat the prosecutor, Mr. Daniel Mayfield. The opposite side was empty. Somewhere in the back of my brain I remembered a defense attorney was on his way from Dutch Flats. Obviously, he wasn't here yet.

Neither were Pokey and the prisoners.

I leaned down to Mayfield. "Where's Smith and Doyle?" I knew they'd escaped again and I would *never*, in a million years, live it down.

He turned his dark-brown eyes on me. "Didn't you bring them?"

I stood up fast, like I'd been poked in the rear.

Damn and double damn. That *would* be my job. Guess my

embarrassment was the high price to pay for drinking. Or at least drinking so much. I leaned back down to him.

"I'll be right back. Don't start without me."

A quick look around the courtroom. I didn't spot the judge, but then again, I may not have recognized him if he stood on my feet. I remembered a man in the street last night, stern, confused brown eyes glaring at me. A man, about Pokey's height, slim with a neatly trimmed gray beard, leaning back as I offered a mud-encrusted hand. If such a man was in the courtroom, I didn't recognize him. Which meant I had time to get the prisoners and not look like the fool I knew I was.

I vowed that was the last time I'd drink so much. Maybe even the last time I'd drink. No wonder Pa warned me away from saloons.

Now I understood.

I pushed my way through the courtroom. Outside, I pulled in fresh California air. The bass drum in my head lessened with each breath. Maybe I'd get through today. Maybe.

"Sheriff Overstreet?"

I spun around at my name. A fellow dressed in a dark wool suit, fancier than I'd seen in some time, trotted up the boardwalk toward me, a narrow leather satchel tucked under one arm. I waited until he was within spitting distance. I didn't recognize him, but he obviously knew me.

"Sheriff Overstreet," the man extended a hand. "I'm Frederick Parmigan, Esquire . . . from Dutch Flats?" He spoke like it was a question. Maybe it was his thick southern accent that made his words sound sort of fuzzy.

"Pleased to meet you. Been expecting you." I pointed over my shoulder. "Courtroom's through those doors. I'm going right now to get the prisoners."

"You mean, the poor men who've been so wrongly accused? Unjustly?" Parmigan said. "You mean Amos Smith and Juan

Doyle? . . . so innocent? . . . and miles away at the time . . . ?"

Oh, boy.

His recital trailed behind me like a swarm of Southern moths, as I sprinted toward the office. Halfway there, I spotted Pokey with Smith and Doyle in tow. People gawked at the shuffling men, manacles around their wrists, shackles on their ankles. Women pulled their children closer as Pokey, a stone cold expression on his face, marched the two criminals toward me.

I grabbed Smith's arm and led him in front of Pokey. I'd be sure to thank my almost-deputy, when we weren't surrounded by Dry Creek citizens eager to watch me mess up . . . again. Although it had been three months since taking the oath, I knew there was still a lot of snickering and finger pointing behind my back. Right now, I didn't care. I was doing a good job, at least to the best of my abilities, and that's all anybody could ask.

With my throbbing head held high, I mimicked Pokey's serious face and marched Smith to the courthouse, Pokey and Doyle right behind me. People parted without my asking, which in itself was pretty amazing. Part of me wanted to smile at that feeling, but the other part told me to be serious.

We parked Doyle and Smith up front in chairs, Pokey and me between them. Pokey slipped me a clean gun, which I recognized as mine. When he had time to do all this and how he made rational thoughts awed me. I'd have to bake him a pie. Two pies.

I leaned in close. "This is Wednesday. Who's taking your place on the mail run?"

"Joe McLaughlin."

Joe had taken over when Pokey'd been hurt, so Joe knew the routine. I smiled at Pokey for his logical thinking.

Fidgeting was something I did well, one of my talents. I half-turned from my seat, my gaze trailing over the faces behind me.

In the first row, to my right, sat Seth. Next to him crammed in three reporters, their pencils poised over notepads. Most people I recognized.

The judge was certainly taking his time preparing. I knew it was well past ten. I envisioned Richfield primping and preening and adjusting his judge's robe. There wasn't much room in the judge's "chambers." It was so small the desk took up most of it. A kerosene lantern, not used often, occupied one corner of the desk. Although the room was undersized, it did have a nice rug and the chair was leather upholstered.

A bailiff I didn't recognize marched into the room. He straightened his shoulders and looked at the fifty-plus people stuffed into the courtroom. "All rise for the Honorable Judge Andrew Richfield."

We did. A man I vaguely recognized swooped in from the back room. The crowd quieted and then sat as soon as he did. Mumbles arose but faded into silence with a stern look from the judge and a solid *thwack* of his gavel.

"The court is now in session."

Richfield's brown eyes locked onto me. Had I missed some mud still on my face?

Without a hint of recognition, he got down to business.

"Sheriff. State your case," he demanded of me, as if we'd never met.

CHAPTER FORTY-EIGHT:
ORDER IN THE COURT!

Each lawyer, in turn, presented what they were going to prove during the trial. The prosecutor claimed the defendants were evil miscreants, of the worst kind. The defense railed about how these poor, innocent boys were sorely misunderstood.

This would take longer than I'd anticipated.

Once opening arguments were presented, Mr. Mayfield invited me to stand near the bench and recall my side of the story, detailing our holdup by Smith and Doyle, their escape and eventual recapture. I explained how badly Pokey had been beaten during the second robbery. Then the Southern lawyer took his turn. By the time Parmigan sat down, I wasn't sure we were talking about the same men and situation. This shyster painted the pair like they had been set up, framed for a robbery and escape they'd never done. He claimed they'd been sleeping off a high good time back behind a saloon when Pokey and I had been robbed. That Pokey and I locked up the wrong men. They were wrongly accused.

Smith and Doyle spent the morning looking hangdog, kicked around and oh, so abused. They hung their heads, kept shoulders slumped, and let out plaintive sighs. I certainly knew better and hoped the judge did, too. On the other hand, that defense legalist was good. Heck, *I* almost believed him.

We broke for dinner, the judge declaring a good noonday meal made for a more "efficacious conductance of the business at hand." The prosecutor would get his turn this afternoon.

Pokey and I marched our duo back down the street, enduring their growls and threats at passing citizens.

Seth declined our offer to accompany us to the office, citing important mayoral business that would take less than an hour. I guessed his business was making amends to Pearl. He'd see us back at the courtroom before the trial started up again.

I relaxed a bit when we locked them in their cell. I sat at my desk; Pokey pulled up a chair. I was queasy. Maybe coming down with something. I put my head on crossed arms on the desk and relaxed. This evening, I could go home and sleep, knowing the house was clean and supper ready. Pokey would sleep here at the jail tonight and I'd relieve him early in the morning.

But, still, I had the afternoon to get through.

Someone shook my shoulder.

"Maud? Wake up. Time to go."

I blinked into consciousness, unfolded my arms, which were more asleep than I had been, and looked up at Pokey. He raised one eyebrow.

"Least you're not dead. You were darn still."

"How long—"

" 'Bout an hour." He waved toward the cells. "They're fine. Still there. And Billy's here to watch the place."

I'd forgotten we had three other "guests," two again sleeping it off and one sitting in the corner, pouting. Down at a saloon he'd been raising a ruckus and refused to put away his gun. So, with some persuasion from my revolver and Pokey's strong hands, the man had ended up behind bars. I told him I'd release him when he was hospitable enough to say "please." He'd also need to cough up the fare for his keep.

Three days and still he pouted. He was getting expensive.

I had more important things to worry about than him right now, so I wiped the moisture from the corner of my mouth, leaned back for a stretch and strained up to my feet. A deep breath or two and I felt better.

In the courtroom, Pokey and I shoved Smith and Doyle into their respective seats. Then we took our own. The fancy southern lawyer looked over at us and smiled. I returned a frosty glare. Judge Richfield swooped into the room, his robe fluttering behind like hawks' wings. We all stood, then all sat. More testimony, more lies. The afternoon dragged on.

When Mr. Parmigan ran out of things to twist, our prosecutor had said his closing piece, and Pokey and I couldn't answer any more questions without repeating ourselves, the trial was over. The judge stood.

"I'll make my decision following a brief recess." He shot from the room like a man in need of a stiff drink. I would bet there was a bottle secreted away in one of the desk drawers.

Everyone spoke in hushed tones. The murmurs grew to cranky grumbles. Mumbles of *supper* and *how long does it take?* and a few other unrepeatable comments made me squirm. Again, I fidgeted.

The rain, having quit the night before, left behind stifling humidity. Late afternoon sunlight streamed in through the west windows, baking us, turning the room into an oven, oppressive with all these warm bodies. I whispered to Pokey, "I'm gonna open some windows, before I faint." Not that I had any intention of fainting; it sounded like a meaningful threat.

All four milk-glass windows were stuck, their wooden frames swollen with the rain. With assistance from another sufferer, we managed to raise one of them, allowing a cool summer breeze to waft its way through the courtroom. Pleased with myself for fixing a problem no man had figured out, I aimed my attention at Seth. But where he'd sat was empty. Maybe he'd scooted out when my attention turned elsewhere. Perhaps he had an early date with Pearl?

I sat back down. I'd catch him up on the trial later.

After what felt like years but was less than a quarter hour, Andrew Richfield strode back into the room. We had barely jumped to our feet when he sat. So, we sat.

"In the case of the village of Dry Creek versus Smith and Doyle . . ." Richfield cleared his throat looking down his considerable nose at my two prisoners. With grave purpose, he raised his gavel, pausing for effect. "I find the defendants, Juan Doyle and Amos Smith—"

Bang!

The gunshot deafened me. The judge's shattered gavel flew out of his hand. The kerosene lantern hanging on the wall beside him exploded in a shower of glass. He turned toward the sound.

Bang!

The shots came from outside the open window. Rifle.

Richfield clutched his chest, flew back in his chair and toppled over to the floor.

People jumped up. Women screamed, everyone scrambling for cover. Those who'd been standing stampeded through the single door. The bailiff and both lawyers rushed to Richfield. I didn't know what to do, where to go. March my prisoners back to jail? Hunt down the shooter? Check on the judge? I needed to be three people.

I turned to look at the people pushing and shoving their way through the door. Weight lifted off my hip. My gun! Before I could move, something hard slammed into the back of my head. Bright lights exploded like fireworks. I went down, my world spinning worse than last night.

I tried to make sense of things. On my hands and knees now, I knew I had to get up.

Sitting back on my knees, I looked behind me for Pokey, now lying on the floor.

Smith and Doyle were running for the door, threatening the scattering public with guns.

I figured one was mine and the other Pokey's.

"Get outta the way!" Smith shoved a woman into the wall. "Move!"

An elderly man and his cane flew backwards, onto the floor. I spotted Ian MacKinney and Harvey Weinberg, two-thirds of the town council, on their hands and knees, scurrying between the benches.

The two crooks would get away and there was nothing I could do, right now. I shook my head, attempting to clear it, and regretted it, immediately. Pokey. Was he dead? Was the judge dead? I'd check on them both, go get another gun and trail Smith, Doyle and the shooter.

But who was the gunman? Could it have been a partner come back to bust them out?

Their leader? Shivers claimed my body. I pushed to stand, but instead of rising, I leaned over and lost remnants of last night's supper.

CHAPTER FORTY-NINE:
IN AND OUT

Thank goodness Pokey wasn't dead. After the doctor had inspected him, I knelt by him, watching his chest expand and contract. A bulbous red lump parted the hair. Apparently, he'd been cracked on the head harder than me, which meant he'd take a long nap on the courtroom floor.

But that was still better than the judge's fate. A bullet right through the upper arm. Dr. Monroe said Richfield would more than likely make a full recovery, except for full use of his shattered limb.

I stood where Richfield had been, traced the bullet's trajectory and confirmed it had come from outside. By opening the window, I'd given a clear view to the assassin. I was responsible for the judge's assault.

Who shot him? Only one person I knew had a reputation for precision shooting like that or who would want to upset the trial.

James Mooney.

Ruthless. Heartless. No morals. Would he have the audacity, the gumption, to shoot a judge? Especially in a crowded courthouse?

I struggled to pull my throbbing thoughts together, while Pokey was still unconscious. I talked to as many people as I could. Nobody had seen anything. They'd all been intent, like me, to hear what the judge had to say. And when the gun went off, people reacted by scrambling out of the way. I couldn't really blame them for not noticing, but I figured *somebody* had to have seen *something*.

And where had Smith and Doyle disappeared to?

On the bright side, with them gone, now I had more jail space.

Once Pokey was able to stand, I walked him over to Dry Creek Mercantile, where he lived in a room in the back. Harvey Weinberg rented it out cheap in exchange for Pokey's help around the store. Pokey made the ideal renter—he was rarely there.

Pokey slumped on the bed, while I made a wet rag compress for his sore head. He swatted my hand away.

"I'm fine. Don't need coddlin'." He leaned back against the pillow I'd managed to shove under his head. "Gonna rest for a while, then I'll come help you."

I patted his shoulder. "Take it easy. Sleep now. I'll get somebody else to watch the jail tonight." Before opening the door, I turned back to him. "Maybe one of our brave town councilmen."

Holding the compress to his head, Pokey snorted and grinned, changing to a grimace. "Ow! It hurts. Please, don't make me laugh."

I tossed him a smile.

On the way to my office, I considered Mooney, my two lost thugs, the shot up judge, injured Pokey and my own poor, throbbing head. At least, I had a lump to show for my misery, a souvenir that a hangover didn't provide.

I'd have to put together another posse and soon, but first I needed to find Seth. His absence disturbed me. I don't know why, it did. It wasn't like him to miss such excitement. And by now, surely he'd heard about the assault on Pokey and me. Why hadn't he rushed to see how I was?

Maybe he really was dead.

Before I reached my office, Councilman Slim Higginbotham hollered from across the street. I stopped mid-stride and waited for him to pick his way across the mud.

"Got a posse yet?" He spurted out over his wheezing.

I shook my head, regretted it. "Next on my list."

"Better get one soon. Those *hoodlums* are long gone, as it is." Slim's pudgy finger started to poke the badge on my chest, but changed direction to point up the street. "We can't have Dry Creek shootin' up judges. Word gets out and we'll be back to nothing but a one-horse town. Nobody'll move here. Buy goods here. Drink here. Nobody. We'll be the laughing stock of northern California."

That carried it a bit too far was my thinking. While I'd never heard of a judge getting shot before, especially in his own courtroom, I didn't think men would stop buying whiskey because of it. They might even buy more to celebrate.

Maybe I was wrong.

"I gotta find somebody to stay with the prisoners tonight." I knew Billy Harsburg couldn't tonight, he'd already told Pokey. I pointed up the street toward the jail. "Then I'll get up a posse and we'll head out. We'll leave first light tomorrow." Maybe with extra hours of sun, the road would have dried out a bit, too. But with several hours lead time, could I really catch them? This time they'd be smarter than last go-round. We'd have to ride hard.

Slim took a long breath. "Do something!"

"I am."

He started off down the boardwalk. I grabbed his sleeve. "You can help round up some men. Get the posse together while I deal with the rest."

A long sigh and then nod.

"Good. Thanks. I'll see you at dawn? You'll be riding with me

253

again?" He had been a real help with the last posse and I could use him.

He huffed, glared and stormed off.

In view of the notion our tight-fisted town council had volunteered to be temporary deputies, now was the time to call on them. Slim Higginbotham was already signed up for posse duty, which left watching the jail to the other two. I wondered what excuses they'd have to avoid it.

I reversed my heading and aimed for Dry Creek Mercantile. As I entered the store, Harvey was hanging his jacket on a peg, having returned recently from the courthouse.

"Took the judge over to Doc Monroe's," he said. "Doc said he was lucky. Apparently the bullet skimmed along the chest and lodged in the arm." Harvey sank into the swivel chair behind his desk in a side office, pulled out a John Rauch, clipped the end, struck a match under the edge of the desktop and turned cross-eyed watching the tobacco catch fire. He sucked on the cigar, his cheeks pulling in, then puffing out. He drew in at least five gallons of air and then let out a ten-gallon cloud of smoke. His shoulders lowered.

I stood in front of the desk and waited. The right time to ask would be coming soon, I was sure. He opened the bottom drawer and held up a whiskey bottle.

"Want a snort?"

That was the *last* thing I wanted. Ever. I shook my head, the pain of which seconded the motion and, again, I regretted doing so. I held up a hand.

"*Ech,* just as well," Harvey said. "Made a couple days ago by that new fella, says he's from some backwards country in Europe." His eyes twinkled. "Aren't they all? Backwards that is?"

I shrugged. I'd never been to Europe, though I knew Harvey

was from there, somewhere. I figured this to be some kind of inside joke.

"Anyway," he poured himself a glass. "Tastes kind of like cherries. Don't particularly care for cherries, myself."

Right now, even cherry pie didn't sound appetizing. To get my mind off of food and whiskey, I got down to the reason for my visit. "Mr. Weinberg, I'm . . . uh, needing another gun."

He froze in the midst of exhaling a smoky *O*.

I soldiered on. "As you know, mine was taken during the escape. Lifted right out of my holster, slicker 'n . . ." I rubbed the knot on my head. "Got walloped pretty good, too." I doubted he'd seen that part of the scuffle, considering he and MacKinney, on hands and knees, heads down, burrowed like badgers to get under benches immediately after the shot.

He stroked his beard. "Town supposed to pay for another gun?"

I hadn't really considered it, but seeing as I was on official business, I figured as much. "They should."

He sat completely still for a moment, I supposed calculating the profit margin, then sighed. *"Oy, vey!"* He rubbed his temples. "Good thing for you I have another one like it. Follow me."

I endured eye rolls and muttered breath laced with *what was the town thinking?* and *female sheriff.* There were more mumblings and others in his odd tongue, but I paid little attention as I followed him through the store. No way could I convince him *this* time it hadn't been my fault. I'd been buffaloed. He wouldn't let facts get in the way of his own opinions.

He handed me a gun similar to my stolen Colt. I inspected it. "Another thing, Mr. Weinberg," I said looking up at him. "You said you'd fill in as deputy, if there was a crisis in town."

"I did?"

"Yep. And we got us a bonafide crisis. I need you to watch

over what's left of my prisoners tonight. Pokey's too hurt and I gotta get a posse together."

"How 'bout Slim? Can't he do it?" Harvey's curls bobbed as he spoke.

"He's riding posse with me at first light."

"MacKinney?"

"Gonna ask him, next." I pointed toward the door. "How about the two of you trade off? You guard for half the night and he takes the other half?"

That proposition brought Harvey's eyes to study whatever was going on outside. A long draw on his cigar, he turned the eyes on me.

"We told you we'd be deputies." He sighed. "With elections coming up, we can't afford not to." His cigar waggled at me. "Be sure to tell that red-headed Scotsman I get first watch."

CHAPTER FIFTY:
PEARL'S CONFESSION

I told him.

Ian MacKinney was none too happy about having to roust out of his comfortable bed at midnight to come down to the jail to keep watch over sleeping inmates. He cursed Harvey out loud and probably me, silently. His Scottish temper certainly flared, but he was a man of his word. He'd be there on time, he promised.

Before I closed the door to his house, I asked, "Have you seen Seth Critoli this evening?"

MacKinney's green eyes rolled upward, while he thought. "Nae, canna say I hav'." He leaned out of his doorway and peered up the street. "Missin' 'im, are ye?"

Taken aback, I stammered, "I'm . . . surprised he didn't show up for the end of the trial."

"Well, hae's a spunky yoong lad. Probably jest oot coortin' tha pretty school marm, noo tha she's coom back tae town." MacKinney tipped his hat to me. "G'day noo."

And that was that with that. All my wrongdoers would be cared for, if reluctantly. And I had at least one other person in my posse. I'd stop by the saloon later to recruit more members.

While I walked back to my office, I crossed things off my mental "to do" list. All I had left was *Find Seth*. How hard could that be?

I changed my course for Pearl's house. She rented one near the school, so she didn't have far to walk.

My fist poised to knock, the door flew open. A red-eyed Pearl stood in the doorway, more unkempt than I'd ever seen her. Strands of hair cascaded down her shoulders, some stuck out at odd angles. Frankly, she reminded me of an old, beat-up porcupine.

"Did you find him?" Pearl's hands shook as she grasped the doorframe.

I shook my head—gently.

"Come in." She stood back and pointed toward the parlor. "I apologize. I forget my manners sometimes."

"I understand." And I did.

Sitting on her fancy Victorian couch and running my hand along its brocade fabric, I took a longer look at her face. Something was going on there, but I couldn't tell exactly what. I'd have to pry.

Pearl McIntyre sat across from me in a matching wing chair. I'd seen some like it in tony hotel lobbies in Sacramento.

"I'm sorry for my tone with you yesterday, Maud." Pearl's voice cracked a bit. "It's . . . I'd been waiting . . . searching . . . and when I couldn't find Seth and then I did—"

"It's all right." My heart went out to her, my jealousy melting into my toes. Truth was, she was nice. I liked her.

"It's all my fault."

"What is?" My curiosity piqued.

Pearl took a deep breath, looked away and then turned her swollen eyes on me. "There's something I need to tell you."

Would she admit to Seth's murder? I hoped not because I couldn't handle one more shred of drama. And besides, the jail was full up. But I desperately needed to know what, exactly, was her fault.

Pearl wrung her hands and then looked at me.

"I'm leaving."

"What?" I sat forward. "Why?" All sorts of scenarios played

in my head, while I crossed various ones off. Would she tell me? Maybe she really *had* killed Seth. That definitely would be her fault—*and* a reason to leave.

She stood and walked to the window overlooking a field of wildflowers. On the far side sat the schoolhouse. "It wasn't supposed to happen like this. It just did. It was an accident."

All right. That was it. I didn't even have my handcuffs with me, but I'd be sure to grip her arm with all my strength, as I marched her down to the jail. Fortunately, I now had my revolver with me.

"Where is he?" I stood, edging toward the door in case she made a run for it.

"Dutch Flats." She turned pathetic eyes on me.

"How'd you get him over there so fast? And why?" Now I was totally confused.

"That's where we promised to meet, after . . ."

"After what?" I gripped her arm and pulled out my gun. It wasn't loaded yet, but it gave me a bit of confidence, anyway.

Pearl dropped her voice to a whisper. "After I told him it was over."

"What was over?" I hated not understanding.

"Us." Pearl turned her eyes on me and frowned at the gun. "What's that for?"

"Pearl McIntyre," I said, "I'm arresting you for the murder of Seth Critoli."

"What?"

"I'm afraid so." I tugged. "Let's go."

"Seth is dead?" She pulled out of my grip. "What're you talking about?"

"Didn't you admit to killing him?"

"No."

"No?" I hung my arm at my side, the gun getting heavy. "But you said . . ."

Pearl brushed back a strand of hair stuck to her cheek. "I told Seth at dinner this afternoon we were through."

"What happened?"

"We had a terrible fight. He hollered and then begged me to reconsider. Even gave me this stupid charm bracelet." She pointed to the round table. The bracelet lay in a silvery pile on the top. "I told him it was too late."

"Too late?" This was beginning to sound like one of those dime novels I'd picked up at Dry Creek Mercantile.

Pearl pulled in air. Her shoulders straightened and she stood inches taller. "Maud. Remember when I left, soon as school was out?"

I raised one quizzical eyebrow.

"Well, I didn't go back home like I said."

"You didn't?" I figured either she was a darn good liar or she was stretching the truth.

"No. Actually . . . I went to Virginia City." She took a breath and in that moment a dazzling smile blossomed on her face. She stuck out her left hand, a diamond ring encircled the appropriate finger. "I got engaged!"

CHAPTER FIFTY-ONE:
A CLUE

So, that was good news. No. *Terrific* news. Pearl was now officially out of the looking-for-a-husband market. I could relax and not worry about running around with Seth behind her back. Now, all I had to do was find Seth.

By early evening, feeling like things had dragged on for days rather than hours, I'd checked each of the ten saloons, talked to some of the calico queens not otherwise occupied, peered around the shelves and back rooms of the two mercantiles, inspected the blacksmith's, sneezed my way behind the hay in the livery stable, and, as a last resort, walked up and down the church pews. Nada. No Seth Critoli. Now I was truly worried.

Had he left town in grief, seeking refuge elsewhere? Maybe he'd ridden over to Dutch Flats to meet Pearl's fiancé and give him a what-for. Or, maybe Seth had drowned himself in Dry Creek. No, wait. Not enough water in there to wet your big toe. We'd get water later in the summer, when the snow melted in the mountains. Right now, the river was leftover rain puddles, mostly mud. If he stuck his face in the thick muck, he'd most likely suffocate.

I frowned at my silly thoughts.

While sundown was still an hour away, I trudged back up the boardwalk toward my office. Too discouraged to go home, too tired to ask anybody anything else, too worried to rest, my sanctuary would provide relief. If I could call a tiny office and crowded cells a sanctuary. Nevertheless, it was mine.

Before I could turn the door handle, I heard my name. Glancing over my shoulder, I spotted Rune Maguire, the telegrapher, waving at me from across the street. I waited for him to catch up. For someone as old as Rune, he hobbled pretty fast.

"Doc sent me. They found Seth, Maud. Found him." Rune jabbed a skinny finger toward the courthouse. "Yep, there he was. A'lyin' there like he was asleepin'. Only he weren't sleepin'."

"Dead?" The word came out squeaky.

"Banjaxed, but not dead." Rune wagged his head. "Got walloped upside the head real good."

"Where's he now?"

"Doc Monroe's got him over to his office. Ol' Seth ain't come to, yet. Doc's saying he might never."

Panic closed my throat and put an end to the beating of my heart. I swallowed . . . painfully.

A cursory thanks to Rune for the news, I checked in with Harvey Weinberg, who reported no problems, then hitched up my skirt and flew up the street and over a block to Doc's house, a well-tended cottage at the end of town. Doc's wife, Charity, served as his nurse, in addition to cooking, cleaning and watching over their three boys, all of which were aged somewhere between grass and hay. Her name served her well.

I knocked softly and let myself in.

"Doc? Mrs. Monroe?" The house was much too quiet, considering all that had to be going on. I hurried to the back of the house, where Doc's office and medical rooms were. Sure enough, the last room held the doc, his wife and Seth, stretched out on an examining table.

His naturally olive skin had taken on an ashen quality and his arms lay at his sides on the table. This was the stillest I'd ever seen the man. Lifeless. Was he now dead?

I moved in closer and that's when Mrs. Monroe noticed me.

Her eyes flitted from my face to Seth's over to her husband's and back to me. Doc turned around.

"Sheriff. Glad you're here."

His words resonated with a gut-wrenching tone of finality. Unsolicited tears filled my eyes. I sniffed as quietly as I could.

Doc turned compassionate eyes on me. "Somebody hit him over the head," he said. "Used something sturdy, probably the end of a rifle or shotgun. Somebody strong."

I wanted to go to Seth, but my feet wouldn't budge. I had to ask the question. "He gonna be all right?" More tears welled.

Mrs. Monroe scurried around the table and slid an arm across my shoulders. "He's strong. Have faith."

Like a tornado, all of the day's events crashed into me, spinning one into another. Out of control, my worry, topped with senses of failure, anger and confusion, plunged me into overwhelming fatigue. Mrs. Monroe's soothing touch released my remaining tears.

I stood there like a six-year-old who'd lost her pet dog, bawling into the shoulder of a woman three inches shorter than me. It didn't matter. I needed her shoulder more than I needed air.

She patted my back.

"Let's get you some tea. Doc's finished with Mr. Critoli for the time being. He'll be checking on the judge now." She guided me into the narrow hallway and down to the kitchen.

She and I sat at the dining table while the water boiled. Tea was not my favorite drink. But right now it was the elixir I needed. I hoped it would calm me down and let me think.

By the time the tea was ready, I felt a little better. I used her wet dishcloth to wipe my face. Something about its soothing coolness rejuvenated me. Tears dried on my blouse and I no longer sniffled.

Other than what I was sure were red, puffy eyes, I was back to my old self, feeling a whole lot better. "Someone notify Seth's mama? She'll be worried sick."

"She's on her way now," Charity said.

The tea, laced with a splash of whiskey Charity added, did the trick. It was delightful. I'd have to remember Irish tea. My world relaxed and brightened.

She sipped her unspiked cup and set it down. "One of my boys found Mayor Seth 'bout an hour ago." She cocked her head toward the back door. "Tommy and his friend were taking a shortcut through the alley, over by the courthouse, and saw legs sticking out from under a bush."

I mentally kicked myself for not checking behind the building. What was Seth doing there in the first place? When he woke up, it would be one of my first questions. Check that. *If* he wakes.

I hated to ask, but I had to. "I know what Doc said, but what do you think? He gonna live?"

She studied the tea leaves in the bottom of her cup. Too long of a breath and her eyes not meeting mine said everything. She shrugged. "I'd say he has a chance. Whatever hit him—shotgun stock, rifle butt or ax handle—did a thorough job. It occurred to me that he might have caught somebody doing something wrong, and they . . . struck him."

I drained my cup and proffered it for more tea. Heavy on the Irish, please.

"So, he got hit in the alley and then fell under a bush?" That didn't make sense. But then, nothing much made sense.

"Tommy said there were drag marks in the mud. Came from the alley. The person who hit him didn't bother to cover up his tracks." Charity filled my cup and sat back down at the table.

A sip from the second cup and I had a plan. First, I needed to tell Pearl they'd found Seth.

Second, I'd go inspect the tracks in the mud. Hopefully, they'd tell me everything I needed to know. At least, how many men were involved and where they'd gone.

Seth wouldn't know or care I'd been here, so I finished my drink and stood. "Thanks for the tea. And the shoulder." I shot her a wide smile. "You're the true lifesaver in this house."

A long hug and she stood back. "You're quite welcome. I'll send word as soon as he wakes."

Well, *that* sounded positive. Then I remembered the judge. "Please tell Doc I'll come look in on Judge Richfield before I take off in the morning."

"I will," Charity said.

I closed the front door and stepped into warm twilight. Breathe. Deep. Still enough time to inspect those tracks, if I hurried. As I sprinted toward the courthouse, a twinge of guilt hit me. I should go tell Pearl first. But I could tell her in the dark a lot better than I could follow tracks in the dark. She would have to wait.

Sure enough. There was the bush, its branches near the bottom broken where someone had crashed into them. And from where Seth had been pulled out. Unfortunately, his rescuers had tromped all over the original tracks. Boot prints smushed into other prints left no room for figuring out whose was whose.

At long last, I spotted them. Prints in the mud, up against another building in the alley. Someone had stood for a while. My gaze followed from there to the open window of the courthouse. A taller person would have had a clear view of the judge from this angle. According to the tracks, it was only one person who'd done the shooting.

A closer survey of the area turned up two brass shell casings. I took one and smelled the open end. Sulfur. It had been fired not too long ago. I guessed the other one was the same. Putting both in my pocket, I decided to ask Harvey Weinberg what caliber these were. If they fit a rifle. They were different from the .36s I carried. These were a bit longer and narrower, and not made of heavy parchment, like mine.

The more I looked at the ground, the building, the bushes, the more clear it became. Somebody stood on this spot, reckoning to eliminate the judge, waiting for a clear shot. I had obliged by opening the window for a picture-clear view. Probably Seth came along before the trial started and the sniper buffaloed him before shooting the judge. That would explain Seth's absence for the second half of the trial.

I hated the idea of Seth lying here, mere feet away from me inside the courthouse. Well, I couldn't change any of it. I'd have to settle for capturing their assailant. I owed both the judge and Seth that much.

Deep shadows played games on my eyes. Grayed light danced in the alley, as I walked through. The new kerosene lanterns hanging on poles provided enough light for me to find the boardwalk. One of the taller teenage boys was in charge of lighting them, and he'd finished by the time I got to Pearl's.

CHAPTER FIFTY-TWO:
ON THE ROAD AGAIN

My second visit with Pearl had taken much longer than I'd expected. I'd explained twice what had happened, revisiting every possible scenario, before she grabbed her bonnet and shawl and took off for the doctor's. She'd have to elbow her way in to see him, as I was sure Mama Critoli was there already, flapping and clucking over her injured boy. Mama somehow always managed to bring chaos into calm. But she had a good heart and loved her son dearly.

My day had been long and wasn't going to get shorter, soon. I had riding to do first thing in the morning and, judging by the way my legs felt, they would scream "bloody murder" and "torture" when I mounted up.

But I would do my job and, by golly, do it to the best of my ability. This time, I mentally packed my bags, doing the real packing later. I'd be sure to be ready at first light.

Pa was none too happy when I pushed open the door. As usual, I was late for supper and probably looking more like something the cat had dragged in from the barn.

He sat in the parlor in his favorite chair looking over his newspaper. He looked up as I hung up my shawl and hat. "Heard about the shooting." Pa folded his paper and eased out of his chair. "Looking a bit disheveled there, Maud. You all right?"

"Tired." I rubbed the receding knot on the back of my head. "Bit of a headache is all."

"Gotta tell you," Pa said. "When I learned you were involved, it worried me. And more than a mite. Sure wish you'd recon—"

"Not a chance." I pointed toward my bedroom. "Gonna get cleaned up before supper."

As I splashed water on my face, scrubbing away dirt and specks of gunpowder, I let my hair down and brushed it, gentle near the lump. I thought about what Harvey Weinberg at the mercantile told me regarding the shell casings I'd found. Winchester, forty-four caliber, he'd said. Any sensible gunfighter would reach for this rifle, when needing long-range accuracy. Could exceed two hundred yards, if necessary. And it held seventeen rounds. The rifle was affordable but certainly not inexpensive. Would James Mooney carry something like this?

I sniffed my way into the kitchen. Before leaving for the day, Mrs. Stevenson had fixed roast chicken with an onion she'd thrown into the mix. It sat on a plate in the warming bin. On the sideboard, recently baked bread slices with pats of butter beckoned.

Taking the chicken and mashed potatoes I'd found pushed to the back of the bin, I called Pa in for supper and we sat at the dining table. Aromas made my mouth water, but did I even have the energy to pick up a fork? A rumbling reminded me my mid-day meal had been . . . Huh, I hadn't had one. I'd slept through it at my desk. And breakfast . . . well, that hadn't happened, either.

I tried a bite. The piece of chicken, with just-right herbs and spices, along with its juices tenderizing it, rejuvenated my starvation. I dug in.

Once my stomach quit complaining, I noticed Pa regarding me, his gaze roving over my face. I didn't know if he'd tried conversing earlier because I certainly hadn't been listening. Now, I slowed and waited. He sipped his coffee, his plate still half full.

Pa pointed his cup at me. "You planning to hire extra deputies for the big doings?"

"Big doings?" I spoke over a final spoonful of potatoes. "What big doings?"

"Fourth of July's coming up in a couple of weeks. Town council's got big plans this year."

"They do?"

"Yup. Haven't you talked to any of them?"

Not about celebrations and festivities. I shook my head. "Been a little busy." Why hadn't anybody mentioned it to me? Shouldn't I be one of the first to know? Outrage, tinged with anger, muddled in my well-packed stomach.

"They have a problem, though." Pa finished his coffee. "No one in town here knows a thing about fireworks. Dry Creek Mercantile is willing to sponsor the display, but there's nobody to run it. Too bad Gunther Gruber died last year. He's the only one I know who could light those things without blowing himself up or half the town down."

Fireworks? He was right. We couldn't have a Fourth of July hoop-de-do without skylights. "I'll ask around."

Pa picked up his fork and studied the tines like they held the key to the universe. "I'm thinking, with the town now twice as big as last year and all, they'll be wanting more hoopla. And there's probably gonna be more opportunity for miscreants to cause a little trouble." He stabbed a piece of meat. "Figure you'll be arresting a passel of drunken cowboys and miners."

Miners. Cowboys. Drunks. Bands. People. *Lots* of people. I speared a slice of my second helping and chewed without tasting. Again, Pa was right. It was going to be a humdinger of a few days.

Maybe I'd go fishing with Old Sheriff Larimore.

★ ★ ★ ★ ★

The sun came up way too early for my liking. Cheerful and unwelcome dawn poured through the window, tossing golden shadows all around my bedroom. I growled and pulled the covers over my head, then thought better of it, admitting, no matter how much I whined, I had things to do.

Check on Seth.

Head the posse.

Ask someone to watch the prisoners.

Find my *escaped* prisoners.

Arrest the judge's attacker.

Enough for anybody's "to do" list. And that was simply for starters. Real soon I'd have to worry about the Fourth of July "big doings." The sun'd had time to dry the muddy roads and possibly erase any tracks. We'd have to look carefully to find our man. Correction. *Men.*

Dressed and coiffed, I said good-bye to Pa, who was none too happy with me after I explained I might be gone a few days. I waved a hello to Mrs. Stevenson, who was arriving for her day's work. What an angel she was turning out to be. And a darn good cook. Kind of like having a ma, again.

Provisions and bedroll under one arm, I gathered my dark-brown skirt, one I'd chosen because it didn't show much mud and dirt, and rushed down to Doc's and let myself in. Nothing had changed, he reported, adding that could be a good sign. Or not.

What I'd envisioned was Seth sitting in the parlor, reading last week's *Sacramento Daily Union* and sipping Charity's tea. Possibly of the Irish persuasion. He'd flash me his famous politician's smile, which always melted me into my shoes.

But it didn't happen. I left depressed.

My spirits picked up, slightly, when I spotted six men waiting for me in front of my office. True to his word, town councilman and saloon owner Slim Higginbotham was there, along with five other men. All rarin' to go, if jovial conversation was any indication. By the sounds of their chatter, you'd have thought they'd already started celebrating our country's birthday. Maybe they'd been nipping the local cherry whiskey.

I deposited my armload of supplies onto the boardwalk and took a brief survey of the posse. Dependable, solid men. All of whom had ridden with me previously.

Slim ambled next to me, cocking his head toward my office. "Weinberg and MacKinney volunteered to watch the jail."

I chuckled at the emphasis he put on *"volunteered."* How much arm twisting and vote getting had they taken into account before they both agreed when I asked? But that was one more item checked off my "to do" list.

Before I climbed into the saddle, I gave the posse a quick rundown of what to expect. We *knew* who we were chasing and who we *thought* we were chasing. I pictured James Mooney as the assailant. Perhaps, it would turn out to be somebody else, but my gut instincts pointed to Mooney.

"Let's go, Sheriff." Slim handed me May Belle's reins. "While you were talking, I took the liberty of loading your gear. Hope you didn't mind."

Why would I mind?

"Faster we get going, Maud, sooner we catch 'em." Slim offered me a foot up into the saddle. With his heave, I about flew over the horse, but I grabbed the saddle horn before ending up on the street.

Instead of butterflies fluttering in my stomach, like the last time, knots of dread and apprehension took their place. This was serious business and, more than likely, one of us would get shot or even killed. I hoped no one would get seriously hurt, but it was clear there would be bruises.

CHAPTER FIFTY-THREE:
BRUISES

As the last house disappeared from view, I spotted three sets of hoof prints. Were these our fellas? I pulled to a stop and slid from the saddle to inspect the tracks. Definitely three horses recently trotted through the mud before it dried.

"You think these're from yesterday afternoon?" I squatted by the prints and played with the drying mud. "Know anything about tracking, Slim?"

Slim Higginbotham and two other men joined me, all contemplating, I supposed, who was the best tracker. As if any. Slim gazed thoughtfully up the road.

"I'd say it's them. Don't do much tracking, but look here." He pointed to a slick spot in back of the print. "They're running full out, I'd say. Not walking. Yep. Definitely three of 'em. Running."

The others agreed, grunting manspeak, all seeming to know what each grunt meant. I stood, wiping my dirty hands on my skirt. Not a very ladylike thing to do, but right now it was a sheriff-like thing to do.

"Think they're hiding out by the stream, where we found Smith and Doyle last time?"

More grunts from the men. Slim shrugged. "Maybe. But it's not very smart of 'em. I mean, they gotta figure that's the first place we're gonna look."

"Criminals aren't smart," I said. "We'll do like last time. Stop back aways from the cabin and sneak in from all sides." More knots fisted in my stomach. This wasn't nearly as much fun. Last time, I had no idea what I was getting into. Now, I did.

We mounted again and rode in silence to the bottom of the hill. The cabin was on the other side. I gave further instructions, sent two men around one side, one around back to look for horses, two around the other, and Slim and I again took the front.

Sidling up to the door, we stood on either side. I pulled out my gun, using it to knock.

"Smith. Doyle. Mooney. Come on out. With your hands up. You're surrounded." A tiny shiver ran down my spine. Calling them out, being in charge, was exciting—but scary, too.

I waited. Silence. No door opening, no rustling around inside, no windows creaking open for men to escape. Nothing.

I tried, again. Same commands. Again, same response. Maybe these men were smarter than common lawbreakers. Right. They weren't common, everyday lawbreakers—these were proven murderers, jail breakers, robbers with lots of experience. I should give them a little more respect, not get too confident of their stupidity and of my "levelheadedness." That arrogance could get me or the others killed.

I took a deep breath, my thumb on the hammer, ready to pull back and shoot. I tried the door handle. Unlocked. I pushed and it swung open.

"Smith? Doyle?" I eased in, Slim on my heels. "Mooney? We know you're here. Come on out."

We checked under the bed, shook out the piles of bedding still wadded on the floor, even looked behind the single chair. Obviously, nobody had been here since the last time we'd stopped by.

I holstered my gun and stepped outside.

"Now what?" I said more to myself than the men who gathered around.

"Go back and check those tracks." Councilman Slim holstered his revolver and cocked his head toward the road. "Must've missed something."

More man-grunting, some I understood to mean the rest agreed. We had missed something. I dug a biscuit out of my saddlebag and munched, while Slim squatted in the road. Two men joined him, discussing the tracks, the rain and Seth's bashed-in head. My frustration turned to resolve. I *would* find whoever hurt Seth and shot the judge. They'd be brought to justice.

By the time I'd finished the snack, I knew this wasn't going to be as easy as the last time. Our fugitive was proving to be smarter than we'd given him credit for. Had to be James Mooney.

The tracks continued on past the cabin for a good ten miles, veering away from Dutch Flats where the road turned south, off toward a forested area known as "Shirt-Tail Bend." I supposed there was a big bend in the road but, since I'd never been there, it was a mystery. The men didn't know how it'd got its name, and only one of the posse members had even been so far. I looked forward to seeing what was up ahead.

However, with more and more trees, and more and more miles, the sun slipped toward the horizon. We followed faint tracks. The escapees had a good lead on us and, as much as I didn't want to stop for the day, we couldn't see. Grudgingly, I called a halt.

"We'll set up here for the night." I pointed toward a creek running close to the road. "There's a nice wide spot right over there where we can pitch some tents." It hit me. Did we even have tents? I certainly didn't.

"Nobody brought tents, Maud," Slim Higginbotham said, exasperation and fatigue tinging his words. He grunted out of his saddle. "Not to worry, though. Looks like it won't rain tonight."

Stars blinked through the dark-gray evening. While I unsaddled May Belle, the men went about making a small fire, heating water and setting up their bedrolls. I unrolled a wool blanket and spread it near the fire. I would stay warm tonight.

The evening passed quickly and I fell asleep much easier than I'd anticipated. Bone tired did that, I supposed.

I awoke to men's murmurs and boiling coffee aroma. I could barely see my hand in front of my face and the men around the fire were more shadows than shapes. Getting off the ground was a challenge. My back popped and ached in places reserved for old people. My legs still wobbled, but now they also hurt. I'd be saddle sore for days. My ribs ached with each breath, but I wouldn't let the men see me wince. I'd be strong and tough, like them.

But first . . . coffee.

We rode all that day, heading south and eventually west. Three sets of tracks.

Then, we lost them. How was that possible? The road dried out, leaving nothing but dust, blowing about in a strong wind that set our nerves on edge. I split the group, some backtracking, some forging ahead and the rest of us fanning out into the forest.

By mid-day the third day, we were done. Enough was enough. Some of my posse had to get back to wives and businesses. As it was, the return trip would be just as long.

We stopped at a wide bend in the road, which we assumed was the area Shirt Tail Bend was named for, and tried talking to a single prospector panning for gold. Addlepated. Too long alone and isolated. I should've chatted with his three mules. They would've made more sense.

I couldn't admit defeat. I couldn't ride back into Dry Creek empty handed. What would I tell the citizens? What would I tell Pa? What would I tell the judge? And Pokey? And Seth?

The seven of us stopped a mile down the road past the prospector.

"Men. We gotta face facts." I hated saying this. "They got away. Smith and Doyle and their accomplice are gone. We'll never find them again."

Bobbing heads didn't make me feel better. They'd probably been ready to turn around long before me, but I'd pushed them on, insisting we'd succeed.

"Maud, look at it this way," Slim said. "Least we know they ain't around here. Don't worry. They'll surface sooner or later."

"But, the town council's gonna take my badge—"

"I'll put in a good word." Slim puffed up. "After all, I *am* one-third of the commission." He winked. "Don't worry."

"That's right," one of the men shrugged. "Sometimes they get away."

Another helpful soul chimed in. "And if they come back into Dry Creek, we'll get 'em, Maud. You're good to ride with. We'll follow you any time."

My saddle seemed to aggravate me a little less, and I smiled.

Chapter Fifty-Four:
Sin

We rode into town under darkness two nights later. Our horses seemed to know intuitively where their hay and homes were. I gave May Belle her head and she strutted to the livery stable like a queen who'd been out of the country sightseeing.

Feeling nothing like a queen myself, more tired and dirty than I could remember, I mumbled a thanks-and-good-bye to the men, as they moseyed on home. Turning over May Belle's reins to Swede Swensen, I made a beeline to Doc's. Now close to a week since the attack, I had no idea what I would find.

Smoothing my skirt and my hair, hopeless of staying tucked up under my hat, I trudged down the boardwalk, eyeballing a couple of dusty miners lingering in front of a saloon. I sure hoped they weren't about to cause trouble, because I was too exhausted to care.

My thoughts turned to Pokey. I'd assumed he was up and about, pretty much healed by now. Though he'd also been bludgeoned, he wasn't in as bad a shape as Seth. I sent a silent prayer upward for both of these friends, who meant so much to me. I included the judge for good measure.

I knocked at Doc's door. Tommy opened it and ushered me in. "Howdy, Miss Maud, Sheriff ma'am." Tommy's adolescent voice cracked as he led me toward the parlor. "Pa's back here."

A napping Dr. Monroe roused and stood, his newspaper falling from his lap. We shook hands.

"Success?" Doc bent over and scooped up the pages.

I shook my head. "Lost their tracks about three days from

here." The question I'd been dreading all the way over had to be asked. "How's Seth?"

"One lucky son of a gun." Doc's smile stretched cheek to cheek. "Sent him home this morning. Still got a powerful headache and two shiners, but he'll be good as new in no time."

A wave of relief sent air rushing from my chest. "How about Pokey?"

"Thick head. He's gonna be all right, too. Been helping out over at the jail." Doc waggled the paper toward a darkened room down the hall. "And Richfield's going to be all right, too, although that arm . . . gonna take a long time to get even partial use again." He tsked. "Damn shame." He glanced over his shoulder as Charity walked in.

"Maud," she said. "Good to see you in one piece. You look tired."

"Long, long ride." Exhaustion filled my body. Would I even be able to drag home? Maybe I could sleep right here on her floor tonight. With effort, I pointed a thumb over my shoulder toward the door. "I'll check on Seth at his house, then go home."

Charity stepped closer, her narrowed eyes cluing me there was more to the story. "He's not at his house, Maud."

I frowned. "Where is he?"

She cleared her throat. "At Pearl's. She's been taking real good care of him." She leaned in my ear and whispered. "I hear tell he's living with her. In sin."

Now I was really confused. Was Pearl simply helping an old friend, or taking advantage of the situation? And taking advantage of Seth? Or had she lied to me? I wanted to tell Charity I'd heard Pearl was now engaged—and not to Seth Critoli—but I kept my mouth shut. Which was really hard to do. Such gossip was almost too juicy to contain. But it wasn't my news to share.

I chewed on my lip.

★ ★ ★ ★ ★

Pearl opened the door on the first knock. With a wide smile, she took both of my hands and drew me inside. Seth sat on a brocade sofa, his bandaged head making him look like a king with a crown. Black bruises cascading down both cheeks made his dark eyes appear darker. He staggered up and wrapped me in a hug. His arms smothered all doubts and misgivings I'd had. He still liked me.

Pearl disappeared into the kitchen. Her voice sailed out like a disembodied spirit. "I'll get you some tea. Seth and I already finished supper, but tea is always the perfect nightcap."

"I'd like some. Thank you." I sat beside Seth as he eased himself down— as though he was made of eggshells and would shatter if touched.

Seth took my hand. Its softness and warmth melted into my arm, spreading upward until I could hardly think. It reminded me of Eli's touch. Tugging my hand away, I struggled to say something meaningful.

"Doc says you'll be fine." Was that the best I had? What I wanted to say was I hadn't found the man who'd nearly killed him and I hadn't found my escaped prisoners and Pearl was engaged and, for Pete's sake, what was he doing staying here anyway? Why aren't you home with your ma?

But I didn't.

"That's what he says." Seth touched the bandage. "My noggin doesn't agree, though. Hurts like sin."

"I'll bet," I said. "Your ma's got salves and potions for injuries like yours, doesn't she?" Was that too obvious? He flat didn't need to be here, alone, with Pearl.

"She does, but . . ." he gazed at Pearl. "I'll go home later."

Uh huh, sure is what I wanted to say. But I kept more irritating comments to myself and asked instead, "Do you know who buffaloed you? And why were you in the alley in the first place?"

Seth leaned back, accepting a fresh cup from Pearl, another to me. I smiled a thanks, sipped as she sat across from us. Seth's voice was soft. "Remember that pretend lawyer, who caused all the problems?"

I cocked my head, definitely not liking where this was going.

"Well, I spotted the same fella heading for the courthouse. I followed him, to ask why he'd cleared out so sudden-like, and figuring he might be up to no good. He sneaked into the alley and, sure enough, he'd stashed a rifle under a bush near the wall." Seth stopped for a second sip of tea.

"Was it a Winchester?" Men somehow seemed to *know* these things.

"Sure was. A nice one," Seth said.

"And this was all before the afternoon part of the trial started?" I could hardly contain myself. I had been right. James Mooney.

Seth spoke slowly. "Guess he hid around the corner when he heard me coming into the alley." He rubbed his left temple. "That's all I remember, until I woke up at Doc's."

"I filled him in on the rest," Pearl said. "The judge's attack, your posse tracking them. The crowd of reporters."

"What?" I sat up straight. "What reporters?"

Pearl frowned at my ridiculous question. "The ones who keep piling into town asking about the near killing of a famous judge . . . and why the posse was led by a woman."

"They still around?" If I stayed here longer, maybe they'd go away.

"Yep," Pearl said. "And more by the day."

Seth had to jump in. "I hear, with you being . . . a *woman* and all, the attempt on the judge, a mayor being clobbered and the gold strike bringing so many people into town, plus the fandango the town council's planning, why, the whole town's making a story as fine as cream gravy."

Great. I stood and somehow made my way into the kitchen, putting my mostly-empty cup into the sink. Energy drained, at this particular moment I didn't really care if Seth and Pearl *were* living in sin. I'd care tomorrow.

I muttered a *so long*. My last stop would be my office to see if any more prisoners had escaped.

Pokey sat at the desk, feet propped up on top, smoking a cigar and reading. He closed the dime novel. "You're back!" He slammed his feet on the floor and jumped up, giving me a quick cupped hand on the arm. "Any luck?"

I shook my head. "Got away clean. Followed them past Shirt-Tail Bend but lost the trail."

A quick look into the cells revealed a full house. Pokey had been busy.

"Got nine boarders." Pokey waved his arm, like presenting celebrities. "Everybody who was in here before you left paid their fines and for their food. Got new ones since you've been gone."

Great. More paperwork.

Trembling with fatigue, I had to go home. Had to get to bed.

"Glad you're all right," I said. "I'll be back in the morning."

"Before you go," Pokey handed me his dime novel. "You should read this. It's good! Just finished it."

I didn't have time to read, but when I did, I enjoyed the short stories, the trials and tribulations of some dashing and daring hero saving the day.

"This one," Pokey said, "has a bank robbery in it. During a big town celebration. They blow up the bank during the fireworks. Pretty exciting!"

"Think I already read it, but sounds exciting." I accepted the novel with a thanks. But I wanted to get home.

I turned the doorknob, the door swung open, and three men with notepads and pencils bustled inside.

"Sheriff Maud? Heard you're back. I'm from the *Sacramento Daily Union*. So . . ." His gaze traveled up and down my body. "You're a woman."

"I am." I didn't want to be there, right then. I wanted to be at home, sleeping. "Thanks for noticing." My sarcasm dripped.

"I meant woman sheriff." The reporter shrugged. "Never heard of one." He glanced toward the cells. "Where's the real sheriff at?"

Another man scribble-scratched something on his pad. "The *Fresno Telegraph* wants to know if you took this job from your husband. Was he killed?"

A third reporter moved in so close, I had to back up. "Where'd *you* go, while the posse was out searching? Did they catch their man?"

I manufactured, undoubtedly, the world's heaviest sigh.

This was going to be one long night.

CHAPTER FIFTY-FIVE:
ABIGAIL

Early morning rays pierced my narrowed eyes, as I bent to tug a weed from my carrot patch. On my way to the privy, the scraggly dandelion had caught my attention. I yanked.

"Takin' your posse out again today?"

I jumped and spun around like a drunken dust devil, only the top half of the dandelion clutched in my hand. Another dang reporter leaned on the fence, pencil and pad in hand, smirking.

Shading my eyes, I took in the man's form. Slender, bowler hat canted on his rounded head, frayed vest over a white shirt. What I'd always envisioned as a typical journalist.

He licked the end of his pencil, poised it over the paper, and raised a shaggy eyebrow. "Goin' searchin' for those reprobates, again? Are ya, Sheriff?"

I mumbled a *no*, excused myself and set my sights on the privy. Surely he'd be gentleman enough not to follow.

When I emerged, fifteen minutes later, not only was he still there but so were three of his cronies, hovering like bees harvesting one lone flower. I dodged a barrage of questions as I raced to the house. Slamming the back door on the swarm, I knew the coffee pot would be my salvation. I aimed for it.

I poured a steaming cup, sat at the table and smelled breakfast cooking. This afternoon, I'd pay Seth a visit and get some campaigning tips from him. The Fourth of July celebration would be a great opportunity to launch "Vote For Maud." Elections were the end of July, so I still had plenty of time to get the word out. Shake hands and kiss babies.

Babies. A familiar knot tugged at my heart. I wanted a baby. I wanted a husband. But . . . did I really? I thought I wanted Eli, but shreds of doubt clung to my mind. Would he be good husband material? Was he steady? Treat his family right? Did he even have a job, other than cowboying, which you took on only when you couldn't find a *real* job?

If he came riding into town on the Fourth of July, a wide smile on his face, his white horse prancing amid the band and pie eating contest, and popped "The Question," would I say yes?

What *would* I say?

And what if it was Seth doing the asking?

I let out a long sigh and realized my fork was suspended mid-air, halfway to my face.

Humming softly, Mrs. Stevenson rattled pans and dishes in the kitchen. Blinking back into the present, I looked at my speared scrambled eggs.

With the extra help, home had turned again into a clean, organized, safe harbor from the world. My office usually provided the same, but lately it was filled with newshounds and drunken cowboys. Not real conducive to shutting out the world.

Mrs. Stevenson appeared with two cups of steaming coffee. "Thought you could use a fresh cup." She set one in front of me. "Mind if I join you?"

I stuffed the fork into my mouth and pointed to a chair. "Please do." It wasn't ladylike to talk over food, either, but lately I wasn't feeling very ladylike.

She eased to the chair, sipped her coffee and stared toward the window. I continued to eat, while she continued to observe whatever the garden view had to offer. I searched for conversation starters and chose a benign one.

"Where'd you learn to cook like this? I mean, you're pretty

young, right?" *Young* being a relative term. I figured she was easily ten years my junior, making me feel ancient.

"Thanks." She ducked her head and produced a genuine grin. "I was in charge of the family after Ma . . . went away. So, guess I've been cooking and tending most of my life."

"Sorry to hear about your ma," I said. "I know what it feels like to lose her." And I did.

Somehow, there was a hole left in your heart and nothing could fill it.

She looked back at the garden, then turned reporter on me. "You like being sheriff? What's been your scariest moment? You gonna try to get elected sheriff, again?"

Had she been listening in on my life? I clanked my fork onto the plate, wiped my mouth with a napkin and leaned back. How much should I answer? I needed to get to the office and why would she care, anyway? She was probably voicing concerns other people had.

"Here's the thing . . ." I stopped, realizing I had no idea what her first name was. Searching my memory, I came up blank. "What's your front name?"

She laughed. "Abigail. After my grandma."

"Well, Abigail, I do mostly enjoy being sheriff, except for breaking up fights and arresting people. But I do it, you know, to protect the citizens. As for running again, I didn't run in the first place. Town council asked me. Turns out, it was a gag they were playing on me. Seems the council was bored, and not much was going on around here. They thought it would be a good joke to have me as sheriff, until election time rolled around."

"I'm thinkin' the joke's on them, Sheriff. I hear tell you're doin' a plum fine job."

I straightened my shoulders and cleared my throat.

Abigail leaned forward like she was interested. "You gonna

run for real, this time?"

"Sure am. Fact is, I'm going to start campaigning during the big celebration."

"You've got my vote." Abigail's face clouded. "If I could vote, that is."

An awkward silence fell on us. I got to thinking women should be allowed to vote and also, if I couldn't vote, how could I hold such an esteemed office? The answers jumbled my head. About the time I gave up, Abigail's next question came from out of the blue.

"You ever gonna get married?"

That stopped me. I'd never considered not marrying. I'd always assumed being a wife and mother were in the stars. Now, of course, being sheriff was a new role. I hated these kinds of dilemmas. I shrugged.

"If the right fella comes along, I'd consider it," I said. And meant it. But would I really give up my tin star? Hang up my gun? I finished my coffee and scooted back the chair. Its wooden legs screeched against the polished floorboards. A rug would be nice under the table. I made a mental note to talk to Pa.

A knock at the door startled both of us. Seeing as I was standing, I answered it. One of the doctor's children stood with an envelope in hand.

"Got a special letter for Mrs. Stevenson, ma'am." He held it up but kept his grip tight. "Mr. Maguire from the mail office sent me right over with it."

"She's inside, Tommy. I'll give it to her." I reached for it, but he jerked it away.

"Supposed to give it to her and her only." He eyed me up and down. "But being you're the sheriff and all, guess it'll be all right to give it to you." Half of a smile crinkled his cheeks. "And you've been to my house."

I let out a chuckle, dug into my skirt pocket for a penny,

exchanged it for the envelope. He turned and trotted away, pocketing his new fortune.

As I walked into the parlor, a quick glance at the handwriting startled me. No return address, but I was sure I knew who the sender was. Elijah J. Goodman. *My* Eli.

Couldn't be. I examined the curlicues. Sure looked like his.

Abigail glanced at the envelope, plucked it out of my hand like it was a dirty handkerchief, and stuffed it into her apron pocket. She tossed me a quick smile. "It's from my cousin. Lonely, I guess." She patted her pocket. "I'll read it later."

Was Eli her cousin? I thought back. Well, he had two brothers somewhere or other, but he'd never mentioned cousins. What was I thinking? That wasn't Eli's handwriting. I looked at Abigail, whose eyes flicked away. I had to ask.

"What's his name?"

There was no hesitation. "Jeremiah Whitson."

Hmmm. Jeremiah. Eli J. Goodman. Interesting. Eli's middle name was John.

I made for the front door as Abigail tagged along.

She handed me my bonnet and leaned in close. "Seeing as you're the bank president's daughter . . . and sheriff . . . I have a question. My cousin," she tapped her pocket. "Well, he's thinking of moving here and he wants to know if the bank's really a secure enough place to keep his money. I went in again yesterday, talked to your pa and he showed me all around . . . even the safe and all, but I mean, now my cousin's got a few dollars saved . . . Well, he'd hate to lose them."

I tied the ribbons under my chin. "Don't worry. My pa won't let anything happen."

Abigail stepped outside with me. "There's talk around town about the big Fourth shindigs. I was wonderin' . . . I mean about your plans, in case the bank gets robbed." She held up a hand. "I'm not meanin' anything by it. It's only that I've been reading one of those dime novels—"

"I know, me, too. Bank's robbed during fireworks." I supposed there was only one dime novel around and we'd all read it.

Abigail shrugged. "Wondering if you've thought about it."

"Don't worry. No fireworks this Fourth. Nobody who can do it." I waved a good-bye and stepped into a soft summer morning.

I hadn't given much thought to a bank robbery. But I sure as shootin' would now.

Chapter Fifty-Six:
A Good Turn

From what I'd seen so far this morning, there must've been fifteen different newshounds from all over the state and territories clamoring for a story. I didn't see the big deal. Just because I wore a skirt and cared about my hair didn't mean I wasn't sheriff material. The more I thought on it, the more I truly wanted this job, and the more important it became to me.

I elbowed my way into my office, past the gaggle of reporters camped out on the boardwalk. Whew! Wouldn't those hacks ever get tired and leave? What other stories could there possibly be? But, the men were good for business, buying food and drink and hotel rooms. I was sure the town council was pleased.

With a week to go before the Fourth of July, more and more ranch hands, stray cowboys, miners, prospectors, ladies of questionable virtue, shopkeepers, push-cart vendors, reporters and even whole families wandered into town. Even a Chinese laundry opened up. Tents sprung up, flap to flap, camped all over the hillsides, even in the apple and cherry orchards, some nestled up as close as possible to the stills.

Samuel Goldstein, owner of the Dry Creek Hotel, tacked up a sign declaring he now rented rooms in halves and quarters. If a visitor didn't mind sharing a bed with a stranger or two, then they'd have a place to lay their heads. Of course, they all paid the full price. Otherwise, the nearest hotel was over in Dutch Flats, twenty miles away.

As I nudged a couple wanted posters around on my desk, the

door flew open. Slim Higginbotham squeezed through and put his back against the door. Reporters tried to push in. Slim won.

Motioning to an empty chair in front of my desk, I stood. Slim always seemed to enjoy my coffee; I automatically filled a cup for him.

"Quite a crowd out there," he said, wiping a trickle of sweat from his sideburn. When I handed him a cup, his eyes returned to the inside of the office. "You know we have nobody to run fireworks, not since Old Man Gruber died."

"I heard." I eased into my chair. Where was he going with this? And why should I care?

One of Slim's eyebrows arched. "You know the Yuans, the Chinese who run the laundry?"

"Uh huh."

"What would you say to us hiring some of them?"

"For fireworks?" I sat forward so quickly coffee sloshed onto the desk. "Do we hafta have fireworks?"

"They offered . . . for a price. Can't have a Fourth without fireworks." Slim aimed his cup toward the window. "Said they shot off displays back home in China and brought some from San Francisco."

All right. A firecracker or two, a single skyrocket would be fine. But more than that . . . I wasn't so sure. "How many?"

Slim turned into a six-year-old in front of me. "A crateful! Biggest we've ever had! Go way up in the air! And firecrackers. Lots of firecrackers! They're even gonna do a Lion dance and a Dragon one, too."

Great. What the heck was a Lion dance? Surely, they didn't use real ones. I'd best have a chat with the one Yuan who spoke English.

"Town council's been talking, Maud. There's money set aside, as you know. Enough for the fireworks."

"So, you want my blessing?" Visions of bank robberies flew

around my head.

"I wanted you to know what we're doing. Don't go around arresting our celestial yellow brethrens, if you see fuses in their hands."

Terrific. Exactly what we needed. First a lion, then a dragon. And now . . . fireworks.

I swore I'd learn to fish.

CHAPTER FIFTY-SEVEN:
CONSPIRATORS

All right. If we're going to have fireworks, we may have a bank robbery. I was jittery. Three times now, I'd heard about bank robberies. I had to make a plan . . . just in case.

Pokey, Seth, Pa and I needed to sit down and strategize. I figured the fewer people who knew the plans, the more likely they were to be kept secret. If I included the three town councilors in on our little meeting, well, it was pretty certain within minutes the entire town would know. I'd bring them in only if absolutely necessary.

Which brought up my next problem. The four of us couldn't meet in my office because of all the criminals and reporters swarming around. We couldn't meet at the bank because that would be too obvious. Seth, tired of Mama Critoli mothering him nearly to death, was still at Pearl's and Pokey didn't really have a place, which left my house.

I invited Seth and Pokey to Pa's house, where the four of us could talk over supper. Maybe Mrs. Stevenson would bake one of her famous chocolate cakes, like those becoming popular in the Old States—New York, for one. I'd read in the Sacramento newspaper they now added chocolate to icing. San Francisco bakers were going crazy with new chocolate inventions. Due to quicker transportation these days, commodities such as Mexican chocolate were more commonplace on grocers' shelves. And the prices were becoming reasonable.

We set the meeting for the next evening. The cover story—in

case anyone, namely, the nosey newspapermen, asked—was I was thanking both Pokey and Seth for their help. In reality, I probably didn't need a cover story, but it was sort of exciting—definitely of dime-novel mystique.

A knock at the door pushed me to my feet. I opened it wide.

"Pokey. Seth." I hugged each and matched their smiles. "Thanks for coming."

They shook hands with Pa and Pokey lowered his rounded body to where I pointed on the sofa. He patted his stomach. "I'll do pretty much anything for a fried chicken supper."

"Me, too," said Seth. He sat at the opposite end of the sofa, where we would wait for Mrs. Stevenson to call us in. Normally, she didn't stay during our evening meal, instead preferring to eat at the boarding house, where she lived alone, waiting for her husband to hit a gold strike and send for her. Pa had offered a bonus to her weekly pay, if she'd stay to serve this evening. She'd agreed, a bit too eagerly. Must really need the cash, I figured.

While the four of us waited in the parlor, smells and crackles of chicken frying melded with cooking potato aromas and what I hoped was chocolate cake. I began to salivate.

At long last, Mrs. Stevenson called supper and I was the first to the table. She'd set out the good company dishes and our best forks and knives, which sparkled with all the polishing she'd done. Aromas of yeast rolls sailed around the room. Compliments caused Abigail to blush, as she scurried off to the kitchen for the remainder of the dishes.

Soon, in front of us sat the biggest plate of chicken I'd ever seen. Had to have been half a flock. A heaping mound of mashed potatoes accompanied steaming turnip greens. The heavenly aroma was laced with snippets of dill and sage. Lettuce, accented with radishes and baby carrots—all out of our garden—rounded out the meal. It was a feast fit for royalty.

Our plates piled sufficiently high, we dug in, obviously famished, a long day of working slumping our shoulders. Gravy clung to Pokey's beard, turning strands of his hairy chin from light brown to lumpy, dark brown.

A couple bites of heavenly chicken, then I swallowed potatoes. "I talked to each of you, briefly, about my concerns for next week. Look at how many new people are already in town."

"Gonna be a whole lot more," Pokey said. "I hear a group from Dutch Flats're coming over 'cause of our barbecue." He flashed a wide grin. "Hiram's sauce is legendary."

I was impressed by Pokey's use of "legendary." He probably didn't know exactly what it meant, but he was right. Hiram Dillon's barbecue sauce made everyone sit up and take notice.

"What about the bank?" Pa placed his fork on the rim of his plate and peered over his glasses perched on the end of his nose. "I feel like a sitting duck." His brown eyes cut to me. "What's the plan to guard it?"

"That's what we gotta figure out."

Seth sipped his fresh-squeezed lemonade. His head was still kept together with a wide bandage, but his black eyes had turned into streaks of green and yellow. He was on the mend.

"What makes you think there's gonna be any trouble, Maud?" One of Seth's eyebrows arched, the other still hidden under gauze. "I mean, did somebody send you a letter or something?"

I hated his sarcasm at times like this. He could be so unfunny.

" 'Course not." I pointed my fork at him and then toward town. "Doesn't mean nobody's planning to. We need to be prepared is all."

"I agree." Pa speared a carrot with his fork. "Can't be too careful nowadays." His scrutiny alternated between Pokey and Seth. "Leastways, it's *your* money that'd be lost, if someone robbed the bank."

Well, things were certainly put in proper perspective, now. Both Pokey and Seth stopped chewing, sat upright and frowned. Guess they didn't like the idea very much. Pa had a way of getting right to the heart of the matter.

Mrs. Stevenson appeared with a pitcher of fresh lemonade and I let a couple of beats fill the room, as she refilled the glasses. Leaning forward, I lowered my voice. "I've got an idea, but it's kind of odd. Hear me out all the way, then tell me what you think."

Nods all around. Mrs. Stevenson returned to the kitchen and I began.

"Seems to me, if I were a robber, I'd wait until night, with all the fireworks and bands and people in the street. And a dragon dance. I'd kick in the back door, open the safe and ride away. Nobody'd miss anything until the next day. By then, I'd be long gone." I reflected, adding, "And I wouldn't bring in many men. Wouldn't want to call attention to myself."

"Exactly," Seth said, caught up in the plans. "Two, maybe three. One as a lookout in front, the other two to do the real robbing." He shook a fork at me. "I like it."

Pokey waved a roll at him. "You sound like a robber, yourself."

Seth let out an exasperated sigh. "What I mean is, it makes sense." He looked from face to face to face. "So, how do we keep this from happening?"

"Post someone in the bank? A deputy with a big shotgun?" Pokey sopped up a last pool of gravy with his bread. "I could do it."

"I'm not comfortable with that," I said. Having Pokey being the "sitting duck," as Pa had so aptly put it, didn't set well with me. We'd have to come up with another plan.

"Pa," I asked. "How hard's it to break into your vault? I mean . . . can anybody open it?"

He paused, staring at his plate, his fork swirling through mashed potato remnants. Finally, he raised one eyebrow. "Pretty hard to crack. It's a Herring and Company—one of their newer models. They say the metal's the stoutest and toughest wrought bar and plate iron." Pa set his fork across his plate, wiped his mouth with our best cloth napkin and lowered his voice.

"Cost a pretty penny, too. But with the right drilling equipment, you might be able to open 'er up. Take some doing, though."

"Herring," Seth said. "Heard of them. Good safes."

"Herring or no Herring." Pokey jabbed his chest with his spoon. "Nobody's gettin' past me, when I'm guardin' the bank. Nobody."

And then I had it. I glanced toward the kitchen. Abigail's soft hum told me she probably wasn't listening in, certainly not paying us any attention.

"Seth." I leaned forward. "Here's what we're gonna do. You'll be out front, looking like you're watching the festivities."

"But I'll really be watchin' the bank. Make sure it doesn't get robbed." Seth's face lit up like the fireworks I sensed he'd be watching.

"And Pa, you and Pokey will be around back and down the alley." I figured the two of them could handle any misdirected soul who tried to get in.

Pa frowned, shaking his head. "What'll you be doing? Don't tell me *you're* going to be inside. Alone. Not with those curly wolves around."

"Bad men are everywhere, Pa. We got the drop on them because we know they're coming. The way I see it, everybody's gonna be expecting me to be on the boardwalk, but I'll be inside, pretty as you please." My cheeks warmed at my own pun. "Any would-be robber worth half his salt, even those curly wolves, would know to stay away, if I wasn't out in public." I shrugged, hoping the doubt invading my chest wasn't obvious. "Nothing to worry about."

The three men sputtered and stuttered, each mulling over their assignments. I didn't think any of them wanted to have a girl guarding the vault, but they weren't brave enough to really say so. It was dangerous, I knew. But standing outside or at the bank's back door was dangerous, too.

Being sheriff in general was dangerous. Apparently, I thrived on danger.

But now . . . I had a plan. I lifted my glass.

"Here's to us. Saviors of Dry Creek." We clinked. Yep. It would be all right.

From my seat, if I craned my neck, I could see into the kitchen. Mrs. Stevenson, in her shawl and bonnet, was backing out of the door, easing it shut. It *was* kind of late and I supposed she would clean up from supper, in the morning. I started to wave and then thought better of it. I'd see her tomorrow.

CHAPTER FIFTY-EIGHT:
I Do Declare!

With no more than a couple more days before the Fourth, I relaxed into worrying about my re-election campaign only. I needed a strategy that was surefire. When campaigning, I had to play down the judge's shooting and my prisoners' escape. That ugly event hung around my neck like the old Mariner's albatross. I'd probably lose the election because of it. Not one for much stretching of the blanket, I told the truth, even if it caused me grief later on. No, I'd not lie to retain my position as sheriff. My actions would have to speak for themselves.

Yep, I was in trouble.

As I hurried across the street toward Seth's office, another covey of correspondents swarmed around me.

"You give up on catchin' that gunman, Sheriff Overstreet?"

"What about the escapees?"

"You ready for the big shindig? What happens if there's trouble?"

"You running for re-election?"

"You gonna stay home and bake pies for a change? Like a normal woman?"

I screeched to a stop in mid-stride. Enough was enough. I'd set these yahoos on their tails, send them packing. There was no story here.

I wanted to pull my gun and shoot them, or curse them, or at least yell impolite and unladylike things. I straightened my shoulders and faced the first man. But I changed my mind.

Suddenly, I was glad they'd stayed. Now was as good a time as any.

"Gentlemen," I said, taking time to make eye contact with each reporter. "I'd like to thank you for your interest in Dry Creek . . . and in me, personally." The intended sarcasm flopped onto the boardwalk, unnoticed. "I do have a statement to make."

They whipped out pencils and notepads. Heads canted, brows furrowed, pencils poised. Passersby stopped to gawk.

"This past spring, as you know, I was asked to become Dry Creek's sheriff to fill out the previous sheriff's term. This I did willingly, not one to shirk my civic duty for our great little town. And to show women can do anything a man can do. Maybe better."

"But you didn't catch—"

"Even men sheriffs aren't always successful. Most of all," I said, "I'm not done looking, yet."

Raised eyebrows shoved bowler hats farther up foreheads. Pencils scritch-scratched across paper.

Several non-reporters crowded around. I continued, hoping I wouldn't be interrupted, again. This was harder than I'd anticipated. "Despite the challenges of being a female sheriff, I've enjoyed my months in office."

"You ever getting married, Sheriff?"

Flashing narrowed eyes at the varmint, I continued. "These months have shown me a different side of life. One in which I am proud to have participated. So . . . I am hereby officially announcing my candidacy to run as sheriff for the next term. A full three years."

You would've thought I'd announced the end of the world. Rapid-fire questions hammered. I spouted short answers until my ears rang. Finally, I held up a hand. "I'll have more to say once I've spoken with my campaign manager."

Why did I say that? I didn't have a campaign manager. Not

officially. In fact, I hadn't even asked Seth, yet, if he'd help me.

"Who's your manager, Sheriff?"

"Your pa?"

"Another woman?"

"Or somebody qualified?"

I ignored their ridiculous insinuations, and only smiled—tightly. I spent a moment or two debating whether I should set them straight. And this is what I'd have to look forward to? I clenched my jaw and raised my eyebrows. Their absurdity and insults pushed aside, insincere, China-doll smile still plastered on my face, I was surprised at my own composure. "That's all I've got for now, gentlemen." I pushed through a dozen. "Thank you."

Changing my mind about going to Seth's, I made an about-face, aimed for my office and managed to slam the door before the horde pushed its way in. Knowing I'd have to deal with them again, all too soon, I reveled in the quiet. Too quiet. The inmates should have been talking or at least snoring. Criminy! Had they escaped, also?

Hand on the handle to the inner door, did I even want to open it to find out? Swallowing dread, I peered into the back room with the two cells.

Relief. Five men behind bars. Two slept, two held cards and one stood looking out the window.

"Grub'll be coming soon." I closed the door wondering why I'd said that.

Late-afternoon sunlight pooled on the office floor, turning the brown floorboards golden. Mayor Seth Critoli occupied the chair in front of the desk and chuckled. It was a quiet chuckle, the kind that pushed the ends of a mouth up and crinkled the eyes. The kind that made me wonder what he was really thinking. His chest rose and fell in short bursts.

"Now, let me get this straight." He slid a hand across his mouth, his eyes searching mine. "You want me to be your campaign manager?"

"Yep."

Seth shrugged. "You expect to win with only three weeks to campaign?"

I shrugged back. "Plenty of time." I'd given this some thought and I didn't see what the problem was. "Dry Creek's not real big. And people're starting to forget about the escaped prisoners."

Seth took a breath but I continued.

"And Judge Richfield's already gone home. Left a couple days ago." I shrugged, again. "Maybe nobody'll bring it up."

It was Seth's turn to shrug, but he squirmed in the wooden chair, instead. Something about his repositioning changed his demeanor. He leaned forward. "They haven't forgotten, Maud. And I don't think your chances are very good, if you don't find them."

That's definitely not what I wanted to hear. "But I went looking. I couldn't—"

"I know." Seth played with a pencil he found on my desk. "However . . . there's talk."

But I'd tried. It wasn't my fault. "Still, if you're my campaign manager, you can tell them."

Seth looked everywhere but at me. "There's something else." The pause stretched for years. "You do know Pokey's going to run, too, don't you?"

Pokey? I crashed back against my chair. "News to me. He's never said a word. Thought he liked being an almost-deputy."

Seth dropped his voice. "The boys down at the Tin Pan put him up to it."

I gazed around Seth's head to peer through the window. People scurried past on the boardwalk, horses clip-clopped down the street, wind kicked up dust.

"Where is he now?" Seth asked.

Pulled back from the street scene, I ran down a mental calendar. "Today's Wednesday. He's driving the mail from Dutch Flats. Be back this evening."

Seth used the end of the pencil to rub his chin. At last he sighed. "All right." He pointed to a piece of paper on my desk. "I got some ideas."

Sitting there, I realized how blind I'd been to Pokey. Of course he'd want to be sheriff. He'd volunteered to help and had served the position well. He'd even been shot in the line of duty. Maybe he deserved to be sheriff.

Now, I didn't want to lose his friendship, but I also didn't want to lose my job. I liked . . . no, *loved* being sheriff. My campaign would have to take on a whole new personality. Plus, I'd have to find those stinking fugitives.

And I'd thought it was going to be easy.

CHAPTER FIFTY-NINE:
A RUN FOR IT

I heard Pokey's "yee haw" and the clatter of mail-coach wheels long before he came around the far bend heading for the edge of town. He pulled back on the reins as gently as one would hold a kitten.

"Slow now, boys."

Setting the brake and wrapping the reins around its wooden handle, Pokey flashed a smile at me and jumped down.

"Hey, Maud." He patted the side of the coach. "Another terrific trip. No robbers, no rain, no delays. This run came together like greased—"

"You plan on running for sheriff?" The words escaped before I had the chance to lasso them. I'd been thinking about it all afternoon. Guess my mind had a mind of its own.

Pokey ran a long-sleeved arm across his forehead and over his mouth. "Good to see you, too." He flashed a quick smile as his eyes narrowed and slid toward me. "Yeah, I've been thinking I might."

"But, I thought you liked driving the mail coach. You'd do it, forever."

He opened the door and lugged out three mailbags, plopping them on the boardwalk. He spoke over his shoulder before turning to me.

" 'Course I like driving. But I think I'd like being sheriff even better." Pokey reached into the coach again. "I ain't been paid for helping out, but figured I might get paid for being sheriff."

The pay wasn't much, but fifty dollars a month was more than the twelve from driving the wagon that he made now. The mail service was prospering, and we'd increased the driver's pay to a dollar a run, better than most other jobs. Difference was I worked every day. He worked three times a week, which made his somewhere close to cowboy wages. And he didn't even get grub with his.

While he staggered into the postal office loaded down with four heavy bags, I tugged a light one out of the coach. Looked like we were now adversaries. This election business was about to get interesting.

The closer it got to the Fourth, the more people flooded into town. Men, women, children of all shapes, sizes and nationalities roamed the streets. I'd never heard so many different languages in one place. French, German, Italian. Several Scandinavian dialects, if that's what they were. More Spanish than ever. Some Chinese, now that they were making Dry Creek their home and opening laundry services. I'd heard an opium den was in the works, but I hadn't seen one, yet. I was curious as to what services or entertainment it would provide.

Even Rune Maguire had met a fellow countryman. They now spent hours sitting in the telegraph office one-upping each other with stories of the Emerald Isle. Many men of various nationalities wore typical wool trousers and vests, denim shirts with long sleeves, but a few— particularly the Chinese and Mexicans— continued to dress in their native costumes. Beautiful silk pants and shirts for both Chinese men and women; serapes and white cotton pantaloons for the Mexican men. The women wore bright skirts, embroidered with symbols representing parrots or other birds. I marveled at how large, and yet small, our world had become.

I smiled at so many people my cheeks ached as I walked up

toward Seth's office. The boardwalks were crowded, lengthening my stroll to twice the time. Of course, I stopped often to shake hands or pat children's heads or *ooh* and *ahh* over a new baby.

I spotted two tallish men up half a block, sombreros riding low on their foreheads and ponchos covering shirts, walking toward me. I took little notice of them as they neared. Simply more visitors to Dry Creek. They strode shoulder to shoulder, allowing me no room to pass easily, forcing me to the boardwalk's edge. Right as we met, one fella shoulder-bumped me hard enough I spun back a step and crashed into the street, barely staying upright. They continued, unperturbed, one mumbling, *"Perdóneme."*

I rubbed my throbbing shoulder, glaring at their receding backs. They slowed, gave a half turn and glanced over their shoulders. I thought one of them snickered, but with so much noise, I couldn't be sure. A glimpse of their faces as they turned back. I'd seen them before . . . somewhere.

I stepped back onto the boardwalk, certain I recognized them. Crazy. I'd seen so many faces, I knew it was crazy to think like that. But, as soon as I got back to the office, I'd check those wanted posters, again.

I reset my sights on Seth's office and my campaign.

Seth sat hunched in his chair. Behind him, a tintype I'd seen often hung on the wall. It was of a couple. The man sat ramrod straight like he was nailed to a board; the woman stood behind, her hand on his left shoulder. Neither looked happy. I studied it. There stood Mama Critoli and more than likely it was Papa Critoli, who'd died a while back.

Seth steepled his fingers, all ten of them tapping out a rhythm only he could hear. This made me not only nervous, but a bit concerned. Would he be a good campaign manager? What exactly qualified him, anyway?

Rejoining the here-and-now, he brought his brown eyes up to mine. "Here's the thing, Maud." He wagged his head. "Pokey's hired me to be his campaign manager, too."

I sat back, all the wind taken out of my sails.

"Hired?" I hadn't given any thought to paying Seth for his advice, figuring he'd do it out of the goodness of his heart and our friendship. "But I asked you first."

"Gave me cash up front." Seth shrugged. "Hard to say no to."

"Guess so." Could I afford him? And how had Pokey been able to pay Seth? Was there somebody else who'd do it for free? Nobody came to mind. All right, I'd have to pony up some coin. I wanted this job. "What d'you charge?"

He held up a hand. "Whoa! I'm gonna have to reconsider helping you. Might smack of conflict of interest." He paused. "Got my reputation to consider. And my own election next year."

Leaning forward from my seat in front of his desk, I dagger-stared him straight in the eyes. I wanted to make my stance clear. "I intend to win this election. I'd like your help. But if you're not willing—"

"Didn't say I wasn't willing." Seth's crooked smile dimpled his right cheek. "I said it might be ethically wrong."

"How can it be wrong if you're only giving advice?" My mind raced with what ifs. "Might be seen as unethical if you took payment from both of us."

His chair squeaked as he leaned back. "Might."

"Tell you what," I said, figuring I had him now. I took a page from Beth Gallaway's book. "What'd you say to a pie every Saturday? We'll start with strawberry and, later, apple."

He contemplated, then licked his lips. "A whole one? For me?"

"Yep. I'll even make a Montgomery pie." When he didn't jump at the pie, I sweetened the pot, so to speak. "How about dinner at my house tomorrow night? Abigail's cooking."

Seth smiled an honest-to-goodness smile, not his practiced politician one. "Okay, I'm in."

"Great." I stood, untangling my green skirt, which seemed always to wrap around my ankles. "We can start planning."

"Looking forward to it," Seth said escorting me to the door. He moved in close and I turned my cheek, right as he planted a kiss on it. There was no doubt in my mind he'd aimed for the lips, but I wasn't ready for such a big step. This time, I was sober. And I had to figure out Eli, first.

Instead, I stuck out my hand for a seal-the-deal handshake.

Back at the office, with the five inmates now fed, I sat studying each surly mug on each wanted poster. Those faces. Those men. Had to be here. Images flashed by. Pretty much, they all looked alike. Beady eyes, weak hairy chins, smirks curling their lips. Nobody I recognized nor wanted to meet.

The last poster caught my breath. Three crudely-drawn faces stared back. Two of them I recognized. Smith and Doyle. No doubt about it. "Same durn brutes on the boardwalk," I muttered, and one or two other embellishments Ma would *not* have approved.

A closer look at the drawing. Nah, who was I kidding? Couldn't have been. Besides, what kind of outlaw in his right mind would come back into a town he'd escaped from? Crazy outlaw, that's for sure.

By now my heart was in my throat. Who was the third face on the poster?

Mooney? Maybe. Possibly.

The caption: *James Mooney. E. J. Andrews, Ben Dunsford, Rowdy Jones. Six foot, light brown hair, brown eyes. Gang leader.* I was right! My eyes riveted on the pencil drawing. Sure looked a lot like somebody I knew. But who? The description could fit about half the population.

I swallowed hard. Was he in town, like Smith and Doyle, and I didn't know it?

Think I'll buy more ammunition.

Chapter Sixty:
The Campaign

I couldn't concentrate on my re-election strategies, so it helped to have my campaign manager coming for supper and pie. Seth appeared at our door at six o'clock, promptly, and I escorted him in. Aromas of cooking roast mingled with the cinnamon wafting from the peach pie, my strawberries not ripe enough for cooking. I was sure Seth would be forgiving. Next pie, I hoped to have fresh strawberries.

Supper announced, Seth sat down and made short work of Abigail's long hours of work. Pa and I didn't pretend to keep up. There was no way we could eat as much.

He wiped his mouth with one of our best napkins, leaned back patting his stomach and then dug into a heaping slice of pie. Peach pieces clung to his neatly-trimmed mustache while he spoke.

"Seems to me you're already campaigning, Maud, by staying visible all day. People like to know they can count on you to be in your office or out patrolling, if they need you."

"If you ask me, she's out too much, as it is." Pa patted his mouth, inspected the napkin for remnants, then pushed back from the table. "Don't get me wrong. I'm proud of her. What she's done. But I still wish she'd reconsider. Too dangerous. She oughta be home—"

"But I'm not, Pa." I cut my eyes sideways to Seth, who seemed desperate to stay noncommittal. I wasn't a hundred percent sure where he stood on this issue, but he better be on my side. After all, wasn't that why he was here?

Pa stood, nodded to Seth and ambled off into the parlor, muttering. I thought I caught *hard-headed woman,* but I wasn't sure. Seth watched Pa go. I watched Seth.

The rattle of his fork upon the plate rim broke the long silence. He swiped at his mouth once more, folded the napkin and placed it next to his plate. Mama Critoli had taught him good manners. I made a mental note to thank her, next time I saw her. His gaze moseyed to my face.

"A debate." He stifled a light belch. "Yep, a debate 'tween you and Pokey. That'd get the town's attention. You'd explain about the escape and get elected."

"You mean a discussion between us? Up at podiums and such?" The thought had never occurred to me I'd go toe to toe with Pokey in some sort of shouting match. What did I have to say? Something new and different? What would we talk about?

Seth's head bobbed. Were there voices in there? It was obvious he listened, because he mumbled an answer.

I pushed my plate back. "What if he's more charming than me? What if he knows what to say and I don't? What if—"

"No 'what if's,' Maud." Seth tossed a disarming smile my way, one that made most women melt. All it did for me was to raise an eyebrow. "By the time we have this debate," he continued, "you'll know exactly what to say. I'll write up the points you need to make, you practice them and, come election time, I'll pin the tin star on you, again."

I remembered how awkward it was for Seth, trying to figure out where on my chest to pin it. Way back then, a mere three months ago, it was embarrassing. Now, it was funny.

"Tell you what." Seth scooted back his chair. "Let's go over the particulars tomorrow, in my office."

"Can't we talk about it right here? Right now?" I was ready to get going and sure didn't want to wait until tomorrow. I'd spend tonight thinking about whatever I was to say and also work on it again, tomorrow.

Seth's lips pursed together and stuck out like he was balancing a pencil on his upper lip, which would've been hidden by his well-trimmed mustache. It felt like five minutes but was probably closer to ten seconds. He shrugged. "Fine. Got paper and pencil?"

We sat and strategized until my eyes crossed. Pa rattled his newspaper every so often, then finally poked his head into the dining room. *Good night*s were exchanged and Seth and I got back to planning our attack. Abigail had cleared the dining room, cleaned the kitchen and was long gone by the time Seth and I had it all figured out.

Seth stretched back in the chair, his arms reaching toward the ceiling. A deep breath in, a longer one out, his gaze riveted on the ceiling. "You heard about Pearl?"

For a moment, I panicked. Was she dead? He would've told me right off, if that had been the case. I kept my voice soft, in case I was wrong. "She's engaged?"

He played with the empty cup, still in front of him. "Some yahoo she met up with again, last month in Virginia City. Says she's known him a while, but things got . . . *serious,* recently."

"She say who he is?" I'd not thought to ask names or details the other night and I sure hadn't had time today.

"No, merely that he was smitten with her." Seth's shoulders sagged. "Thought she was smitten with *me.* Anyway, I hope he's not 'smitten' because her Pa's a big banker over there. He's rich, you know." He paused a moment, as if gathering thoughts, peeked into his tea cup—maybe hoping there was some left. Finding none, he pushed back from the table and stood to leave. "I wish them all the happiness in the world."

Somehow, he sounded sincere. Were those his politician's

sentiments or his heart's?

"Me, too," I said, and meant it. "How soon's she leaving?"

"Gonna wait for her man to send for her. She said a month or so."

Boy, did that sound familiar. I'd definitely make it a point to visit with her tomorrow, tell her what a rotten idea waiting was, she should know better, and who was this mystery man, anyway?

Seth stood on the porch, me in the doorway. Stars twinkling behind him framed his head, while lanterns' soft glow from neighboring houses bathed him in gold. At this time of night and from this angle, some sort of magnetism pulled me toward him. I wanted to kiss him. A lot.

He caressed my arm, then drew me into his chest. Tingles ran up both arms. His lips—soft and tasty—reminded me of tonight's supper. The kiss and his embrace turned me into mush. Standing was hard, my knees unwilling to hold me upright.

I could have stayed this way forever. Heaven. Now I knew exactly what Heaven was like. And then . . . Eli's face popped into my brain. What was I doing? This wasn't Eli I was kissing! This was Mayor Seth Critoli nuzzling my ear, breathing warm desire into my soul.

I pulled away. What kind of woman was I? Certainly not a two-timer. No, siree, I was a one-man woman. Elijah J. Goodman's woman, doggone it.

Strong arms pulled me back. Obviously, Seth had gotten over Pearl. Quickly, too. And why was I about to push him away? Here Seth was right in front of me, ready to be my beau, and I hadn't seen Eli for over a month. Even that was under mysterious circumstances.

One more delicious kiss and I took a breath. This wasn't right. I owed it to Eli. Or did I? Confused, I shook my head.

"Thank you, Seth," I whispered, not really sure what I was

thanking him for. "I'll see you tomorrow."

I stepped inside, closed the door and leaned on it . . . hard.

CHAPTER SIXTY-ONE:
DEAD EYE MAUD

The morning came despite my not sleeping a wink, all night. I'd tossed and turned, visions of Eli and Seth parading through my mind, across my bedroom, into my heart. Breakfast turned into a half-hearted attempt to push food into my mouth, washing it down with coffee. I assumed I ate because Abigail pointed out the soft egg parts clinging to my blouse, as I started for the door. Pa was already up and gone to the bank.

I changed into the light-blue blouse, which matched my skirt. I'd always liked this combination; somehow the color reflected in my eyes. At least, Eli said it did.

Three days away from the "big doings" and I was nervous as a cat in a gunnysack. My claws were out and I was ready to dig into anything or anyone. Along the way to my office, I stopped frequently to shake hands with the fine citizens of Dry Creek and pat the heads of their children. By my usual standards, these were not my finest handshakes or smiles, my mind not truly on campaigning, at the moment.

Despite everyone's well-wishing, by the time I pushed through the office door I knew one big event was dead ahead and I wasn't quite prepared for it. The "Fourth of July Possible Bank Robbery" weighed heavy on my mind. When was the last time I'd practiced shooting my gun? Or cleaned it? Did I have enough bullets? How many would I need? Thanks to the holdup, I was reasonably comfortable with the idea of shooting a man, if he was shooting at *me*, but how many bullets would it take to do the job? Too bad ol' sheriff Larimore was busy up in the hills, somewhere, snagging the biggest bull trout in the territory. He'd probably know. I couldn't ask Pa nor Seth . . . certainly not Pokey. I couldn't show any weakness around my adversary.

I sat behind my desk glancing at the wanted posters, my mind drifting. What was Eli doing right now? Still driving a herd of cattle? Shouldn't it be over pretty soon? Would he come back or continue his journey? Without me—again. What had started as a good day quickly turned sour. I loved Eli but it was becoming clear he didn't reciprocate the feeling. I blinked back tears. Right now, with Seth's kiss still on my lips, reality hit. Eli didn't love me.

Had he ever? Really?

The office door squeaked open, bringing my attention back to the here and now. Councilman Slim Higginbotham, my partner on the last two forays to track down outlaws, stepped in.

"Had a couple of thoughts on The Big Doin's, Maud." Slim glanced at the open inner door to the cells. He closed it. "Thinkin' there might be some trouble."

Now he had my undivided attention. Did he know something I didn't? We now had fireworks, despite my misgivings. What else could there be? "What kinda trouble?"

He chose the sturdiest of the two wooden chairs, pulled it close to my desk, huffed to sit and dug into his vest pocket. Extracting a cigar, he held it up and raised eyebrows at me. I grimaced.

"Not sure, exactly." Slim bit off and spit the cigar's tapered end, then struck a match, using the underside of my desk. The orange flame flared up and down, as he held it against the Two Brothers' end. He puffed gray clouds and, when satisfied, shook out the match.

I waited 'til I could no longer stand the suspense. "Why'd you say there's going to be trouble, if you're not sure?" I hated this kind of guessing game. Either he knew or he didn't.

Slim shook his head, shrugging. "Nothing I can put my finger on. Down at the Tin Pan, last night . . ." He pointed his cigar in the general direction of his saloon, down the street. "Couple ol' boys come in sayin' they'd heard a couple other men talkin' about plannin' a bank robbery. Got me to thinkin'. What if they're talkin' about here?"

"Were they wearing serapes? Did one speak Spanish?" I sat forward. "Either one look like Smith or Doyle?" I explained I thought I'd spotted both men in town a couple days back, but hadn't seen hide nor hair of them since. And I'd been keeping a sharp eye out. Both eyes.

Slim blew more smoke. "Nope. Hadn't seen either man before."

For the first time in a long while, I felt confident. I had a plan.

Leaning back in my chair, I allowed a grin to twinkle on my face. "No problem then. Already thought about it and we're ready." Not exactly ready. I still had to do some target practicing. But we were mostly ready.

Slim puffed and blew smoky O's, while he thought. I assumed he was thinking because his eyebrows knitted, as he gazed at the ceiling. He examined it so long, I followed his stare and looked up there, too. Nothing but white wood, needing a good coat of paint.

He pushed his chair back and groaned up to his feet. "Guess if you needed my help you would've asked." As he reached for the door handle, he turned around to me. "You know if you need help, I'm here."

I did know. "Thanks, Slim. I appreciate it. I'll holler if I do."

A wave over his shoulder with the cigar and Slim was gone.

As I sat, my gut told me something was about to happen. This was more times than I could count trouble had been forecast.

Both of my rabble-rousers were busy sleeping off too much celebrating last night. They'd be fine by themselves, for a while; no need to get Pokey or Billy Harsburg. I locked the outside door and walked down to Dry Creek Mercantile. I bought six boxes of cartridges and four of shells, knowing it was at least two boxes too many. But I wasn't going to take any chances. Ten boxes equaled at least a hundred rounds. If I couldn't hit a bank robber in a hundred shots, then I deserved to lose my sheriff's badge. I didn't want to lose my life in the process.

Now would be as good a time as any for some target practice. Still in the store, I spotted one of the doctor's boys, gave him a couple of pennies and asked him to get Mr. Harsburg to watch the prisoners. Guess I'd need his help after all.

Toting a sack of tin cans, I walked farther out of town for target practice than last time, as more people were camping on the town's edges. I sure didn't want to spook them or their animals. I found a clearing close to a mile from town and sat under a tree to catch my breath.

It was under such a tree where I'd last seen Eli. Elijah J. Goodman. *My* good man. Not so good any more. More like a liar and heart breaker.

Ruminating on him, envisioning those deep-brown eyes and soft lips pressed upon someone else's, I loaded my gun, jamming the parchment cartridges into the little round chambers, spinning the barrel, like a professional. That Eli. Where did he get off having another girlfriend? Why hadn't he written? Or stayed longer? He'd ridden off with somebody else, probably a woman younger than me, and left me here, waiting. I sighted down the barrel and snarled at his image.

Bang! Right between the eyes.

Then again . . . Had he really been unfaithful? Maybe he

hadn't been close to a town with mail service. *Maybe* I was being unfair.

On the other hand, what about that letter to Abigail? She said it was from her cousin, but I still had my doubts. I looked at the return address. How many men write using curlicues like Eli? I pushed speculation to one side and focused on the afternoon's purpose.

I released the hammer gently, not wanting to shoot when I wasn't ready. I realized how far I'd come in a couple of months. No longer was I afraid of guns, nor shooting, nor telling people what to do.

It dawned on me I'd developed into more than "levelheaded." I'd grown confident. Elevated to assertive.

Become *sheriff*.

I set up a row of cans, most sporting holes from my last target-practicing adventure a couple of weeks ago. Standing back at least five yards, I aimed for the one on the far left. Squinting with one eye helped; the can plinked when my bullet hit it. It leaped backwards as though jerked with a string. I inspected the can and found the new hole to be dead center. Quite pleased with myself, I recognized practicing showed positive results.

Spurred on by the success, I pressed on with renewed determination. Not surprisingly, I hit more than half of my targets.

The morning rolled by and I was about to declare victory over the cans, having reloaded only three times, when I caught movement out of the corner of my eye. I spun around to discover Seth Critoli standing behind and to my right. His raised eyebrows brought my own smile.

"Impressive, Maud. Mighty impressive." Seth strode down the line of riddled cans, eyeing each, resembling a general inspecting his troops. He stopped, turning to me almost like I was an equal. "Where'd you learn to shoot like that?"

I stood up straighter and tilted my chin. "Practice."

"Must've practiced when I wasn't around." Seth ran his hand over his mustache. "Guess you don't need my help anymore."

A compliment of the highest order. "But I *do* need your help. Well, maybe not for shooting." I finger-spun my Navy revolver and missed the holster. Fortunately, I didn't drop it into the dirt. Only a small snort from Seth and I recovered quickly. "Still don't know quite what to say in a speech, or in a debate. I gotta be honest with people. What's the first thing I say?"

Pointing to the nearest tree, he took my elbow, leading me. "Let's get outta the sun and do some more figuring. I hope you know that's why I hiked all the way out here—to talk."

"And *strategize*." I smiled my best smile, pleased at my use of such a sophisticated word.

We sat and he whipped out a pencil and pad from his vest pocket. He'd already written notes. Were these for me or were some for Pokey? Would Seth use the same strategy for both of us?

"First things first." Seth regarded his scribbling, the paper resting on his crossed legs. "I've given it some more thought, especially what with that fine supper Abigail fixed. The fact you occupy the position—still—and the fact the town fathers felt you were the one to take over Larimore's job, is about all you need to win the election."

"But—"

"It's all about being an incumbent."

"Pokey's well liked and our town's first mail coach driver. That counts for something, doesn't it?"

"It does." He stared at the holey cans. "Nice." He flashed me a drop-dead smile. "You'll win. Don't worry."

Visions of me losing, returning to run Pa's household,

bombarded me. I couldn't lose. I sat up straighter.
I *wouldn't* lose.

CHAPTER SIXTY-TWO:
BIG DOIN'S

Seth had been little or no help; I'd have to strategize on my own. I mean, how hard could it be to get up and give a speech in front of strangers and everyone you'd ever known?

I was terrified.

The morning of the Fourth, I woke as the sun peeked through a lightly clouded sky. I cat-stretched, soothing my nerves. I peered out the bedroom window, wondering what the day would hold. With clouds so early in the morning, there was a chance it would rain this evening, which meant no fireworks. So, maybe, just maybe, no bank robbery. Would I be so lucky?

By late morning, the blue sky was crystal clear. I couldn't have bought a cloud with all the gold in California. I paraded up and down Main Street, greeting everyone, cooing over babies, shaking millions of hands, and trying to look very sheriff-like without looking mean.

The debate was scheduled for noon and, although I wished otherwise, the hands of the clock continued to move. Now, they both stood straight up, due north, and I knew there was no denying the inevitable.

Slim Higginbotham had a couple carpenters erect a platform in the middle of Main Street. On it perched two wooden chairs and two lecterns, probably borrowed from the church. I didn't care if they'd stolen them from the Vatican; my focus was to keep my knees from folding.

Pokey and I shook hands and took our respective seats as

men, women and children of all aspects stood in the street peering up at us. I supposed how celebrities felt when they came to town to put on a play or something. Not that it happened very often. It was purely unnerving to stand there having people stare up at you, like you were important, maybe some kind of saint. Subconsciously, a tiny part of me took flight, bringing a smile to my face. In an odd way, this *was* fun.

I gave a tiny wave to Pa, who, despite his grumblings and mumblings, had decided to attend, standing over to one side. Opposite him stood Dr. Monroe, his wife, Charity, and their brood. All three town councilmen, along with Mayor Seth, sat down front. That was the first time I'd even noticed chairs placed in the middle of the street. I didn't remember seeing anybody doing that. They'd simply sprung up like weeds in a garden.

Standing near Pa were Abigail Stevenson, our housekeeper, Rune Maguire, the telegrapher, and Beth Gallaway, officially now Post Mistress. Squeezing into the mix, Pearl McIntyre made her way to stand next to Beth. They all waited expectantly, anticipating hifalutin' words to emanate from my mouth, I guessed. I greeted individuals and reporters I recognized and turned back to Pokey. His face, normally a light tan, now was drained of any color. He blinked like he had dirt in his eyes.

I leaned over to him and spoke so no one else could hear. "You'll do fine. Take a deep breath and pretend you're talking to me or your horse."

"Why would I want to talk to my horse?" Pokey's voice carried over the crowd and they snickered.

Fine. You're on your own from here on out.

Seth jumped up on the platform, only about three feet off the ground, but high enough so everyone could see us. He stood on the front edge, directly center stage, and faced the crowd. "We've gathered here today—"

"This ain't no weddin', Seth," someone yelled from the crowd.

Laughter.

"Sounds more like a funeral," another shouted.

More chuckles and guffaws.

Seth Critoli turned on his mayoral façade. He produced a toothy smile and held up his hands. "In many ways, folks, this *is* like a wedding. A wedding . . . marriage . . . is a commitment . . . a promise . . . between two people. A man and a woman. The election of our sheriff is no different. We're bringing together two entities. One—these candidates for sheriff, and the other—the fine citizens of Dry Creek. It's a union fraught with ups and downs, but, in the end, stands firm in the commitment to the betterment of all. It's—"

"We wanna hear Maud and Pokey. Not you!"

"Yeah. Get on with it." Another voice, closer to me, drowned out Seth's oration.

Seth surrendered and turned to us. "You heard 'em. Give 'em what they came for." He spread his arms wide. "It's my esteemed honor to introduce our current sheriff of Dry Creek, Miss Maud Overstreet . . ." He gestured to me and I held a hand up to the crowd. Most clapped, politely. "And Dry Creek's mail coach driver, Mr. Pokey Johnson."

Pokey leaped up and bowed, grandly. The crowd roared.

Seth stepped off the platform, leaving us to our own devices.

Since I was the incumbent and a girl, I went first. I rose and gripped the lectern with both hands, cleared my throat and peered into the crowd. "I'm not going to make this speech long because we have a band to listen to, barbecue to eat and *fireworks* to liven things up."

Cheers and applause bolstered my spirits. Maybe I was on the right path.

"As you know, I've been your sheriff now for over three

months. It's been a challenge, but I've risen to the occasion. I could list the progress made in the sheriff's office, but I don't want to bore you with so many details."

Another, somewhat smaller, cheer went up.

"I'd like to look to, and talk about, the future of Dry Creek. It's pretty obvious to everyone we're growing, and—"

"Hey! She's a girl!" An intoxicated range cowboy, who'd staggered out of the Tin Pan Saloon, swayed on the crowd's back edge and pointed at me. "D'ja know you're a girl?" He elbowed the person next to him, who happened to be my pa.

"She's my daughter, you drunken sot. Get your hands off me." Pa pushed him away, probably harder than was necessary. The inebriate toppled into the street. Pa glared down at him. "Of course I know she's a girl. And she's the sheriff."

"Girl sheriff? Ain't no such thing. You're lyin'!" The drunk sprang up, landing a Texas roundhouse into Pa's cheek. Immediately, it was impossible to tell whose fists went with whom. All I could see were at least thirty men pushing, punching and pummeling one another. Women shrieked, pulling their children out of the reach of flailing long arms. A few of the older, more distinguished gentlemen edged back but, from where I stood, every man from the age of fifteen to fifty jumped in. I'd never seen so many arms, legs and bodies cartwheeling around in the dirt.

Tearing my gape away from the brawl, I turned first to Pokey, his attention riveted on the fight, then down to Seth, who grinned back up at me. He pointed over his shoulder.

"Gotta get this stopped, Maud. You're still the sheriff."

He was right. Depending on how I handled this, I'd either get elected or run out of town on a rail by the none-too-happy citizens. Because Pokey was my unofficial part-time deputy, I grabbed his arm and pulled him to his feet.

"We gotta break this up before this gets outta hand." By now, several of the nearest saloons had emptied out, the bartenders in their aprons standing at the doors, watching the melee.

"How?" Pokey shrugged, pulling his gun.

"We can't shoot 'em," I said.

"Ain't gonna do that. Fire in the air. Get their attention."

I pointed at his gun. "Bullets come back down." I'd already considered it, my gunbelt snugged around my waist, the holster warm against my hip. "Put it away. Don't want anybody accidentally shot."

He offered no further comment and holstered his Colt.

And then it hit me. "Come on," I said and jumped off the stage, my skirt bunched in my hand. Pokey followed, as we threaded our way through to the combat.

"Grab those water buckets." I pointed to the several wooden pails lining the street. These were kept full in case of fire, which happened all too often. Having such buckets ready had saved many a building. "Dump 'em on their heads. Should cool 'em off."

With a couple of water barrages, followed by several more for good measure, the sputtering, drenched men turned on Pokey and me.

"What the—?"

Language a lady doesn't use, even when I'm mighty angry, sprayed over me right as I'd sprayed them. Five or more wet, dripping constituents staggered about in the middle of Main Street on that hot Fourth of July. But they stopped fighting. People on the edges, women and children mainly, laughed and pointed. Pa's face sported bright red knuckle prints and several men held handkerchiefs to their bloodied noses. As far as I could tell, nobody was seriously hurt.

"Go on now. Nothing to see here," I said over the crowd's grumbling. To my amazement, many of them turned and wandered off, trudging through mud puddles. More than a few slapped me on the back, muttering things like "Good idea, Maud" and "He needed a bath, anyways."

Seth pushed his way through the crowd, until he stood in front of me and Pokey. "Can't believe this. I can't believe this. I go to all this trouble and look what a shambles the first-ever debate turns into." He planted his hands on his hips, a gesture I'd never seen him use before. "Son of a—"

"Not all's lost," Pokey said. "We put on a show nobody'll ever forget. I think it'll bring everyone out to the polls on election day."

I had to agree with Pokey on that one. Nobody, but nobody would forget this Fourth of July. And I didn't even have to finish my speech.

The day progressed more to my liking. Given I hadn't had to arrest anybody, I didn't have any paperwork to do. I spent the remainder of the afternoon walking the street, taking in people's comments on the fight and checking in with each saloon to be sure nobody was getting too roostered. I didn't want any man too drunk to navigate his way home. Or to start another fight. Somebody might actually get hurt.

Right before sundown, an idea hit me I was sure would work. At least, it would make potential robbers think twice. With the fireworks display set for full dark, I wouldn't have much time. I located Pokey coming out of a saloon.

"See all these horses up and down Main Street?" I pointed at the rows of mounts tied to the hitchin' rails. A quick count added up to about thirty.

"Course I see 'em, Maud. Clear, too," Pokey said. "Ain't had but one beer."

I pulled him closer to the street. "How about, starting right now, we get these horses out of the way and into a stable or off a ways, tied to the trees? They're liable to get spooked during the fireworks, anyway, and more importantly . . ." I leaned in close to my current almost-deputy. "Robbers can't make a quick getaway if they gotta hunt for their mounts. Right?"

Pokey straightened up, surveyed the horses, then back to me. His head cocked side to side, while he thought. "Ain't that stealin'?" His hand rubbed his throat. "They hang people for horse stealin'."

"They do. I know." Time was running out. I rushed. "We're not stealing them, we're . . . *relocating* them. And since I'm a duly-appointed law officer, I can do that." I wasn't sure if that was correct or even legal, but it would have to do, for now.

Pokey shrugged. "You're right. That'll keep outlaws on their feet and outta the saddle. Only problem is, how're we gonna get all these horses into the stable?"

"I'll hire a couple a kids and I'm sure the bank'll be well-disposed to pay the stable fees, if that keeps it from getting robbed." I knew, just *knew* my plan would work.

He untied a rein. "I'll take a couple with me right now and you go find Doc's boys to help."

He started off but I grabbed his arm, again. "Soon as we get them off the street, we gotta position ourselves for the Possible Robbery."

Pokey patted his holstered gun. "Gonna get the shotgun from the office and then nobody, but nobody'll get past me. Don't worry."

But I was.

Chapter Sixty-Three: Surprise!

By the time we got all the horses off Main Street and posted boys at either end to direct incoming riders to hitchin' posts outside of town, it was close to full dark. Still with a couple of minutes to kill, I decided to change into a different blouse, one a mite looser than the one I'd picked for my speech. I needed something not binding on my arms, if I needed to take down a criminal. The dark blue one sporting tiny white flowers would be a better choice. And maybe some of Abigail's pie was left over. I'd snag a slice on my way out of the house.

Abigail had left a lamp burning in the parlor—bless her heart. Even though it wasn't safe to leave a flame burning, it was nice to come home to a lighted house. I hung up my bonnet and, as I turned for my bedroom, out of the corner of my eye I caught a figure. Someone sat on the sofa. Someone who wasn't Pa . . . or Seth . . . or even Pokey.

I spun, pulling my gun, pointing it. Heart pounding so hard I couldn't breathe, I squinted at the figure, now grinning at me.

"Good to see you again, Maud."

I swallowed. Hard. "Eli?" I know I frowned because my face hurt. Moving closer, I edged across the room as he stood, then holstered my weapon.

He stretched his shoulders back as he stood. "Surprised?"

The man I'd come to love and hate, depending on my mood, stood inches from me. The man I'd dreamed of, mounted on a white charger and carrying me away as his princess, was right here. Just us. The two of us.

"Shouldn't surprise a body like that. Almost shot you."

"Glad you didn't." His heart-melting smile still dazzled me.

"How'd you . . ." The words wouldn't come.

"Your housekeeper let me in. She was on her way out. Told her I was an old friend come to surprise you." Eli's brown eyes sparkled in the lantern's golden glow. "Guess I did."

He was so good looking I wanted to eat him, right then and there. Then I called to mind he'd left me alone for way too long. I was sheriff now, not some moonstruck teenager. In fact, I had to get going right now, or more than likely they'd start the show without me and the bank'd get robbed before I was in place and the town would lose all their money and Pa and Seth and Pokey would get hurt and—

"Come away with me, Maud. I've waited for this moment a long time." Eli moved in close and enveloped my body in his. Whispered love notions mushed my insides. "At the end of the cattle drive up in Oregon, I got paid. I've got money. Enough for us to start a life together."

Something new for Eli. He'd rarely had even pocket change, when we were dating. Cattle business must be booming.

More sweetness from Eli. "Leave with me. I'll take you anywhere you want to go. We'll have children. And a house. With a garden. A white picket fence. What you've always wanted."

Was it?

Eli's purring melted me. "Let's leave tonight, Maud. We'll run away. Make our own lives. You and me."

His breath in my ear . . . I'd fantasized of this moment for years.

My world spun.

"I love you. You know that, don't you?"

His body pressed against mine. His heart beating with mine.

His arms holding me.

Why was I not dabbing tears of joy?

I heard a voice, much like my own, but it declared an impossible. "Not tonight. Let's wait 'til tomorrow. I have sheriff duties." Doubting myself, I pulled back, but he pulled me close.

"No. Tomorrow's too late. Tonight." Eli relaxed his hold enough for both of us to breathe, together. "To hell with the town. To hell with being sheriff. Be with me. Come." His strong arms nudged me toward the door.

Every fiber of my body wanted to go with him but, deep down, I knew my duty. I'd given it a lot of thought and effort and I wanted to continue being a peace officer. Really. I did.

By the time we reached the front door, my resolve was firm. I stopped and gazed into those mouth-watering eyes. The eyes I'd prayed to see again. "Eli, I can't go with you. I want Pa's blessing and I'm sheriff, now. I like being sheriff. *This* is what I want. Not some house, children or garden."

"What's got into you?" He held my shoulders and pierced me with his eyes. "I thought you loved me, no matter what."

I do. Or did. I stood there, emotion and conflict caught in my head.

He lowered his voice. "You sure?"

No. Of course I wasn't. But it was all I had, right then. I'd wanted to trust, to believe in Eli. But he'd let me down too often. I took a deep breath . . . slowly.

His lips brushed the top of my head. "All right. Gotta respect you for knowing your mind. But I gotta get going. Tonight. How about you walk me down to Swensen's stable; it's only a couple of blocks. I'll saddle up, ride outta here. Never bother you again."

It wasn't what I wanted, but I agreed. We walked, arms around each other's waist, my mind racing with possibilities. Maybe I wouldn't get elected. I could find Eli and become Mrs.

Elijah J. Goodman. Or, he could come back in a couple of weeks to see for himself.

We discussed it all the way to the livery.

"Don't know if I can, Maud." Eli tugged open the wooden stable door, took down a lantern from its peg, slid the glass chimney up to light. "Tell you what, though. I'm planning to head down to San Diego, see the ocean, do some exploring. Maybe all the way to Mexico. Got fine tequila down there, I hear."

"Write me a letter. Tell me where you went." I hoped he'd wait in town for a few days, but knew better.

"I'll do that, Honey. I'll write. Promise." Eli and I sauntered to the end stall, where a magnificent black stallion stood, its rump wide and shiny. He picked up the saddle draped over the top rail, then put it down, mumbling.

"What's wrong?" I asked.

"Forgot the blanket in the tack room." Two steps, he turned around and held out his hand. "Come with me?"

Wanting to be near him every second I could, I walked with him, my hand in his, its warmth making me regret my decision to remain in Dry Creek. To be sheriff.

He lifted the two-by-four wooden bar set across the door, leaning it against the wall. Hinges squeaked as the door opened. I peeked inside. Rows of blankets, harnesses, bridles, bits, curry combs, lanterns and other items I couldn't name lined the small room. There was barely enough room for him to squeeze in. From the very back, he bent over, examining something on the ground. "Look here, Maud. Ain't never seen one like this before. You'll be interested."

"What is it?" I couldn't imagine, but if Eli said it was interesting, it must be. I threaded my way to him, watching the floor for more of whatever it was. His arms around me brought us into a welcomed embrace. But I couldn't breathe. Between all the tack and him, there wasn't much room for air.

A long, passionate kiss. I wanted more, much more. I squeezed my eyes tight.

I love you, Maud caressed my ears. If only this moment would last forever. Our lips parted. He let go and I lingered, eyes still closed, in a dream state, memorizing the moment before it evaporated.

Weight lifted from my hip. I forced one hesitant eye open.

My gun. The other eye springing open, I stood watching Eli bolt for the door. Baffled, I started after him. He slammed the wooden door in my face and dropped the heavy bar into its receivers. His footsteps faded.

"Eli? What're you doing? Eli?" I slapped at the door with an open palm.

Within a minute, horse saddled and reins in hand, Eli paused by the tack room door. I peered through slits between the wood planks. He held up my gun. "Sorry, Maud. Don't want you hurt."

"This a joke?" I said. "Not funny. Give it back."

Eli, mouth turned down and shoulders slumped, moved closer to the door. His voice turned velvety smooth with a tinge of sarcasm. "If I can't get your pa's money one way, I'll just have to do it the other way." Then he tossed a parting shot over his shoulder. "And I won't have to put up with you."

And he was gone.

I rattled the door, pushed against it, banged on the wood, but it held tight. No amount of kicking and cursing worked.

I hollered. In the distance, a dog barked. Nobody came.

Out on the streets, people laughed, music played and an occasional gunshot peppered the festivities. No one would hear me over all the noise. I screamed, shouted, pushed, banged, cursed, cried. The wooden bar held.

I slid down to the ground, my shoes pushing aside straw and

lumps of something foul-smelling. A couple deep breaths and my head cleared enough for me to wonder what the heck Eli meant. Why were his words, that last part, so icy? They hurt.

Tired and confused, part of me wanted to sit in the filtered darkness and kick myself for believing in Eli, for falling for his ploy. But, if I was going to get out of this situation any time soon, I needed to break out of this tack room. Now.

It was up to me to save myself.

Then it hit me. Eli planned to rob the bank during the fireworks! It was *him* all along!

I scrambled to my feet and rummaged through the far corners of the room, looking for anything I could use to get me out of here. Peering behind bridles and harnesses hanging on the walls, picking up saddles to look under, finally I spotted it. A branding iron, shoved behind some long leather straps used for stagecoach suspension.

Long and heavy, it would pry the boards. Smashing through them was my last option, as it would be destructive and probably spook the horses. They were already antsy enough with the outside noise. They'd probably not enjoy the fireworks, either.

I pried and pried, a small "yes!" when the first board popped off. The squeaks and groans of boards separating from their nails filled the stable. A couple more and I was a free woman. I wiggled out and made a mental note to tell Mr. Swensen what had happened to his tack room wall and also I'd make good on the damages.

Emotions collided, all fighting for elbow room. A few jostled around in my head, as I stormed outside, around the corner two blocks and down the boardwalk. Fireworks exploded in the clear, summer sky. Crowds cheered. Dogs howled.

Still blocks from the bank, I came face to face with Pokey and Pa. Seth slid to a stop behind them.

"Maud?"

"You all right?" Pokey gripped my arm.

I sputtered, "He's gonna rob the bank."

"Who? What? Huh?" The three men grunted at me.

I shot off a quick explanation of Eli, what he said, and of my being locked in the tack room.

"Eli?" Pa demanded. "What the hell is Eli doing back here? And why'd he treat you like that? I have a mind to—"

"I know, Pa. But not now." I didn't have time to listen to ranting. Instead, I peered around Pokey's shoulder and pointed. "Bank." I took off at as close to a run as my skirt would allow.

Seth, Pa and Pokey not only kept up with me, but somehow overtook my stride. The one thing I needed to know, so that possibly a modicum of the events would make sense, was how did they know where to find me?

Seth filled me in. "Mrs. Stevenson came to the bank. She was flustered and said you were in trouble. Injured. We all should come. She pointed this direction."

"Then high-tailed it down the boardwalk the other way," Pokey continued. "Figured she was going for the doc."

"I yelled and yelled. Nobody came." I turned from worrying about myself. "Did any of you see Eli?" Before they answered, another question hit me. "What's Mrs. Stevenson got to do with it?

Shrugs and grunts answered me.

Too many unsolved questions. My mind reeled with possibilities. As we trotted, the men argued over who found me first. It didn't matter who did, I was just glad to be out. The four of us dodged drunks, zigzagged around hollering children, and threaded through gaggles of women and men filling the street. Aromas of barbecue and sulfur filled the air. Strings of firecrackers brought shouts from the children.

Bank now in sight, I slowed and then stopped, not sure what I'd find. The men halted, also. Pa sucked in air, Seth's chest pumped and I found my heart pounding. "Eli's gonna rob the bank," I said, "and wanted us all out of the way."

Pokey half turned toward downtown. "If Eli's robbing the bank, wanted us gone, how'd Mrs. Stevenson know you were in trouble?"

"And how's she involved with Eli?" Pa asked.

That stopped me. Until this minute I'd not put two and two together. Then it clicked. They were in cahoots. Like Pokey and me, only we weren't outlaws.

"Or . . ." Seth said, interrupting my thoughts. "Maybe, just maybe, nobody's gonna rob the bank and Eli didn't want you following him. And, maybe, Abigail hadn't seen you and was worried about you and went looking for the doc."

"She probably heard you yelling from the stable," Pa said.

I repeated Eli's parting words. They sounded hollow. "None of this washes," I said. A bit rested, I hitched up my skirt and sliced through the three men. "I'm gonna check the bank."

Although I was focused on the bank, I couldn't help but notice Chinese men carrying a thirty-foot-long silk dragon banner with a wagon wheel–sized head, red and green eyes and a forked tongue. They placed it over their heads as they paraded through town, stopping and bowing before each Chinaman they met. Lion-head puppets on long poles bobbed throughout the crowd. I wished I'd been able to stand and enjoy the celebration. But I was sheriff. With a job to do.

Drums beat. Horns tooted. Cymbals crashed.

Flashes of orange, red, blue, gold infused the sky. *Pop! Pop! Pop!* More orange, red, gold and, now, green.

I ran. Pokey, Pa and Seth dogged close on my tail. A cacophony of noise, light and smoke enveloped me. I collided with a man made up to resemble a monkey wearing a crown. Somehow, he seemed oddly appropriate.

No time to appreciate the grandeur of the festivities. I ran full out. No way was Eli going to steal the bank's money. And my badge.

Without bothering to check the bank's front door, not wanting anybody to notice me, I bolted through the alley to the back door. Icy cold jolts shot through my veins. The door stood open at least six inches.

The three men slid to a stop behind me, their gasping and wheezing only bringing more tension. My hand automatically reached for my gun. Gone.

I wasn't about to go inside without a weapon of some sort. Pa didn't carry and Pokey would need his. I held out a hand to Seth. "Gimme your gun."

"You know I don't—"

"Yes, you do. Now!" I wiggled my fingers.

Reluctantly, he pulled out a one-shot pocket pistol from his vest. "Be careful. Got a hair trigger."

It was ridiculously light in my hand, but still, I liked the idea of having *something* to shoot. I pushed the door open and eased inside. I knew they followed me; I heard them panting.

Dark. Almost too dark to see. Light from various bonfires and the fireworks displays flashed through the window, dancing grotesquely on the walls. Fortunately, it was enough for me to make out no outlaws were still hiding behind the counter or under a desk.

No villains or robbers lurked in the room.

"Get a couple lanterns up, so we can see if anything's missing," I said. Please don't let the vault door be unlocked, I thought. Please.

Sometimes, prayers aren't meant to be answered. When the two kerosene lanterns came to full brightness, sure enough, the singed vault door stood open an inch. Pa swung it wide, as we all crowded together to peer inside.

Nothing was inside. A whole *lot* of nothing.

With a collective groan, we straightened up and exchanged guilty glances. Some security team we were.

"Hell and damnation," I blurted. The profanity garnered no response. They were probably thinking along those same lines, themselves, and took no notice.

"We gotta go get whoever did this," Pokey said.

"I *told* you who did this." I cocked my head toward the stable. "He's the only one with a horse."

"Eli?" Seth said. "That's crazy."

"You think?" I returned Seth's miniature gun and mentally listed my priorities. Weapon, ammunition, then horse. Find Eli, right now. I spun around and faced the men. "Pa, get a posse together. Half of them go east, the other head south. Pokey and I'll go west."

"Wait for a big posse, Maud. I don't want my little girl—"

"No time." I narrowed my eyes and spoke as clearly as I could. "This was our money. Yours and mine. The people of this town. We gotta go get it back. *Now!*"

Pa let out the loudest, longest, deepest sigh I'd ever heard. He took both of my shoulders in his soft hands. "I'll get everybody with a horse and gun. Just you be safe."

"I will, Pa." It wasn't like him to get all mushy, and as much as I wanted to be his little girl again, I couldn't right now. I gave him a quick peck on the cheek. "I'll be fine. Thanks for your help. Watch the town, will you?"

He nodded, pursed his lips into a tight smile and headed out the door.

Pokey shook his head at the open vault. "Eli doesn't have much of a lead. I'll get the horses, go with you."

"What can I do?" Seth asked.

"Gun," I said. "Get me a gun and ammo." He stood there, looking like I'd asked him for a roadmap to the moon. I shooed him toward the door. "Now, Seth. Find Harvey, have him get me something that works."

"Give me ten minutes," Seth said.

"You got five." I escorted him to the door and the moment Seth stepped out Councilman Slim Higginbotham stepped in.

He jumped and a little-girl "eek" escaped him. "Didn't expect to see you here. Startled me. Thought I'd look around, and spotted the open door." Slim pointed at the door. "Everything all right in there?"

Of all the town officials, Slim would be the only one I would trust with this kind of news. I tugged him in and shut the door.

I caught him up on the current situation, trying to keep panic, anger and confusion out of my voice. I didn't do it well. I pointed to the safe. "Empty."

"My money?" Slim mumbled and pushed past me to the safe. He inspected it more thoroughly than we had, then stood, shoulders stooped and dejected. "All of it."

"We'll get it back. I promise." A promise I vowed to keep.

Slim gripped the safe's door, then straightened up. "Wait. Eli Goodman? He's in town?" His eyes widened then narrowed. "Thought he was sweet on you."

"Was," I said. "Guess he's moved on." An awkward pause, a fidget. "Pokey and I are heading out, now."

"I'm coming with you," Slim said. "You're gonna need my help."

I'd need all the help I could get. "Thanks," I said, again moving toward the door. He slipped between me and the door.

"Don't want to add any more pressure, or scare you, but MacKinney and Weinberg are watchin' you—close. If you don't catch these bank robbers, you can kiss your badge good-bye."

Behind those kind eyes shone stone-cold sincerity.

He was right, of course. It was time for do or don't do . . . there was no more try.

CHAPTER SIXTY-FOUR:
MOVING ON

Pokey, Slim and I let our horses pick their way under the dim light of a half moon. The road lay smooth, despite drenching summer rains. We managed to avoid most of the muddy patches reflecting the night's light. Galloping, which I would have done in daylight, tonight would surely prove suicidal. So we risked a hurried trot. Or rather, we bounced along following Eli's trail. I knew he couldn't have much of a head start. Fifteen minutes, tops.

"Got any idea where he might be headed?" Slim loped next to me, Pokey behind, to my right.

I knew where. "San Diego."

"San Diego?" both men chorused.

"That's a far piece!" Pokey said. "Gotta be clear on the other side of Sacramento."

"More'n that." Slim looked over at me. "How exactly do you know? How is it you're privvy to his plan?"

"What?!" I couldn't believe he'd insinuate I was an accomplice, or at least knew about it. But, I wasn't willing to explain further, especially Eli's comment about not having to put up with me. I simply shrugged. "He mentioned it. A while back. When I thought I . . . knew him."

This seemed to satisfy their curiosity. At least, they stopped asking.

As we rode, I thought about Eli and my feelings and how we'd both changed. It was sad, but not so tragic as I'd once imagined. We had both moved on, both grown and changed. Even if I'd said yes to his offer—if it had been legitimate—I wouldn't have been happy with children, a house and a garden. And damn that picket fence! There was so much more to life I'd discovered, and I wanted a part of it. To *be* a part of it. Crying about a bad past was a waste of good tears. Nope. No going back.

We'd ridden most of an hour, I figured, and just when doubts about the surety and *sanity* of my actions crept into my mind, I heard voices up ahead. I pulled back on the reins. Pokey and Slim followed suit. Somewhere near by, a man and woman argued.

"You'll be fine. Just get back on and let's go." Sounded a lot like Eli.

"Stupid horse. Fell into that chuckhole on purpose. My head's still pounding." Could that be Mrs. Abigail Stevenson? Sounded like her, only whinier. What was she doing out here? Eli? Abigail? What in tarnation was going on?

Mutterings I couldn't make out. Bushes shook. Then the man's voice again. "Your horse is fine. Mount up. We gotta go."

That voice. Definitely Eli's. I caught Pokey's attention and hoped my whisper was low enough Eli wouldn't hear. "Head around to the right here. We'll cut 'em off." I turned to Slim. "You go left."

They nodded, urged their horses into the forest and disappeared. Alone now with my pounding heart, I counted a slow ten. Any second now, the woman would be on her horse and she and Eli would ride away.

No way was I going to let them get away. Not with my money. At nine, I gigged May Belle—hard. I galloped around the bend and sure enough, there was Eli perched in the saddle and Abigail standing with one hand gripping the saddle horn and one foot in the stirrup.

"Hold it right there!" I commanded.

But Eli didn't hold it.

A quick hand down, up again and an intense orange flame leapt from Eli's gun, headed right toward me. It whizzed past my head and the blaze sailed off into the night, just like those fireworks.

I was stunned. Eli had just tried to kill me! He took off, leaving his accomplice hanging. Literally. Abigail swung into the saddle and gigged her horse. "Haw!" I hollered as I kicked my shoe heels into May Belle's sides. I rode fast, reaching Abigail's side within seconds. Eli rode full out.

He wasn't going to get away. Not again. I pulled out my gun, but I didn't want to shoot him, or her for that matter. However, he had no such reluctance shooting me. I pulled back on the hammer, aimed and released.

Bang! An orange streak zipped over his right shoulder. Sulphurous spent gunpowder filled my nose. He hunched lower over the saddle, poked a gun out from under his arm and fired. At me. Again. The bullet pinged into the ground.

"Stop, Eli!" I shouted. "There's posse all around."

He didn't stop. Didn't even slow down. Another deep breath. I aimed again, hoping, praying my bullet wouldn't hit him. But if it did, then at least he would stop. But just wounded. And he'd be all right.

"I said stop!" I fired again.

"Stop, yourself!" Abigail screamed at me.

Riding next to her, I was close enough to see her lips pull back into a snarl and her eyes narrow. Rage wasn't a becoming feature on her.

I hollered back, "Just stop before somebody gets hurt."

Abigail fumbled with a quirt hanging from the saddle horn. Those short whips were strong medicine for half-broken saddle broncs, but her mount seemed to be running just fine.

Whack! The rawhide braiding ripped part of my right sleeve. My skin burned like all the fireworks put together. I pointed my gun at her. So close, I couldn't miss.

"You won't shoot me!" She snapped the quirt again. The rawhide dug farther into my arm.

She was right, of course. I wouldn't shoot her. I jammed the gun into my holster, leaned as close as I could and grabbed for the reins. Instead, I got braiding and yanked. It about took her out of the saddle. She pulled back. I pulled harder. She let go.

Still side by side, she kicked out of her stirrup and at my leg. She connected, but it didn't hurt half as much as my stinging arm welt.

"Stop it!" I yelled and threw the quirt. "You're under arrest!"

"Suck an egg!" she hollered back and kicked again.

Ready for a catfight, I flailed at her, hoping she'd fall and stop. She didn't. Instead, she smacked and backhanded my sore arm. We slapped and kicked like schoolgirls.

To the right, Pokey thundered out of the forest. His muzzle flashed, lighting up his own face. The shot went over Eli's head. Slim crashed through a bush on the left in front of Eli, forcing him to pull up. With them trapped in my posse snare, I mentally handcuffed both and led them back to town.

But Eli jerked his reins sideways, kicked his horse and headed off down a trail I'd failed to notice earlier. Abigail followed on his heels. Within seconds, both had disappeared into the forest.

The posse convened. Pokey pointed. "Ain't that the way to the old Cavanaugh cabin?"

I blew out. "Another cabin? Again?"

"Ain't very original, are they?" Pokey said.

"Road ends at the house. Creek runs right behind it." Slim said. "Mousetrapped for sure."

So, that was both good and bad news. Good, they weren't

going anywhere. Bad, they had nowhere else to go. They'd hole up there and shoot it out.

We urged our horses onto the trail, taking the chance we'd all stay upright and out of chuckholes or worse . . . ambush.

The trail wound around elderberry bushes and evergreens, their branches so dense they created a wide tunnel.

The low roar of the nearby rain-swollen creek echoed in the darkness. If they had any brains, they'd see it would be suicide to try to cross it tonight. We reined up in sight of a ramshackle shack, dismounted and tied our horses to the closest juniper. Hunkering down behind a scrub oak, its branches providing minimum coverage, we somehow managed to take in air and hold our breath at the same time. Heart pounding in my ears, I pushed an errant strand of hair out of my face and checked my arsenal. I pushed new ammo into the Navy Colt Slim had procured and stuck it in my holster. Ten extra cartridges from Slim went into my skirt pocket. Vexed, yet determined, I was loaded for bear.

"What d'you think?" I asked.

"That we're crazy?" Pokey shot me a sideways glance.

For once I agreed, but I'd never admit it. "Let's go," I said, low.

Using saplings and undergrowth for cover, I made it to the edge of the corral with only a snagged skirt and scratched cheek. Pokey and Slim arrived unscathed A horse nickered to our left and another one answered the call. Slim was right. They *were* here. I let out a breath. Cooing softly to the animals, I moved in closer. Sure enough, one was black with a wide rump. Eli's horse, all lathered up.

"Pokey, you go around back. Watch the other door. Slim," I whispered, "you're with me."

My plan was to go in the front and arrest everyone. Slim and I scurried to both sides of the door. From inside, furniture crashed to the floor, scraping sounds near the door. I heard that clear enough. Just like defenders at the Alamo, they were fortifying themselves. As each of us rushed through that door, we'd be easy enough to pick off. Would Eli really shoot to kill? Could I?

Slim and I stood plastered against the wall, my head a whirlwind of battle strategies. Without a sound, a dark figure appeared next to me. Out of the corner of my eye, I was sure the boogeyman had me! Recoiling, I rolled into Slim on the other side of the door and thrust out my Colt.

"It's me, Maud." The voice whispered out of the darkness. "Pokey."

I could breathe again, but I couldn't decide whether to hug him or shoot him. "You scared the bejeezus outa me!" I hissed. "Don't ever sneak up—"

"Sorry. But there ain't no back door."

I exhaled long and low while my heart returned to its accustomed location. "Gotta be careful going in there. Duck low and head for the side."

I cocked my pistol and listened. For a long moment, silence. Then, a male voice, asking about grub.

Of course. Men always want to eat. I wasn't surprised at the raspy response, either. "Are you *serious*?"

How to go about capturing them without getting anyone hurt? Then again, I hadn't come chasing all the way out here merely to stand around and speculate. A fluttery, empty feeling filled my chest. My hands tingled. Now or never! I used the borrowed handgun to rap on the door. The heavy *thud-thud-thud* was impressive.

I hollered. "Eli, come out with your hands up." Like he would actually do that!

A bustling of boots. A chair crashed to the floor.

I pushed the door open and announced my intentions. "You're under arrest! Both of you."

A shot splintered the wooden doorframe over my head. Instinctively, I flinched, ducking, trying to make myself small. I darted inside, stopping near the door. I scuttled to my right, taking refuge behind an overturned chair. I called out with as much authority as I could dredge. "No need for shooting. Somebody's gonna get hurt."

My eyes adjusted to the dim light. Next to the stove, the table was on end, creating a perfect defensive position.

Moonlight seeped through the dirty window. I peered into the darkness and made out two tops of heads over the upturned table. "Give up!" I said.

I felt more than saw Pokey rush into the room, taking cover behind a cot. Slim knelt outside the door, peeking around, his pistol ready, too.

Eli's second shot took off a chair leg and almost my ear. Every fiber in my body screamed at me to get out, run for cover. But I knew why I had to stay. I knew, for the first time, who I was.

So I stayed put, aimed my gun at the table and pulled the trigger.

Bang!

The cabin's window shattered.

Bang!

Eli returned fire, his bullet notching the open door.

Pokey and Slim joined in. A barrage of gunfire lit the room. Trails of orange light arced overhead. Bullets whizzed past me and chunked into a wall. One sailed out the doorway, behind me. I fired blindly over my head, counting my shots.

Three left. Ten cartridges in my pocket. How could I reload in the dark?

But enough was enough. I took aim at a leg sticking out from behind the table.

Bang!

345

"Ow! I'm hit! Abby, I'm hit!" Eli grabbed his leg and rolled away from the table and onto the floor.

Abigail rushed to him. "James? Oh, my God! James!"

Who the heck was James? It was Eli who'd just robbed the bank. Had to be *Eli* I just shot. I peered from behind the overturned chair. Abigail picked up the gun Eli had dropped, aimed at my head and fired.

I ducked back. Something hot and angry tore into the upper part of my left arm, knocking me back and onto my rear. Despite the searing fire, I took aim and returned the favor.

The stovepipe exploded. Chunks of tin cylinder rained down on Abigail, knocking her flat. A cloud of soot obliterated the pair.

The air turned opaque and suffocating. Coughing, I scrambled to my feet and stood over them, gun gripped with white knuckles. "It's over, you two. Toss the gun, over here." To my surprise, she did. I tucked it into my waistband. Everyone coughed, choked, sneezed.

"Pokey?" I croaked over my shoulder, as I wiped soot out of my eyes.

"Here, Maud. I'm all right." Pokey found a broken lantern, lit it and held up the flickering light.

"Slim?" I asked.

"I'm good." Slim wheezed.

I turned my attention to Elijah J. Goodman, cradling a sobbing Abigail Stevenson. They were covered in soot, the two of them resembling every bit of an old blackface traveling minstrel show. Abigail swore a guttural and most unladylike oath.

Eli turned those beautiful, sinful eyes on me, eyes that once held love and tenderness. Now they radiated hot, spearing anger. "Got no call to shoot at her."

"She shot *me*! And whipped me!" I countered, pointing to each injured appendage. Where were his loyalties anyway? I holstered the gun and gripped my wounded arm. Warm blood oozed between my fingers.

Pokey moved in. He waved his gun toward Eli. "Up. Don't try anything."

"Can't," Eli said. "My leg."

"Where's the money?" I asked.

"Here!" Slim reached into the corner behind the ruined stove. He clutched a saddlebag. His face beamed as he held up cash stuffed inside. I pressed a blood-smeared palm to my heart and let out a long stream of air. "Is it all there?"

" 'Course it is, Maud." Eli's sarcasm punctuated each word. "Think I spent it 'fore riding out of town?"

I focused narrowed eyes and tight lips on him for his rudeness. One more tick on this cur. A long pause, then I unloaded the million-dollar question.

"Why'd she call you 'James'?"

Heavy silence filled the room. Eli shrugged. "Mean to tell me, you still don't know? Ain't smart enough to figure it out?" He snorted. "A high and mighty sheriff, like you?" His sharp scorn both stung and irritated me.

"Humor me."

He sneered, refusing clarification. Pokey kicked Eli's injured leg. "The lady asked you a question."

Eli *yowled* and grabbed at the injury, but didn't reply. He only threw his head back and glared, menacingly. Pokey toed Eli a second time, threatening a third. "Speak up."

Eli grimaced. "All right, all right. I'll talk slow, so even Maud can get it."

A smirk curled his upper lip and lit his eyes. "Given name's . . . James Mooney."

Chapter Sixty-Five:
What's Love Got to Do with It?

My arm throbbed, my throat closed and my heart ached. We rode slowly back to town, the yellowed full moon resting on the horizon. How could I lock up Eli, or James Mooney, much less escort him to trial, only to watch him hang? How could I? And what was the relationship between Eli and Abigail? Brother-sister? Boyfriend-girlfriend? Husband-wife? He'd told me he loved me. He'd lied. Were the last five years a lie, too? Why'd I wait for him for so long? I agonized over all of it.

That's when I realized I'd apprehended the infamous James Mooney! If all I'd read about him were true, he was a real desperado. Maybe Pokey would get some reward money, after all. He'd have to share it with Slim, of course, but still, it should be sizeable.

And I hoped that Juan Doyle and Wink Smith would be caught any day now. The posse was on their trail. They'd all stand trial.

Some of the time we rode in silence since it was so dark and late at night. I thought about my skirt—I'd torn strips from the hem, wrapping them around my arm and Eli's leg. I'd have to find time to sew a new one.

Eli fluctuated between fuming and spouting angry curses, to complaining about his leg, to threatening me with all sorts of mayhem because not only had I caught them but shot him, as well. And so quickly. He hadn't had time to even bury the booty.

Pokey kept an eye on both Eli and me, riding between us,

probably worried we'd slug it out while we rode. Eli was safe, however. My left arm was numb and throbbing at the same time; my right, hurting but able to hold the reins. No way could I reach over and pop him a good one, though he deserved it . . . and so much more.

The five of us plodded into town as the sun spread its first vermillion rays across the landscape. Must've been a heckuva party last night, if broken bottles littering the street and ripped banners waving in the early morning breeze were any indication. Even at this time of day, a saloonkeeper or two were busy sweeping out their places. They stopped, leaned on their brooms, watching us pass. A man "slept it off" on the boardwalk near the Tin Pan Saloon.

Yep. Quite the celebration.

Harvey Weinberg turned from unlocking his mercantile. "Catch 'em, did ya?" He surveyed our ragtag group. "Back sooner'n expected."

I returned the greeting, smiling weakly. By now, it was obvious the entire town knew about the holdup. Up ahead to my left, Seth stepped out of the new restaurant, napkin clutched in hand. Behind him came Pearl. They both moved into the street, waiting for us to ride in close.

"Posse that went south, Maud?" Seth pointed. "They caught Smith and Doyle, already brought 'em back in."

"Already?" As glad as I was they'd been found, and that I wasn't the one running after them, I felt a tad bit of disappointment at not being there.

"Yep. Locked behind bars." Seth eyed my two prisoners. "Got the rest of 'em, I see." He frowned at my bloodied sleeve. "You hurt?"

"Shot, whipped is all," I said. "I'll be . . ."

Pearl flew over to Eli and grabbed his good leg, gawking up at him. "Benjamin? What are you doing here? I'm so happy to see you. Thought you weren't coming for another month."

"You know him?" Confusion caught in my throat.

Pearl held Eli's hand and turned wide eyes on me. "Well, sure I know him. He's my fiancé."

"What?" Pokey, Slim, Seth and I barked in unison. Could've flown an entire flock of geese through my open mouth.

Pearl's head swiveled from Eli to me and back to Eli. "What're you doing, Ben, honey?" Her eyes grew wider, if that was possible. "You hurt? What happened to your leg?"

Eli's chin pointed at me. "She shot me."

Pearl drew in breath and glared at the same time. "You shot him? You had no call. He could've been seriously hurt."

I didn't want to get into a catfight, here in the street, but I was in no mood to be overly civil. "He robbed the bank." I took a breath. "Why'd you call him Benjamin? Don't you know who he is?"

"Benjamin Dunsford."

"Eli Goodman," I said.

"James Mooney," Pokey said.

"Ben? Benny?" Pearl turned pleading eyes on Eli. "Tell 'em who you really are."

In some ways, I felt sorry for the man. But not that sorry. Silence hung over the party, despite more and more townsfolk gathering around. Must've been twenty people. I spotted a reporter headed our way. There were bound to be more momentarily. Now, finally, was a good reason for them to be here! I'd be sure they spelled my name correctly.

I didn't wait for Eli to explain to Pearl. There would be plenty of time for that while he was locked up. "C'mon," I said and gigged May Belle. Pokey and Slim tugged the prisoners' reins. The whole mob paraded down the street to the office. I was surprised to see Pa standing on the boardwalk. He helped us off the horses.

Seth kept me on my feet, my knees wanting to buckle. "Glad you're back in more or less one piece. I was worried about you." He hugged me lightly but let go way too soon.

"We were lucky," I said, gripping Abigail's arm and tugging her into the office. Pokey followed, dragging along a gimpy Eli. Slim brought up the rear.

"I'll get the doc." Seth pointed over his shoulder. Surveying the quantity of injuries, he added, "Probably need Miss Charity, too."

The clanging of cell doors and the clicking of locks brought peace to my soul. I smiled for the first time that day. These four bandits, and especially Eli, would surely get what they deserved.

I glowered at him, now perched and skulking on the cot. "I don't get it," I said. "I expected better from you."

The glacial scowl from him thawed. He eased to his feet and hobbled in close to the bars. He dug into his vest pocket, pulling out something small.

"I've changed my mind about you, Maud. Saw you in a new light. Take back everything I said." His voice turned soft, smooth. "I do have feelings for you. Deep feelings." He took a breath, then continued. "Wanted to give this to you yesterday." Eli pressed it into my hand. "Got it just for you."

In my palm . . . a gold band. I've never been one for being speechless, but I was.

He dropped his voice so low I strained to hear him. His voice . . . so sweet. "Can't marry you if I'm locked up. Get me out of here and we'll find a justice and tie the knot. Today, if you want."

I examined the treasure. What I'd always wanted. But, wait . . . a tarnished ring with a chip? Then things clicked.

Now I had plenty to say. "You stole this outta my desk drawer! *You're* the one who busted those two out." It all crashed together. "This's Annie Perkins's ring."

"Could've been yours." He snorted.

"A cheap, stolen ring? It that all I mean to you?"

"No, I—"

I shook it at him. "How dare you offer this . . . this ring! How *dare* you!" Certain to be out of control if I didn't rein in my anger, I took a deep breath and zeroed in on Eli's eyes. "I don't know whether to be disappointed or disgusted with you."

I spun on my heels and marched through the inner door, slamming it behind me. I would *not* let him see me cry.

CHAPTER SIXTY-SIX:
THE BIG DAY

So, I had been wrong about many things. Eli being the one that stood out most. But right up there at second was how I felt about being sheriff. Initially, I'd figured it would be something to do, something to get me out of the house. But now, despite getting shot, despite the jeering, despite the general lack of respect and threats to take my badge—I loved it. So much had changed in the last three months, I couldn't begin to count it all.

Today, three weeks after James Mooney's capture, was the big day. For me, even bigger than the Fourth of July. This was Election Day and my fate was in the hands of the voting citizens. I'd done everything I could to win them over, and now it was all over but the shouting—and ballot counting.

It had felt odd, watching the people walk past my office window this morning. I knew where they were headed. I was as nervous as a long-tailed cat under a rocking chair. I should be able to vote, too. Why were women relegated to the back seat? Weren't we equal to men? Who did they think they were? I buried this line of thinking and got busy.

Sequestering myself in the office, I saw to the prisoners, dusted, swept, rearranged the bulletin board, cleaned the coffee pot and my gun, all more easily now that my arm was close to healed and out of a sling. I cleared breakfast dishes from the cells and checked the Regulator, about every ten seconds. At very long last, Seth stopped by with Ian MacKinney in tow, to relieve me for the next few hours.

"Almost suppertime, Maud," Seth said. "Come on, I'm buying."

MacKinney welcomed the opportunity to oversee such illustrious captives, with his typical hubris. "The stout horse aye gits the hard work." No doubt, this service would reflect well in the eyes of the voters, helping to get him re-elected, next year. I double-checked the inmates, before stepping out with Seth.

As the sun set, Seth and I occupied a corner table in the new Dry Creek Bakery and Restaurant. Here they had pressed linen napkins, as stylish as the ones in Dutch Flats, and menus on fine parchment. Like the election, for the first time ever there were choices to be had.

My arm still aching from the bullet wound, I nursed a broken heart as well. My pride had taken a major beating and was still raw and bruised. But I had some help with the healing. Pa now believed in me and said so, every chance he got. He'd even put up a "Thank You" banner in the bank with Pokey's and my names on it. Councilmen Ian MacKinney and Harvey Weinberg declared a "Maud, Pokey and Slim Day," where we got free beer and food. I even managed to drink a whole beer without getting silly. Pokey was in seventh heaven. Slim darn near bankrupted his own saloon.

"Much longer?" I nursed my stemmed glass of fancy local wine, hoping Seth would pull out his watch and tell me the poll had closed.

"Few more minutes." He reached across the table, patting my hand. "Relax."

Easy for him to say.

I thought about Pearl. It had taken some time for her to figure things out. Eli-Jimmy-Benjamin-James fancied women whose fathers were bankers. Thankfully for Dry Creek, she agreed to stay another year to instruct the younger denizens.

She enjoyed it and was good at teaching. And I believed we'd remain friends, despite the irritating fact she had been engaged to my boyfriend.

And Annie Perkins went back to work at the bank after her near-fatal wedding, becoming one of Pa's finest tellers. She hadn't heard from her almost-husband and probably never would. And feisty Virginia Bouvier? She returned to San Francisco . . . with her money.

The biggest surprise was Eli . . . the *James* and Abigail connection. Turned out they were first cousins, their pas being brothers. Both were still cooling in jail, waiting for a new circuit judge to ride into town. It had been a month already since Richfield got shot, and two more weeks would ripen in the waiting.

And I had been right. According to Eli, Smith and Doyle had been in town during the celebrations. Keeping a low profile, their jobs were to scout the bank and bushwhack anybody who followed Eli's getaway. But, without them noticing, Pokey and I stabled their horses. They couldn't get out of town in time to meet up with Eli and Abigail before we arrived. They'd had to steal some nags and ride like the wind, as it was.

And, even without her admission, I deduced that Abigail had taken up as our housekeeper only to ascertain everything she could about the workings of the bank and me as sheriff. She had sent letters to Eli regularly, detailing my every move.

In some ways, I was gonna miss her. I'd grown used to having someone else cook and clean. Her pot roasts melted in my mouth. And her cakes. Oh, those heavenly chocolate cakes. Looked like I'd have to learn to juggle jobs again. I wondered . . . would she share her recipes?

My half-eaten ham and potatoes supper had grown cold. Seth pointed his fork at me. "You're looking a bit off your feed. Feeling all right?"

"Yeah. Just nervous." I'd be right as the rain, soon.

Every time the door swung open, I flinched, hoping for election news. Seth checked his pocket watch for the umpteenth time. "Poll's closed," he said, reaching across the table for my hand. "Should know in about an hour."

"An hour?" I whined. This was torture.

I pushed down as much supper as I could. We ordered pie and coffee and made small talk. Things had certainly changed between us. A while back, my feelings for Seth had been intensifying. But now . . . I wasn't so sure. He was a nice enough fellow, fun to talk to, even better to kiss. But I wasn't wanting anything more, right now. It was enough to go out on the town with him, from time to time.

Pokey jaunted into the dining room and seated himself at our table. He perched on the edge of his chair, elbows on the table, that pervasive Cheshire cat grin. "Soon enough, I reckon. Almost time." He leaned in close. "Don't worry. You're gonna win. I even voted for you, myself."

Tears pushed against my eyes and my nose dripped. Not very fitting for a sheriff.

More small talk only accented the plodding pace of the clock's hands. A snail's pace.

Before the full hour was up, the door flew open. Slim Higginbotham and Pa barreled into the room, faces lit up, smiles stretching to the moon.

Pa beamed, sweeping me into an embrace and hugging me close to him. "By a landslide, Maud. By a landslide!"

Pokey thumped me on the back. "Well, butter my butt and call me a biscuit!" He beamed.

Great. Now I really did cry.

ABOUT THE AUTHOR

New Mexico native **Melody Groves** has a deep love for anything cowboy and Old West. Melody was raised in southern New Mexico, but spent a few "growing up" years on Guam and in the Philippines. Besides being a freelance writer, she plays rhythm guitar in the Jammy Time band.

Winner of five first-place writing awards, Melody is a member of Western Writers of America. She writes magazine articles, screenplays, novels and non-fiction books and contributed to a collegiate history encyclopedia.

Melody is a contributing editor for *Round Up* magazine for Western Writers of America. She lives in Albuquerque, New Mexico, with her photographer husband, Myke.

www.melodygroves.net